THE MAN

VOLUME III

Robert Musil was born in Klagenfurt in 1880. Initially
destined for an Army career, he turned instead to
engineering and took a diploma at the Technical
University of Brno in 1901. Then in a further switch, he
went on to read philosophy at the University of Berlin,
taking his degree in 1908. Publication of his first novel,
Young Törless, in 1906, encouraged him to turn down
professional academic opportunities and to make a living
as a freelance. He was working as an editor in Berlin
when war broke out, and went on to serve as an officer
with the Austrian Army. He began work on *The Man
Without Qualities* in the 1920s, and the first volume
appeared in 1930. Financially ruined by inflation, and
moving from Berlin to Vienna and ultimately to Switzerland to evade the enveloping tide of Nazism, Musil was
revising the third volume when he died in Geneva in
1942.

THE MAN WITHOUT QUALITIES

VOLUME III

INTO THE MILLENNIUM
(THE CRIMINALS)

ROBERT MUSIL

*Translated from the German
by Eithne Wilkins and Ernst Kaiser*

Minerva

A Minerva Paperback
THE MAN WITHOUT QUALITIES VOLUME III

First published in Great Britain 1960
by Secker & Warburg Limited
This Minerva edition published 1995
by Mandarin Paperbacks
an imprint of Reed Books Ltd
Michelin House, 81 Fulham Road, London SW3 6RB
and Auckland, Melbourne, Singapore and Toronto

A CIP catalogue record for this title
is available from the British Library
ISBN 0 7493 9588 5

Printed and bound in Great Britain
by Cox & Wyman, Reading

CONTENTS

THIRD BOOK

INTO THE MILLENNIUM
(THE CRIMINALS)

FOREWORD

THE MAN WITHOUT QUALITIES tends to overshadow Musil's other work, to the disadvantage of both. From the time when the first volume appeared in German, amid impressive celebrations on the occasion of his fiftieth birthday in November 1930, German critics practically ceased to mention his previous books except in passing; and up to the present day, when his Complete Works are available in German, no one has tried to evaluate his work *as a whole*. In Italy and in France, where his immense unfinished last book is now acclaimed as a masterpiece, the problem does not arise so long as none of the other works is translated. In English-speaking countries the situation is rather different. On the one hand, we also have *Young Törless* and translations of two long stories, where echoes and correspondences become apparent, suggesting a larger unity. On the other, English readers, unlike those on the Continent, have shown a tendency to regard *The Man Without Qualities* as primarily, if not wholly, a satirical work and largely to ignore certain aspects of it. It would therefore seem opportune to refer to these aspects, which English taste has obscured and which knowledge of Musil's earlier imaginative writings would instantly have illuminated. Indeed it becomes necessary to refer to them on the appearance of the third volume, which is remarkably different from the previous two, not least in the way that these aspects of Musil's thought and imagination come into prominence. It is only in this volume that the book's main theme becomes explicit, the theme that in the end he calls ' the last love-story of all '. It is present, in the previous volumes, by implication only; until Agathe appears it is dealt with in roundabout ways, often by caricature, and Ulrich's *princesse lointaine* presides chiefly as an idea—an idea about the nature and quality of life itself. The previous volumes are in fact a sort of prologue, and the story begins only now, at the point where Musil originally intended to begin it, before he knew where it was going to lead him and into how deep waters. In 1925 and 1926 his title for the novel in progress was ' The Twin Sister '; and that Agathe, whose name means The Good One, is, though cryptically, still more truly the central figure than her brother is can tell us something important that we need to know. For she, the 'forgotten' sister, is at last the embodiment of that great and homeless love which Ulrich thought of in the chapter on his 'forgotten' but nevertheless 'exceedingly important' infatuation with the Major's wife; it is that unfocused love, that homelessness, which impels him, as it does the main figures of Musil's other works. It may be disconcerting to realise that now we shall need to re-read over a thousand pages of prologue to the story. But Musil is a disconcerting writer. And one of his characteristics is to reward every re-reading with a profusion of new insights.

His fundamental problem has two elements: love and belief. At first sight this may not look like one problem. But even in his first novel, *Young Törless*, he is insistent that the anguish and frustration of sexual love as the boy experiences it is a token of that 'something else' which is a constant reference throughout this and all his later works. The particular object of love is a mere eidolon. The loved person (or even thing, for Musil is much concerned with childhood experience) is not a potential source of fulfilment, but—more and more clearly, it appears with each work—an obstacle to fulfilment. Beyond any loved person or thing is the intangible 'something stronger, greater, more beautiful, more passionate, and darker than ourselves' that Törless perceives, something implicit in art and, for him especially, in mathematics; it is the mysterious, indefinable, quintessential x to which in *The Man Without Qualities*, with characteristic ambiguity, Musil repeatedly gives the name 'God'. Love, in whatever form it is experienced, is an approximation only: as it were, an experimental approach to living in a condition that he calls 'Other'. In most of his work, and even in the studies made during the 'twenties for the novel that was gradually to become *The Man Without Qualities*, the forms of love that obsess his characters are all the cause of agonising inner conflict. Some are also comical, or at least grotesque. Some are hideous and terrifying. At one extreme longing turns into destructive fury, as in Moosbrugger and, more crassly, in the exhibitionist watched by Clarisse and her friends; and short of that it is tinged with abnormality and risks coming up against immemorial social taboos. At the other extreme all desire, physical, emotional, or spiritual, seems to cause only infinite frustration in a world that is by nature ' partial ' and which can supply only ' partial solutions '. Up to the time of *The Man Without Qualities*, and to some extent still in this book, Musil's work is wrung by an ultimate denial: there is no ideal lover, no complete friend, and above all no God. Yet in the face of this unbelief there is always, and from the very beginning, a haunting paradoxical faith that all this can be found; and the attempt to identify it culminates in Ulrich's declaration, near the end of the present volume, that he is dedicated to this search and setting out on an adventure of life and death.

In *Young Törless* the erotic experience is homosexual, with a floating background of incestuous yearnings. Incest did subsequently become an important motif for Musil; but whether as the erotic relationship of son to mother or, later, of brother to sister, he never treated it in explicit terms in any work that he completed. Each time he dropped it, as though the kind of drama involved were too crudely realistic to satisfy his imagination. So the forbidden union remains symbolic, an implication of that ' Other ' which is the completion of the self. The problem of fidelity, which much engaged him in his early period, notably in *The Perfecting of a Love*, is essentially bound up, for him, with the problem of identity. Thus the problem of love becomes almost indistinguishable from the problem of reality. The ideal lover who cannot be found anywhere is the other half of the seeker, whose longing is not to possess another person but to be literally one with the other person and so become whole. One can interpret this on several levels, from the psychological to the mystical. Musil's enquiry covers the full range. It is significant that in a note on mediaeval mystics' sayings all referring to the *unio mystica* and often, of course, in erotic symbolism, he puts ' God ' and ' frustrated love ' side by side as examples of the unattainable.

The clue is in the concept ' union '. When he gave the title *Unions* to the volume of two stories published in 1911, he was quite aware that here was the central problem of his work and life. Union means, after all, the becoming one of this and that, whether male and female, subject and object, intellect and imagination, or science and art—and with Musil it is all of these.

The last chapters of *The Man Without Qualities*, written in his Swiss exile between 1938 and 1942, which follow directly on those of the present volume, are almost exclusively dedicated to reflections on this subject. And here it becomes overwhelmingly clear what all the earlier work, from *Young Törless* onward, was saying by poetic suggestion: becoming one with the ' Other ' is an experience more complex, more complete, and therefore more desirable than any union that can be physically enacted. A human ' other '—and Ulrich's sister is his ' other self ', the mirror-reflection and transformation of himself—is an image of an ' Other ' that is nameless. As Agathe says: " I am in love, but I don't know with whom ".

An expedition, a journey of exploration through territory of the mind and spirit—such was Musil's description of his last book. It is not solely Robert Musil in search of himself; it is a portrayal of intellectual European man in search of another self. The old images, old beliefs, old methods will no longer answer, Musil observes. Yet why—he instantly asks—why, since all the great religions offer the same answer and its life-and-death importance is obvious, cannot we accept it any longer? In 1932, preparing the German original of this volume for the press, he wrote:

the main problem here is the search for right living. I seek to show what I call ' the pocket in European morality ' (as in billiards, where the ball sooner or later gets stuck in such a pocket), because it hinders right action: it is, briefly, the wrong treatment that has been accorded to mystical experience.

He rejects all such answers as are supplied, too readily, by tradition or by emotion. Far from proclaiming any allegiance, he questions every type of experience. Far from being a sceptic, he investigates the types of experience with the utmost precision, testing them always for their ultimate value. Like Ulrich, he is a man of faith who merely happens not to believe anything. The man who in his youth had admired Maeterlinck insisted, in his maturity, that ecstasy was not authentic if it was cloudy and solemn, and that any mystical condition must stand up to the brilliant light of day. To discover how to achieve such a way of living, in the modern world, is the task Ulrich and Agathe set themselves. These ' Trappists of modern life ' go about a

very ancient task in a way that is new and perhaps startling.
Musil supposes, in the second of their Holy Conversations, that
it may even outrage the reader. His own statement of what this
book is about also has its outrageous ambiguity, for it is made by
one who ' had not believed in God since the age of eight ' and
who yet wrote, in the continuation of this volume:

Ulrich was in the habit of thinking along lines that were not so
much god-less as god-free—an entirely scientific attitude that leaves
all the heart's God-seeking to the heart, because that is, after all, not
what profits the intellect but only what leads it astray. And he did
not in the least doubt that this was the only right approach, since the
human mind has achieved its most tangible successes only since it has
begun to avoid God. But the notion that haunted him was this: ' Supposing precisely this ungodliness were the appropriate contemporary
way to God ! Every era has had its own way there, corresponding
to its most potent spiritual resources: might it then not be our destiny,
the destiny of an era of ingenious and enterprising experience, to reject
all dreams, legends, and sophistries solely because on the heights of
discovery about the natural world we shall turn towards him again
and shall begin to achieve a relationship based on experience ? '

Such statements as those quoted offer some hint, though they
certainly do not explain, why ' Into the Millennium ' has a
parenthetical sub-title ' The Criminals '.   Behind that parenthesis
there is a long and fascinating story—the story of this book, as
Musil said, which was ' never told '. Fortunately he left the
extraordinary traces of it, discarded snake-skins, as it were—glittering, tortuous, real in a curiously implausible way that may yet
cause the unwary to start back in alarm: snake-skins that are
evidence at once of many deaths and of something alive elsewhere.
However, this is a story to come to later. For the purpose of
these thirty-eight chapters it is enough that the sub-title that
prevails is ' Into the Millennium ', and to realise that if Ulrich
and Agathe are ' criminals ', it is in the sense of infringing border-
lines of which most people are scarcely aware at all.   Their
situation is what Musil calls ' a border-line case '.   ' Border-line '
is indeed a key word in this book; and it is relevant that the heading he gave to the pages on which he copied out the mediaeval
mystics' sayings for use in it is ' Border-line Experiences '.

                                        EITHNE WILKINS

ACKNOWLEDGMENT

The translators wish to thank the Bollingen Foundation for continued assistance in their work.

THIRD BOOK

INTO THE MILLENNIUM
(THE CRIMINALS)

1 *The forgotten sister.*

ARRIVING in X—— towards evening of the same day, as Ulrich came out of the station he saw ahead of him a wide, shallow square with streets debouching into it at each end, and the sight of it affected his memory almost distressfully, in the peculiar way a scene does that one has often seen and always forgotten again.

" Take it from me, wages have gone down by twenty percent, and the cost of living's gone up by twenty percent: forty percent that makes ! " " Take it from *me*, there's nothing like a sporting marathon for promoting good will among the nations ! " The voices came right out of his ear—railway-compartment voices. Then he quite distinctly heard one saying: " Still, I always say there's nothing like the opera." " Hobby of yours, is it ? " " It's my passion."

He tilted his head as though to shake water out of his ear. The train had been crowded, the journey long. Drops of the talk around him had seeped into him during all that time and now they were oozing out again. And the station exit was like the mouth of a vast pipe through which the jolly hustle and bustle of arrival poured out into the quiet of the square. Ulrich had waited in the midst of it until it was no more than a trickle. Now he stood in the vacuum of silence that follows upon noise. And while his ears were still tingling with the unrest this sudden stillness caused, he was struck by unaccustomed restfulness before his eyes. All visible things seemed more intensely there than he was used to; and when he looked across the square, the cross-bars of perfectly ordinary windows on the other side stood out as black—in the evening light on the pallid incandescence of the glass—as though they were the crosses of Golgotha. And everything that moved also seemed to detach itself from the immobility of the place in a way that never happens in really large cities. Both the mobile and the immobile here clearly had scope to

expand their significance. It was with a trace of the curiosity
one feels on seeing something again after a long time that he
observed this, gazing out into the large provincial town in which
he had spent brief and not exactly pleasant periods of his life.
Its character had, as he very well knew, a touch of exile, of the
colonial. Here of old a body of ancient German burgher stock,
centuries ago transplanted to Slavonic soil, had flourished and
gradually withered into decline, so that apart from a few churches
and some family names there was hardly anything left to remind
one of it; nor was there much to recall the fact that the town had
later been the seat of the provincial Diet except a well-preserved
fine old palace. But in the era of absolute rule this past had been
overlaid by the huge levy of imperial administration, with its
provincial headquarters, its schools and universities, barracks,
law-courts, prisons, bishop's palace, assembly rooms, and theatre,
and with all the people who kept all this going, and the merchants
and artisans who followed in their train, until finally industrial
concerns were also set going by newly arrived entrepreneurs,
whose factories, roof to roof, filled the suburbs and had a greater
influence on this territory's fate than anything else had had for
generations. This town had a history, and it had a face too, but
one in which the eyes did not match the mouth or the chin the
hair, a face bearing the traces of a life intensely active but inwardly
empty. Perhaps it was this that, in certain special circumstances,
encouraged the development of the outstanding and extraordinary.

Ulrich had—to sum it up in terms that do not explain anything
either—a sense of something ' spiritually insubstantial ', something in which one lost oneself so entirely that there was a danger
of falling a prey to unbridled imaginings. In his pocket he had
his father's eccentric telegram, which he knew by heart: " Here-
with notify you of my decease of current date." This was the
message that the old gentleman had had conveyed to him—or
should one say, that he had conveyed to him? as was actually
indicated by the telegram's being signed: " your father." His
Excellency the Privy Counsellor never jested about serious matters. And there was indeed something deucedly logical in the
weird formulation of the message: it was he himself who had informed his son when, in expectation of his end, he wrote or dictated the wording of it and gave orders that it was to be despatched

the instant he had drawn his last breath; all in all, it seemed as if the situation could hardly be more accurately summed up. And yet from this act, in which the present had tried to dominate a future it would not live to experience, there was wafted down the passage of time the eerie cadaverous odour of a wrathfully disintegrating will.

This attitude, which by some process of association reminded Ulrich of the downright meticulously undiscriminating taste of provincial society, also made him think, and not without misgiving, of his married sister, who lived in the provinces and whom he was doubtless going to meet in a few minutes now. Even during the journey he had been wondering about her; for he knew hardly anything of her. From time to time his father's letters had included regulation items of family news, such as: " Your sister Agathe has married "; this last had been followed by supplementary details, since Ulrich had been unable to travel home for the occasion. And it must have been only about a year later that he had received news of the young husband's death. And it was three years after that, if he was not mistaken, that the announcement had come: " To my great satisfaction, your sister Agathe has decided to marry again." At this second wedding five years ago he had been present and had seen his sister for several days; but all he recalled of it was that these days had been a ceaseless whirl, like a Giant Wheel of white cambric and lace. He also remembered the bridegroom, whom he had disliked. Agathe must have been twenty-two then, and he himself twenty-seven; he had just got his doctorate. That made his sister twenty-seven now, and during all this time he had neither seen her again nor exchanged any letters with her. All he remembered was that his father had more than once written such things as: " In your sister's marriage, it grieves me to say, all does not seem to be as well as it might be, although her husband is an excellent man." There were also such remarks as: " I have been extremely pleased by the recent successes gained by your sister's husband." That was more or less the gist of his father's comments in letters to which, deplorably enough, he had never paid much attention. But once, as he now suddenly remembered quite clearly, there had been a disapproving remark on his sister's childlessness, with the appended hope that she was nevertheless contented in her married life, even though her character would never allow her to admit it.

'I wonder what she looks like now,' Ulrich thought to himself.

It was in keeping with the character of their father, who so punctiliously supplied each with news of the other, that he had sent them away from home at a tender age, straight after their mother's death. Their schools had been at a great distance from each other, and Ulrich, who was a difficult boy, was often not allowed to come home for the holidays, so that since their childhood, when they had been extremely fond of each other, he had scarcely seen anything of his sister, except for one longish period when Agathe was ten.

To Ulrich it seemed natural that in these circumstances they did not write to each other either. What could they have written to each other about?! At the time of Agathe's first marriage, as he now recalled, he had still been a lieutenant in the army, and had been in hospital recovering from a bullet-wound received in a duel. Lord, what an ass he had been! Come to think of it, how many different asses in the course of time—for he now remembered it was not the duel that had kept him away, but that by then he had been an engineer and had had something 'important' to do, which prevented his attending the ceremony. And later he gathered that his sister had been very much in love with her first husband. He could not remember who had told him—but, after all, what does 'very much in love' mean anyway? It is the sort of thing people say. She had married again, and Ulrich could not endure her second husband: so much, at any rate, was certain! It was not only that he had a bad impression of him personally; equally bad was the impression he got from several of the man's books he had looked into, and it might well be not entirely without intention that he had let his sister drop out of his thoughts since then. It had not been quite right of him; still, there it was, and he had to admit to himself that even in this last year, during which he had thought about so many things, he had never given a single thought to her, not even when he received the news of their father's death. On his arrival, however, he had asked the old man-servant who came to meet him whether his brother-in-law was there yet; and he was delighted to hear that Professor Hagauer was not expected until the day of the funeral. Although it could not be more than two or three days till then, it felt like a respite of indefinite duration, a period of solitary retreat that he would spend together with his sister as though they were the most intimate friends in the world. There was no sense in asking himself exactly what made him think of it that way: probably the notion of the 'unknown sister' was one of those spacious abstractions in which there is room for many feelings that are not quite at home anywhere.

And while his mind was occupied with such questions, Ulrich had walked on slowly into this town that opened up before him, at once strange and familiar. His suit-cases, into which he had stuffed quite a number of books in the last minute before leaving, he had sent on in a cab in the charge of the old servant he remembered from his childhood, a man who combined the functions of caretaker, butler, and library attendant in a way that with the years had become less and less clearly definable; it was probably to this self-effacing taciturn man that Ulrich's father had dictated the telegram announcing his own death. Ulrich took an astonished pleasure in letting his feet carry him along the way homeward, while his senses were all inquisitively alive to the fresh impressions that every growing city springs on someone who has not seen it for a long time. At a certain spot that they remembered before he did Ulrich's feet turned off the main street, and after a short time he found himself in a narrow lane between garden walls. Obliquely facing him there was the two-storeyed house, the central part of it higher than the wings, and there was the old stable at one side and, squashed up against the garden wall, the little cottage where the old servant and his wife lived; it looked as if in spite of all his confidence in them the master had kept them as far away from himself as possible, though at the same time enclosing them within his walls.

Sunk in thought, Ulrich had gone up to the low locked door in the garden wall and had let the big ring-shaped knocker, which served instead of a bell, fall back against the age-blackened timber, when the servant came running along the street to put him right. They had to walk round the wall to the main door, where the cab was drawn up. And only now, in this moment, with the shuttered façade of the house before him, was Ulrich struck by the fact that his sister had not met him at the station.

He was told that she had retired after lunch, with migraine, giving instructions that she was to be called when the young master arrived. Ulrich asked whether his sister often suffered from migraine, and instantly regretted his awkwardness in drawing attention to his own estrangement when talking to the old family servant, touching on family relations it was better to pass over in silence. "Madam gave orders for tea to be served in half an hour," the old man said respectfully, with the blank face of a well-trained servant, carefully conveying the assurance that he knew nothing of matters beyond the limits of his duty.

Involuntarily Ulrich glanced up at the windows, with a vague notion that Agathe might be up there watching his arrival. He wondered whether he would get on with her, and was uneasily aware that his stay would be anything but agreeable if he did not like her. However, the fact that she had neither come to the station nor met him at the door was somehow confidence-inspiring. It showed a certain congeniality of feeling: after all, there would have been as little warrant for her hastening to meet him as in his rushing to his father's coffin the moment he set foot in the house. Leaving word for her that he would be down in half an hour, he went to have a wash. The room that had been prepared for him was in the attic-like second storey of the central part of the house; it was the room he had had as a small boy, but now the old furniture was curiously supplemented by several random pieces meant to contribute to an adult's comfort. 'There's probably no way of arranging it differently till after the funeral,' Ulrich thought, installing himself, not without some difficulty, among the ruined vestiges of his childhood, and yet invaded by a faintly pleasing sensation that seemed to rise from these surroundings like a vapour. As he was changing, it occurred to him to put on a pyjama-like garment, a sort of play-suit, that he had come across while unpacking. 'Really, she might at least have come down to say hello as soon as I got here!' he thought and there was an element of retaliation in his choice of this extremely informal garb. Still, he did not lose the feeling that his sister would be sure to have some reason for her behaviour that would appeal to him; and this, again, lent his choice of dress something of the courtesy that lies in the spontaneous expression of being at home and at ease with another person.

This loose, soft, woollen pyjama-like suit he put on was checkered black and grey, close-fitting at wrist and ankle, as at the waist, and altogether faintly resembling a pierrot's costume; he was fond of it because it was so comfortable, and particularly now after his sleepless night and the long journey. Relaxed then, he went downstairs. But when he entered the room where his sister was waiting for him, he was struck with the full sense of his peculiar garb, for by some mysterious workings of coincidence he found himself face to face with a tall, fair pierrot clad in a striped and chequered suit of delicate grey and rust, who at a first glance looked exactly like himself.

" I didn't know we were twins ! " said Agathe, and her face lit up with amusement.

2 Confidences.

THEY did not kiss by way of greeting, but merely stood looking at each other in a friendly way. Then they moved apart, and Ulrich was able to survey his sister. They matched in height. Agathe's hair was fairer than his, but her skin had the same bloom and dryness that was the only thing he liked about his own body. Instead of the voluptuous bosom that was the fashion of the time, she had small, firm breasts, and her limbs seemed to have the long, slender spindle shape in which natural vigour combines with beauty.

" I hope you've got over your migraine," Ulrich said. " You don't look any the worse for it."

" I haven't been having migraine, I only told them to say that," Agathe explained. " It was too complicated to tell them anything else. I was just lazy. I was asleep. I've got into the habit of sleeping in every free minute I have here. I'm a lazy person anyway—out of desperation, I suppose. And when I heard you were coming, I said to myself: I hope this is going to be the last time I shall be sleepy, and then I gave myself up to sort of sleeping myself wide awake. The servants had to have something to tell you, and I thought it all out very carefully and decided to call it migraine."

" Don't you play games at all? " Ulrich asked.

" A bit of tennis. But I loathe games."

While she was talking he went on considering her face. It did not seem to him very like his own; but perhaps he was mistaken and it resembled his as a pastel portrait might resemble a woodcut of the same face, so that the difference of medium distracts one from seeing the correspondence of line and plane. There was something about this face that disquieted him. After a while he realised it was simply that he could not tell what it expressed. It lacked that element in a face which makes it possible to draw conclusions about the person. There was a great deal in it, but nothing was emphasised, nothing combined in the usual way to form what one generally calls characteristics.

" What made you dress up this way? " Ulrich asked.

" I didn't work it out," Agathe replied. " I just thought it was nice."

" It's very nice! " Ulrich said, laughing. " But positively a conjuring trick of coincidence! And I gather Father's death hasn't upset you very much either? "

Agathe rose slowly on to her toes and then slowly sank back again.

" Is your husband here yet? " her brother asked, for the sake of saying something.

" Professor Hagauer will arrive only in time for the funeral." She seemed to relish the chance to utter the name so formally, as it were to pick it up and set it down at a distance, like some strange object.

Ulrich did not know what answer to make to this. " Oh yes, that's what they told me," he said.

Once again they gazed at each other; and then they went, as propriety required of them, into the little room where the dead man lay.

All day long this room had been in darkness, with the curtains drawn; it was saturated with blackness. Flowers and lighted candles gave off their glow and fragrance. The two pierrots stood straight and tall before the dead man, and it was as if they were watching him.

" I'm not going back to Hagauer ! " Agathe said, to get it over and done with. It seemed almost as though the dead man were meant to hear it too.

There on his catafalque he was laid out according to his own directions: in full evening dress, the stiff shirt-front gleaming above the pall, which was drawn only half-way up his breast, leaving the decorations showing, and his hands folded upon it, without a crucifix. The curving brows were small, hard ridges, the cheeks and lips sunken. He was as though sewn up tight in the corpse's dreadful, eyeless skin, which is still part of the personality and yet already different, an alien thing: life's travelling-bag. In spite of himself, Ulrich felt a shock somewhere at the core of his being, deep down where there is neither emotion nor thought: but nowhere else. If he had had to put it into words, all he could have said was that a tiresome and loveless relationship had come to an end. Just as a bad marriage makes the people bad who cannot get free from it, so do all those bonds that lie heavy and seem as though they must last for ever: they too make people bad when time shrivels away from under them.

" I should have liked you to come a good deal sooner," Agathe went on. " But Papa wouldn't hear of it. He made all the arrangements in connection with his death himself. I think he would have found it embarrassing to die with you looking on. I've been here for a fortnight. It was horrible."

" Was he at least fond of *you* ? " Ulrich asked.

" He gave all his instructions to old Franz, and after he had everything settled he was just like someone who has nothing to do and feels his occupation's gone. But every quarter of an hour or so he would lift his head to see if I was still in the room. During the first few days, anyway. Later on it was only about every half-hour, and then every hour or so, and during that frightful last day it only happened two or three times. And all that time he never spoke a word to me except when I asked him something."

As she was telling him this, Ulrich thought to himself: ' She's hard, really. Even as a child she had a quiet way of being incredibly obstinate sometimes. Still, she looks tractable, doesn't she ? ' And suddenly he remembered an avalanche and how he had almost lost his life in the forest that it had devastated: it had been no more than a soft cloud of powdery snow and yet the irresistible force behind it gave it the impact of a toppling mountain.

" Was it you who sent off the telegram ? " he asked.

" No, of course not—old Franz did ! It was all settled beforehand. He wouldn't let me look after him, either. He can't possibly ever have been fond of me, and I don't know why he sent for me. I felt perfectly miserable, and I shut myself up in my room as often as I could. It was during one of those times that he died."

" He probably did it just to put you in the wrong," Ulrich said bitterly. " Come on ! " And he drew her towards the door. " But perhaps he wanted you to stroke his forehead or kneel down beside the bed ? Even if only because he always read that that's the proper way for children to take their last leave of their father. Only he couldn't bring himself to ask you."

" Perhaps," Agathe said.

They had stopped and were looking at him.

" You know, the whole thing's horrible ! " Agathe said.

" Yes," Ulrich answered. " And one knows so little about it."

As they were leaving the room, Agathe stopped again and, looking straight at Ulrich, said: " I'm springing something on you that can't of course interest you in the slightest, but it was during Father's illness I decided not on any account to go back to my husband."

Her brother could not help smiling at this insistence. There was now a vertical furrow between Agathe's eyes, and she had spoken vehemently. She seemed to be afraid he would not take her side. She was rather like a cat that is terrified and for that very reason rushes bravely into the fray.

" Does he agree ? " Ulrich asked.

" He doesn't know yet," Agathe said. " But he won't agree ! "

The brother looked questioningly at his sister.

But she shook her head violently. " Oh no, it's not what you think ! There's nobody else," she said.

With this the conversation was over for the present. Agathe said apologetically that she really ought to have shown more consideration for Ulrich, who must be hungry and tired, and she led him into the room where tea was waiting. Something was missing from the tray, and she went to get it herself. Left alone,

Ulrich did his best to recollect what her husband was like, the better to understand her. Professor Hagauer was a man of medium height who bore himself very erect and whose stumpy legs were encased in baggy trousers; he wore a bristly moustache over his rather thick lips and he had a fondness for large-patterned ties, which was doubtless meant to indicate that he was no common schoolmaster but one with progressive views. Once again Ulrich experienced his old misgivings about Agathe's choice; but it was impossible to believe that this man, Gottlieb Hagauer, pursued secret vices and that the candid radiance shining from his brow and eyes was only a mask. ' Oh no, it's simply the enlightened, efficient type, the worthy man who promotes the cause of humanity in his own field, without meddling in things outside his scope,' Ulrich concluded, and at the same time he remembered Hagauer's writings and sank into thoughts that were not entirely agreeable.

Such people can be picked out for what they are even in their schooldays. They work not so much conscientiously—as people call it, mistaking the effect for the cause—as in an orderly and practical way. They organise every piece of work first, the way one needs to arrange tomorrow's clothes the night before, down to the collar-studs and cuff-links, if one is to dress quickly in the morning without wasting any time; there is no thought-process that they cannot fix firmly in their brains by the aid of half-a-dozen such studs, which they keep always in readiness, and it must be granted that the result is fit to appear in public and will stand up to scrutiny. In this way they get to the top of the class without acquiring a reputation for priggishness. And people like Ulrich, even if they are much more gifted, people whose nature lures them now into slightly overdoing things, now into just as slightly underdoing things, gradually get left behind, and this by a fatality that asserts itself imperceptibly, like a lingering disease. He now admitted to himself that secretly he was rather daunted by these, life's ' top boys ', for their mental exactitude made his own romantic enthusiasm for exactitude look a little shady. ' They haven't a trace of soul about them ', he thought, ' harmless, good-hearted people as they are. After the age of sixteen, when adolescents get worked up about intellectual problems, they seem to get left a little behind the others and haven't quite the ability to appreciate new ideas and feelings, but they carry on with the aid of their half-dozen studs, and the day comes when they can produce adequate evidence of always having understood every-thing, " of course without going to untenable extremes ", and finally it is they who introduce the new ideas into practical life, but only at a time when for others those ideas have faded away with their dreams and the solitary extravagances of adolescence.'

And so, by the time Agathe came back into the room, although Ulrich still had no picture of what had been going on in her life, he felt that war waged against her husband—and even though it were an unjust war—was likely to afford him pleasure of an entirely frivolous kind.

Agathe apparently regarded it as futile to try to explain her decision rationally. As was to be expected, considering Hagauer's character, her marriage was outwardly all that a marriage should be. There was no quarrelling, scarcely any difference of opinion, if for no other reason than that Agathe—as she herself recounted —never confided in him what her own opinion was on any subject. Naturally Hagauer was not the man to commit excesses; he neither drank nor gambled, nor had he even clung to any of his bachelor habits.

Their income was fairly apportioned. Their finances were in order. Their social life was quietly regular in its alternation between sociability with their acquaintances and boredom when they were alone.

" What it comes to," Ulrich said, " is that if you simply leave him for no reason at all *he* will get the divorce on grounds of your desertion. That is, assuming he files a petition."

" I want him to ! " Agathe said challengingly.

"Perhaps it would be a good idea to offer him some small financial compensation in return for an amicable settlement ? "

" All I took with me," she replied, " is what one needs, going away for three weeks, and a few childish things and mementoes of the time before I married him. He can keep all the rest, I don't want it. But for the future he's not going to get anything out of me at all—nothing ! "

She had again spoken with surprising vehemence. What it perhaps conveyed was that she wanted her revenge on this man whom she had formerly allowed to get too much out of her. Ulrich's own pugnacity, his competitive spirit, and his ingenuity in overcoming difficulties were now aroused, although he felt some compunction about it; for it was like the effect of a stimulant, which releases the grosser impulses, while the finer aspects of the personality remain untouched. He gave the conversation a slightly different turn, groping for some orientation.

" I know some of his writings and something of his reputation," he said. " I gather he's regarded as a coming man in the educational field."

" Yes," Agathe replied, " he is."

" It seems to me from what I know of his work that he's not only a sound educationist, but one of the pioneers of reform in higher education. I remember once reading a book of his where there was talk on the one hand of the unique value of history and the humanities generally as moral disciplines and on the other, similarly, of the unique value of science and mathematics as intellectual disciplines, and thirdly, of the unique value that the concentrated activity of sport and para-military training has in developing initiative and a sense of responsibility. Am I right ? "

" I dare say," Agathe answered. " But did you notice the way he quotes ? "

" The way he quotes ? Let me see—I do seem to have a vague memory of being struck by something. Yes, he quotes a great deal. He quotes the classics. And of course he quotes the moderns too. Now I know what it is: he does something that's positively revolutionary for a schoolmaster, he doesn't only quote the established great of the school textbooks, but the aircraft engineers, politicians, and artists of our own day as well. Still, that's only what I was saying just now, isn't it ? " he ended, with the rather discouraged feeling one has when a recollection suddenly comes to a standstill without having got one anywhere.

" The way he quotes," Agathe elaborated, " is this: for instance, in music he has no qualms about going as far as Richard Strauss, or in painting as far as Picasso. But what he'll never do, even to give an example of something he thinks wrong, is to mention a name that hasn't become more or less established currency in the newspapers, at least by way of adverse criticism."

That was how it was. That was what Ulrich had been groping for in his memory. He looked up. He was pleased by the acuity and indeed the whole attitude revealed in Agathe's reply.

" So that's how he's become a leader in the course of time—by dint of being one of the first to follow in time's train," he added, laughing. " All those who come after see him there ahead of them ! But do you care for the great figures of our day ? "

" I don't know. Anyway, I don't quote."

" However, let's try to be humble," Ulrich suggested. " Your husband's name stands for a programme that many people nowadays look upon as supremely important. His activities constitute a small piece of solid progress. It can't be long before he rises higher in his profession. The least he'll achieve before long is a university chair, even though he bears with him the odium of having earned his living as a schoolmaster. But just look at me ! All I had to do was to go straight along the course laid out for me, and what I've made of it probably wouldn't even get me a lectureship. What d'you think of that ? "

Agathe was disappointed, and that was probably the reason why her face became a porcelain-smooth, non-committal, ladylike mask as she replied, graciously: " I don't know—perhaps you ought to keep on the right side of Hagauer ? "

" When exactly is he supposed to arrive ? " Ulrich asked.

" Just in time for the funeral. He won't spare any more time than that. But he's not going to stay in this house—I won't have it ! "

" Just as you like ! " Ulrich said with unexpected decisiveness. " I'll meet him at the station and drop him at a hotel. And if that's what you want, I'll just tell him: ' Here's your room, I hope you like it.' "

Agathe was surprised, and suddenly enthusiastic. " That'll annoy him frightfully, because it'll cost money, and of course he's expecting to stay here." Her expression had instantly changed, and her face now wore the gay, wild look of a child contemplating mischief.

" What actually is the position ? " her brother asked. " Does this house belong to you, or to me, or to both of us ? Is there a Will ? "

" I've been given a big package Papa left—apparently with all the information we need."

They went into the study, which was beyond the room where the dead man lay.

Once again they moved quietly through candlelight and the scent of flowers and through the territory of those closed and sightless eyes. In the flickering half-light Agathe was for an instant no more than a shimmering haze of gold, grey, and pink. The packet containing the Will was there and they took it back to the tea-table with them; but there they put it aside and forgot to open it.

For as they sat down again, Agathe told her brother that she had been living to all intents and purposes apart from her husband, even though under one roof; she did not say how long this had been so.

The first impression this made on Ulrich was a bad one. Many married women tell a man this sort of tale when they begin to look on him as a possible lover. And although his sister had imparted the information with embarrassment, even a trace of defiance, and yet obviously with a sort of awkward determination to set something going, it irritated him that she should not be able to think of any better way of trying to impress him; he thought the whole thing an exaggeration.

" Frankly," he responded, " I've never been able to understand how you could live with a man like that."

Agathe said it was what her father had wanted. And how— she asked—could she have opposed him?

" After all, you were a widow at the time. It wasn't as if you were a little girl, not yet of age ! "

" That was just it. I'd come back home. Everyone thought I was still too young to go and live on my own, even though I was a widow. After all, I was only nineteen. And then, the fact is I just couldn't stand it here."

" But why didn't you find yourself some other man? Or go to the university and equip yourself for a career and independence ? " Ulrich asked bluntly.

Agathe merely shook her head. It was only after a little pause that she replied: " I told you before: I'm lazy."

Ulrich could not help feeling this was no answer. " So then you had some special reason for marrying Hagauer ? "

" Yes."

" You were in love with someone else whom you couldn't have ? "

Agathe hesitated. " I loved my first husband."

Ulrich regretted having used the word ' love ' in such a banal way, as though he himself attached importance to the social institution thus customarily referred to and regarded it as inviolable. ' All the consolation one ever offers is no better than giving a dry crust to a beggar,' he thought. All the same, he felt tempted to go on talking in the same way. " And so then you realised what you'd let yourself in for, and you began making things hard for Hagauer," he remarked.

" Yes," Agathe admitted. " But not at once. Quite late in the day," she added. " In fact, very late."

At this point they got into a little argument.

It was obvious that these confessions cost Agathe an effort, although she made them of her own free will and clearly, as was in keeping with her years, regarded problems of sex-life as a subject of great interest to everyone. She seemed determined to force the issue and discover at once whether she was going to meet with sympathy or the lack of it; she was in search of someone to confide in; and, not without candour, as well as passion, she was putting up a fight to win her brother over. But Ulrich, being still in the mood to dispense gratuitous moralisms, was not yet able to meet her halfway. For all his strength of spirit he was by no means always free from the prejudices that his intellect rejected; and he had often had to let his life take one course while his mind followed another. He had time and again exploited and misused his power over women by taking a hunter's delight in stalking and cornering his quarry, so he was quite in the habit of thinking of women as the prey that is struck down by the amorous male's assault, and he well knew the relish that lies in humiliating a woman, who in love succumbs to it, whereas the man is far from experiencing anything like surrender. This assumption of male superiority over female weakness is a standard one even today, although every new generation adds its own new and different ideas. And yet he was almost pained by the naturalness with which Agathe implied her subordination to Hagauer. It seemed to him that, without being quite aware of it, his sister had delivered herself up to outrage when she made herself over to that man he so much disliked, and she had gone on submitting to it for years. Although he did not say so, Agathe must have seen something of this in his face, for she suddenly said: " After all, I couldn't run away from him straight after marrying him, could I ?   It would have seemed pretty hysterical ! "

Ulrich was suddenly jerked out of his elder-brother rôle and the state of patronisingly edifying narrow-mindedness he had been in.   " Would it really have been hysterical," he exclaimed, " to feel abhorrence and immediately draw the logical conclusions from it ? "   He tried to soften the blow by immediately smiling and looking at his sister in as friendly a way as possible.

Agathe looked at him too.   Her face was as though rendered defenceless by the effort she was making to decipher the expression on his.   " Surely a normal healthy person isn't so sensitive to minor miseries ? " she retorted.   " What does it matter, after all ? "

Ulrich now pulled himself together, no longer letting his thoughts be governed by one aspect of his personality.   He was once more all objective intelligence.   " You're quite right," he said.   " After all, what do the processes as such matter ?   What matters is the system of concepts by means of which one contemplates them, and the personal system into which they are fitted."

" What do you mean by that ? " Agathe asked dubiously.

Ulrich apologised for his abstract mode of expression.   But while he was looking for a readily comprehensible analogy, his brotherly jealousy reasserted itself and influenced his choice of terms.   " Let's assume that a woman whom we care about has been raped," he said.   " Within the framework of a heroic system of ideas the consequence would inevitably be vengeance or suicide. In a cynical-empirical system, we should expect her to shake it off like a hen.   And what would really happen today would doubtless be a compromise that's neither here nor there.   But this lack of a touchstone within ourselves is more sordid than all the rest of it."

However, Agathe did not accept this way of putting the problem either.   " Do you really think it so terrible ? " she asked him quite simply.

" I don't know.   It struck me as humiliating to live with a person one doesn't love.   But now—just as you like ! "

" Is it worse than if a woman wants to marry in less than three months after her divorce and is compelled by law to be examined by an officially appointed gynaecologist to see whether she's pregnant or not, because of the laws of inheritance ?   It's difficult to believe, but I've read about it." Once again the little vertical furrow of defiant anger appeared between Agathe's eyebrows, crumpling her smooth forehead. " And there's none of them who doesn't get over it all right, if it comes to the point! " she said contemptuously.

" I don't doubt what you say," Ulrich responded. " Once they're actually there, all the things that happen to us pass over like rain and sunshine. You're probably much more sensible than I am, if you look at these things in such a natural way. But a man's nature isn't natural. It's nature-altering, and therefore sometimes tends towards extremes." His smile was a plea for friendship.

Looking at her, he saw how young her face was. In excitement it did not pucker up, but was made tenser and smoother than ever by what was going on behind it, as a glove is when the hand inside clenches into a fist.

" I've never thought about it in such general terms," she said now. " But what you've been saying makes me think I've been leading a dreadfully wrong life."

" It's all just because, of your own accord, you've told me so much," her brother said, lightly glossing over their mutual admissions of error, " and still haven't told me the decisive thing. How am I to get things right if you won't tell me anything about the man you're leaving Hagauer for at long last ? "

Agathe looked at him like a child that has been unjustly accused by its governess: " Has there got to be a man ? Can't it happen just by itself ? Is it wrong of me to leave him without having a lover to go to ? I'm not going to try to make you believe I've never had one, that would be absurd. But I haven't got one now, and I'd be very cross with you if you thought I had to have one in order to leave Hagauer ! "

Ulrich had no choice but to assure her that passionate women sometimes left their husbands without having a lover and that he actually thought this the more dignified thing.

Tea had almost imperceptibly been extended and enlarged into a somewhat haphazard early supper, at Ulrich's suggestion, because he was very tired and wanted to go to bed early, to get a good night's sleep and be fit for the next day, which seemed likely to bring with it all sorts of bothersome affairs to be attended to.

Now they sat smoking a last cigarette before separating. Ulrich still did not know what to make of his sister. There was neither anything emancipated nor anything bohemian about her, even though she sat there in those wide trousers in which she had received the brother who was almost a stranger to her. It was more something hermaphrodite, as it struck him now: as she moved and gestured, talking, the light semi-masculine garb gave a hint of the delicate forms of her body beneath it, like blurred outlines seen through the semi-transparency of water; and in contrast with the independent, free display of her legs, she wore her beautiful hair up in orthodox feminine style. But this impression of ambiguity was conveyed above all by the face, which had a high degree of charm that was wholly feminine, and yet with some minus quantity, some modification, that he could not quite define.

And knowing so little about her and sitting there together with her so intimately, and yet not at all the way it would have been with a woman for whom he would count as a man—it was all very pleasant to him, especially now that he was beginning to yield to his fatigue.

'A great change since yesterday!' he thought.

Being thankful for it, he made an effort to say something especially cordial and brotherly to Agathe as they said goodnight. But since this was something he was not accustomed to, nothing occurred to him. So he merely put one arm round her and kissed her.

3   *Daybreak in a house of mourning.*

THE next morning Ulrich woke early, as smoothly as a fish leaping from the water; he had slept dreamlessly and soundly and felt no trace of the previous day's fatigue. He explored the house in search of breakfast. The ritual of mourning had not yet been fully resumed; there was merely a hovering funereal atmosphere in all the rooms; it made him think of a shop with its shutters opened early in the morning when the street is still deserted. Then he got some of his scientific work out of his suitcase and took it into his father's study. The stove was lit and the room, as he sat there, felt more human than on the previous evening. Although it was a pedantic mind, a mind given to weighing every pro and con, that had made the room what it was, right to the plaster busts symmetrically facing each other on the top of the bookshelves, still, the many little personal things left lying about—pencils, eye-glass, thermometer, an open book, boxes of nibs, and the like —did give it the touching emptiness of a habitation that had only just been abandoned by its inmate. Ulrich sat in the midst of it— actually not far from the window, and yet at the room's ideal centre, at the writing-desk; and he felt a peculiar weariness, a slackening of the will. On the walls there were portraits of his forbears, and some of the furniture dated from their time. The man who had lived here had used the broken egg-shells of their lives to form the shell of his; now he was dead, and though his belongings still stood there, sharp-edged as if he had been scooped out of these encasing walls, the order of things was already on the point of crumbling, of yielding to his successor, and all these inanimate objects, in their greater longevity, began perceptibly, almost visibly, to quicken behind their rigid air of mourning.

Under such impressions Ulrich spread out his work, which he had put aside weeks, indeed months, ago, and he was instantly confronted by the equations of hydrodynamics where he had broken off. He remembered vaguely how his thoughts had drifted to Clarisse while he had been using the three main states of water in the application of a new mathematical operation, and how thinking of Clarisse had distracted him. Still, there is a way of remembering not so much words as an atmosphere in which they were uttered; and so, with the word ' carbon ' all at once floating through his mind, Ulrich got the feeling, as it were from nowhere, that it would get him somewhere if only he could say instantly in how many states carbon occurred; but he could not remember, and instead of trying he thought: ' Man is found in two states: male and female.' He went on thinking this for some time, seemingly paralysed with amazement, as though he had made heaven alone knows how great a discovery in noticing that man occurs in two different permanent states. But behind this deadlock in his mind something quite different was going on. For one can be hard, selfish, and eager, as it were sharply profiled against the world, and then suddenly also feel oneself, this same Ulrich What's-his-name, quite otherwise, deeply absorbed within, recollected, a selflessly happy being partaking also of an ineffably tender and somehow equally selfless condition of all surrounding things. And he asked himself: 'How long is it since I last had this experience?' To his surprise, it was scarcely more than twenty-four hours. The silence around him was having a reviving effect, and the condition that he was now reminded of did not strike him as so abnormal as it generally did. 'After all, we're all organisms,' he thought, relaxing, ' all having to assert ourselves against one another with all possible vigour and greed in an un-friendly world. But each of us, together with his enemies and victims, is still a particle of this world, and born of it, by no means so detached from the rest, by no means so independent, as he imagines.' And if that was so, surely it was no wonder if sometimes a fleeting sense of unity and love rose from the world, almost a certainty that it was only the material stringency of life that ordinarily prevented one from recognising more than one half of the pattern of living things. There was nothing in this that need offend a man mathematically and scientifically exact; on the contrary, it made him think of the work of a psychologist whom he happened to know personally. This work assumed the exist-tence of two main opposing groups of ideas, the one based on the condition of being enveloped by the content of experience, the other on the enveloping of this content by the subject. The inference was that this sort of ' being inside something' and ' looking at something from outside ', this ' sense of concavity' and ' sense of convexity ', this being ' spatial' or 'corporeal ', this ' introspection ' and ' contemplation ', occurred in so many pairs of opposites both in experience and in language that it was justifiable to assume that behind them there was an archetypal ambivalence common to all human experience. This work did not belong to the class of austere, strictly objective enquiry; it was of that fantastical kind which often gropes far ahead into the future and which originates in some stimulus outside the scope of every-day scientific activity. However, it was built on sound foundations and there was much plausibility in its deductions, which pointed to there being a unity of experience hidden behind the ultimate nebulosity of our feeling and perception. Indeed, Ulrich himself assumed that the scattered and displaced fragments of that unity were perhaps what had produced the present-day attitude, the core of which lay obscurely in the contrasting male and female modes of experience and which was everywhere mysteriously overshadowed by ancient dreams.

At this point Ulrich tried to secure his position—in exactly the same way as one uses ropes and crampons for the descent over a dangerous rock-face—and began the following reflection:

' The most ancient philosophies that have come down to us, obscure and almost incomprehensible as they are to us, often speak of a male and a female " principle ".'

' The fact is,' he went on thinking, ' these goddesses that in primeval religions existed side by side with the gods are no longer within our emotional range. If we tried to have any relationship to those superhumanly mighty females it would be sheer masochism.'

' Nature,' he thought, ' provides men with nipples and women with a rudimentary male sex organ, but this doesn't necessarily mean that our ancestors were hermaphrodites. And there's no more reason to suppose they were psychological hybrids either. In that case, they must at some stage have been endowed from outside with the dual possibility of the ' giving ' and the ' receiving ' vision corresponding to the dual face of Nature. And somehow all this is much older than the differentiation of the sexes, and the sexes later adopted this duality as a supplement to their psychological garb . . .'

Thus he reflected. But after a while an image from his childhood arose in his mind; and because the memory gave him pleasure, in a way that had not happened for a long time, he allowed his thoughts to be deflected. It must here be put on record that his father had in earlier days been something of a horseman and had kept his own horses, a fact to which the empty stable by the garden wall still bore witness—the stable that had been the first thing Ulrich caught sight of on his arrival. This had probably been the only aristocratic taste that his father had presumed to adopt in imitation of his feudal friends' much-admired way of life. Ulrich had been only a little boy then: and here and now, in his recollection, he experienced all over again the sensations that the huge, muscular equine body aroused in the marvelling child—that sense of the seemingly infinite, the immeasurably vast, an awe-inspiring mountain landscape in fairyland, with hair growing on it as grass grows on the slopes, and the ripples of the skin running over it like the waves of the wind. It was, he realised, one of those memories whose splendour had its origin in the child's helplessness and inability to fulfil its wishes. But these are poor words for the vastness of that splendour, which was nothing less than supernatural. Nor do they convey anything of that no less miraculous splendour which, only a short time later, the little boy touched with his fingertips while he was in quest of the earlier one. For at that time the town was placarded with posters announcing a circus; depicting not only horses but lions and tigers as well, and magnificent big dogs that lived on good terms with the wild beasts. He had spent a long time staring at these brightly-coloured posters before he managed to get hold of one for himself; and he cut out the animals and stiffened them with little wooden supports so that they would stand up on their own. But what happened then can only be compared with drinking and never quenching one's thirst however long one goes on; it was without form or limits, and for weeks it went on expanding without showing any progress, a permanent state of being drawn out of himself and into those creatures which he so much admired, gazing at them with the unutterable happiness of a solitary child, now believing that he possessed them just as intensely as he felt there was some last thing missing, some fulfilment that nothing could bring about; and the very absence of this last fulfilment was what gave his yearning that immense radiance, which seemed to flood his whole being. But together with the memory of that strangely boundless experience the feeling of another, somewhat later, childhood experience now came back to him and for all its childish irrelevance took possession of the big adult body sitting here, dreaming open-eyed. It was the little girl who had consisted of only two elements: that of belonging to him alone and that of the fights he had to have with other boys for her sake. And of these two only the fights were real, for the little girl herself did not exist. What a weird time it had been, when he had gone out like a knight errant, roaming through lonely, mystery-laden streets, seeking his antagonist always among strangers and preferably one bigger than himself, taking the other by surprise, leaping at his throat. Quite often he got a thrashing, though sometimes he won great victories; yet however it ended, he felt cheated of the satisfaction he had expected. His feelings utterly rejected the obvious thought that the other little girls, those whom he knew in reality, were creatures of the same kind as that secret little girl for whom he fought. Like all boys of his age he was silly and awkward in the presence of girls. And then one day something happened that was an exception to the rule.

Ulrich remembered it as distinctly as if he were looking at the circular picture at the far end of a telescope trained, across all the intervening years, on that incident in the past: it was an evening when Agathe was dressed up for a children's party. She wore a velvet dress and her hair flowed down over it like waves of brighter velvet. Although he was himself menacingly encased in knightly armour, at the sight of her he suddenly felt an indescribable longing similar to that which had overwhelmed him at the sight of the animals on the circus posters—only this time it was a longing to be a girl himself. At that age he still knew so little about the difference between the sexes that he did not think it entirely impossible for his wish to be fulfilled, yet he already knew enough about it not to do what children so often do, dashing into some impulsive attempt to *make* the wish come true; and today, as he tried to define that paradoxical state, tried to find words for it, it seemed to him that it had been like groping in darkness for a door and suddenly encountering some blood-warm, warmly delicious resistance, pressing against it, trying to penetrate through whatever it was that seemed to be all tender yielding to his desire without ever actually giving way before him. Perhaps too it might be likened to some harmless form of vampirism, devouring the object of desire; and yet what that infant male had wanted was not to draw the infant female to himself, but to be entirely in her place, to be himself the little girl. And all this had happened in that dazzling haze of tenderness which belongs only to the experience of immature sexuality.

Ulrich stood up and stretched his arms, marvelling at these day-dreams. No more than a few paces away from him, on the other side of the wall, his father's body lay, and only now did he become aware that all around them both the place was swarming with people, as though they had shot up out of the ground: this house, which had seemed dead and desolate, was now alive with bustling activity. Old women were laying carpets and lighting fresh candles, there was a sound of hammering on the staircase, floors were being polished, and flowers were being delivered. And now he too was drawn into this activity: he was expected to see a number of people who were out and about so early because they were all after something, even if it was merely information. And it went on like this for hours. The university needed some information about the funeral; an old-clothes man came submissively asking if there was anything for sale; a local secondhand-bookseller appeared with profuse apologies, to make an offer, on behalf of a bookshop in Germany, for a rare legal work that he surmised was in the deceased's library; then a curate asked to see Ulrich about some point that was not clear in the parish register, and after him a man from the insurance company, with some long and complicated problem to do with the deceased's insurances. Somebody wanted a piano cheap. An estate agent left his card in case the family should wish to sell the house. A superannuated clerk offered to address envelopes. And so it went on all through the precious morning hours, down at the front door, where the old servant turned away as many as he could, and upstairs, where Ulrich perforce saw all those who slipped through: a continual coming and going, enquiring and soliciting, all with matter-of-fact reference to the death and all of it asserting, by word of mouth or in writing, its own claim on life. He had never before realised how many people are always politely waiting for other people's death and how many hearts one sets throbbing the moment one's own heart ceases to beat. He was considerably astonished, contemplating it: a dead beetle lying somewhere in the woods, and other beetles, ants, birds, and flickering butterflies gathering around. For in all this commotion, this profit-seeking activity, there was everywhere a fluttering and stirring of darkness as in the deep woods.

Now he looked into eyes veiled with emotion, through which self-interest gleamed like a lantern that had been left burning in bright daylight: a man stood before him, wearing mourning-crape on the black sleeve of a suit that seemed to serve the dual purpose of conveying the wearer's condolences and attiring him correctly for business. This man paused on the threshold, somehow appearing to expect that in the next moment either he or Ulrich would burst into tears. But when after the lapse of a few seconds neither of them had done so, he seemed to consider that sufficient proper feeling had been shown and, entering the room, introduced himself, quite in the manner in which any ordinary tradesman would have, as the manager of the undertakers' firm. He asked if Ulrich was satisfied with the style in which the arrangements were being carried out. He assured Ulrich that all further operations would also be carried out in a style with which even the late lamented would most certainly have found no fault— and it was well known that the late lamented had never been an easy gentleman to please. He pressed into Ulrich's hand a form on which there was a great deal of print, with columns, dotted lines, and squares for ticks, and forced him to read through what turned out to be a contract-form intended to cover all possible classes of funerals, and to give his attention to such items as eight horses or two horses . . . wreath carriage . . . number . . . harness, style of . . . with or without outrider, silverplated . . . mutes, style of . . . torches, Marienburg style . . . Admont style . . . mutes, number of . . . illumination, style of . . . illumination, duration of . . . quality of coffin . . . pot-plants . . . name, date of birth, male or female, occupation, firm does not accept liability for any unforeseen. . . . Some of these archaic-sounding phrases Ulrich had never before heard and he asked the funerary director what their history was. The man looked at him in amazement; he had no idea. He stood there before Ulrich like a reflex-track in the collective human brain, a link between stimuli and actions, something that does not develop a consciousness of its own. Ancient customs, the heritage of centuries, were entrusted to this merchant of mourning, who was at liberty to turn the archaic words into a list of wares. He obviously sensed that Ulrich was trying to loosen some screw on his machinery that was better left untouched, and he quickly tried to prevent this by bringing their conversation back to its purpose and their business to a conclusion. He explained that unfortunately all these classifications were required by the statutes of the national association of undertakers, but that it did not matter in the least if they were ignored

—as a matter of fact they always were—if Ulrich would just be good enough to sign the form, since madam, his sister, had yesterday had misgivings about doing so without consulting her brother— all it amounted to was that Ulrich would be declaring his agreement with the instructions previously given by his late father, and he could rest assured . . . could rely entirely on first-class execution of the order.

While Ulrich was signing he asked the man if the town yet had any of those electrically driven sausage-machines with a picture on their housing of St. Luke in his capacity as patron of the guild of butchers and sausage-makers. He was just adding that he had seen such a machine in Brussels when he realised he was talking to someone else. There was now a different man there, a reporter from the leading local newspaper, who needed information for the obituary. Ulrich handed the signed form to the undertaker, who had respectfully stepped back and, having got rid of him, tried to give the journalist an account of the most important aspects of his father's life. But as soon as he began, he realised that he did not know what was ' important ' and what was not ' important ', and his visitor had to come to his aid. Only then, with the promptings of the specialist whose professional inquisitiveness was like forceps gripping the essential, did the interview get under way, and Ulrich felt increasingly as if he were present at the creation of the world. The reporter, a young man, asked whether the old gentleman had died after a long illness or whether his death had occurred un- expectedly, and when Ulrich answered that his father had continued his lectures right up to the last week of his life, the young journalist moulded this into: . . . still enjoying the full vigour of his mental and bodily powers. And then the chips began to fly from the old gentleman's life until nothing seemed left except a few ribs and joints: born at Protiwin in 1844 . . . educated at . . . and the university of . . . appointed . . . subsequently to the post . . . until finally, with the listing of honorary degrees and other distinctions, five of them in all, the main points seemed to be exhausted. There was the incidental mention of his marriage. There was the list of the few books he had written. And once he had just missed becoming Minister of Justice (there had been opposition from some quarter). The reporter wrote, Ulrich read through what he had written, and passed it as correct. The reporter was content; he

had filled the necessary number of lines.   Ulrich looked in wonder
at the little heap of ashes that was all that was left of a long life.
For every piece of information supplied the reporter had his cut-
and-dried magnificatory phrase, which came rolling along like a
coach-and-six: distinguished scholar . . . wide sympathies and
deep understanding . . . forward-looking but statesmanlike policy
. . . mind of truly universal scope . . . and so on.   It was as if
nobody had died for a considerable time and the long unused words
were hungry for employment.   Ulrich reflected for a moment;
he would have liked to wind up by saying something good and kind
in memory of his father.   But the journalist had got his facts and
was putting his notebook away, and the rest was like trying to pick
up a glass of water without the glass.

Now the bustle had subsided.   All the people whom Agathe
had the previous day referred to him had been and gone away,
and when the reporter took his leave Ulrich remained alone.   For
some indefinable reason he felt embittered.   Had his father not
been right after all, to go carting along the sacks of knowledge,
to go on shifting some grains from the great heap of all the grains
of knowledge, and for the rest simply to submit to those powers
of life which he deemed the strongest ?   He thought of his own
work, which lay untouched in a desk drawer.   Probably no one
would even be able to say as much of him some day—that he had
spent his life shifting the grains from one heap to another.

He went into the small room where the dead man lay in state.
Amid the ceaseless stir and bustle of which it was the cause, this
rigid, straight-walled cell was fantastic, uncanny.   Stiff as a
floating log the body drifted on the current of activity; but now
and then the image would for an instant be reversed, and then it
was as though all the life around were petrified and this dead body
were floating onwards in uncannily quiet movement.   ' What
does the traveller care,' it said, ' for the cities and towns he has
left behind, with their harbours and their stations ?   Once I lived
here, acting as was expected of me—and now I am on my way
again.'   Ulrich was assailed by the uncertainty of a man living
among others and wanting something different from what they
want; and it constricted his heart.   He looked into his father's
face.   Perhaps all he held to be his own, his whole individuality,
was no more than the result of opposition to this face, opposition

originating far back in childish antagonism? He glanced about him in search of a looking-glass; but there was none. The only thing here that reflected light was this blank face. He scrutinised it for some resemblance to his own. Perhaps there was some. Perhaps it was all there, the race from which they had sprung, their dependence on all the past, all the non-personal, the great river of heredity on which each individual is only a tiny ripple, and the limitation and the disillusion and the eternal repetition and sameness, the mind's everlasting circumambulation, which he hated with every fibre of his deep-rooted will to live.

Suddenly he was overwhelmed by such discouragement that he thought of packing his bags and leaving instantly, not even waiting for the funeral. If there was anything he might yet achieve in life, what then was he still doing here?

But in the doorway to the other room he collided with his sister, who had come to look for him.

4   " Lest old acquaintance be forgot . . ."

FOR the first time now Ulrich saw her dressed in a woman's clothes, and, after the impression he had received the previous day, it positively affected him like a kind of masquerade. Through the open door came artificial light, mingling with the tremulous grey of the advancing morning, and this black-clad fair-haired figure seemed to be standing in some ethereal grotto irradiated with light. Agathe's hair was now drawn back closer to her head, and this lent her face a more feminine expression than he remembered from yesterday. Her severe black dress held her delicate breasts as in a frame, in a perfect balance between yielding and resistance, making him think of the feathery lightness and yet the hardness of a pearl. The slim long legs of yesterday, so similar to his own, were now curtained by skirts. And because today her appearance as a whole was less like his, he began to notice the likeness of their faces. It was as if it were he himself who had come through that door and was now walking towards himself: only this other being was quite beautiful and surrounded by an aura in which he never saw himself. For the first time it flashed on him that his sister was himself all over again, transformed as in a dream; but it was the merest flash of a thought, vanishing an instant later.

Agathe had come hurrying in to remind her brother of duties that were on the point of being left till too late, for she had been asleep all this time. She had her father's Will in her hands, and now she began to draw Ulrich's attention to various points that must be dealt with instantly. Above all there was a rather eccentric stipulation of the old gentleman's with reference to his decorations, a matter on which the old servant Franz had also been given instructions. Agathe—all zeal, though somewhat deficient in proper respect for a Last Will and Testament—had sidelined the passage in red pencil. It had been the old man's wish to be buried wearing his decorations, of which he possessed a fair number, and since this wish had not been born of vanity he had set down his reasons in writing, with philosophic profundity and at some length. His daughter had read only the beginning of it and now handed it over to Ulrich to explain the rest to her.

" Well, it's rather abstruse," Ulrich said, after reading the passage through. " Papa wished to be buried wearing his decorations because he considered the individualist theory of the State to be mistaken. He recommends the universalist one to us. It is only through the creative community which is the State that man acquires a purpose reaching beyond the limits of the merely personal, and with it his sense of the good and his sense of justice. Man alone is nothing. This is why the monarch is a symbol of the spirit. The long and the short of it is that at his death man should have himself wrapped in his orders as a dead sailor is wrapped in the flag when his body is consigned to the sea."

" But surely I've read somewhere," Agathe said, " that these orders have to be returned ? "

" The dead person's heirs have to return the orders to the Chamberlain's office. So Papa got himself a spare set. But evidently he seems to think those he bought himself are not quite so authentic as the others, and that's why he wants us not to exchange them for the genuine ones pinned to his breast till the very last moment when the coffin's going to be fastened down. That's really the whole problem. For all we know this may be his own silent protest against the regulation, which he didn't like to express in any other way."

" But by that time there'll be hundreds of people here, and we're bound to forget ! " Agathe said, slightly worried.

" We might just as well do it now, at once."

" There's no time now. You'd better read the next bit, what he's written about Professor Schwung. Professor Schwung may turn up at any moment. In fact I was expecting him all day yesterday."

" All right, then let's do it when Schwung's gone."

" Only it's not very nice," Agathe objected, " not to fulfil his wish."

" Well, he doesn't know any more about it now."

She looked at him doubtfully. " Are you quite sure ? "

" What a question ! " Ulrich exclaimed, laughing. " You sound almost as though you weren't ! "

" I'm not sure about anything," Agathe answered.

" And even supposing it weren't certain—we never could do things right for him anyway."

" That's true," Agathe said. " All right then, we'll do it afterwards. But tell me," she added, " do you never bother about what people ask of you ? "

Ulrich hesitated. ' She goes to a good place for her clothes,' he thought. ' I needn't have worried that she might turn out to be provincial.' Her words somehow became associated with the whole of the previous evening, and that was why he wanted to find an answer that would really meet the case and be of use to her. But he could not think of any way of putting it that might not cause misunderstanding. Finally he said, with inappropriately youthful lightheartedness:

" It's not only Father that's dead. So is all the pomp and ceremony going on around him. His Will is dead too. All the people who turn up here are dead. I don't want to sound beastly—heaven knows, one probably ought to be grateful to all those who contribute to the solidity of the world we live in. But all that is the limestone of life, not the great ocean ! " He caught an expression of doubt in his sister's eyes and realised how obscurely he was talking. He laughed. " Society's virtues," he concluded, " are vices to the saint."

He put his hands on her shoulders with an air partly patronising and partly exuberant; it was embarrassment that made him do it. But Agathe would not fall in with his mood. She stepped back gravely and asked: " Did you make that up ? "

" No. It was said by a man of whom I think very highly."

There was something about her now of the indignation one finds in children who are forced to think very hard, as she summed up Ulrich's answer: " So I suppose you wouldn't call someone good if he's honest simply from habit ? But a thief stealing for the first time, with his heart in his mouth, you would call good ? "

Ulrich was surprised by the oddity of what she had said, and became more serious. " I really don't know," he said abruptly. And he added: " Frankly, in certain situations I don't very much care whether a thing's considered right or wrong, but I can't give you any rules to go by."

Slowly Agathe lowered her querying gaze; she picked up the Will again. " We must get on with it," she said, as though calling herself to order. " There's something else sidelined."

Before taking to his bed for the last time the old gentleman had written a number of letters, and his Will contained explanations and directions concerning these letters and the way he wanted them despatched. The passage that was sidelined concerned his old colleague, Professor Schwung, who, after a lifetime of friendship, had so very much embittered the last year of his life by taking the opposite point of view on the law relating to diminished responsibility. Ulrich instantly recognised the long-drawn-out and long-familiar arguments about illusion and will, the precision of law and the vagueness of Nature, all of which his father had summarised for him shortly before his death. Indeed it appeared that what had chiefly occupied the old gentleman in the last days of his life was denouncing the social school of thought, to which Professor Schwung had declared his allegiance, as a manifestation of the Prussian spirit. He had just begun working on a pamphlet to be entitled " The State and the Law, or Consequence and Denunciation ", when he felt his strength beginning to fail and realised, with much bitterness, that he was about to leave the enemy in sole possession of the field. In solemn phraseology such as is inspired only by the approach of death and the struggle to preserve that sacred possession, one's reputation, he exhorted his children not to let his work fall into oblivion, imposing especially on Ulrich the duty of cultivating the influential connections that he had made thanks to his father's unwearying admonitions, in order that all Professor Schwung's hopes of achieving his aims might be utterly frustrated and annihilated.

Still, after writing in such fashion, having completed one's task—or rather having paved the way for its completion—one may feel the urge to forgive an erstwhile friend those errors of his that arise from his gross conceit. Severe illness, and the sense of how the mortal coil is quietly working, will make a man inclined to forgive and seek forgiveness; but the moment he feels better, he will take it all back again: for the healthy body has an innate tendency towards intransigeance. It was evident that the old gentleman must have experienced both these states of mind during the fluctuations of his last illness, and both of them must have struck him as equally justified. But since this is an intolerable situation for a distinguished lawyer to be in, his logically trained mind had devised a means of leaving his Last Will in such a state that its validity as his Last Will should not be impaired by any reversals of emotion: he wrote a letter of forgiveness and left it unsigned and undated, charging his son Ulrich with the task of entering the day and hour of his death and then, together with his daughter, signing the document as a proxy, as is sometimes done when a dying person no longer has the strength to write his name. Actually, although he would never have acknowledged it, in his quiet way he had been rather a quaint old bird—this little old man who had always subordinated himself to the hierarchies of this world, making himself their zealous servant and champion and all the while harbouring a multitude of rebellious impulses to which, having chosen his course, he could never give vent. Ulrich could not help thinking of the telegram he had received, in which his father announced his own death; it had probably been the result of a similar logical process. Indeed, here Ulrich almost recognised some kinship with himself, yet this time not irritably and resentfully, but compassionately, at least in the sense that he began to understand how the old man, having always stifled his own urge for self-expression, must have been infuriated to the point of hatred by this son of his who made life easy for himself by permitting himself unpardonable liberties. For this is the way the sons' approach to life has looked to fathers all down the ages, Ulrich reflected and, thinking of all that was still unresolved in himself, he suddenly felt a twinge of filial feeling. But he had barely begun trying to give the thought an appropriate form, which would also be comprehensible to Agathe, when, with long buoyant strides, a man swept into the candlelit room.

He strode in as though throwing himself forward with each step, right into the nimbus of candlelight, and it was only there, one pace from the catafalque, that he came to a halt and was caught up with by the old servant scurrying along to announce him.

" Revered friend ! " the visitor sonorously declaimed.

And there his enemy, Schwung, stood over the little old man who lay with clenched and stiffened jaws.

" Ah, my young friends," Professor Schwung continued: " above us the majesty of the starry firmament, within us the majesty of moral law ! " With veiled eyes he gazed down upon his colleague. " Within this breast now cold there lived indeed the majesty of moral law ! "

Thereupon he turned to face the brother and sister and shook hands with them.

Ulrich took the opportunity to acquit himself of his task at once. " If I understand rightly, sir," he said, approaching the subject with some caution, " there was recently some unfortunate disagreement between yourself and my father ? "

It seemed that the white-bearded visitor needed a moment to grasp the question's import. " Divergencies of opinion, not worth mentioning," he then replied magnanimously, turning an affectionate gaze upon the body on the bier.

But when, in the politest possible way, Ulrich persisted, conveying that his question related to the deceased's Last Will and Testament, the atmosphere in the room suddenly became tense as in a backstreet tavern when everyone knows that under cover of the table one of the gang has just drawn his knife and the next moment they will be in the thick of a brawl. So even at his last gasp the old boy had managed to think out ways of annoying his colleague Schwung. Enmity of such long standing had of course long ceased to be a matter of the emotions; it had become a mental habit. Whenever there did not happen to be any new cause of irritation, the hostile impulses simply ceased to exist; what had happened was that the accumulated memories of countless disagreeable episodes in the past had piled up, taking on the form of a disparaging opinion that each held of the other—and this was as independent of the flux of emotion as any objective truth could be. Professor Schwung felt this exactly as his dead antagonist had felt it. To him it seemed utterly childish and superfluous to forgive; for the one tolerant impulse just before the end (and that merely an expression of emotion, nothing at all like a considered recantation of erroneous views) naturally counted for nothing over against all those years of controversy, and it was indeed, as Schwung saw it, quite shamelessly intended to serve no other purpose than that of putting him in the wrong the moment he exploited his victory. The fact that Professor Schwung felt the urge to take leave of his dead friend was of course something entirely different. Good lord, they had known each other away back in their bachelor days, when they held their first lectureships ! You remember drinking to the setting sun that time in the Palace Gardens, arguing about Hegel ? However many sunsets there may have been since then, that's one I've never forgotten. And you remember our first difference of professional opinion, which nearly made adversaries of us even then ? Ah, those were the days ! Now you are dead, and I am still on my feet, I'm glad to say, even though standing beside your bier.

Such, it is well known, are aged people's feelings when their contemporaries die. When one falls into the sere, the yellow leaf, poetry breaks through. Many people who have not turned a verse since they were seventeen suddenly produce a poem at the age of seventy-seven, when drawing up their Will. Just as at the Last Judgment the dead will be called forth one by one—even though they and their bygone centuries have been lying on the ocean-bed of time like the cargoes of foundered ships—so too in Wills things are summoned by their names, and the personalities that were gradually worn away in use are now restored to them. " The Bokhara rug in my study with the cigar-burn . . ." that is the sort of thing one reads in such last screeds; or " the umbrella with the rhinoceros-horn handle purchased by me at Sonnenschein & Winter's in May 1887 . . ." Even the packets of stocks and shares are named and referred to by their numbers.

And it is no accident that as this last light is shed on each individual object a desire also flares up to attach a moral to it all—some admonition, some blessing, the enunciation of some rule of conduct, one completely effective formula for all this undreamt-of multiplicity, looming up for the last time round about what is sinking out of sight for ever. And so what awakens now is not only the poetry of Will-making time, but the philosophy as well; and, understandably enough, it is usually an ancient and dusty philosophy, brought out of a drawer where it has lain forgotten for the last fifty years. Ulrich suddenly realised that neither of these two old men had been capable of giving way. ' Let life do what it will, but let our principles be unimpugned ! ' is a very sensible attitude to take when one knows that in a few years, or even months, one will have been outlived by these one's principles. And it was clearly to be observed how in the old Hofrat the two impulses were still contending with each other: his romanticism, his youth, all the poetical side of his being, demanded a fine, sweeping gesture and some high-sounding, noble utterance; his philosophy, on the other hand, required that he should demonstrate the immaculate aloofness of the law of reason, which must not be blemished by any sudden eruptions of feeling or weak and transient sentimentalities such as his dead adversary had laid in his way like a snare. For two days past Schwung had been nurturing the thought in his mind: ' Well, so he's gone, and now there's nothing to interfere with the Schwungian view of diminished responsibility.' And so his emotions had flowed in great waves towards his old friend, and he had worked out the farewell scene as carefully as a chief of staff prepares his mobilisation plan, so that all it needs is the signal that puts it into operation. But a drop of vinegar had fallen into his overflowing cup, and its effect was clarifying. Professor Schwung had begun with a great sweep of sentiment, but now he felt like someone writing a poem who suddenly comes to his senses and then cannot think of anything for the last lines. Thus they confronted each other, a white stubbly beard and white beard-stubble, and each with jaws implacably clenched.

' And what'll he do now ? ' Ulrich wondered, intent on the scene before him. In Hofrat Schwung the cheerful certainty that now Paragraph 318 of the Penal Code would be emended in accordance with his own proposals finally gained the supremacy over his annoyance; and so being liberated from resentful thoughts, he could almost have begun to sing ' Lest old acquaintance be forgot And never brought to mind . . .' as the only way of giving vent to his now entirely benevolent emotion. And since he could not very well do that, he turned to Ulrich and said:

" Believe me, young son of my departed friend, it is the moral crisis that develops first. Social decline follows in its wake ! " Then turning to Agathe, he added: " It was the mark of greatness in your late lamented father that he was always ready to help an idealistic view to prevail in re-formulating the foundations of our law."

Then he seized one of Agathe's hands and one of Ulrich's, shook them, and exclaimed:

" Your father attached much too much importance to minor differences of opinion, which cannot always be avoided in long years of collaboration. It was always my conviction that his delicate sense of justice compelled him to do so lest it suffer self-reproach. There will be many eminent scholars bidding him a last farewell tomorrow, but not one of them half the man he was ! "

Thus the encounter ended on a conciliatory note; and, on leaving, Schwung had even assured Ulrich that he might count on his father's friends should he decide to take up an academic career after all.

Agathe had listened, wide-eyed, contemplating the uncanny final form into which life moulds human beings. " Heavens," she said to her brother afterwards, " that was like being in a forest of plaster trees ! "

Smiling, Ulrich replied: " I feel as sentimental as a dog by moonlight ! "

5   *They do wrong.*

" DO you remember," Agathe asked him after a while, " one time when I was still quite small—you were playing with some other boys and fell into the water, right up to your waist ? You sat there at lunch, with the top half of you dry, trying to hide the fact that the lower half was soaking. But your teeth chattered so much that it gave you away."

When as a boy Ulrich had come home from school for the holidays—and actually that occasion had been the only one in a long period—and when this small, shrivelled cadaver here had still been a man almost almighty in the children's eyes, it was not infrequent that Ulrich refused to confess some misdemeanour or was unwilling to show any sign of remorse even though he could not deny or conceal the offence. So it was too on that occasion: he had caught a chill and had had to be packed off to bed, running a high temperature.

" And all you got to eat was soup," Agathe went on.

" That's true," her brother agreed, smiling. How remote it was now—that punishment of long ago—something that had as little to do with him as if he had suddenly seen his tiny baby shoes on the floor beside him!

" You wouldn't have got anything but soup anyway, with such a high temperature," Agathe said. " Still, it was also meant as a punishment."

" That's true," Ulrich once more agreed. " Only of course he didn't do it to be horrid, but because that was how he saw his duty to us." He was not sure what his sister was getting at. He himself was still having that vision of the baby shoes, not really seeing them at all, only with the feeling of somehow having them before his eyes. And it was in the same way that he felt the insults and humiliations he had outgrown. What he thought to himself was: 'This no-longer-concerning-one is somehow symbolic of the way one is never quite a proper fit for oneself at any stage of one's life.'

" And you wouldn't have been allowed anything but soup anyway ! " Agathe repeated. " You know," she added, " I think I've spent my whole life being afraid I might be the only person incapable of understanding that sort of thing ! "

May it be, when two people are talking of their common past, that their memories suddenly not only supplement each other but coalesce, and this even before they are given utterance ? Certainly what happened at this moment was something of the kind. Brother and sister were both overtaken by the same state of mind, a shared experience; and they were startled, even bewildered, as hands might be, unexpectedly emerging from somewhere under cloaks and one suddenly feeling the touch of the other. Each of them all at once knew more of the past than either had previously supposed. Once again Ulrich was aware of the fever-haunted light: very much in the same way as the flickering of the candles seemed to creep up the walls of this room they were standing in now, that light had crept up from the floor, and then Father had come in and, passing through the cone of light cast by the table-lamp, had sat down beside the bed. ' If you did not fully appreciate the possible consequences of your action, a milder view might be taken of it. But in that case you must first admit to yourself that it was so.' Well, perhaps that was not exactly how it had gone; he might be superimposing on the image some phrases that occurred in the Will, or in one of those letters about Paragraph 318. Normally, he had no memory for detail, no verbal memory, so there was something quite unusual in this recollection of whole sentences, standing out so clearly. It was all somehow connected with having his sister here beside him, as though it were her proximity that had brought about this change in him.

" ' If you were capable spontaneously, and independently of any compelling necessity, of the resolve to commit a wrong act, then you must also realise that in so acting you have incurred guilt,' " he went on aloud. " He must have talked that way to you too."

" Perhaps not quite the same way," Agathe demurred. " In my case he generally took into account the mitigating circumstances arising from my psychological constitution. He was always trying to make me realise that volition is linked with the intellect, that it isn't an instinctual operation."

" ' It is the will,' " Ulrich quoted, " ' that, in the process of gradual development of the understanding and the reason, must dominate the desires, which is to say the instincts, by means of reflection and the resolves consequent upon reflection.' "

" Is that true? " his sister asked.

" Why do you ask? "

" I suppose because I'm stupid."

" You're not stupid ! "

" I always found it hard to learn things. And I never really knew what anything was about."

" That doesn't prove much."

" Well then I suppose it just means I'm wicked, because I don't really take in what I understand."

Face to face, close to each other, they lounged in the doorway to the other room, the door having remained open when Professor Schwung departed. Daylight and candlelight played on their faces, and their voices intertwined as in a responsory. Ulrich went on intoning almost liturgically, and Agathe's lips moved quietly in response. That old torment of admonition, which for the tender, uncomprehending childish mind meant having a hard alien pattern impressed upon it, merely amused them now, and they toyed with it.

And all at once, entirely without any prompting from what they had been talking about, Agathe exclaimed: " Now just imagine that extended ad infinitum, and you have Gottlieb Hagauer ! " As pertly as a schoolgirl, she began imitating her husband: " ' You mean to to say you really don't know that lambium album is the white dead-nettle ? ' ' How else should we progress but by taking as our trusty guide that same strenuous process of induction which, in the course of millennia of strenuous if often mistaken labour, has brought mankind, step by step, to the present-day level of understanding ? ' ' My dearest Agathe, surely you must realise that thinking is also a *moral* obligation ? *Concentrating* means perpetually overcoming one's own natural indolence.' ' And mental discipline is that training of the mind by means of which man becomes steadily more capable of working out expanding series of concepts rationally and with constant scepticism towards his own notions, that is to say by means of deduction, that is, by means of faultless syllogisms, whether categorical, hypothetical or disjunctive, or by means of induction, and of submitting the final conclusion to verification for as long as may be necessary to create harmony between all the concepts ! ' "

Ulrich was amazed by his sister's feat of memory. It seemed to afford Agathe immense delight to recite these schoolmasterly pedantries in which she had made herself word-perfect. Heaven alone knew where she had taken them from—some book, probably, though she asserted it was simply the way Hagauer talked.

Ulrich did not believe it. " How could you memorise such long complicated sentences by just hearing them spoken ? "

" They stuck in my mind," Agathe retorted. " That's the way I am."

" Have you any idea," Ulrich asked, still nonplussed, " what a categorical syllogism is, or a verification ? "

" Not the slightest ! " Agathe disclaimed, laughing. " And perhaps he'd only read it somewhere too. But that's the way he talks. And I learnt it by heart by listening to him, just parrot-fashion. I think I did it because I was so furious with him for talking like that. You're different from me. Things go on lying at the bottom of my mind because I don't know what to do with them—that's all there is to my good memory. Being stupid makes me have an awfully good memory ! " She conveyed the impression that there was some mournful truth in this that she must rid herself of in order to be able to go on, all exuberance : " It's the same with tennis. Hagauer's just the same about that. ' In learning to play lawn tennis, when I first consciously place my racquet in a certain position with the intention of propelling the ball in a certain direction, when it has hitherto been travelling to and fro to my satisfaction, I am intervening in the processes of phenomenal reality : I am *experimenting* ! ' "

" Does he play well ? "

" I beat him six-love."

They laughed.

" Do you realise," Ulrich said, " that if Hagauer does say all these things you've been attributing to him, objectively speaking he's quite right ? It's merely that he's ridiculous."

" It may very well be that he's right," Agathe replied. " I wouldn't know. But how about this ? The boys in his class were sèt a Shakespearean speech to translate into German—' Cowards die many times before their deaths '—and one of them did it quite literally, in a rather touching and inspired way. I saw the copybook with Hagauer's corrections, and do you know, without the slightest feeling for what the child had done, he'd crossed it all out and replaced it by—of course !—the Schlegel-Tieck rendering !

" And another time I remember, he touched up a passage from —I think—Pindar, which was translated : ' The law of Nature, the king of all mortals and immortals, reigns, approving the most violent things, with almighty hand.' He gave it a gloss by making it: ' The law of Nature, reigning over mortals and immortals all alike, rules with almighty hand, approving even violence.'

" You see what I mean! But really, don't you think it was lovely," she urged, " the way that little boy, who couldn't even get half-marks for it, had translated the words so hair-raisingly literally, just as he found them, like a little heap of stones fallen out of a mosaic? "

And, standing with one arm raised, her hand outspread on the door-post as though she felt it to be a tree-trunk, once again she flung out the schoolboy's uncouth and floundering version of Caesar's speech:

> *Seeing that death, a necessary end,*
> *Will come when it will come.*

She flung it out with a wild and lovely enthusiasm that made the words, all naively ungrammatical as they were, ring true; and this she did without paying any heed to the poor shrivelled corpse that lay there under her gaze, while her eyes were alight with the pride of youth.

Frowning, Ulrich stared at his sister. ' The man who won't restore an old poem, but insists on leaving it weather-worn, semi-meaningless, and fragmentary, belongs to the same type as the man who'll refuse to put a new marble nose on an antique statue that's lost its own,' he mused. ' One might equate that attitude with " sense of style ", but really it's nothing of the sort. Nor has the person got it whose imagination is so vivid that he doesn't mind if something's missing. I'm more inclined to think that " sense of style " goes with the type that simply attaches no importance at all to completeness and therefore never expects even his own feelings to be " whole ", to go to the limit. And ', he concluded, with a sudden leap of his thoughts, on a different level, ' I dare say she'll have kissed a man before now without wholly taking leave of her senses.'

It seemed to him this ardent recitation was all he needed to know of his sister in order to be sure that she never ' completely fitted ' either, that she too was being made up of fragments, all passionate piecemeal, like himself. The thought so fascinated him that he quite forgot the other half of his own temperament, the half that insisted on moderation and control. He could now have told his sister, with certainty, that none of her actions would ever fit into her immediate environment, whereas all of them were related to some far larger environment of a highly ambiguous nature, which began nowhere and had no limits anywhere. Thus the conflicting impressions left by their first evening together would have been propitiously explained. But the reserve to which he had trained himself was still stronger than the impulse; and so he waited, curious and not without scepticism, to see how Agathe would descend from the heights to which she had soared. She was still standing there, her raised arm tense against the doorpost, and only a fraction of an instant too much would spoil the whole scene. He detested women who behaved as though they had been put into the world by a painter or a producer, or who modulated from a moment of intensity, such as this of Agathe's, into an all too artistically muted *pianissimo*. 'Perhaps,' he reflected, ' she'll suddenly glide down from the peak of enthusiasm with that rather imbecile, somnambulistic expression a medium has on " coming round ". I dare say she'll have no choice. All the same, it'll be rather embarrassing.'

But Agathe evidently realised this herself, or perhaps something in her brother's gaze had given her a hint of the danger lying in wait for her. She gaily dared the leap from the heights and, suddenly putting her tongue out at Ulrich, landed safely on both feet.

But instantly she became grave, and she went off in silence, to return after a moment with the old man's decorations.

So it was that they set about acting in defiance of their father's last wishes.

It was Agathe who actually did it. Ulrich seemed shy of touching the old man lying there defenceless; but Agathe had a way of doing wrong that made it impossible to think of it as wrong. The deftness of her hands, the quickness of her glance, gave her all the air of a woman tending a sick person; and then momentarily they would have the spontaneous and appealing quality of young animals that suddenly pause in their romping to make sure the master is watching them. Ulrich took over the decorations that had been removed and handed her the replicas. He could not help thinking of the thief stealing for the first time, his heart in his mouth. And if it seemed to him that the stars and crosses twinkled more brightly in his sister's hand than in his own, indeed that they positively turned into things of fairy-tale magic, perhaps it was really so in the greenish darkness of this room, with all the glimmering light reflected from the many big pot-plants, or perhaps it was simply that he was letting himself be dominated by his sister's will, which was here taking the initiative—hesitantly and yet with youthful eagerness. And since there was evidently no deliberation in all this, now in this moment of untarnished communion there arose—almost without dimension, amorphously strong—a sense of their joint existence.

Agathe paused. It was done. Then it occurred to her that there was just one little thing more they might do, and after an instant's musing she said with a smile: " How about each of us writing something nice on a scrap of paper, to put in his pocket ? "

Ulrich instantly knew what she meant, for there were not many such shared memories for him to search among. He recalled how at a certain age they had both been very fond of mournful poetry and stories about people who died all alone and forgotten. It was perhaps the loneliness of their childhood that gave them this taste; however it might be, they often made up such stories between them. But even then Agathe had been given to acting the stories out, whereas Ulrich had merely been the one who took the lead in more masculine enterprises, in those that called for audacity and hardness of heart. So it was Agathe who had one day evolved the plan, which they carried out, that each should cut off a bit of finger-nail and bury it in the garden; and she indeed had added a tress of her own fair hair to the nail-clippings. Ulrich had vaingloriously declared that in a hundred years someone might dig it all up and wonder whose it could have been. What he was mainly thinking of was going down to posterity. But little Agathe had been more concerned with the burial as an end in itself; it made her feel that she was hiding part of herself, removing it permanently from the vigilance of a world whose schoolmasterly demands intimidated her even though she had scant respect for them. At that time the servants' cottage was being built at the bottom of the garden, and they agreed to do something really special. They would write some wonderful poems on two pieces of paper, putting their own names and address underneath, and this was to be bricked up in one of the walls. But when they set about writing the poetry that was to have been so especially splendid, they could not think of anything. So it went on day after day, and the foundations were finished, and the walls were rising higher and higher. Then at last, at the eleventh hour, Agathe copied a sentence out of her arithmetic book, and Ulrich wrote: " I am—" and at length added his own name. However, it was with thudding hearts that they crept down the garden and up to the two bricklayers who were at work there, and Agathe simply dropped her piece of paper into the wet mortar and ran away. But Ulrich, being the elder and feeling himself a man and therefore even more afraid of being stopped by the bricklayers and asked what he was up to, was so paralysed with excitement that he could not move hand or foot. Then Agathe, emboldened by the fact that nothing had happened to her, came back and took his piece of paper from him, whereupon she strolled along with an exaggeratedly innocent air, inspected a brick at the far end of a row that had just been laid, lifted it, and slipped the piece of paper with Ulrich's name on it into the wall before there was time for anyone to send her away. Ulrich had followed her rather hesitantly, and in the moment when she performed the deed he felt the suffocating pressure on his heart suddenly turn into a wheel with spokes like knife-blades, which whirled round inside his chest so fast that it burst into flames, throwing off sparks like a catherine-wheel on fireworks night.

It was to this, then, that Agathe was alluding, and for quite a while Ulrich gave no answer, merely smiling deprecatingly, for he could not help thinking it indecorous to play the same game with the dead.

But before he could bring himself to say anything, Agathe had bent down and slid a wide silk garter from her leg: then she lifted the pall and slipped the garter into her father's pocket.

Ulrich could scarcely believe his eyes when he saw that childhood memory re-enacted. He almost jumped forward to stop her, simply because the action seemed utterly out of place. But then he caught, in his sister's eyes, a flash of such pure and dewy freshness, such early-morning candour, unspotted by any trace of the day's toil and moil, that he did not move.

" What on earth are you up to ? " he said softly, disapprovingly.

He did not know whether she was trying to conciliate the dead man because he had been wronged, or to give him some kindly token because he himself had done so much wrong. He might have asked, but the barbaric notion of sending the icy dead on its way with a garter in its pocket still warm from a daughter's thigh constricted his throat and created upheaval in his mind.

6 *The old gentleman goes to his last rest.*

THE short time that remained until the funeral was taken up with innumerable unaccustomed little tasks and passed quickly; and in the last half-hour the number of black-clad callers trickling in all through the morning had expanded into something like a celebration in black to give the old gentleman a send-off. The undertaker's men had redoubled their noisy efforts, going about it with the gravity of a surgeon, who cannot be argued with once one has put one's life in his hands; and through the comparative normality of the rest of the house they had as it were laid a gangway of solemn emotion leading from the front gate and up the steps right into the room where the coffin was. The flowering and evergreen pot-plants, the black baize and crape draperies, and the silver candelabra with little tremulous gold-tipped flames, which received the visitors, knew their role better than Ulrich and Agathe knew theirs. For brother and sister, standing there, representing the family, receiving all who came to pay their last respects to their father, had very little idea who anyone was and would have been lost without their father's old servant, who unobtrusively prompted whenever particularly eminent persons arrived. All the arrivals glided up to them, glided on past them, and then somewhere in the room, either alone or in a little group with others, dropped anchor and so remained—quietly observing this son and daughter. And over the faces of these two a mask of solemnity gradually congealed, a stiffness of the upper lip—which stayed there until at last the undertaker (manager, proprietor, or whatever he was, the man who had presented his printed forms to Ulrich and during this last half-hour had dashed up and down the steps at least twenty times) hastened up to Ulrich and, with the studiously modulated self-importance of an adjutant reporting to his general on parade, informed Ulrich that everything was now ready.

It had been arranged that everyone was to enter the carriages only after the funeral cortège had passed slowly and ceremonially through the town. So they all set forth on foot, with Ulrich leading the way, walking with, on his one side, His Imperial and Royal Majesty's representative, the Governor of the province, who had appeared in person as a token of respect to a deceased member of the Upper House, and, on the other, a gentleman of similarly lofty rank, the senior member of a delegation of three representing the Upper House. Behind them came the two other noblemen of the delegation, followed by the Rector and Senate of the University. Only after these, though ahead of the seemingly endless stream of silk hats topping public persons of gradually diminishing importance and dignity, came Agathe, surrounded by black-clad women: which indicated the point where, between the peak of officialdom, private grief had its allotted place; and the place for ' unorganised attendance ', for those ' merely demonstrating sympathy ', was only after those who appeared in their official capacity, and possibly indeed it was occupied by none but the old cook-butler couple trudging along in solitude at the tail-end. The procession was therefore predominantly male. And walking at Agathe's side was not Ulrich but her husband, Professor Hagauer, whose apple-cheeked face with the bristly caterpillar of a moustache across the upper lip had meanwhile grown very strange to her; through the thick black veil that enabled her to observe him without being observed, it even looked dark blue. Ulrich himself, who had spent all the immediately preceding hours in his sister's company, all at once felt that the age-old traditional pattern of precedence, which dated from the time of the university's foundation, had positively torn her away from him. He missed her, and he could not even turn round to see where she was. He was thinking out a joke to greet her with when they met again, but his thoughts were hampered by his consciousness of the Governor's being there at his side, pacing with lordly bearing, in silence for the most part but occasionally addressing a quiet word to him, a murmur that he was obliged to catch if he could; and indeed this was only one among the many attentions shown to him by their many and various Excellencies, Magnificences and Worships, for he was held to be Count Leinsdorf's very shadow, and the mistrust with which His Highness's patriotic campaign was gradually coming to be regarded cast a nimbus about his own head.

On the pavement and at windows along the way there were also little groups of curious onlookers. And although he knew that in another hour it would all be over, exactly like a performance at the theatre, he still could not help having an especially vivid awareness of all that was going on; and the general interest in his destiny enwrapped him like a heavily braided cloak about his shoulders. For the first time he fully experienced the pomp and ceremony of tradition. The awe that was like a wave running ahead of the procession, through the people crowding the pavements, who paused in their chat and then, as the procession passed, breathed freely again; the ecclesiastical magic; the premonition of the dull thud with which earth would fall on wood; the dammed-up silence in the procession itself—all this plucked at the vertebrae as at the strings of an immeasurably ancient musical instrument, and with astonishment Ulrich heard an indefinable resonance within him, a tone that buoyed him up physically as though he were actually being borne along by the measure of the surrounding solemnity. And being, as he was, nearer to the rest of people than on other days, he built up this impression by imagining how much more so it would all be if at this moment he had been what would have been appropriate to the original meaning of this pomp and ceremony, more or less obliviously adapted to present-day general use: if he had, that is to say, been pacing along as truly the heir to some great position of power. At this thought the sadness vanished and death ceased to be a horrifying private affair: it became an act of transition that was performed ceremonially and in public. There was no longer the gaping void that one stares into, appalled, that void which every human being whose presence one is used to leaves behind in the first days after his vanishing from the earth. The place was already filled, the dead master's successor already walking there in his stead, the crowd breathing out its loyalty to him, the rite at once funereal and a coming of age for him who now assumed authority and, now for the first time yielding precedence to none, paced on alone towards his own end.

' I ought to have closed my father's eyes,' Ulrich involuntarily thought. ' Not for his sake, nor for mine, but——' and he could not finish the thought. The fact that he had not liked his father, and his father had not liked him, now, confronted as he was with this ritual order of things, seemed a pettifogging irrelevance, and to think of it was to overvalue a man's personal importance. Indeed any personal way of thinking had a thin savour of triviality in the face of death, whereas all that was now significant seemed to emanate from the gigantic body of this cortège meandering slowly through streets lined with human beings, and this even though it might be riddled with idle curiosity and mere unthinking compliance with the conventions.

And yet the music went on playing, it was a splendid, light, clear day, and Ulrich's emotions swayed this way and that like the canopy that is borne overhead when the Host is carried in procession. Now and then he would glance into the plate-glass panes of the hearse in front of him, and see his reflection, hatted head and shoulders; and occasionally he would catch a glimpse, on the floor of the hearse, beside the armorially resplendent coffin, of little droppings of candle-grease left over from previous funerals and never properly cleaned away. Then he felt sorry for his father, quite simply and unreflectingly sorry for him as for a dog that had been run over in the street. Then his eyes grew moist, and when he gazed away across the black-clad figures around him at the onlookers on the pavement they were like many-coloured flowers a-twinkle with dew; and the thought that it was he, Ulrich, who was now seeing all this, and not the man who had always lived here and who was, besides, so much fonder of ceremony than he himself, was so queer that it seemed downright impossible for his father not to be able to be there too to see himself taking his departure from a world that he had, on the whole, regarded as good.

Moving as this was, however, it did not escape Ulrich that the overseer or supervisor whose job it was to conduct this Catholic procession to the cemetery in an orderly manner was a Jew, a tall thickset man in his early thirties, graced with a drooping fair moustache. He carried papers in his pocket, like a courier, and dashed up and down along the procession seeing to things, now making some tiny adjustment to a horse's harness, now whispering some instructions to the band. Somehow this reminded Ulrich that on this last day his father's corpse had not been in the house. It had been returned to the house only at the last minute after having been placed at the disposal of science, in accordance with the old gentleman's last wish, which had doubtless been inspired by a humanistic attitude to science; and it was only natural to assume that after such anatomical intervention the old gentleman had been only cursorily stitched up again. And so there, then, behind the glass panes that reflected Ulrich's image back to him, was an untidily cobbled-up object being conveyed along as the focal point of this great, beautiful solemn act of imagination and illusion. 'With or without his decorations?' Ulrich suddenly wondered in dismay. He had forgotten all about that, and indeed he did not even know whether his father had even been dressed again in the dissecting-room before the closed coffin was returned to the house. Yes, and there was also Agathe's garter. It might have been found, in which case he could guess at the sort of jokes the medical students would make. It was all extremely embarrassing. And in this way the minor frictions of the present dissolved his emotion into many smaller elements, after it had, for a moment, almost rounded out into the smooth shell of a living dream.

All he felt now was the absurdity, the confused oscillating nature of all human order and of himself. ' Now I am all alone in the world,' he thought. ' A mooring-rope has snapped. And I ascend! ' This echo of the first sensation he had had on receiving the news of his father's death was what now summed up his feelings as he walked along between the two walls of onlookers.

7   *A letter from Clarisse.*

ULRICH had not left his address with anyone he knew, but Clarisse had it from Walter, to whom it was as familiar as his own childhood.

She wrote:

" My dar*ling*—my lord*ling*—my *ling* !

" Do you know what a *ling* is? I can't work it out. I think perhaps Walter's a weak*ling*." (All the ' -ling's ' were heavily underlined.)

" Do you think I was drunk when I came to you ? ! I *cannot* get myself drunk! (Men get drunk sooner than I do. A re*mark*able thing.)

" But I don't know what I said to you. I can't remember. I'm afraid you imagine I said things that I didn't say. I didn't say them.

" But this is going to be a letter—in a moment! First, though: you know how dreams open up. Sometimes in a dream you know: you've been there before, you've talked to that person before, or —it's as though you had got your memory back.

" *What I have when I'm awake is knowing I've been awake!*

" (I have sleep-fellows.)

" Do you even remember who Moosbrugger is ? There's something I must tell you:

" *Suddenly his name was there again.*

" Those three musical syllables.

" But music's just a swindle. I mean when it's by itself. Music by itself is aestheticism or something of that sort: vital weakness. But if music combines with vision, then the walls sway and the life of those to come rises out of the tomb of the present. I didn't just hear those three musical syllables, I saw them as well. They *loomed up* in my memory. Suddenly you realise: where they loom up there's something else as well! Yes, once I wrote a letter to that Count of yours about Moosbrugger—how one forgets things! Now I hear-see a world where things are and people move just the way you've always known them to do, but *resonantly visible*! I can't describe it exactly. So far only three syllables of it have loomed up. Do you understand ? Perhaps it's still too early to talk about it.

" I said to Walter: ' I want to get to know Moosbrugger! '

" Walter said: ' And who is Moosbrugger ? '

" I told him: ' Ulo's friend the murderer.'

" We were reading the papers. It was in the morning and it was time for Walter to be going to the office. Do you remember the time we were all three reading the newspaper ? (You have a *poor* memory, you *won't* remember!) So I had opened out the part of the newspaper Walter had given me—one arm left, one

arm right: suddenly I feel hard wood, I'm nailed to the Cross.
I ask Walter: ' Wasn't it only yesterday there was something in
the paper about a railway accident near Budweis ? '

" ' Yes,' he says. ' Why do you ask? A small accident, one
person killed, or two.'

" After a while I say: ' Because there's been an accident in
America too. Where's Pennsylvania ? '

" He doesn't know. ' In America,' he says.

" I say: ' Making their trains collide on purpose is something
the engine-drivers never do! '

" He looks at me. It was obvious he didn't understand. ' Of
course not,' he says.

" I ask when Siegmund's coming. He isn't sure.

" And so there you are: Of course the engine-drivers don't
make their trains collide on purpose, out of spite. *But what do
they do it for ?* I'll tell you. In that immense network of rail-
way-lines, points, and signals that's cast all over the globe, we all
lose our strength of conscience. If we had the energy to test
ourselves once again and to take one more look at our task, we
should always do everything necessary and avoid the disaster.
The disaster's our stopping at the step before the last !

" Of course Walter can't be expected to realise that instantly.
I believe I can attain that immense strength of conscience, and I've
had to shut my eyes sometimes so that Walter wouldn't see the
lightning flashing in them.

" For all these reasons I regard it as my duty to get to know
Moosbrugger.

" You know my brother Siegmund's a doctor. He'll help me.

" I was waiting for him.

" Last Sunday he came to see us.

" When he's introduced to someone, he says: ' But I'm neither
—nor musical.' That's his sort of joke. Because he's called
Siegmund, he doesn't want to be taken for a Jew or for musical.
He was conceived in a Wagnerian rapture. It's impossible to get
a rational answer out of him. So long as I kept on talking to
him, he would only mutter nonsense. He threw a stone at a bird
and bored holes in the snow with his stick. And then he wanted
to shovel the snow off a path. He often comes up to us to work
at something, he says because he doesn't like being at home with

his wife and children. It's a wonder you've never come at the same time. ' You two have *les fleurs du mal* and a vegetable garden! ' he says. I pulled his ears and boxed him in the ribs, but it didn't make any difference.

"Then he went indoors where Walter was, at the piano of course, and Siegmund had his jacket under his arm and his hands all dirty right up to his cuffs.

" ' Siegmund,' I said to him in front of Walter, ' when do you understand a piece of music ? '

"He just grinned and what he said was: ' Absolutely never.'

" ' When you *play it inside yourself*,' I said. ' When do you understand another human being ? You have to *play along with* him.' Play *along*! There's a great secret there, Ulrich! You have to be like him: but not putting yourself *into* him, putting him *out into* you! We redeem *outwards*! That's the *strong* form! We fall *in* with people's actions, but we fill them *out* and climb away over them.

"Forgive me for writing so much about it. But the trains collide because conscience doesn't take the last step. The worlds don't rise to the surface if one doesn't draw them. More about this another time. *The man of genius has the obligation to attack!* He has the uncanny power to do so! But Siegmund, the coward, looked at his watch and reminded me about supper because he had to go home. Do you know, Siegmund always keeps the balance somehow between the blasé attitude of an experienced doctor who doesn't think over-highly of what his profession can do, and the blasé attitude of the contemporary man who has gone beyond intellectual tradition and come back to the hygiene of the simple life and gardening. But Walter exclaimed: ' Oh for God's sake! Why do you two talk such nonsense ? ! What do you *want* with this Moosbrugger, anyway ? ' And that helped a bit.

"Because then Siegmund said: ' He's either insane or a criminal, that's true. But what if Clarisse imagines she can make him better ? I'm a doctor and I have to let the hospital chaplain go round imagining the same thing! Redeem, she says ? Well then, why shouldn't she at least see him ? '

"He brushed his trousers down, adopted a great air of calm, and washed his hands. Then at supper we worked it all out.

" And so now we've been to see Dr Friedenthal; he's the deputy medical officer Siegmund knows. Siegmund came right out with it, said he'd take the responsibility for bringing me in on false pretences as a writer wanting to see the man.

" But that was a mistake. Having been asked so openly, the M.O. could only say no. ' If you were Selma Lagerlöf herself, I should be delighted by your visit, as of course I am in any case, but I'm afraid only scientific interests receive recognition here.'

" It was rather nice pretending to be a writer. I gave him a straight look and said: ' In this case I count for more than Selma Lagerlöf, because I'm not doing it for reasons of research.'

" He looked at me and said: ' The only thing I can suggest would be for you to approach the superintendent himself with a letter of recommendation from your embassy.' He took me for a foreign writer, not realising that I was Siegmund's sister.

" Finally we agreed that I would not see the insane Moosbrugger but the prisoner Moosbrugger. Siegmund got me a letter of introduction from a charitable organisation and a permit from the *Landesgericht*. Afterwards Siegmund told me that Dr Friedenthal regards psychiatry as partly a science and partly an art, and he calls him the ringmaster of a demon circus. But I'd like that.

" The nicest thing about it was that the hospital building was once a monastery. We had to wait in the corridor, and the lecture-hall is an old chapel. It has high arched windows, and looking across the courtyard I could see right into it. The patients wear white clothes and sit on the dais with the professor. And the professor bends over their chairs as if they were all old pals. I thought to myself: perhaps now they'll bring Moosbrugger. I had the feeling that then I'd want to fly through the tall glass window into the lecture-hall. You will say I can't fly. Jump through the window then? But I wouldn't have jumped, oh no, that wasn't the feeling.

" I hope you'll come back soon. One can *never* express things. Least of all in letters."

And thereunder, heavily underlined: " Clarisse."

8   *Two in family.*

" WHEN two men or women have to share a room for some time,"
Ulrich said, " when travelling, in a *wagon-lit* or a crowded hotel,
they often strike up an odd sort of friendship. Everyone has a
different way of brushing his teeth or bending down to pull his
shoes off or getting into bed. Clothes and underclothes are
broadly the same, but in each individual case there are innumerable little differences that then reveal themselves to the eye. At
first—it's probably because of the extreme individualism of our
modern way of living—there's a resistance, a faint revulsion,
warding off any too close approach, any infringement of one's
own privacy. Once that is overcome, you get a community of
feeling that bears the mark of its unusual origin like a scar. After
that transformation many people behave more cheerfully than
usual—most of them more innocuously, many more talkatively,
and almost all more amiably. The personality is changed. One
might almost say, under the skin it has been exchanged for
another that is less idiosyncratic. The place of the I has been
taken by the first rudimentary form of something that is felt to
be distinctly uncomfortable and a reduction, but nevertheless
irresistible—the rudimentary beginnings of a We."

" This revulsion from close contact is particularly true of
women," Agathe replied. " I've never been able to get used to
women."

" You find it between man and woman too," Ulrich remarked.
" Only in that case it's overlaid by the obligations of love-making,
which are what instantly claim attention. But then it quite often
happens that those who've become involved with each other wake
up out of the love-making state and—with astonishment, irony,
or an impulse to escape, according to their temperament—what
they see is a total stranger ensconced at their side. This may
even happen after the passage of many years. Then they find
it impossible to say which is more natural: their union with
another being or their ego's hurt recoil from that union into the
imaginary realm of personal uniqueness—both of which have their

place in our nature, after all! And both are tangled up in the concept of the family. Family life is not a full life. Young people feel themselves deprived, diminished in stature, not in full possession of themselves, so long as they're in the family circle. Just look at elderly unmarried daughters: they're sucked dry by their family, drained of their blood. What they've turned into is rather queer hybrids of I and We."

For Ulrich Clarisse's letter was an intrusion. The spasmodic outbursts in it he found far less disquieting than the calm and apparently rational process going on, deep within her, towards the realisation of an obviously demented plan, and he told himself that on his return he must really talk to Walter about it. Then he deliberately bent his mind to talking about other things.

Agathe was lying at her ease on the divan, with one knee drawn up. "By saying what you do," she responded eagerly, "aren't you yourself explaining why I had to marry again?"

"And yet, you know, there is something in what's called the sanctity of the family, that merging of person with person, that living for the other, that whole selfless movement in a closed circle"—Ulrich continued, without taking any notice of what she had said. Agathe was puzzled by the way his words so often withdrew from her at the very moment when they seemed to have come closest. "Usually this collective ego is nothing but a collective egoist, and this makes strong family feeling the most insufferable thing anyone can imagine. On the other hand, I can picture that unconditional leaping into the breach for one another, that fighting shoulder to shoulder, that suffering one another's wounds, as one of the archetypal pleasures, going back to the very beginnings of the human race, and fairly well developed even in the instinctual life of gregarious animals." Agathe listened, but she could not make much of this. Nor could she make much of what he said next: "The fact is that this condition easily degenerates, as is the case with all ancient conditions whose origin can no longer be traced." And it was only when he concluded with the words: "And one probably has to insist that individuals must be particularly orderly and organised if the totality they form is not to deteriorate into a meaningless distortion!" that she felt secure again in his companionship. And she felt she had to keep from blinking while she watched him, lest he should vanish while her eyelids were lowered; for it was amazing that he should be sitting there and saying things that disappeared high in the air and then suddenly came down again like a rubber ball that had been momentarily caught in the branches of a tree.

It was late in the afternoon and they were together in the drawing-room. Several days had elapsed since the funeral.

The drawing-room was a long room, furnished in the good old Biedermeier taste with genuine pieces of the period. Between the windows hung the tall rectangular mirrors in their plain gilt frames, and the stiff discreet chairs were ranged along the walls, so that the empty floor seemed flooded with the dark brilliance of the parquet, like a shallow basin filled to the brim, into which one hesitated to set foot. At the edge of this elegant austerity— for the study, where he had settled down on the first morning, had been made over to Ulrich's use—more or less in an alcove where like a severe column the huge tiled stove stood, on the top of it a vase and on a ledge surrounding it about half-way up, approximately at waist-height, one lone candlestick, Agathe had created an eminently personal peninsula for herself. She had had a divan moved in here and had spread beside it a rug whose ancient red and blue, in conjunction with the senselessly repetitive Turkish pattern of the divan, flung a voluptuous challenge at the delicate grey and the soberly elusive lineaments of this traditional room. She further outraged the room's chaste dignity and discipline by introducing a large-leaved green plant about as tall as a man; it was one of those that had been provided for the funeral decorations; and she had kept it, including tub, and set it up as a sort of ' grove ' at the head of the divan—juxtaposing it to the tall standard-lamp in whose bright light she could read in comfort while lying down and which stood out, in the semi-classical setting of this room, like a searchlight or an aerial mast. This drawing-room with the coffered mouldings of its ceiling, its pilasters, and its slim glass cabinets, had changed little in the hundred years or so of its existence, because it had been used but rarely and had never really formed part of the lives of its latterday owners. Perhaps in ancestral days the walls that were now painted pale grey had still been covered with delicate fabric, and the chairs had probably been covered somewhat differently too;

however that might be, the room's present appearance was that which Agathe had known since her childhood, without even being sure whether it was her great-grandparents who had furnished it thus, or people not of her family at all. For her what counted was that she had grown up in this house, and the only special thing she knew about it was that she had always entered this room with that sense of awe instilled into children in relation to something that they might easily damage or dirty. But now she had discarded the last symbol of the past, the mourning that she had worn, and was once again wearing her lounging pyjamas. She had been lying on the divan, that token of rebel invasion into this sphere, almost all day, reading whatever books, good and bad, she had scrambled together, now and then breaking off this occupation in order to eat something or fall asleep. And when the day thus spent was fading into evening, she gazed through the darkening room towards the pale curtains, now merging with the twilight, which ballooned out from the windows like sails, and it made her feel as if, enclosed in the corona of brittle lamplight, she had been travelling through the stiffly delicate room and had just come to a halt. So she had been found by her brother, who appreciated her illuminated encampment at a glance. He too remembered this drawing-room well, and he was even able to tell her that the original owner—so the story went—had been a rich merchant who later did not do so well, which had enabled their great-grandfather, the *k. & k.* notary, to acquire this pleasant property at a price well within his means. There were all sorts of other things besides that Ulrich knew about this drawing-room, which he now examined thoroughly. Agathe was especially struck when he told her that in their great-grandparents' days this sort of stiff furniture was felt to be particularly natural; she did not find it easy to understand this, for to her way of feeling it was like some monstrous emanation from a geometry lesson, and it was some time before she could begin vaguely picturing an era when people were so satiated by the ostentation of Baroque forms that their own rather rigidly symmetrical taste was veiled in the exquisite illusion that they were being true to the spirit of a Nature pure and rational and unadorned by superfluous curlicues. When, by the aid of all the details that Ulrich supplied, she finally succeeded in understanding this shift of ideas, she was delighted

with the thought of knowing a great deal about things that everything in her life up to then had caused her to despise. And when
her brother wanted to know what she was reading, she quickly
hid her store of books, rolling over on top of them, even though
at the same time she boldly insisted that she enjoyed reading
trashy books just as much as good ones.

Ulrich had spent the morning working and had afterwards
gone out. Until today he had not been able to concentrate in
the way he had hoped; the good effect he had expected from this
interruption of his normal life had been outweighed by the dis-
tractions of the new circumstances he was in. Only now, when
the funeral was over, did a change come about; for the relations
with the outer world that had been so intense at the beginning
had now ceased entirely. It was merely as their father's children
and, as it were, vicariously that they had for some days been the
focus of general sympathy and interest and as such had become
aware of the network of connections converging upon this position;
but apart from Walter's old father there was no one in the town
whom they would have cared to visit and out of respect for their
mourning they were not invited anywhere. Their solitude was
broken by no one but Professor Schwung, who not only came to the
funeral but also appeared the next day in order to enquire whether
his late friend had not left a manuscript on the problem of
diminished responsibility that one might hope to see published
in due course. This sudden transition from a commotion that
had been in unceasing hubble-bubble to this leaden stillness was
almost like a physical shock. The state of mind it brought about
in Ulrich was heightened by the fact that here he and his sister
were sleeping in the rooms they had occupied as children. Since
the house had no guest-room, they had had to be put upstairs
in these attics, on camp-beds; and there they were surrounded
by the odds and ends of furniture left over from the nursery,
whose bareness somewhat suggests that of a padded cell, a bareness that, with the insipid sheen of the oilcloth on the tables and
the linoleum on the floor—that desert of linoleum in which, once
upon a time, the little bricks reared up in the rigid fantasies of
toy architecture—invades the sleeper's dreams. These memories,
which were as meaningless and boundless as the life for which
that past was supposed to have been a preparation, made brother

and sister feel it a relief that at least these bedrooms of theirs were adjacent to each other, separated only by a closet; and since the bathroom they shared was on the floor below, they could scarcely help encountering each other on the stairs as soon as they woke in the morning. Living together, they had to consult each other's wishes and to share responsibility for settling all the problems of unfamiliar domestic affairs of which they were suddenly in charge. Naturally enough they felt the comic aspect of this coexistence, as intimate as it was unexpected; it resembled the adventure-story comedy of a shipwreck that had left them marooned on the solitary island of their childhood. All this meant that after the first few days, on the course of which they had had no influence, they tried to re-establish their independence, each of them doing so, however, more out of consideration for the other than from any inner need.

So Ulrich had got up some time before Agathe and had slipped quietly into the study long before Agathe came down to build her peninsula. He had taken up his interrupted mathematical work, actually more as a way of passing the time than with any intention of really finishing it, but to his considerable astonishment in the few hours of one morning he finished—except for some minor details—all the work he had not been able to make himself touch for months. What had helped him to the unexpected solution of his problem was one of those incalculable ideas about which one might say not so much that they come only when they are no longer expected as that they flash upon the mind in a startling way reminiscent of another sudden recognition—that of the beloved who has been merely one girl among the other girls till the moment when the lover is suddenly amazed that he could ever have supposed any of the others to be her equal. Such inspirations involve more than the intellect: there is always some element of passion at work too. In that moment Ulrich felt as though he had to be finished and done with it, in order to be a free man; and then, because there was no apparent reason or purpose to be seen in the thing, he positively struck himself as having accomplished his task prematurely, and the balance of energy he was left with carried him on into a mood of reverie. He perceived the possibility that the method by which he had solved his problem might be applied to the solution of considerably more complex problems, and he began idly conjuring up the outlines of the theory. In this moment of happiness and relaxation he even felt tempted to yield to Professor Schwung's tempting suggestion and return to his career, to seek the path leading to an established position and influence. But when, after some minutes of indulging in this intellectual luxury, he pictured to himself in all sobriety what it would lead to if he were to succumb to ambition and make his way back belatedly on to the academic road, he realised for the first time that he felt too old to undertake anything of the sort. Since his boyhood he had never felt this semi-impersonal concept ' age ' to be anything with a content of its own. Not till now had he ever been assailed by the thought: This is something you're no longer capable of doing.

Later that day, when afternoon was shading off into evening, he told his sister about this, and it happened that he used the word ' destiny '. It stirred her interest. She asked him what ' destiny ' meant.

" Something halfway between ' my toothache ' and ' King Lear's daughters '," Ulrich answered. " I'm not the sort of person who goes in for the word much."

" But for young people it's part of the great song of life. Young people long to have a destiny, even though they don't know what it is."

" In times to come," Ulrich answered, " when people know more, the word ' destiny ' will probably have acquired a statistical meaning."

Agathe was twenty-seven, young enough still to have some of those hollow modes of feeling, those empty moulds, that are what one first evolves, and old enough already to have some inkling of the other content that reality pours into them. " I suppose growing old is in itself a destiny," she answered, and was very much dissatisfied with this remark, which expressed her youthful melancholy in a way that struck her as banal.

But her brother passed this over. By way of illustration, he recounted: " When I took up mathematics I wanted to achieve something in my field, and I applied all my energy to that end, even though I regarded that only as a preliminary to something else. And even though of course still in a rough-and-ready form, like all beginnings, my first papers really did contain ideas that were new then. But they were either overlooked or actually met with opposition, though the rest of the work was well received. Well, perhaps it might be called ' destiny ' that I soon lost patience with hammering at the wedge I was trying to drive in."

" Wedge ? " Agathe queried, as though the mere sound of such a masculine and craftsmanly-sounding word connoted something unpleasant. " Why do you call it a wedge ? "

" Because it was only the way of beginning. I wanted that work to be the thin end of the wedge. But then, you see, I lost patience. And today, when I'd finished what may well be the last piece of work of that kind I shall do—a piece of work I began in those early days—I realised I might really have become the leader of a new school of thought if I'd had better luck at that period—or shown a little more persistence."

" You could still do it! " Agathe said. " After all, a man doesn't get too old for things as quickly as a woman does."

" No," Ulrich replied. " I don't want to. However astonishing it may seem, actually that wouldn't have changed anything in the course of events, in the development of my subject. Perhaps I was about ten years ahead of my time. But rather more slowly and by different roads, without my aid, other people have reached the same point, and the most I could have done would have been to get them there a little faster—while it remains questionable whether the effect on my life would have been enough to stimulate me to advance again beyond that first goal. And so there you have a piece of what is called personal destiny. But what it amounts to is something remarkably impersonal.

" Altogether," he went on, " the older I get the more often it happens that subsequently, and by devious routes, something I have hated comes to take the same direction as my own road, so that from a certain point onwards it becomes impossible for me to deny its right to exist. Or else it happens that ideas or measures I was once enthusiastic about begin to show up as defective. And so in the long run it seems to be a matter of indifference whether one gets excited or not and if so what cause one gets excited in. It all comes to the same thing in the end, and everything contributes to a process of evolution that is both unfathomable and infallible."

" Once that used to be called God working in mysterious ways,"

Agathe remarked, frowning. Her tone was that of one speaking from experience, and it was not precisely respectful.

It reminded Ulrich that she had been educated in a convent.

Sitting at the foot of her divan, he gazed at her as she lay there in her ankle-bound trousers, and the glow of the standard lamp fell around them, making on the floor a great leaf of light on which they floated in darkness. " Nowadays," he said, " destiny makes more the impression of the autonomous movement of some larger mass: one is inside it, rolling along with it." He remembered that once before he had been struck by the idea that nowadays every truth comes into the world divided into two half-true halves, and that here was a tricky and nimble process that nevertheless resulted in a total achievement greater than what would have resulted if everyone had gone about doing his whole duty in a solemn and solitary way. This idea, which was like a hook sticking into his complacency and yet somehow not without a touch of grandeur about it, was one that he had already advanced once before, with the frivolous corollary that therefore one could do whatever one liked. Nothing was in fact further from him than that conclusion. And now more than ever, now when his destiny seemed to have dismissed him, leaving him no more to do, now in this moment so dangerous to his ambition, when, impelled by an inexplicable stimulus, he had actually finished the last piece of work linking him with his earlier days—that long-drawn-out work, that straggler of a task—now, that is to say, in the very moment when he felt himself to be utterly a clean sheet, instead of feeling a falling off in strength, what he was aware of was the new tension that had come about since his departure and journey hither. There was no name for it. For the present one might put it this way: that a younger person, kin to him, was seeking his advice. Or one might just as easily see it differently: and with astonishing clarity he saw the glittering mat of bright gold against the black-green of the room, and on it the delicate lozenges of Agathe's clown-costume, and himself, and the super-lucidly outlined chance—this chance scooped, as it were, out of the darkness—the sheer chance of their being so companionably together.

" Can you say that again ? " Agathe asked.

" What's still referred to, nowadays, as one's personal destiny,"

Ulrich repeated, " is being gradually replaced by collective processes that can finally be expressed in statistical terms."

Agathe thought about this for a moment, then laughed. " Of
course I can't follow that. But wouldn't it be wonderful," she
suggested, " to be dissolved by statistics ? I mean, after all, love
can't do it any more! "

And this suddenly led Ulrich to tell his sister all about what
had happened to him when he had finished his work and had
gone out of the house and walked into the heart of the town in
order to ' fill himself up with something ', being left so vague and
empty now that his task was done. He had not meant to speak
of it, for it seemed too private. Whenever, on his travels, he
found himself in a city where he had nothing in particular to do,
he took intense pleasure in the special sense of solitude that it
gave him; and seldom had this feeling been so acute as this time.
He had seen the colours of the trams, the carriages, shop-windows,
archways, the shapes of church towers, faces, and the façades of
buildings, and though they all had a general European resemblance
to each other, the glance flew about over them like an insect that
has gone astray over a field bright with unfamiliar colours that
prevent it from settling anywhere, though that is what it really
wants to do. This walking that had no aim and no clear function,
in a town that was so self-absorbed, going about its own affairs
with such animation, this intensity of perception that increased
as the foreignness of the surroundings increased, heightened still
further by the conviction that it is not oneself that matters, but
only these totals, these masses of faces, these movements wrenched
loose from the body to become armies of arms, legs, or teeth, to
all of which the future belongs—all this can evoke the feeling
that, walking along by oneself, keeping to oneself, still all of one
piece, one is positively antisocial and criminal. But if one goes
on yielding to this, it may suddenly give rise to a physical sense
of pleasure and irresponsibility so foolish that it seems the body
no longer belongs to a world in which the sensual ego is encased
in thin skeins of nerves and blood-vessels, but to a world all flooded
with somniferous sweetness.

In such words did Ulrich describe to his sister something that
was perhaps the result of a state of mind lacking all aim and
ambition, or perhaps the result of a diminished sense of one's own

existence—that illusion that one is a personality—or perhaps, after all, nothing more or less than the 'primal myth of the gods', that 'double face of Nature', that 'giving and taking vision' which he was after with all the alertness of a hunter. Now he paused, curious to see whether Agathe would make any sign of agreement or indicate that she too had felt such things. And when nothing happened, he tried another way of explaining it: "It's like a little split in one's consciousness. You feel yourself being embraced, enfolded, penetrated to the very heart by a pleasant sort of involuntary helplessness. But at the same time you remain wide awake, your taste remains critical, you're even prepared to go to war with these things and people that are full of stuffy presumption. It's as though there were two comparatively independent layers of life within us, which are nevertheless profoundly balanced. And, talking about destiny, it's also as though one had two destinies: one active-unimportant, which fulfils itself, and one inactive-important, which remains beyond one's ken."

Now Agathe, who had been listening for a long time without stirring, suddenly said out of the blue: "It's like kissing Hagauer."

She had propped herself up on one elbow, laughing, with her legs still stretched out full-length on the sofa. And she added: "Of course it wasn't anything like so beautiful as the way you describe it!"

Ulrich laughed too. It was not entirely clear what they were laughing at. This mirth that had befallen them seemed almost to have come out of the air or out of the very fabric of the house, or perhaps out of the traces of amazement and uneasiness that the last few days had left in them, with all that solemn procedure which touched, all futile, on the Beyond; or perhaps it came out of the unwonted delight they took in this conversation: for every human custom that is developed and refined to the utmost bears within it the seed of change, and every sort of excitement that exceeds the normal very soon mists over with a patina of melancholy, absurdity, and satiation.

In such a way, by such round-about roads, they came in the end—and as it were for recreation—to a less exacting theme, and talked about 'I' and 'We' and 'the family', arriving at the conclusion, somewhere midway between mockery and astonishment, that the two of them together constituted a family. And while Ulrich talked about the desire for fellowship—once more with the eagerness of a man inflicting some mortification on his nature, though without knowing whether on his essential or only on his assumed nature—Agathe listened, noticing how his words would come closer to her and then again disappear into the distance. And he realised that for a long time, as he looked at her, lying there defenceless in that bright light and in that capricious garb, he had been searching, as, alas, his habit was, for something to repel him; but he had not found it, and for that he was thankful with an unadulterated, simple affection that he was not used to feeling. And he was utterly delighted with their talk.

Then, when it had come to an end, Agathe asked him point-blank: " Tell me now, are you actually for what you call ' the family ' or against it ? "

Ulrich replied that this was not the point at all, for what he had in fact been talking about was the world's inconclusiveness, and his own personal indecisiveness.

Agathe reflected on this.

Then, after some time, she exclaimed: " Well, that's something I can't judge. But I must say I should like to be entirely in harmony with myself for once and—well—somehow to live accordingly. Wouldn't you like to try it too ? "

9   *Agathe when she cannot talk to Ulrich.*

THE moment that Agathe got into the train, starting out on her unexpected journey to her father, something had happened that strongly resembled a sudden rupture, and the two sections into which the moment of departure was instantly rent tore so wide apart that it seemed they could never have formed a unity. Her husband had seen her off. He had raised his hat, he had held that stiff, round, black bowler hat out a little sideways in front of him, as is customary when saying goodbye, and as Agathe's train began to move and the hat grew smaller and smaller, it seemed to her as if the station were travelling backward as fast as the train was travelling forward. Although only an instant earlier she had still believed she would not stay away any longer than the circumstances absolutely required, in this moment she resolved not to return at all, and the shock of it left her mind throbbing like the heart of someone who has just escaped a danger unseen until the moment when it was past.

When Agathe reflected on this later, she was not entirely satisfied. What she disapproved of in her own behaviour was that the form it had taken reminded her of a strange illness she had had as a child, soon after she had begun going to school. For more than a year she had suffered from a feverish condition that neither became acute nor yielded to treatment, and she had become so thin and frail as to arouse anxiety in the doctors, who could not diagnose any cause. Nor had an explanation of that illness ever been found. Now, doubtless Agathe had enjoyed seeing how the great doctors from the university, each of whom would make his first entry into her room full of dignity and wisdom, gradually, from week to week, lost something of their confidence; and although she obediently took whatever medicine was prescribed, and would really have liked to get well, because it was expected of her, she was still pleased at how, with all their efforts, the doctors simply failed; and she felt herself to be in a supernatural or at least extraordinary state as less and less of her remained. She was proud of the fact that the grown-ups' order of things had no power over her so long as she was ill, and she did not know how her little body had managed it. But in the end it recovered of its own free will and in a way that seemed to be just as uncanny.

Almost all she remembered about it now was what the servants had told her later. They said she had been bewitched by a beggar-woman who often came to the house, but who one day was brusquely turned away from the door. Agathe had never been able to find out how much truth there was in this story; for although the servants enjoyed indulging in dark hints they were never willing to come out with an explanation, being obviously intimidated by the strict ban that Agathe's father was said to have put on the subject. Her own memory of that period amounted to no more than one single but vivid image: she saw her father in a towering rage, lashing out at a sinister-looking woman whom he several times slapped in the face. Only that once in her life had she seen that small man, who was always rational and even painfully just, so utterly changed, almost taking leave of his senses; but to the best of her recollection this had happened not before but only during her illness. For it seemed to her that at the time she had been in bed and that instead of being in the nursery the bed had been in a room on the floor below, ' with the grown-ups ', in one of the living-rooms that the servants should never have allowed the beggar-woman to enter, even though she was by no means a stranger in the kitchen and below stairs. Indeed, it seemed to Agathe that this incident must have occurred more towards the end of her illness and that she had suddenly recovered a few days afterwards, roused from her bed by some strange impatience; and so this illness ended as inexplicably as it had begun.

Of course she did not really know to what extent these memories related to facts or whether they were merely fantasies conjured up by her fever. ' Probably the only remarkable thing about it all ', she thought moodily, ' is the way these images have survived in my mind, hovering between reality and imagination, without my ever finding them really odd.'

The jolting of the taxi-cab, as it drove over bumpy cobbled streets, made conversation impossible. Ulrich had suggested taking advantage of the dry winter weather and having an outing; and he had proposed a goal that was actually not a goal in the usual sense of the word, but more like an expedition into a re-awakening landscape of their memory. And now they were in this cab, which was taking them to the outskirts of the town.

' I'm sure that's the only remarkable thing about it,' Agathe thought to herself all over again. This was just the way she had learned her lessons at school, so that she never knew whether she was stupid or clever, a willing or an unwilling pupil: the answers that were expected of her imprinted themselves on her mind with the greatest of ease, without her ever discovering the purpose of the questions, against which she felt herself to be insulated by some deep inner indifference. After her illness she had liked going to school neither more nor less than before, and because one of the doctors had been inspired with the idea that it might be a good thing to remove her from the solitary life she led at

home and give her more company of her own age, she had been
sent away to school, to a convent. There too she was regarded
as a cheerful, docile child. Later she was sent to a grammar-
school. Whenever she was told something was necessary or true,
she accepted it, and she willingly put up with all that was required
of her because that seemed least trouble; it would have struck her
as absurd to rebel in any way against the established system,
which had no real relevance to herself and which was clearly part
of a world constructed according to the ideas of fathers and teachers.
But she did not believe a word of anything she learned, and because
in spite of her apparent docility she was far from being a model
pupil and wherever her wishes came into conflict with her convictions calmly did what she liked, she enjoyed the respect of her
schoolmates, enjoyed indeed that admiring affection which can
be earned at school by those who know how to make life easy for
themselves. It was even thinkable that her strange illness had
been a device of this kind, for with this one exception she was, as
a matter of fact, always healthy and by no means a neurotic child.
' Plainly and simply then, an idle, good-for-nothing character ',
she concluded dubiously. She remembered how much more
vigorously than herself the other girls had often revolted against
the rigid convent discipline and what principles of moral indignation they had supplied to justify their offences against law and
order; yet so far as she had had the chance to observe it was
precisely those who had been most passionately mutinous in
matters of detail who later most completely came to terms with
life as a whole: those girls turned into well-adjusted women who
brought up their children not very differently from the way they
had been brought up themselves. And so in spite of her dissatisfaction she was not entirely convinced that it was better to
be an active and good character.

Agathe abominated the emancipation of women just as intensely
as she despised the female craving to breed that demands a man
to build a nest for it. She liked to remember the time when
she had first begun to feel her dress tightening over her breast
and had borne her glowing lips through the cooling air of the
streets. But the sort of feminine erotic activity that emerges
from the veils of girlhood rather like a round knee from pink
tulle was something that had aroused her contempt ever since

she could remember. When she asked herself what she really believed in, a feeling told her that she was destined to experience something extraordinary, something of a different order—and this even then, at a time when she still knew practically nothing of the world and did not believe the little she had been taught. And she had always seen a mysterious kind of activity, somehow in keeping with that feeling, in the fact that, whenever it had to be, she was prepared to let things happen to her just as they came, without rashly over-estimating their importance.

Agathe glanced obliquely at Ulrich, sitting there grave and stiff, being rocked to and fro by the jolting of the cab. She recalled how hard it had been to make him see, that first evening, why she had not simply run away from her husband on her wedding-night, liking him as little as she did. She had been in utmost awe of her big brother so long as she had been waiting for his arrival, but now she smiled, secretly recalling the impression Hagauer's thick lips had made on her in those first months whenever they rounded into an uxorious pout under the bristles of his moustache: his whole face would be drawn in thick-skinned folds towards the corners of his mouth, and she would feel, with something like satiety: ' Oh, how ugly this man is ! ' His mild pedagogic vanity and benevolence were also something she had endured like a merely physical nausea, as something pertaining more to the exterior than to the interior world. After the first shock was over, she had now and then betrayed him with other men. ' If one can call it that,' she thought, ' when to a young thing without experience, whose sensuality lies dormant, the advances of a man not her husband seem to come like a thunderous knocking on the door.' For she had proved but little gifted for infidelity: no sooner had she got to know her lovers a little than they struck her as by no means more irresistible than husbands, and it soon seemed to her that she might just as easily take an African tribe's ceremonial masks seriously as the erotic masquerading adopted by European men. Not that she had never lost her head over it: but at the very first attempts to repeat the experience that state would fail to reappear. The manifested realm of imaginings, the theatrical quality, of sex could not in-toxicate her. These stage-directions for the heart, developed mainly by the male, all amounting in the end to the notion that life, being hard, should now and then contain an hour of weakness —with all the variations of weakness: the going under, the fainting away, the being taken, the giving of oneself, the surrender, the being translated into another state, and all the rest of it—all struck her as being in the nature of over-acting, ham-acting, since she, for her part, never felt herself anything but weak in a world so superbly constructed by the strength of the male.

The philosophy that Agathe acquired in this way was simply that of the female who refuses to be taken in, while she cannot help watching the male going through his paces for her benefit. Or rather, it was not a philosophy at all, but merely disappointment defiantly concealed—yet mingled, too, with a restrained readiness to some still unknown act of dissolution, a readiness that perhaps even increased in the same measure as the external defiance diminished. Since Agathe was well-read, but by her very nature unsympathetic to theorising, she often had occasion, when comparing her own experiences with the ideals set before her in books and in the theatre, to marvel at two facts: one was that her seducers had never entangled her as the snare entangles the wild animal of the woods, which would have matched the Don-Juanish portrait that men painted of themselves in those days for use in their escapades with women; the second was that her life together with her husband had not taken on the somewhat fashionable form of a Strindbergian war of the sexes, in which captive woman used her resources of cunning and weakness in order to torment the despotic but hopelessly clumsy master to death. Quite the contrary: her relations with Hagauer, in contrast with her deeper feelings about him, had always remained quite good. On that first evening Ulrich had used strong words like panic, shock, and violation, which did not meet the case in the least. And even now she became quite stubborn, remembering what he had said. She was sorry (she had told him), but she could not pretend to outraged innocence; the fact was that everything about the marriage had taken a very natural course. Her father had supported the man's suit with reasonable arguments; she herself had decided to marry again. All right then, one did it. One had to put up with all it involved. It was neither especially wonderful nor excessively unpleasant. Indeed even now she felt sorry about deliberately hurting Hagauer, even though it was what she was absolutely set on! Love had not been included in her hopes; she had thought it would work out somehow, for he was, after all, a decent sort of man, a good man.

Or rather, he was more one of those people who always do good, without having any real goodness in them. That was what Agathe thought to herself. Apparently the goodness disappears out of people in the same measure in which it turns into goodwill or good actions. How had Ulrich put it? A stream that turns factory wheels loses its force. Yes, yes, he had said that too, but it was not what she was trying to remember. Now she had it! ' It seems it's really only the people who don't do much good who manage to preserve their goodness intact.' But in the very instant that she recalled the saying, which must have seemed so meaningful when Ulrich had uttered it, it struck her as completely nonsensical. It could not be detached from the now forgotten context of their conversation. She tried re-shuffling the words and replacing them by similar ones; but now it became evident that the first form was the right one, for the alternatives were a preaching to the winds, nothing at all remained of them. And so that was the way Ulrich had put it. But: ' How can one call people good if they behave badly?' she thought. ' Really, that *is* nonsense!' And she realised that in the moment when he made this assertion, without its having any more real substance, it had been quite brilliant! ' Brilliant' was not even the word for it: it had made her almost sick with happiness. Sayings of this kind explained her whole life. This one, for instance, had been uttered during their last long talk, after the funeral and after Hagauer had left; and suddenly she had realised how carelessly she had always acted, including the time when she had simply thought it would ' work out somehow' with Hagauer, because he was ' a decent sort'. Ulrich often said things that for a moment would fill her to the brim with happiness or unhappiness, though one could not ' save up' those moments. When was it, she wondered, that he had said he could imagine being able to love a thief, but never a person who was honest from habit? She could not instantly remember when he had said it; and the funny thing was that she very soon realised it was not he who had said it, but she herself. As a matter of fact, a great deal of what he said she had already thought herself, only without putting it into words: for left to herself, as she had been previously, she would never have made such definite assertions.

Up to now Agathe had been feeling quite comfortable, being jogged and jolted along in the cab, bumping over the cobbled streets leading out of town, the two of them rendered incapable of conversation, wrapped as they were in a net of mechanical vibrations; and her husband's name had cropped up among her thoughts without in any way disturbing her, merely as a term of reference for a certain period and its content. But now, without any particular reason, quite slowly, an infinite horror went through her: Hagauer had actually been there with her in the flesh! All the fairness with which she had been thinking of him now vanished, and her throat contracted in bitterness.

He had come on the morning of the funeral; had, despite this late arrival, affectionately insisted on having a last glimpse of his father-in-law; had gone to the dissecting-room; had delayed the closing of the coffin; had, in a tactful, sincere, well-moderated fashion, been extremely moved. After the funeral Agathe had excused herself on grounds of fatigue, and Ulrich had had to take his brother-in-law out to lunch. As he told her later, several hours of Hagauer's unrelieved company had made him as frantic as a tight collar, and for that reason alone he had done all he could to get rid of him as fast as possible. Hagauer had intended to travel up to the capital for an educationists' congress and to spend another day there calling on various people in the Ministry and doing some sightseeing, before which he had planned, attentive husband as he was, to stay with his wife for two days, going into the matter of her inheritance. But Ulrich, mindful of his agreement with his sister, invented a story that made it seem impossible for Hagauer to be put up at the house and told him he had booked a room for him in the best hotel in town. As expected, this made Hagauer waver: the hotel would be uncomfortable and expensive and in decency he would have to pay for it himself; on the other hand, he might well give *two* days to conferences and sightseeing in the capital, and if he travelled by night, he would save one night's hotel bill. And so Hagauer had insincerely expressed regret at its being so difficult for him to take advantage of Ulrich's thoughtful arrangements, and had finally announced his plan, which would scarcely be modified now, to leave that same evening. Thus all that remained to discuss was the Will.

At this thought Agathe smiled again, for at her desire Ulrich had told her husband that the Will was not to be read for some days yet. Agathe would be there, after all—Ulrich had told Hagauer —to look after his interests, and he would in any case receive a proper legal statement of the position in due course. As for whatever there was in the way of furniture, mementos and the like, Ulrich, being a bachelor, would make no claim to anything that his sister might happen to want. Finally he had asked Hagauer whether he would agree to their selling the house, which was really no use to any of them—without committing himself, of course, since none of them had yet seen the Will. And, without committing himself, of course, Hagauer had said that at the moment he could see no objection, though he must of course reserve the right to adopt whatever attitude he thought fit in the event of any steps actually being taken. All this had been at Agathe's instigation, and her brother had spoken accordingly because it meant nothing to him one way or another and he wanted to be rid of Hagauer.

But suddenly Agathe felt miserable again. For after they had contrived all this so ingeniously, her husband had after all come to her room together with her brother, to say goodbye to her. She had behaved as unamiably as could be, declaring that there was simply no telling when she would be returning. Knowing him as she did, she had instantly realised that he was unprepared for this and resentful at now being forced into the position of the inconsiderate husband who had no time to spare; and he was suddenly annoyed in retrospect at being expected to put up at a hotel, and in general at the cool reception he had met with. But being a man who did everything according to plan, he said nothing, resolving to make the suitable reproaches only at a later date; he picked up his hat and dutifully kissed her on the lips.

The memory of this kiss, with Ulrich looking on, made Agathe feel utterly crushed. ' How on earth,' she wondered in dismay, ' could I stand living with that man so long ? But—come to think of it—haven't I let my whole life happen to me just as it came, without putting up any fight ? ' And she passionately reproached herself: ' If I were worth anything at all, it could never have come to this.'

Agathe averted her face from Ulrich, whom she had been watching, and looked out of the window. Low tenement buildings, frost-bound streets, people all muffled up—it all gave one the feeling of a bleak desert, and it seemed to mirror the desert, the blank, of her own life, which she felt was the result of her own lack of principle. Now she was no longer sitting up straight, but had gradually slid down into the cab's upholstery, with its mildewy odour of antiquity, for in this position it was easier to see out of the window, and she did not bother to change this ungraceful posture even though the jolting of the cab went right through her pelvis, and she was jarred worse than ever. This body of hers, being tossed about like a bundle of rags, became quite uncanny to her: for there it was, the only thing that belonged to her.

As a girl at school, sometimes, waking in the half-darkness of the morning, she had felt as if she were drifting along inside her body as though lying stretched full-length on the planks of a small boat, drifting into the future. Now she was roughly twice as old as then. And here in the cab, too, there was semi-darkness. But she could not form any picture of her own life and had no notion of what it ought to be. Men were complementary to one's own body, a completion of it, but no spiritual content; one took them as they took one. Her body told her that in only a few years it would begin to lose its beauty: which meant losing the feelings that, arising directly out of its self-certainty, were expressible only to a slight extent in words or thoughts. Then everything would be gone, without anything ever having been there. It occurred to her that Ulrich had spoken of the futility of his sporting activities in a similar way, and while she doggedly kept her face averted, looking out of the window, she resolved to question him about that.

10

Further progress of the expedition to the Swedish Rampart.
The moral principle of the Next Step.

BROTHER and sister had left the cab at the last, small, now quite rural-looking houses at the edge of the town and set off on foot along a wide, furrowed, slowly rising country road uphill. The frozen earth between the wheeltracks crumbled beneath their tread, and their shoes were soon covered with the dismal grey of this ground proper to carters and' peasants, which contrasted sharply with their own smart town clothes. Although the day was not cold there was a stiff wind blowing down the hill towards them, making their cheeks glow and their lips almost glassily brittle, so that it was hard to talk.

The thought of Hagauer impelled Agathe to explain herself to her brother. She was convinced that this ill-considered marriage must be entirely incomprehensible to him, even in the simplest social terms; yet although the words were there ready in her mind, she could not bring herself to the point of overcoming the resistance set up by the steep road and the cold air beating against her face. Ulrich strode a little ahead of her, in a broad track left by a dragging brake, which they were using as a path; looking at his lean, broad-shouldered form, she hesitated. She had always imagined him hard, unyielding and with a touch of the adventurer about him, perhaps only because of the disapproving remarks she had heard made about him by her father and occasionally also by Hagauer; and the thought of this estranged brother, who had cast off the family ties, had made her ashamed of her own yieldingness in life. ' He was quite right not to bother about me,' she thought, and once again she felt a shock at the way she had so often gone on putting up with discreditable situations. But in fact she had in herself the same tempestuous contradictory passion; this was what had made her break out into declaiming those lines of poetry, standing in the doorway of the room where their father's dead body lay. She pressed on to catch up with

Ulrich, which left her short of breath. And then suddenly this sober road rang with questions such as it had probably never heard before, gasping questions that cut through the clod-hopping hill-wind with a meaning that had never before been carried by any wind among these hills.

" You remember——" she began, raising her voice, and referred to several well-known instances of crime in literature. " You didn't tell me whether you could exonerate a thief. But you'd say these murderers were good, I suppose ? "

" Of course ! " Ulrich shouted back. " Well—no, wait a minute. Perhaps they're potentially good, valuable human beings. They don't lose that even as criminals. But no, they aren't good ! "

" But why then do you go on loving them even after their crime ? Surely not merely because they did have the makings of good people once, but because you still like them ! "

" That's always the way it is," Ulrich said. " It's the man that gives the act its character, and not the other way round. We distinguish Good and Evil, but in our hearts we know they form an entity."

Agathe's wind-whipped cheeks flushed even brighter red because the passion of her questions, at once explicit and concealed in her words, had been able to find its examples only in books. The habitual misuse of ' culture ' has reached such a pitch that one tends to feel its apparatus is out of place wherever the wind blows and there are trees—as though man's culture were not the summary of all the patterns in Nature ! But she had fought down her feelings bravely, and, linking her arm in her brother's, now (close to his ear, so as not to have to raise her voice any more) with a peculiar boisterousness that changed her face she said: " I suppose that's why we kill off the bad people, but first of all kindly give them a good breakfast."

With some intuition of the passion raging at his side, Ulrich inclined his head to his sister's ear and said, though without lowering his voice: " Everyone's given to thinking *he* can't do any evil, because after all *he*'s a good person."

Talking thus, they had reached the top of the hill, where the road levelled out and cut straight through a wide, treeless moor. The wind had suddenly dropped, and it was no longer cold, but in this pleasant stillness they stopped talking, as though the thread had snapped and they could not go on.

" What on earth started you thinking of Dostoievsky and Stendhal in the midst of that gale ? " Ulrich asked after a while. " If anyone could have overheard us, he'd have thought us quite crazy."

Agathe laughed. " He wouldn't have understood us any more than the cries of the birds.—As a matter of fact, only the other day it was you who were telling me about Moosbrugger."

They walked swiftly on.

After a while Agathe said: " But I don't like him."

" I'd nearly forgotten all about him," Ulrich answered.

After they had walked on for a while in silence, Agathe stopped. " Tell me," she said, " you must have done all sorts of irresponsible things yourself ? For instance you were once in the hospital with a bullet-wound, weren't you ? Surely you don't always think things out carefully before you do them ? "

" The questions you're asking today ! " Ulrich exclaimed. " What do you expect me to say to that ? "

" Aren't you ever sorry about what you've done ? " Agathe went on quickly. " It seems to me you never feel remorse. You once practically said so."

" Heaven knows," Ulrich replied, beginning to walk on, " there's a plus in every minus. Perhaps I did say something of the sort, but it really needn't be taken quite literally."

" A plus in every minus ? "

" Some good in everything bad. Or at least in much of what's bad. In human minus-variants there are usually unrecognised plus-variants: that's probably what I meant to say. And being sorry you've done something is just what gives you the strength to do something better than you could otherwise. What one *does* is never the decisive thing—it's always only whatever one does next."

" And if you've killed someone, what can you do then ? "

Ulrich shrugged his shoulders. He felt inclined to answer, for the mere sake of being consistent: ' It might enable me to write a poem that would give spiritual life to thousands, or, say, make some great invention.' But he controlled himself. ' That would never happen,' it struck him. ' Only a lunatic could imagine such a thing. Or perhaps an eighteen-year-old aesthete. Such ideas, God only knows why, are contrary to the laws of Nature. Still—' he thought in rectification, ' for primeval man it was like that. He killed because human sacrifice was a great religious poem.'

He did not utter either of these thoughts aloud.

And Agathe went on: " You may think I make silly objections, but the first time I heard you say what matters isn't the step one takes, but always only the next step after that, I thought to myself: If a person could fly inwardly, as it were be in moral flight, always moving at top speed from one improvement to the next, he wouldn't know any such thing as remorse ! I envied you terrifically ! "

" That's nonsense," Ulrich said emphatically. " What I said was: not the wrong step is what matters, but the next step after it. But what matters after the next step ? Obviously the one that follows after that. And after the *n*th the *n*th-plus-one step ? Anyone living on that pattern would have to live without ends or decisions, in fact without any reality at all. But it still remains true that what matters is always only the next step. The truth is we have no proper method of dealing with this perpetually moving series. My dear," he concluded without ·transition, " sometimes I feel remorse for my whole life."

" But that's the very thing you can't manage ! " his sister remarked.

" And why not indeed ? Why precisely not that ? "

" I myself," Agathe replied, " have never really done anything, and so I've always had time to feel remorse for the few things I've done. I'm quite sure you don't know any such benighted state. The shadows come, and what's past gains power over me. What I've done is there again down to the smallest detail, and I can't forget anything and can't understand anything. It's an unpleasant state to be in . . ."

She spoke without emotion, quite unassumingly. It was true, Ulrich did not know that backwash of life, since his own life had always been organised for expansion, and it merely reminded him that his sister had several times lamented over herself in fairly strong terms. But he did not take this up, for they had meanwhile reached the top of another hill, which he had set as the goal of their excursion, and were approaching the steep slope at the farther side of it. This was a huge rising of the ground, which legend associated with a siege by the Swedes in the Thirty Years' War because it looked like a fortification, even though it was much too big to be one; it was a green natural rampart, without bush or tree upon it, and the side overlooking the town fell away as a high, bright rock face. An empty world of low-lying hills extended far and wide around this place. There was no village, no human habitation, only the shadows of clouds and grey pasture-land. Once again Ulrich felt the spell of this place, which he remembered from his youth; just as then, far in the distance below, the town lay timorously huddled around a few churches, which were like hens with their chickens around them, and one involuntarily felt the urge to take one great bound into the midst of it or sweep it all up into the palm of one's gigantic hand.

" It must have been a glorious feeling for those Swedish adventurers, reaching a place like this after jogging along for weeks and then from the saddle catching their first sight of their quarry," he said to his sister, after he had explained to her the meaning of the place's name. " It's really only in moments like that that the weight of life is lifted from us—the burden of our secret grievance that we must all die, that everything's over so soon and probably all for nothing."

" What sort of moments do you mean ? " Agathe asked.

Ulrich did not know how to answer. He did not want to answer at all. He remembered how, when he was very young, this place had always made him feel a need to clench his teeth in silence.

After a while he replied: " I mean the romantic moments when events gallop away with us—what it really comes to is: the sense-less moments." As he spoke it seemed to him his head was like an empty nut poised on his neck, and rattling round inside it old phrases such as ' Death the Great Leveller ' or ' I care for no-body, no, not I ' and with them came back the long-faded *fortissimo* of the years when there was as yet no dividing-line between life's hopes and life itself. ' What experiences have I had since then,' he wondered, ' that were unequivocal and entirely happy ? None.'

He heard Agathe say: " I've always acted senselessly, and it only makes one unhappy."

She had walked ahead, right to the edge of the cliff. Her ears

were deaf to her brother's words; what he said meant nothing to
her.   Gazing straight ahead, she saw only a solemn, barren landscape of a sadness that matched her own. When she turned
round, she said: " It's a sort of place to kill oneself in," and smiled.
" The emptiness in my head would dissolve with infinite mildness
into the emptiness of the scene."   She took a few steps back to
Ulrich.   " All my life long," she went on, " I've been reproached
for having no will-power, for not loving anything, not respecting
anything, in fact for not being a person with a real will to live.
Papa used to hold it against me, and the man Hagauer is always
lecturing me about it.   And now will you tell me, for God's sake,
tell me at long last what are the moments when there's anything
in life that's necessary ? "

" When one turns over in bed," Ulrich gruffly declared.

" And what does that mean ? "

" I'm sorry," he said.   " It's a mundane example.   But there's
truth in it: you're dissatisfied with your position; you keep on
thinking about altering it and you make one resolution after another without actually doing anything; in the end you give it up;
and all at once there it is—you've turned over !   One really ought
to say: you've been turned over.   It's exactly the same pattern
one acts on both in passion and after long-thought-out decisions."
He did not look at her as he spoke; he was giving the answer to
himself.   He still had the feeling: ' Here I stood, wanting something, with a yearning that has never been satisfied.'

Agathe smiled again, but it was a smile that twisted her mouth
as though with pain.   She returned to where she had been standing and gazed in silence out into distances full of romance and
adventure.   Her fur coat was darkly outlined against the sky,
and her slim form was in intense contrast to the wide stillness of
the landscape and of the shadowy clouds passing over it. The
picture gave Ulrich an ineffably strong sense of action. He was
almost ashamed to be standing there in a woman's company
instead of beside a saddled horse.   And although he was perfectly
conscious that this was caused by the tranquil pictorial effect
emanating from his sister at this moment, he could not help
feeling that something was happening not to him but somewhere
in the world and that he was missing it.   He told himself he was
being ridiculous.   And yet there had been some justice in his

thoughtlessly uttered declaration that he felt remorse for his life. He sometimes yearned to be involved in events as in a wrestling match, and even if they were senseless or criminal, so long as they were authentic—definite, not of that perpetually provisional nature that events have so long as a man remains superior to his experiences. ' In other words, events that are authentic in that they are self-contained,' Ulrich reflected, now seriously groping for a way to say it, and without his being aware of it this thought stopped roaming around imaginary events and focused on the sight offered by Agathe, who at this moment seemed no more than a mirror of herself.

There then each of them stood for some time, apart and solitary, and a hesitation that was filled with conflicting feelings made it impossible for them to move. But perhaps the strangest thing was that nothing was farther away from Ulrich's thoughts than that something had indeed happened when on Agathe's behalf and out of his own wish to be rid of his unsuspecting brother-in-law he had told him the downright lie that there was a sealed Will, which was only to be opened in a few days, and had assured him, equally against his better knowledge, that Agathe would look after his interests; this was what Hagauer later termed Ulrich's being an accessory before the fact.

Still, they did somehow together leave that place, where each had been so deeply sunk in private thought, and walked on without having opened their minds to each other. The wind had freshened up again, and because Agathe seemed rather tired Ulrich suggested resting in a shepherd's cottage that he knew of nearby. They found it soon, a stone cabin, so low that they had to stoop going through the door. The shepherd's wife stared at them in almost hostile embarrassment. In the mixture of German and Slavonic phrases that was used in this part of the country and which he still vaguely recalled, Ulrich asked if they might come in for a while out of the cold and eat their sandwiches there, and he supported his request with a tip so generous as to make the woman break out into apologetic lamentations about her wretched poverty, which prevented her being able to offer ' such fine gentry ' any better hospitality. She wiped the greasy table by the window, set a fire of twigs blazing in the stove, and put some goat's milk on to heat. Agathe had at once squeezed past the table to the window, paying no attention to any of all this, as if it were a matter of course to find shelter somewhere and not of the least importance where. She looked out through the dim little square of four panes on to the countryside; they were now on the far side of the ' Rampart ' and had lost the wide view they had had from it, and what she saw there was rather more reminiscent of what a swimmer sees when surrounded by green billows. Though it was not yet evening, the day had already passed its zenith and the light had somewhat faded.

Agathe suddenly asked: " Why do you never talk to me seriously ? "

Ulrich found no better answer than to glance up at her with an air of innocence and surprise. He was busy spreading out ham, sausage and eggs on a piece of paper between himself and his sister.

But Agathe went on: " If one happens to bump against you, one gets bruised, one gets a shock at the terrific difference between your body and one's own. But if I try to get a definite answer out of you, you dissolve into thin air." She did not touch the food he pushed towards her, indeed in her disinclination to wind up the day with a jolly picnic she was holding herself so straight it seemed she did not even want to touch the table. And now something happened that was almost a repetition of what had happened on their way up the hill. Ulrich moved aside the mugs of goat's milk that had just been brought to the table from the stove and which emitted an odour very distasteful to nostrils unfamiliar with it; the faint nausea that it caused him had a sobering and stimulating effect such as one sometimes gets from a sudden welling up of bitterness.

" I've always talked to you seriously," he retorted. " If you don't like it, I can't help it. For whatever you dislike about my answers is neither more nor less than the morality of our time." He suddenly realised he wanted to explain to his sister, as completely as he possibly could, all that she needed to know in order to understand herself and something of her brother too. And with the determination of a man who does not expect to be interrupted by idle remarks, he began a speech of some length.

" The morality of our time," he said, " whatever else anyone may say about it, is the morality of achievement. Five more or less fraudulent bankruptcies are all right if the fifth is followed by a period of prosperity and patronage. Success has the capacity to obliterate whatever went before. When you reach the point where you swing elections with your money and set up as a collector of paintings, you have also gained the State's indulgence. All this has its unwritten rules: if someone gives money to the Church, charity and political parties, it need not be more than a tenth of what he'd have to lay out if he wanted to prove his good will by patronising the arts. Apart from this, success has its limits. One cannot yet achieve every end by every means. Some of the principles associated with the Crown, the aristocracy, and society exert a braking influence on the *parvenu*. On the other hand, where its own suprapersonal person is concerned, the State blandly adheres to the principle that one may rob, murder, and cheat so long as the result is power, civilisation, and glory. I don't of course wish to assert that all this is acknowledged even in theory. On the contrary, the theory of it is all very obscure. But what I've just said sums up the basic facts. As for moral arguments, they're only one more means to the end, a weapon that's used in pretty much the same way as lies are. There you have the world that men have made, and it would make me want to be a woman if it weren't that women fall in love with men.

" The things that nowadays pass for good are whatever gives us the illusion that it will get us somewhere: but this conviction is precisely what you called the flying man who knows no remorse, and what I've said is a problem we can't solve because we lack a method. Having had a scientific education, what I always feel is that my knowledge is incomplete, merely a pointer, and that even tomorrow I may easily have some new experience that will make me think differently from today. On the other hand, even a man entirely in the grip of his emotion, man ' in ascension ', such as you have pictured him, will feel each of his acts to be a step carrying him upwards to the next. So there is something in our mind and in our soul that we may call the morality of the next step. But is it merely the morality of the five bankruptcies ? Does the *entrepreneur*-morality of our time extend so far into the interior life ? Or is there only the appearance of identity ? Or is the careerists' morality a miscarriage of something else, a caricature, prematurely born, of more fundamental phenomena? At the moment I wouldn't know what answer to give."

The little breathing-space that Ulrich here allowed himself in this disquisition was entirely rhetorical, for he intended to elaborate his views further. But Agathe, who had been listening in a way she often did, at once alertly and passively, carried the talk forward on to quite different ground with the simple remark that she was not interested in any such answer, she only wanted to know where Ulrich himself stood, for she was quite incapable of grasping the whole range of intellectual possibilities. " But," she added, " if you're going to expect me, in any way at all, to do anything in life, then I'd rather not have any sort of morality."

" Thank God for that! " Ulrich exclaimed. " I'm delighted every time I look at your youth, beauty, and strength, and then hear you say you have no energy! Our age drips with practical energy anyway. It's stopped caring for ideas, it only wants action. This frightful energy springs solely from the fact that people have nothing to do. Inwardly, I mean. But, after all, even outwardly everyone spends his whole life simply repeating one and the same action: he takes up an occupation and goes ahead in it. I think this brings us back to the question you put to me out there in the open air. It's so easy to have the energy to act and so difficult to find a meaning for action! There are very few people who understand that nowadays. That's why the men of action look like men playing ninepins, knocking down those nine lumps of wood with the gestures of a Napoleon. It wouldn't even surprise me if they ended up by assaulting one another, frantic at the towering incomprehensibility of the fact that all their actions will not suffice . . ." He had begun in a lively tone, but he had gradually become thoughtful and even fell silent for a while. At last he glanced up with a smile and simply said: " You say that if I were to demand any moral exertion from you you would disappoint me. And I say if you were to turn to me for moral advice I should disappoint you. It seems to me we mustn't expect anything definite from one another—all of us, I mean. What it comes to is we oughtn't to demand action from one another, but to start by creating the preconditions for it. That's the way it seems to me."

" But how is that to be done? " Agathe asked. She realised

that Ulrich had abandoned the big generalising speech that he had begun and had gone over into something more personal to himself, but even this was too general for her taste. She had, after all, a prejudice against general analyses and regarded every exertion that extended, so to speak, beyond the limits of her own skin as more or less futile; she was sure of it wherever there was any question of her own effort, and she had a fairly good idea that it applied equally to the generalisations made by others. Still, she understood Ulrich pretty well. She watched him sitting there with bent head, quietly denouncing practical energy, and all the time unconsciously holding his pocket-knife in his hand, cutting little notches in the surface of the table; all the sinews of his hand were tense. The unthinking but almost impassioned activity of this hand and his having so frankly said she was young and beautiful was something like an absurd duet high over the orchestra of all the other words; and she did not even try to give it a meaning otherwise than by sitting there and watching.

"What should be done?" Ulrich countered in the same way as before. "Once at our cousin's I proposed to Count Leinsdorf that he should found a world secretariat for precision and the spirit so that even the people who don't go to church should know what to do. Of course I was only joking. For although it's ages since we created science to cope with truth, the idea of wanting something similar to cope with everything else seems so foolish that one's quite ashamed of it. And yet all that the two of us have been talking about would logically lead to that secretariat!" He had abandoned the great speech and was now leaning back in his chair. "I suppose I'm just dissolving into thin air again if I add: but how would that turn out, in this age of ours?"

Since Agathe did not answer, a silence fell.

After a while Ulrich said: "Incidentally, I myself sometimes think I can't keep up this conviction of mine. When I saw you standing there a while ago," he went on almost under breath, "on the edge of the Rampart, I don't know why, I had a wild urge to rush and *do* something. As a matter of fact I used really to do rash things at times. The magic lay in the fact that when it was over I had the feeling of having an additional something beside me. Sometimes it seems to me possible for a person to be made happy even by committing a crime, because it gives him a certain ballast and hence, perhaps, keeps him on a more even keel."

Once again Agathe offered no answer. He looked at her quietly, perhaps even searchingly, but without feeling any repetition of the experience he had just described, indeed without really thinking anything at all.

Then after a while she asked him: " Would you be angry with me if I committed a crime ? "

" What on earth do you expect me to say to that ? " Ulrich exclaimed, once again bent over his knife.

" Isn't there any decision ? "

" No, nowadays there isn't any real decision."

At that Agathe said: " I should like to kill Hagauer."

Ulrich forced himself to keep his gaze lowered. The words had penetrated his ear lightly and softly, but when they had passed they left something like a broad cart-track in his memory. He had instantly forgotten the tone in which they were uttered; he would have had to see her face in order to know how to interpret the words; but he did not want to accord them even that much importance. " All right," he said. " And why shouldn't you ? There can't be anyone alive who hasn't wished something of the sort. Go on, do it, if you really can ! " Only now did he straighten up again and look at his sister. Her face was stubborn and surprisingly full of excitement. Keeping his gaze fixed on her face, he explained slowly: " Look, there's something there that doesn't make sense. On this frontier between what goes on inside us and what goes on outside there's some communicating link missing nowadays, and the two spheres only transform into each other with enormous losses in the process. One might almost say our evil wishes are the shadow-side of the life we really lead, and that the life we really lead is the shadow-side of our good wishes. Just imagine you'd really done it: it wouldn't be anything like what you'd meant. You'd be terribly disappointed, to say the least of it. . . ."

" Perhaps I might suddenly be a different person: you admitted that possibility yourself ! " Agathe burst out.

Glancing aside at this moment, Ulrich was reminded that they were not alone; there were two people listening to their conversation. The old woman—she might well have been no more than

forty, but the old shawl she was wrapped in and her care-worn
face gave her an aged look—had amicably sat down by the stove,
and sitting beside her was the shepherd, who had returned home
to his cabin during the conversation, though his guests, deeply
absorbed as they were in their own affairs, had not noticed his
entry. The two peasants sat with their hands on their knees,
listening to the talk in wonderment, it seemed, and almost as
though it brought some credit upon them; they were well content
to have their cabin filled with such talk, even though they did
not understand a word of it. They saw the milk was not being
drunk, the sausage was not being eaten; it was a spectacle for them
and an elevating one at that. They did not even whisper to each
other. Ulrich's eyes met their widened eyes and, feeling a little
awkward, he smiled at them. But only the woman smiled back,
while the man remained grave, mindful of his place.

" Il faut manger," Ulrich said to his sister. " On s'étonne de
nous."

Obediently she toyed with some bread and meat, and he himself
resolutely began to eat and even drank a little of the milk. Meanwhile Agathe went on, aloud and unembarrassed: " If I think
about it seriously I don't like the idea of really hurting him. So
perhaps I don't really want to kill him. But I should like to blot
him out! I'd like to tear him into little bits, pound them in a
mortar, and throw the dust into the water—that's what I'd really
like! Simply wipe out all that has been! "

" You know, it's really a little funny, the way we're talking,"
Ulrich observed.

Agathe was silent for a while. But then she said: " The very
first day, you promised you'd stand by me against Hagauer! "

" And of course I shall. But not that way, you know."

Agathe was silent again. Then she said suddenly: " If you'd
buy a motor-car, or hire one, we could drive there by the Iglau
road and come back the longer way round, through Tabor, I
think it is. It wouldn't even dawn on anyone that we were there
in the night."

" And what about the servants? Fortunately I have no idea
how one drives a motor-car, anyway." Ulrich laughed. But
then he shook his head in annoyance. " Those are just the sort
of ideas people have nowadays! "

" It's all very well for you to say that," Agathe remarked. She was pushing a little piece of ham to and from with her fingernail; and it looked as if the fingernail, which had acquired a greasy shimmer from it, were doing this all by itself. " But you also say: society's virtues are vices to the saint ! "

" Only I didn't say that society's vices are virtues to the saint ! " Ulrich pointed out. He laughed again, caught hold of her hand and cleaned the nail with his handkerchief.

" You always take everything back, that's what it comes to," Agathe scolded and she smiled ruefully, while the blood mounted to her cheeks as she tried to free her finger.

The shepherd and his wife, who were still sitting by the stove, watching them intently, now beamed all over their faces as though in response.

" When you talk to me like this, first this way and then that," Agathe said in a low voice, but sharply, " it's as if I were looking at myself in the splinters of a broken looking-glass: with you one never sees oneself as a whole ! "

" No," Ulrich said, not letting go of her hand, " these days one never sees oneself whole and one never moves as a whole. That's just it ! "

Agathe yielded, suddenly abandoning her hand to him. " I'm certainly anything but a saint," she said quietly. " In my in-difference perhaps I've even been something worse than a kept woman. And I'm certainly not enterprising either, and I don't suppose I'll ever be capable of killing anyone. But when you first said that about the saint—it's a little while ago now—it made me see something ' as a whole '." She bowed her head, either in thought or to avoid letting him see her face. " I saw a saint, perhaps a figure on a fountain. As a matter of fact I didn't actually see anything, but I did feel something in a way you can only call seeing. The water was flowing, and all that the saint did also came brimming over the rim, as though he himself were a fountain gently overbrimming on all sides. It seems to me that's the way one ought to be. Then one would always do the right thing, and yet it wouldn't matter in the least what one did."

" Agathe sees herself standing in the world, overflowing with sanctity and trembling because of her sins, incredulously observing how snakes and rhinoceroses, mountains and ravines, serenely lie down at her feet, all even smaller than she is herself," Ulrich said, gently teasing her. " But where does Hagauer fit in ? "

" That's just the trouble. He doesn't fit in at all. He must be removed ! "

" Now let me tell you a little story," her brother said. " Whenever I've had to take part in anything collective, any sort of thorough-going general human affair, I've been like a man who steps outside the theatre before the last act, for a breath of air and, seeing the great dark void with all those stars in it, walks off, leaving behind his hat and coat and the whole show."

Agathe gave him a searching look. It was the right answer and yet it wasn't right.

Ulrich met her gaze. " I gather you too are often tormented by a dislike of things where there is no liking to counterbalance it," he said. And he wondered: Is she really like me ? Once again it seemed to him that perhaps she did resemble him as a pastel portrait resembles a woodcut. He thought himself the more solid of the two. And she had a beauty he had not got ; she was a joy to behold. He shifted his grip from her finger to her whole hand: it was a warm, long hand full of life, and up to now he had held it in his own only for so long as it took to shake hands. His young sister was agitated, and though she had not actually tears in her eyes, there was a moist glimmer there. " In a few days you'll be going away from me too," she said. " And then how am I to cope with everything ? "

" Well, we can stay together. You can come and be with me."

" How do you picture that ? " Agathe asked, the little thoughtful frown appearing on her forehead.

" Oh, I haven't pictured it at all. It's only just occurred to me." He got up, leaving some money ' for the damage to the table '.

Through a haze Agathe saw the shepherd and his wife grinning and bobbing, and heard them uttering some brief exclamation of delight in words she did not understand. As she passed them she felt those four eyes bent on her, all hospitable kindliness and frank curiosity, and she realised that Ulrich and she had been taken for lovers who had had a quarrel and made it up again.

" They thought we were lovers ! " she said. Impetuously she linked her arm with her brother's, and suddenly a great gladness

welled up in her. " You ought to give me a kiss ! " she insisted
and, laughing, pressed Ulrich's arm to her side as they stood
there on the threshold of the cabin and the little door opened
before them into the darkness of the evening.

11 *Holy conversations : Beginning.*

DURING the rest of Ulrich's stay little more was said about
Hagauer; nor did they return for a long time to the idea that they
should make their reunion permanent and take up life together.
Nevertheless, the fire that had shot up in a high flame in Agathe's
outburst about getting rid of her husband went on smouldering
under the ashes. It spread in conversations that reached no end
and yet time and again began anew. Perhaps it would be best to
say: Agathe's feelings were seeking a vent, in order to break out
into a blaze.

She would as a rule begin such talk by asking a definite, personal
question, the inner meaning of which was: ' May I or may I not ? '
Her anarchic nature had hitherto held the sad and weary conviction: ' I may do as I like, but I don't even want to '. And so
his younger sister's questions sometimes, and not unjustifiably,
gave Ulrich the same feeling as a child's questions, which are as
warm as the helpless little creature's hands.

His own answers were of a different kind, which was no less
characteristic of him: as usual, he expressed himself in a way as
candid as it was intellectually adventurous. It was never long
before he arrived at ' the moral ' of whatever his sister was telling
him, summing it up in formulae, always inclined to bring himself
in by way of illustration, and in this way telling Agathe a great
deal about himself, especially about his more unruly life in earlier
years. Agathe told him nothing about herself, but she admired
his ability to talk about his life like this, and it suited her very well
that he subjected all the problems she raised to moral scrutiny.
For morality is nothing more or less than orderliness in the soul
and among things, embracing both, and thus it is not strange that

young people, whose will to live is not yet entirely blunted, talk about it a great deal. When the same thing occurs in a man of Ulrich's age and experience some explanation is needed, for usually men only talk about morality when the subject arises professionally, when it is part of their occupational jargon, and for the rest the word is swallowed up in the business of living and never escapes again. So when Ulrich spoke of morality, it indicated a profound disorder, which attracted Agathe because it corresponded to something in herself. She was now ashamed of having rather naïvely confessed that she meant ' to live in complete accord with herself ', for she was beginning to get some inkling of the tangle of preconditions that had to be fulfilled first. Yet she impatiently wished that her brother would move faster towards some conclusion; for it often seemed to her that everything he said was moving in that direction, and the more distinctly the further he went on. But always at the last step he stopped just short of the threshold: there, each time, he abandoned the attempt.

The locus of these last steps and this about-turn—and its paralysing effect did not escape Ulrich—can be broadly indicated by saying that every proposition in European morals leads to such a point, where there is no going any further: so that a man taking stock of himself feels like one wading in shallow water for as long as he knows he has firm convictions underfoot, but then suddenly, as he goes a little farther, is plunged into the terror of one drowning, as though the solid ground of life had abruptly fallen away into an abyss of uncertainty. In the discussions between brother and sister this came out in a specific manner: Ulrich was capable of talking calmly and expositorily on any subject he brought up so long as only his intellect was involved, and Agathe's interest, as she listened, was of a similar kind; but then, when they paused and fell silent, another sort of eagerness, a tension, came into their faces. And so it once happened that they found themselves on the far side of the frontier that they had hitherto unconsciously kept within. Ulrich had made the assertion: " The one infallible distinguishing-mark our system of morals has is that its commandments contradict each other. The most moral of all propositions is: the exception proves the rule! " Probably all that provoked the assertion was his distaste for a moral procedure that sets up to be unyielding and in practice has to be entirely flexible, which means that it is the opposite of an exact operation, which always begins by taking account of experience and deduces the law from its observations. He was of course aware of the distinction drawn between laws of Nature and moral laws, the former being the outcome of observing Nature, which is amoral, the latter having to be imposed on human nature, which is not so stubborn. Yet it seemed to him something in this distinction was no longer valid, and what he had actually meant to say was that this left morals in a state that was intellectually a hundred years behind the times, which was why it was so difficult to apply them to present-day needs. But before he reached that point in his explanation, Agathe interrupted with a comment that seemed very simple but which at that moment disconcerted him.

" So being good isn't a good thing at all ? " she asked, and there was a light in her eyes reminiscent of that time when she was doing something with her dead father's decorations that most people would probably not have termed ' good '.

" You're quite right," he answered eagerly. " The fact is one's got to start by constructing some such proposition if one wants to get back the feeling of the word's original meaning. But children are still at the stage of liking ' being good ' in the same way they like sweets."

" And being naughty too, for that matter," Agathe added.

" But has ' being good ' any place among adult passions ? " Ulrich wondered. " It's one of the principles that adults have ! They aren't ' good '—that would strike them as childish—they just behave in a ' good ' way. A good man is one who has good principles and does good works, and it's an open secret that he may at the same time very well be a perfect horror ! "

" Gottlieb Hagauer," Agathe commented.

" There's something paradoxically nonsensical in those ' good people '," Ulrich reflected. " They turn a condition into a requirement, a grace into a norm, a state of being into a goal ! This household of the ' good ' all its life long sets nothing on its table but left-overs, but keeps the rumour circulating that once upon a time there was a feast-day, which the scraps are supposed to be left over from ! Admittedly, from time to time a handful of virtues come back into fashion, but as soon as that happens they begin losing their freshness again."

" Didn't you once say," Agathe asked, " that the same act may be good or bad according to the circumstances ? "

Ulrich agreed. That was his theory: moral values were not absolutes, they were functional concepts. And when we moralise and generalise, we detach them from their natural context, from the totality. " And that," he said, " is probably the point where something's gone wrong on the road to virtue."

" Otherwise why should moral people be so dreary," Agathe supplemented, " when their intention to be good ought to be the most delicious, the most difficult, the most enjoyable thing anyone could possibly imagine ! "

Her brother hesitated. But all at once he let slip an assertion that soon brought them both into an extraordinary relationship.

" Our morality," he declared, " is the crystallisation of an interior movement that is entirely different from it. There's something out of joint in absolutely everything we say ! Take any proposition you like—what's just occurred to me is: ' Prison should be a place of repentance.' It's a statement one can make with a perfectly clear conscience. But nobody takes it literally, or else one would logically arrive at hell-fire for the prisoners ! And so how is one to take it ? Indubitably few people know what repentance is, but everyone's prepared to say where it should prevail. Or simply think of something that elevates you: how does *that* find its way into morality ? When did we ever lie with our faces so in the dust that it was bliss for us to be raised up again, to be *elevated* ? Or try to form a literal picture of being ' seized ' by an idea: the moment you experienced that corporeally you'd already be across the frontiers of the lunatic realm ! But that's just the way every word needs to be taken, literally, otherwise it rots away into a lie. Yet one mustn't take any word literally, else the world turns into a madhouse ! There's some great intoxication emanating from the Word, an obscure memory, and sometimes one wonders if everything we experience isn't just scraps of some ancient wholeness of things destroyed long ago, shreds that we once fixed together into one piece again and got it all wrong."

It was in the library-*cum*-study that they were talking, and while Ulrich sat over several books he had brought with him from home, his sister was looking around the shelves of legal and philosophic works that in a way had become hers too now; it was to some extent they that stimulated her questions.

Since their excursion they had both scarcely left the house. They spent most of their time in this manner. Sometimes they strolled in the garden, where winter had stripped the leaves from plants and trees, leaving the earth exposed and bare, swollen with rain. The sight of it was somehow disturbing. The air was pallid, like something that had long been left lying in water. The garden was not large, and the paths soon turned back on themselves. And the state of mind in which the two of them walked along those paths was also self-involved, turning in a circle, like eddies in water gradually rising behind a dam. When they returned to the house the living-rooms would be dark and like a refuge, and the windows like deep shafts that made the daylight filtering through them as delicate and brittle as thin ivory.

Now, after Ulrich's last, vehement words, Agathe had descended from the library ladder on which she had been sitting and had put her arms around his shoulders without answering. This was an unusual show of tenderness, for apart from the two kisses they had exchanged—one on the evening of their first meeting, the other a few days ago, on leaving the shepherd's cabin—their natural fraternal prudishness had not dissolved further than into words or little acts of attentiveness; and on both those occasions, too, the effect of the intimate contact had been overlaid by its unexpectedness or, the second time, by sheer flamboyance. But this time Ulrich instantly thought of the garter that his sister had so warmly bestowed, instead of wasting words, upon their dead father. And what went through his head was: 'Of course she must have a lover! Not that she seems to care for him much, or she wouldn't have the patience to stay on here the way she's doing.' It was borne in on him that she was a woman, that she had led a woman's life independently of him and would continue to lead it. Merely from the distribution of weight in the arm resting on his shoulders he felt the beauty of that arm, and on the side where his sister was standing he had a shadowy sense of her blonde armpit, so close to him, and the outline of her breast. In order not to go on sitting there like that, defenceless and abandoned to the mute embrace, he reached up and took hold of the fingers of the hand lying near his neck, thus blotting out one contact with another.

" You know, it's a bit childish the way we're talking," he said, not without exasperation. " The world is full of active decision, and here we sit talking, all voluptuous indolence, about the sweetness of ' being good ' and the theoretical vessels one could pour it into ! "

Agathe freed her fingers, but let her arm return to where it had been resting. " Tell me, what's this book you're always reading ? "

" Oh, you must know what it is," he replied. " You're always looking over my shoulder, peering into it."

" Yes, but I don't quite know what to make of it."

He could not make up his mind to discuss the matter. Agathe, who had now drawn up a chair, was kneeling up on it behind him and had simply and tranquilly laid her face in his hair, as though going to sleep like that. In some odd way it reminded Ulrich of the moment when his enemy Arnheim had put one arm round his shoulders and he had been penetrated with a sense of another being's casual pressure like a current pouring into him as through a breach. But this time his own nature did not resist the other; on the contrary, something moved towards it, something that had lain buried under the rubble of mistrust and resentment which fills the heart by the time a man has reached a certain age. Agathe's relationship to him, which floated undefined, with something about it of ' sister ' and something of ' woman ', something of ' stranger ' and something of ' friend ', yet without her being exactly what any of these things meant for him, did not—as he had already quite often mused—consist in any particularly far-reaching agreement of thought or feeling between them. But it could, as he now realised with something like amazement, be summed up in the fact that after no more than these comparatively few days, with their innumerable impressions too various to hold clearly in his mind, Agathe's mouth could rest on his hair just like that and that his hair became warm and moist from her breath. This was something as spiritual as it was physical. And when Agathe pressed her question about his reading, Ulrich was overcome by a kind of solemnity that he had not felt since the days of his youth, when he had still had faith in things. And before this cloud of imponderable solemnity had evaporated—a cloud that, passing right through his body, extended from the presence behind his back to the book in front of him, on which his thoughts rested —he had given an answer that astonished him less by its substance than by its total lack of irony. What he said was: " I'm seeking instruction in the ways of the holy life."

He stood up and moved several steps away: not in order to avoid his sister's proximity, but in order the better to see her.

" You needn't laugh," he said. " I'm not religious. I'm surveying the road to holiness with the question whether it would stand up to one's travelling along it in a motor-car."

" I only laughed," Agathe replied, " because I'm so eager to hear what you have to say. I don't know any of these books you brought with you, but I can't help feeling I somehow know what they're about."

" You have that too ? " her brother asked, already quite sure that she did. " One may be bang in the middle of the most terrific upheaval, and then suddenly one's eye is caught by the play of—any old God-forsaken, man-forsaken thing—and you simply can't tear yourself away from it. All at once its trifling existence bears one up like a feather floating on the wind, weightless and effortless . . ."

" Except for the terrific upheaval you make such a point of, I think I know what you mean," Agathe said and could not help smiling at the almost ferocious look of embarrassment on her brother's face, which was so little in keeping with the delicacy of his words. " Sometimes one becomes oblivious of sight and hearing, and quite loses the power of speech. And yet it's precisely then, one feels, that one comes to oneself for a moment."

" The way I'd put it," Ulrich eagerly went on, " is that it's like looking out across a wide glimmering sheet of water: the eye seems almost to be seeing darkness, everything's so bright, and on the far bank things don't seem to be fixed on solid ground but floating in the air, in a delicate over-distinctness that's almost painful . . . bewildering. The impression one gets is both of intensification and of loss. One is linked with everything and at the same time can't get right *to* anything. There you are on the one side, and the world on the other, over-individuality and over-objectivity, but all almost agonisingly clear, and what at once

separates and unites these generally fused elements is a dazzling
darkness, an overbrimming and an extinction, a swinging in and
out. You float like the fish in the water or the bird in the air,
but there simply is no bank and no branch and nothing but this
floating!" Ulrich was doubtless being poetical; nevertheless,
the fire and the firmness of his language stood out in metallic
relief against its delicate, hovering content. He seemed to have
cast off his habitual cautiousness.

Agathe gazed at him in astonishment, but also with uneasy
delight.

" So you think," she asked, " there may be something behind it ?
More than a mere ' freak of fancy ' or whatever dreary phrase one
might use to play it down ? "

" I do indeed ! " He sat down again in his previous place and
began leafing through the books spread out there, while Agathe
got up to make room for him. Then he laid one of them open,
saying: " The saints describe it like this——" and read aloud:
" During these days I was exceeding restless. Now I sat a while,
now I wandered up and down through the house. It was like
an anguish and yet more to be called a sweetness than an anguish,
for there was no vexation in it, but a strange and supernatural
pleasantness. I had transcended all my faculties, reaching all
the way to the hidden strength. Then I heard without sound,
then I saw without light. Then my heart became groundless,
my spirit formless, and my nature insubstantial."

It seemed to them both that this description resembled the
unrest by which they themselves had been driven through house
and garden, and especially Agathe felt surprised that the saints
too called their heart groundless and their spirit formless. But
Ulrich soon seemed to be caught up again in the trammels of his
irony.

" The saints," he declared, " say: once I was immured, then
I was drawn out of myself and sunken without knowing in God.
The emperors out hunting, about whom we read in our story-
books, describe it differently: they tell of how a stag appeared to
them with a cross between its antlers, so that the murderous spear
dropped from their hands; and then they had a chapel built on
the spot so that they could carry on hunting none the less. And
the rich, clever ladies with whom I consort, if you ask them about

such things, will instantly give you the answer that the last to
paint such experiences was van Gogh. Or perhaps instead of
talking of a painter they'll talk of Rilke's poetry. But on the
whole they prefer van Gogh, who represents an excellent capital
investment and who cut off his ears because his painting wasn't
enough for him compared with the burning rapture of things
themselves. The majority of our people, on the other hand,
would say cutting off one's ears is not a *German* way of expressing
one's emotions—the German way is that unmistakable vacancy
of the gaze from on high, such as is experienced on mountain-
tops. For them solitude, pretty little flowers, and rippling brooks
are the quintessence of what man can experience in the way of
sublimity. And even in that exalted bovinity, with its crude
enjoyment of Nature, there is the misunderstood last by-product
of a mysterious second life, and so all in all there must be such a
thing—mustn't there?—or must have been once!"

"Then you oughtn't to make fun of it," Agathe objected,
sombre with earnest curiosity and radiant with impatience.

"I only make fun because I love it," Ulrich replied curtly.

12   *Holy conversations : Continued with inter-*
ludes.

IN the time that followed there were always a large number of
books lying on the desk, some of which he had brought with him,
some of which he had bought since; and sometimes he talked in
his own way, sometimes he looked up quotations in them, either
to illustrate his point or because he wanted to have the exact
wording of a passage, these places being marked with little slips
of paper. It was for the most part accounts of mystics' lives or
their own writings that he had before him, or scholarly works
concerned with them, and he would usually go off at a tangent
with some such remark as: "Now let's look at this as soberly as
possible, to see what's going on here." This was a cautious
attitude that he did not find it easy to abandon of his own free

will, and that was why he once said: " If you could read straight
through all these descriptions that men and women of past
centuries have left of their states of divine ecstasy, you'd find that
there's truth and reality somewhere there in all the printed words,
but all the same, the assertions that the words form would call
forth strong protest from the commonsense by which you live."
And he went on: " They speak of an overflowing radiance. Of
an infinite expanse, an infinite brilliance of light. Of a floating
' unity ' of all things and all spiritual faculties. Of a wonderful
and ineffable uplifting of the heart. Of flashes of knowledge so
swift that everything is simultaneous and like drops of fire falling
into the world. And on the other hand they speak of a forgetting
and no longer comprehending, of everything utterly sinking away.
They speak of an immense peace, an utter detachment from
all passion. Of growing mute. Of a vanishing of thought and
intentions. Of a blindness in which they see clearly, of a clarity
in which they are at once dead and supernaturally alive. They
call it an undoing of the self, and at the same time they declare
they live more fully than ever. Aren't these, even though
flickeringly veiled by the difficulty of expressing them at all, the
same sensations one has even today when it chances that the
heart—' ravenous and satiated ', as they say !—suddenly finds
itself in those utopian regions that lie somewhere and nowhere
between an infinite tenderness and an infinite loneliness ? "

In the brief pause for thought that Ulrich made, Agathe raised
her voice: " Is that what you once called the two layers lying one
upon the other within us ? "

" I did—when ? "

" You'd gone to town without any object in mind, and you felt
as though you were being dissolved into the town itself, but at the
same time you didn't like the town. And I told you that sort of
thing often happened to me."

" Oh yes ! In fact, what you added was ' Hagauer ' ! "
Ulrich exclaimed. " And we laughed. Yes, I remember now.
But we didn't mean that quite literally. Anyway it's not the only
time I've talked to you about the giving and the taking kinds of
vision, about the male and female principles, and the herm-
aphroditism of the primal imagination, and all that sort of thing—
I can go on for hours about these things !—and it's as though my

mouth were as far away from me as the moon, which is likewise always on the spot at night if one needs someone to chat to confidentially. But what these religious people recount about their spiritual adventures," he went on, and once again there was an overtone of objectivity and also of admiration intermingled with the bitterness of his words, " really, sometimes it's written with the strength and ruthless conviction you get in Stendhal's analytical probings. Though as a matter of fact," he said, modifying that, " only so long as they stick to the phenomena, without their judgment getting involved, for that's falsified by the flattering conviction that they've been singled out by God to have direct experience of Him. For from that moment on of course they stop telling us about their perceptions, which are so hard to describe—having, as it were, no nouns or verbs in them—and start talking in sentences with subject and object, because they believe in their soul and in God as in two doorposts with the great miracle about to open between them. And so they come to such statements about how the soul is drawn out of their body and absorbed into the Lord, or that the Lord enters into them like a lover. They are captured, swallowed, dazzled, rapt, violated by God, or their soul expands to meet Him, enters into Him, tastes Him, embraces Him with love and hears Him speak. The earthly model for all this is something one can't fail to recognise. And at this point descriptions cease to resemble enormous discoveries, they resemble nothing more than the rather monotonous imagery with which a love-poet decks out his theme, on which only one opinion is permissible. At least so far as I'm concerned, having been brought up as I was to maintain reserve, these accounts are frantically tantalising, because the elect, having reached the point of declaring that God spoke to them or that they understood the language of trees and animals, omit to tell me the one thing more—namely what the message was! Or if they ever do, all that comes out is private affairs or standard theological stuff. The eternal pity of it is that people trained in the exact sciences never have visions!" he said, concluding his long reply.

" D'you think they could?" Agathe probed.

Ulrich hesitated for an instant. Then he answered, like one confessing his faith: " I don't know. Perhaps it might happen to me." And while he heard himself speak these words, he smiled in order to limit their implication.

Agathe also smiled. Now, it seemed, she had the answer she had been craving, and her face reflected the little moment of helpless disappointment that follows on the sudden cessation of a tension. And perhaps the only reason why she raised an objection was that she wanted to stimulate her brother to go on.

" You know," she said, " the convent-school I was sent to was a very strict one. With the result that I have an irresistible tendency to caricature these things, and it becomes positively scurrilous the moment anyone talks about religious ideals. Our teachers wore a habit with two colours which formed a cross, and I suppose that was a reminder of one of the sublimest thoughts we were supposed to have before our eyes all day long. But we never thought of it for an instant, we simply called the good sisters the cross-spiders —both because of their habit and because of their soft, silky talk. And so that's why, while you were reading that stuff, I felt half like crying and half like laughing."

" You know what that proves ? " Ulrich exclaimed. " Just one thing: that the power for Good that really does seem to exist in us in some way immediately eats its way through the walls if it gets shut up in some solid form, and through the hole it flows straight out into Evil! It reminds me of when I was in the army, when my brother-officers and I were the mainstays of Throne and Altar: never since in all my life have I heard such loose language used about those two things as I did then! The emotions will not endure being tied down, and there are certain emotions that endure it least of all. I'm quite sure your worthy nuns themselves believed what they preached to you. But faith mustn't be even an hour old! That's the thing! "

Although in his haste Ulrich had not expressed himself to his own satisfaction Agathe did realise that those nuns' faith, which had taken the heart out of her own faith, had been something ' canned '. Admittedly what it was as it were preserved in was its own nature, and it had lost none of its essential property as faith; nevertheless it was no longer fresh: in some undemonstrable way it had simply passed over into a condition different from the original one. And the original one was perhaps at this moment

hovering as an intuition here, in the mind of those godly ladies'
truant and rebellious pupil.

This, with all the rest of what they had already said in talking
about morality, was one of the heart-stirring doubts that her
brother had implanted in her mind, and was part and parcel too of
the state of inner re-awakening that she had been feeling ever since,
without having become clear about what it was.   For the state of
indifference that she made such a point of outwardly displaying
and inwardly encouraging had not always reigned in her life.
Once something had happened, causing this need for self-punishment to spring straight out of a profound dejection that made her
regard herself as ' no good ', because she believed it was not
granted her to keep faith with lofty emotions; and since then she
had despised herself for her heart's sloth.

This episode lay between her life as a girl in her father's house
and her incomprehensible marriage to Hagauer, and it occupied
such a narrow strip of her life that it had even escaped Ulrich's
attention and for all his sympathy he had not asked her about it.
What had happened is soon told.   At the age of eighteen Agathe
had married a man very little older than herself, and on their
honeymoon, when they had barely had time to think of setting
up house, he was snatched away from her within a few weeks by a
fatal illness with which he became infected while travelling.   The
doctors called it typhus, and Agathe repeated the word and found
a sort of appearance of order in doing so, for here was the side of
what was happening that was polished smooth for worldly use:
but on the unpolished side it was different.   Up to then Agathe
had lived together with her father, whom everyone respected, so
that she took it rather dubiously for granted that she was doing
wrong in not loving him; and at school her mistrustful uncertainty
as to what she was really like, the long-drawn-out waiting to
become ' herself ', had also done nothing to stabilise her relation
to the world.   But when later, with a suddenly awakened will to
live and in common effort with her childhood playmate, she had
in a few months overcome all the obstacles that both families set
in the way of the marriage on grounds of the two young people's
extreme youth—though the families had no objections to each
other—, she had all at once ceased to be lonely and as a result
had become herself.   And so this was what is called love.   But

there are two kinds of people in love: there are those who gaze into love as into the sun and are simply blinded, and there are those who in amazement see life for the first time when it is illumined by love. It was to the second kind that Agathe belonged, and she had not even yet found out whether it was her mate or something else that she loved when the thing came that in the language of the un-illumined world was called an infectious disease. It was a storm of horror breaking in with disastrous suddenness out of the alien territories of life—a struggling, flickering, and extinction, a visitation upon two human beings who clung to each other, a simple unsuspecting world going to its doom in vomiting, excrement, and terror.

Agathe had never acknowledged the reality of what had happened then, the thing that had destroyed her capacity to feel. Frantically, desperately, kneeling at her dying husband's bedside, she had made herself believe that she could conjure up again the strength with which as a child she had overcome her own illness. As the decline nevertheless continued and when consciousness had already gone, there she had knelt in the dreary hotel-room, incapable of grasping the thing, staring into that desolate face, and, without regard for danger, had held the dying man in her arms—had, without regard for the realities to which an indignant nurse attended, done nothing but go on for hours muttering into an ear now past hearing: ' You mustn't, you mustn't, you mustn't ! ' But when it was all over she had got to her feet in amazement; and, without believing or thinking anything in particular, acting simply out of her solitary nature's stubbornness and capacity for dreaming, from that instant of empty amazement onwards she had inwardly treated what had happened as though it were not final. A tendency to something similar of course becomes apparent in every human being when he refuses to believe bad news or gives a comforting colouring to something irrevocable. But the special element in Agathe's behaviour was the force and extent of this reaction: in a word, her suddenly manifest disregard for the world. Anything new she made a point of considering less as a fact as though it were still entirely uncertain—an attitude that came to her more easily through the mistrust with which she had always confronted reality. The past, on the other hand, had petrified under the shock she had suffered and was worn away by time much more slowly than usually happens with memories. But in all this there was nothing of the obsessions, the distortions, the derangement, that cry out for the psychologist. On the contrary, Agathe went on living, outwardly perfectly lucid, undemandingly virtuous, only that she was a little bored, with a slight accentuation of her reluctance to live, a state that was in fact very like that fever she had suffered from in such an oddly willing way as a child. In her memory, which in any case never easily dissolved its impressions into generalisations, every hour of the terrible past remained ever-present, like a corpse under a white sheet; and this was a source of happiness to her despite all the anguish of such an exact remembrance, for it was like a mysterious belated hint that everything was not yet over, and even while her spiritual resources withered it kept her still in a vague but somehow noble state of tension. What all this really amounted to was that she had again lost her sense of life's having a meaning and was deliberately putting herself into a state that did not suit her years; for only old people live in such a way that they linger among the experiences and successes of the past and are no longer touched by the present. But unfortunately for Agathe, although the age at which she was then is one that makes its resolves for all eternity, it is also an age at which one year almost has the weight of half an eternity; and so it was only to be expected that after some time repressed Nature and fettered imagination violently reasserted themselves. The exact way in which it came out was pretty unimportant: a man whose advances would in other circumstances never had succeeded in disturbing her balance did succeed in becoming her lover, and this attempt at reliving the past ended, after a very short period of fanatical hope, in passionate disillusionment. Agathe now felt herself as it were cast out by her unreal life and unworthy of lofty aspirations. She was one of those intense people who are capable of remaining quite still and waiting for a long time, until at some point, all at once, they become involved in every possible kind of confusion; and so in her disappointment, she soon made another, equally ill-considered resolve, which consisted, in short, of punishing herself in a manner complementary to that in which she had sinned, namely by condemning herself to sharing her life with a man who inspired her with a faint revulsion. And this man whom she sought out for her own punishment was Gottlieb Hagauer.

Admittedly that was neither fair nor even considerate towards him, Agathe confessed to herself, and it ought to be added that this was actually the first time she did so; fairness and consideration are virtues that young people do not much practise.   However, the self-punishment involved in this marriage was no inconsiderable one either.   Agathe now went on examining the matter.   She had strayed a long way in her mind, and meanwhile Ulrich was looking through his books for something and seemed to have forgotten all about their talk.

' In earlier centuries,' she thought, ' a person in my state of mind would have gone into a convent,' and the fact that what she had done was to marry was not quite without a certain innocently comical quality that had hitherto escaped her.   This comical aspect, which had not been apparent to her youthful mind, was as a matter of fact simply that of the present era, which offers a refuge from the world—a need that people still feel—in the shape of an Alpine hotel, at the worst in that of a little tourist inn; and it even does what it can to prettify prison cells.   This is a symptom of the profound European urge never to go too far in any direction. No European any longer scourges himself, daubs himself with ashes, cuts his own tongue out, or really abandons himself or even really withdraws from the rest of mankind; he never swoons with passion, or impales anyone or breaks anyone on the wheel now. But everyone at times feels the urge to do it.   And this makes it hard to tell which is the more undesirable: the desire to do such things or its repression.   Why for instance should precisely an ascetic starve himself?   Surely it only conduces to disturbing fantasies ? !   A rational form of asceticism consists of a dislike of eating that is balanced by the taking of regular sound nourishment ! That kind of asceticism holds out the promise of permanence and permits the spirit the very freedom it does not have so long as it is bound to the body in passionate rebellion.

Such bitterly amusing points of view, picked up from her brother, did Agathe a great deal of good, for they dissected ' the tragic '—in which, in her inexperience, she had long thought it an obligation to believe quite rigidly—into irony and a passion that had neither name nor goal and for that reason alone did not end with her own experiences.

In this way she had, since she had been together with her brother, a general awareness that something was happening to the great split in her own being between irresponsible living and spectral imagination: there was movement, at once a loosening up and a re-binding of what had been loosened. Now for instance, in this silence deepened by the presence of books and memories, she recalled Ulrich's account of how, going for a walk nowhere in particular, he had entered into the town and the town had entered into him. It reminded her very acutely of the few weeks of her happiness. And it was true, too, that she had laughed; she had indeed laughed entirely without cause, senselessly, when he told her about it, because it struck her that there was something of this turning-inside-out of the world, this blissful and absurd inversion of which he spoke, even in Hagauer's thick lips when they pouted in preparation for a kiss. Of course it made her shudder; but, she thought to herself, there was sometimes a shudder even running through the bright light of high noon. And somehow she had felt this meant all possibilities were not yet exhausted so far as she was concerned. Some mere nothing, some hiatus that there had always been between the past and the present, had recently disappeared. Secretly she glanced about her. The room they were in was one of the rooms in which her destiny had taken shape; this occurred to her now for the first time since she had come. For it was here that she had come with the friend of her childhood when she knew her father was out, in the time when they made the great decision to love each other; it was here too that she had more than once received 'that worthless wretch', had stood at the windows with furtive tears of rage or desperation; and it was here, finally, that Hagauer's wooing had been conducted, reinforced by paternal approval. After so long having been merely the unregarded background to what happened, this furniture and these walls, this peculiarly enclosed light, now in this moment of renewed recognition became weirdly tangible, and all those past events that they had romantically surrounded now became so corporeally, so quite unequivocally, the past that it all was almost like ash or charcoal. All that remained now was the comically shadowy sense of things over and done with, that eerie titillation one feels when confronted with old, now dry-as-dust traces of one's own existence and which, for that moment, one can neither dispel nor grasp; and it became almost unendurably strong.

Agathe made sure that Ulrich was paying no attention to her and then she stealthily opened the neck of her dress, where she wore next her skin the locket containing the miniature that she had not ceased to wear through all the years. She went to the window, pretending to look out. Gently she snapped open the thin lid of the tiny scallop-shaped gold locket and gazed on her dead beloved. There were the full lips and the soft, thick hair, and all the swagger of a young man still in his early twenties flashed out at her from a face that was, as it were, not yet quite free of the eggshell. For a long time she did not realise what she was thinking; and then all at once she said to herself: ' Good heavens, a boy of twenty-one ! '

What do such young people talk to each other about ? What meaning do they give to their affairs ? How funny and presumptuous they often are ! How the intensity of their ideas deceives them about the value of those ideas ! Curiously Agathe unwrapped from the tissue-paper of memory old assertions that she had preserved there, thinking the world of them. ' Heavens, some of the things we said were almost important ! ' she thought. But even that was something one could not definitely proclaim without also recalling for instance that garden where they had talked, with those queer flowers whose names they did not know, the butterflies settling like weary revellers, and the light flowing over their faces as though heaven and earth were melted together in it. If she measured herself against that, she was today an old, experienced woman, even though the number of years that had passed was not so very great. She was a little bewildered to notice the discrepancy that here she was, at twenty-seven years of age, having been in love up to now with a boy of twenty-one: he had grown much too young for her ! ' What would my feelings be like,' she wondered, ' if at my age this mere boy were really the most important thing in the world to me ? ' Doubtless they would be very odd feelings; it conveyed nothing to her, she could not even form a clear picture of them. It all really dissolved into nothing.

With a great expanding sensation Agathe acknowledged that in the one single proud passion of her life she had been the victim of a mistake, and the core of that mistake was a fiery mist that could not be touched or grasped, and it was all the same whether what one said about it was that faith must not grow an hour old, or anything else. And it was always this that her brother had been talking about since they had been together, and it was always herself whom he talked of, even though he hedged it with all sorts of philosophical complications and his caution was often too slow for her impatience. They always came back to the same subject, and Agathe herself blazed with the desire that his flame should not grow less.

Now when she spoke to Ulrich, he was not even aware how long the pause had lasted. But anyone who has not already picked up the clues to what was going on between this brother and sister had better now lay this account aside, for what is narrated is an adventure he will never be able to approve of: a journey to the furthest limits of the possible, skirting the dangers of the impossible and unnatural, even of the repulsive, and perhaps not always quite avoiding them: a ' border-line case ', as Ulrich was later to call it, one of limited and specific validity, reminiscent of the freedom with which mathematics at times resorts to the absurd in order to arrive at the truth. He and Agathe found themselves on a path that had a great deal in common with the ways taken by those who are possessed by God; they went along it without a faith, without believing in God or the soul, indeed without even believing in a beyond or another life. They had entered upon it as children of this world and went along it as such: and precisely this was the significant thing.

Though at the moment when Agathe spoke again Ulrich was still absorbed in his books and the problems they set him, he had not for an instant forgotten the course of their conversation, which had broken off at his sister's resistance to her teachers the nuns and his own demand : or ' exact visions '. And he at once replied: " There's absolutely i o need to be a saint in order to experience something of the kind ! One can just as easily be sitting on a fallen tree-trunk or on a bench in the mountains, watching a herd of cows grazing, and even so doing feel oneself all at once transported into a different life. One loses oneself and all at once comes to oneself. It's what you yourself were saying."

" But what actually happens ? " Agathe asked.

" To know that you must first of all decide what constitutes the normal, O sister in the spirit ", Ulrich declared, trying to brake the too swift inspiration with a little pleasantry. " The normal state of affairs is that a herd of cattle means nothing to us but grazing beef. Or else it is something paintable with a background. Or it hardly registers at all. Herds of cattle beside mountain paths are simply part of the scenery, and what one experiences at the sight of them is something one would *notice* only if they were replaced by a big electric clock or a block of flats. Normally one wonders whether to get up or stay sitting there; one is bothered by the flies swarming around the cows; one looks to see whether there's a bull among them; one wonders where the path leads: there are innumerable tiny intentions, worries, calculations and observations, and they form, as it were, the paper on which one has the picture of the cows. One isn't aware of the paper at all, one's aware only of the cows on it——"

" And suddenly the paper tears ! " Agathe exclaimed.

" Yes. That's to say: what tears is some tissue of habit in us. Then it's no longer something edible grazing there. No longer something paintable. Nothing blocks your way. You can't even form the word ' graze ' any more, because it has a lot of purposeful, useful connotations that you've suddenly lost. What's left on the pictorial plane is something perhaps best called a billowing of sensations, rising and sinking or breathing and twinkling, as though it filled your whole field of vision without any outlines. Of course there are innumerable individual perceptions contained in all this as well—colours, horns, movements, smells, and everything that goes to make up reality. But that's no longer acknowledged, even though it may still be recognized. I should like to put it in this way: the details no longer have that egoism of theirs which makes demands on our attention, they are now fraternally and fondly, truly inwardly, linked with one another. And of course there isn't any ' pictorial plane ' there any more either. Everything somehow merges illimitably into you."

Again Agathe took up the description. " Now," she exclaimed enthusiastically, " all you need to say instead of the egoism of the details is the egoism of human beings, and then you've got what it's so hard to express: that ' Love your neighbour ' doesn't mean love him on the basis of what you and he *are*. What it means is a sort of dreamlike condition ! "

" All moral propositions," Ulrich confirmed, " refer to a sort of dream condition that's long ago taken wing and flown away out of the cage of rules in which we try to hold it fast."

" Then there's actually no such thing as Good and Evil, but only faith—or doubt! " Agathe cried. And the buoyant immediate state of faith now seemed as tangible to her as the way it disappeared out of morality, the disappearance her brother had spoken of when he said faith could not grow an hour old.

" Yes, the moment one slips out of non-essential life everything shifts into a fresh relationship to everything else," Ulrich agreed. " I'd almost go so far as to say: into non-relationship. And this is a condition we know nothing about, we've no sort of systematic knowledge of it at all. All other relationships are extinguished. But for all its obscurity this one is so distinct that one can't deny its existence. It's strong—but impalpably so. It's tempting to say: ordinarily one looks at a thing, and the gaze is like a little stick or a taut thread with the eye at one end and the thing seen at the other end, and there's some great trellis-work of that kind supporting every instant of our experience. But in this instant of which we speak it's rather that there's something at once agonising and sweet that pulls the beams of the eye apart."

" One possesses nothing in the world, one no longer holds anything fast, one's not held fast by anything," Agathe said. " It's all like a tall tree with no leaf stirring. And one can't do anything mean in that condition."

" They say everything that happens then can't but be in harmony with the condition itself," Ulrich supplemented. " The desire to ' belong ' is the only ground, the loving ordinance and the sole form, of whatever action and thought takes place in it. It's an infinitely reposeful and comprehensive condition, and everything that happens while it lasts enhances its significance, which goes on quietly intensifying. Or if it doesn't enhance it, then it's something bad, but nothing bad can happen while the condition lasts; the very moment it does happen, the stillness and clarity tear to shreds and the miraculous condition ceases." He looked at his sister searchingly, without meaning her to be aware of it; he kept on having the feeling that it was very nearly time to stop.

However, Agathe's face was shut: she was thinking of things long ago. " It makes me wonder at myself," she answered, " but there really was a short time once when I didn't know envy, malice, vanity, greed and the rest of it. It seems scarcely credible now, but it seems to me that at that time they'd suddenly disappeared not only out of my heart but right out of the world! When it's like that it isn't only that one can't behave in a beastly way: other people can't either. A good person makes everything that comes into contact with him good, no matter what other people may do to him: the moment anything falls within his scope, by the mere contact with him it's changed."

"No," Ulrich cut in, "it isn't quite like that. On the contrary, that's one of the oldest misunderstandings. A good person doesn't make the world good at all, he has absolutely no effect on it, he simply separates off from it."

"But he does stay right in the midst of it, doesn't he?"

"He stays right in the midst of it, but for him it's as if things had been drained of all the space within them or as if what was happening were imaginary. It's hard to know how to put it."

"All the same, I have the idea that a 'high-minded' person—it's just a word that's occurred to me!—never has anything rotten crossing his path. It may be nonsense, but it's something that does happen, all the same."

"It may very well happen," Ulrich retorted, "but so does the opposite! Or do you suppose the soldiers who crucified Jesus didn't feel rotten? Yet they were the instruments of God! Anyway, according to the evidence of the ecstatics themselves there are bad feelings: they lament that they fall from the state of grace into unspeakable wretchedness, they experience fear, anguish and shame and perhaps even hate. It's only when that quiet blaze flares up again that remorse, anger, fear and anguish turn into bliss. It's so hard to know what to make of it all!"

"When were you so much in love?" Agathe asked abruptly.

"Me? Oh well, I've told you about that: I fled a thousand miles from the woman I loved, and once I felt safe from any chance of her real embraces, I let myself go like a dog howling at the moon."

Now Agathe confided to him the story of her love. She was excited. Even her last question was something she had let go of as if it were an over-tightened violin-string, and what followed was in the same manner. She vibrated inwardly as she revealed what had been hidden for so many years.

Her brother was not particularly overwhelmed. " Memories generally age along with people," he expounded, " and passionate experiences after a while become comical in a changed perspective, as though one were seeing them at the far end of a series of ninety-nine opened doors. But sometimes, if they're associated with very strong feelings, certain memories don't age; then they keep a hold on whole strata of the personality. It was like that with you. There are such points in almost everyone, points where the psychic proportions are slightly distorted. The person's general attitude pours away over them like a river over an invisible boulder. With you it just happened to have been on a very large scale, so that it almost dammed things up entirely. But you did free yourself in the end. You're moving again ! "

He said it with the calm of something like a professional approach. How easily he got off the subject ! Agathe felt miserable. She said obstinately: " Of course I'm moving, but that's not what I'm talking about ! I want to know where I almost got to at that time ! "

She was also annoyed, without meaning to be, simply because her excitement had to find an outlet somehow. Still, she went on talking in the direction her emotion had originally taken, and she felt quite dizzy between the tenderness of what she was saying and the annoyance in the background. In this way she told him about the peculiar state of heightened receptivity and sensibility that brings about a welling up and sinking away again of the perceptions, giving rise to a feeling of being united with everything as in the soft mirror-surface of a sheet of water and giving and receiving without exertion of the will: that wonderful sense of a lifting of all bounds, the boundlessness of things external and interior, this feeling that is common to love and to mysticism. Agathe did not of course use these words, which amount to explanation as well as description; she merely threaded together, like beads, some passionate fragments of her memory.

But although Ulrich had given much thought to these things, he too was incapable of offering any explanation of such experiences. Indeed, he did not even know whether in trying to work one out he should resort to the terms of the experience itself or use the usual logical operations; both forms were equally natural to him— though not to his sister, with her obvious passion. And so what

he said in answer was merely a compromise, a sort of testing of
the possibilities. He pointed out how remarkably akin thought
and the moral sense were when one was in this exalted condition
of which they were talking; each thought was felt to be happiness,
an event, a gift, and did not end up in the store-rooms of the
mind or become associated in any way with feelings of appropriation and mastery, with the urge to hold fast and observe.
Thus in the mind no less than in the heart pleasure in possessing
oneself was replaced by a boundless shedding of oneself and
interweaving with everything.

" Once in one's life," Agathe replied with dreamy decisiveness,
" everything one does is done for another's sake. One sees the sun
shining for him. He is everywhere, and one is oneself nowhere.
Still, it isn't ' egoism extended to two ', for precisely the same
thing must be going on in the other person. In the end both
practically cease to exist for each other, and what's left is a world
for people all in twos, which consists of respect, surrender,
friendship, and selflessness ! "

In the darkness of the room her face glowed with enthusiasm
like a rose blooming in the shade.

And Ulrich pleaded: " Now let's come down to earth again a
bit. There tends to be far too much flummery in discussion of
these problems."

This too struck her as quite right. Perhaps it was the annoyance, which had not yet quite faded, that combined with Ulrich's
realistic attitude to somewhat repress her rapture; but this vague
trembling of the border-line was a not unpleasant sensation.

Ulrich began by saying what folly it was to interpret the experiences they were concerned with as though what took place
were not merely a peculiar change in one's mental processes, but as
though a supernatural thinking replaced the normal kind. Whether
it was called divine illumination or, in the modern style, merely
intuition, this, he considered, was the main impediment to a real
understanding of the phenomenon. In his view there was nothing
to be gained by giving oneself over to illusions that would not
stand up to careful investigation. That, he exclaimed, was just
like Icarus's wings of wax, which melted in the high air. If one
wanted to fly not merely in one's dreams, one must learn to do it
on metal wings.

And, pointing to his books, he went on after a brief pause: "Here are Christian, Judaic, Indian and Chinese testimonies. Between some of them there lie as much as a thousand years. And yet in all of them one recognises the same pattern of inner movement, one that diverges from the normal but which is in itself integral. Almost the only way in which they differ from each other at all is just in whatever comes from being connected with theological constructions, as it were a doctrinal edifice that supplies them with a sheltering roof overhead. What it comes to, then, is that we can assume the existence of a characteristic second, extraordinary condition, a highly important condition that man is capable of entering into and which has deeper origins than the religions.

"On the other hand," he added, "the churches, that's to say, civilised communities of religious people, have always treated this condition with pretty much the sort of mistrust a bureaucrat has for any individual spirit of enterprise. They've never unreservedly recognised this visionary mode of experience. On the contrary, they've directed great and apparently justified efforts towards replacing it by a properly regulated and intelligible scheme of morality. So the history of this condition resembles a progressive denial and evaporation, something rather like the draining of a swamp.

"And when the spiritual despotism of the churches," he concluded, "and their terminology became obsolete, not surprisingly this condition of ours came to be regarded as no more than a flight of fancy. Why after all should a bourgeois civilisation, taking over from a religious civilisation, be more religious than its predecessor?! Now that other condition has gone to the dogs, in fact it's been reduced to the status of a dog fetching and carrying scraps of illumination. There are masses of people nowadays who complain about intellect and try to persuade us that in their wisest moments they think by the aid of a special faculty that's superior to the faculty of thought. That's just a last, perfectly rationalistic, communal vestige of the thing itself: what you get at the bottom of the drained swamp is a bit of mushy rubbish! And so, apart from its occurrence in poetry, this ancient condition is considered permissible only to uneducated people in their first weeks of being in love, as a transient state of mental confusion.

Those are as it were belated green leaves that may burgeon from the timber of writing-desks and double beds. But if the growth tries to burst out into its original immense proliferation, they rush to dig it up, they abolish it root and branch! "

Ulrich had been talking for just about as long as it takes a surgeon to wash his arms and hands, to avoid carrying any germs into the field of operation, and also, for that matter, with the same patience, concentration and calm, all in contrast with the excitement involved in the job ahead. But after he had sterilised himself, he thought almost yearningly of some slight infection and fever, for it was not for its own sake that he loved sobriety.

Agathe was sitting on the ladder used for fetching books from high shelves, and when her brother fell silent she showed no sign of further interest. She gazed out into the endless, oceanic grey of the sky and listened to this silence as she had just been listening to his words.

And then Ulrich began to talk again, with a trace of defiance that he scarcely managed to conceal under a light-hearted tone.

" Let's get back to our bench on the mountain-side, with the herd of cows," he suggested. " Imagine a civil servant, executive grade, sitting there in his brand-new leather shorts with ' Grüss Gott' embroidered on his green braces: he represents the 'real' content of life, on holiday. Now the fact that he's on holiday means that his awareness of his own existence is, of course, temporarily altered. When he looks at the cows he doesn't count them, he doesn't classify or codify them, he doesn't try to evaluate the living weight of them as they graze there before him: he's forgiving his enemies and thinking tolerantly of his family. The cattle have for him changed from a practical into a moral object. Naturally it may also happen that he does slightly evaluate and codify and doesn't quite forgive, but then at least it's all in an aura of woodland murmurs, purling streams, and sunshine. One can sum it up by saying: what generally makes up his life now seems to him ' far away' and ' rather unimportant really '."

" Simply a holiday mood," Agathe said mechanically.

" Just so! And if it makes his non-holiday life seem ' rather unimportant really ', that only means: for as long as his vacation lasts. So that's the fact of the matter today: man has two states of life, of consciousness, and of thought, and he saves himself from the deadly terror of the confrontation by regarding one as a holiday from the other, an interruption, a rest, or anything else that he thinks he knows all about. Mysticism, on the other hand, would be connected with the intention of going permanently on holiday. Our civil servant should properly regard that as irresponsible and disgraceful and instantly feel—as he always does, as a matter of fact, towards the end of his vacation—that *real* life is there waiting for him in his tidy office. And are our feelings different? The question whether something needs tidying up or not is always what finally decides whether one takes the thing completely seriously or not. And here these experiences are out of luck, for in all these thousands of years they've never got beyond their original, primeval disorder and incompleteness. And there's a term ready for it too: mania—religious mania or the infatuation of love, whichever you prefer. Take it from me: nowadays even most religious people are so infected with the scientific mode of thought that they don't trust themselves to look into what burns in the innermost recesses of their hearts, and at the slightest provocation they'd look at that ecstasy from a medical point of view and regard it as a delusion, even if that's not the way they talk officially."

Agathe looked at her brother with a gaze in which something crackled like fire in the rain. "Now you've gone and manoeuvred us right out!" she reproached him, when she realised he did not mean to go on.

"You're right about that," he admitted. "But the odd thing is: though we've covered all this up like a well that we think may be contaminated, there's still some left-over drop of that uncanny miraculous water burning a hole in all our ideals. None of our ideals is quite what we mean, none of them makes us happy. They all point to something that isn't there. Well, we've already said plenty about that today. Our civilisation is a temple of something that if it were at large would be called mania, and at the same time the prison where it's kept, and we don't know whether what we're suffering from is an excess or a deficiency."

"Perhaps you've never dared to give yourself right over to it," Agathe said wistfully, getting down from her ladder.

She got down because they were supposed to be sorting their late father's papers and had let themselves be distracted from this task, which had gradually become fairly pressing, first by looking

at the books and then by talking about them.   Now they went back
to checking through the instructions and notes referring to the
division of their inheritance, for the day of reckoning with Hagauer
was imminent.   But before they had really got going again,
Agathe lifted her gaze from the papers and put another question:
   " To what extent do you yourself believe in all you've been
telling me ? "
   Ulrich answered without looking up.   " Imagine that in that
herd of cattle, all the time your heart was detached from worldly
things, there was a dangerous bull.   Try really to think that mortal
illness you told about would have taken another course if your
feelings hadn't slackened for one single instant ! "   Then he raised
his head and pointed at the papers he had been sorting.   " And
law, justice, moderation ?   Do you believe all that is superfluous ? "
   " So then to what extent do you believe ? " Agathe pressed him.
   " Yes and no," Ulrich said.
   " That means: no," Agathe concluded.
   Chance then intervened in their talk.   As Ulrich, who neither
had any inclination to resume the discussion nor was composed
enough to think in a business-like way, now picked up the papers
spread out before him, something fell on to the floor.
   It was a loose bundle of all sorts of things, which had been
pulled, together with the Will, out of the very back of the desk
drawer where it must have been tucked away for decades, forgotten by its owner.   Ulrich absent-mindedly glanced at it as he
picked it up and he recognised his father's writing on several pages;
but it was not the writing of his old age, it was that of his prime.
And investigating more closely, Ulrich discovered that besides
pages of manuscript the bundle contained playing-cards, photographs and all sorts of oddments.   And suddenly he realised what
he had found.   The drawer was of course ' private and confidential '.   And here were painstakingly recorded jokes, mostly
smutty; nude photographs; postcards to be sent sealed, with
pictures of buxom peasant-lasses whose panties could be opened
behind; packs of cards that looked quite respectable but which,
when held up against the light, revealed very startling things indeed;
mannikins that performed surprisingly if squeezed on the belly;
and so on.   Undoubtedly the old gentleman had long quite forgotten these things there in the drawer, for else he would have

destroyed them, not have left them for others to find. They obviously dated from the years in which quite a few ageing bachelors and widowers heat their fancy with such trivial obscenities. Yet Ulrich blushed at this exposure, this relic of an imagination now dissolved by death. The connection with the discussion that had just been broken off was instantly clear to him. Nevertheless his first impulse was to destroy this evidence before Agathe saw it.

However, Agathe had already seen that he had stumbled on something out-of-the-way. So he changed his mind and called her to his side.

He wanted to wait and hear what she would say. All at once he was again predominantly aware that she was, after all, a woman who must have had her experiences—something he had been quite unconscious of during their more profound conversation. But from her face there was no telling what she was thinking. She looked gravely and calmly at the discreditable relics, and once or twice she smiled faintly. So, contrary to his resolve, Ulrich himself spoke.

" There's the fag-end of mysticism for you ! " he said in angry amusement. " There in one and the same drawer was the Will, with its austere moral admonitions, and this muck ! "

He had risen and began walking up and down the room. And, having started to talk, he was provoked by his sister's silence to go on.

" You asked me what I believe," he began. " I believe that all the ordinances of our morality are concessions to a society of savages.

" I believe none of them is right.

" There's another meaning glimmering behind them. A fire that ought to melt them down, melt them into something else.

" I believe that nothing is at an end.

" I believe that nothing is in equilibrium, but that everything tries to rise up by the leverage of everything else.

" That's what I believe. That was born with me, or I with it."

He had stood still after each declaration, for he did not raise his voice, and he had to give his confession emphasis somehow. His gaze was now fixed on the classical plaster busts on the top of the bookshelves: he saw a Minerva, a Socrates; he recalled that

Goethe had set up an overlife-size plaster head of Juno in his room.   How alarmingly remote that taste seemed to him: what had once been an idea in full flower was withered away into dead classicism.   It had become the rearguard action fought by his father's contemporaries with all their dogmatism, their opinionated sense of duty.   It had all been in vain.

" The morality that has been handed down to us," he said, " is comparable to sending us out to walk a swaying rope suspended over an abyss, without giving us any advice except: Hold yourself straight and stiff!

" It's none of my own doing that I seem to have been born with a different moral sense.

" You asked what I believe.   I believe it can be proved to me a thousand times by all the usual sturdy arguments that something is good or beautiful, and it'll be all the same to me, I shall take my bearings solely from whether its presence makes me feel a rising or a sinking.

" Whether it rouses me to life or not.

" Whether it's my tongue and my brain that talk of it, or the radiating shudder that goes to my very fingertips.

" But I can't prove anything either.

" And I'm even convinced that anyone who surrenders to this is lost.   He lands up in twilight.   In mist and mush.   In unarticulated ennui.

" If you take the unequivocal element out of our life, all that's left is a carp-pond without a pike.

" I believe that then even the most vicious depravity is a guardian angel to us!

" And so: I don't believe!

" And above all I don't believe in the holding down of Evil by Good, which is what our hotch-potch civilisation represents.   That I abominate!

" And so I believe and don't believe!

" But I believe perhaps that some day before very long human beings will be—on the one hand very intelligent, on the other mystics.   Perhaps our morality is even today splitting into these two components.   I might also call it: mathematics and mysticism —practical amelioration and adventuring into the unknown."

It was years since he had been so frankly excited.   The ' perhapses' in what he had said did not disturb him; to him they seemed only natural.

Agathe was kneeling before the stove. She had the bundle of photographs and papers on the floor beside her, looked at each one of them once more, and then put it into the fire. She was not entirely insusceptible to the vulgar sensuality in the indecencies she was contemplating. She felt her body stirred by them, and yet that was as little herself as if somewhere on a bleak moor she could sense a rabbit scuttering past. She did not know whether she would feel ashamed if she told her brother that; but she was inwardly tired out and did not want any more talk. Nor did she listen to what he was saying. Her heart had by now been too much shaken by these risings and fallings and could no longer follow. Oh, others had always known better than she what was right. She thought of that, but she did so—perhaps because she was ashamed—with secret defiance. Walking a forbidden or secret road: in that she felt herself superior to Ulrich. She heard him time and again cautiously revoking all that he let himself be carried away into confessing, and his words beat against her ear like big drops of happiness and grief.

13 Returning home, Ulrich is informed by the General about all that he has missed.

FORTY-EIGHT hours later Ulrich was back in his house, from which he had been absent so long. It was early in the day. The rooms were meticulously tidy, all dusted and polished; and exactly as on his hasty departure he had left books and papers lying on the tables, so they still lay, tended by his servant's hand, either open or bristling with markers that had since lost their meaning, and this or that pamphlet even still with a pencil between the pages, as he had left it. But it had all cooled off and hardened like the contents of a melting-pot when one has failed to keep the fire going under it. Painfully disillusioned and uncomprehending, Ulrich contemplated the imprint of a vanished hour, the matrix of its intense excitements and ideas. He was immensely disgusted at the thought of coming into touch with these remnants of his own existence.

' And this,' he thought, ' extends beyond the doors, all through the house, right to the imbecility of those antlers down there in the hall. What a life I've led in this last year ! ' Standing there, he shut his eyes in order not to see any of it. ' What a good thing she'll soon be coming,' he thought. ' We'll change everything ! '

And then after all he was lured into recollecting the last hours he had spent there. It seemed to him he had been away for a very, very long time, and he wanted to compare then and now.

Clarisse: that episode counted for nothing. But before that and afterwards: the strange excitement in which he had hurried home, and then that insomniac state when the world had melted ! ' Like iron softening under some very great pressure,' he brooded. ' It begins to flow and yet remains iron. A man penetrates the cosmos by force,' he imagined, ' but suddenly it closes around him and everything looks different. There are no more connections. No longer any road on which he has come and must go further. Only a glimmering enclosement in the place where a moment earlier he saw a goal, or, rather, the sober void that lies this side of every goal.' Ulrich kept his eyes shut. Slowly, a shadow, the feeling came again.

It was returning to the place where he had stood then and was standing now: a feeling more in the room outside than in the mind within; or rather, it was not a feeling at all, nor a thought either, but some uncanny happening. If one was as over-stimulated and solitary as he had been then, it was easy enough to believe the nature of the world was being turned inside out. And suddenly (the incomprehensible thing was that it should happen only now) it became clear to him, lying there like a tranquil, open vista in retrospect, that even then his feelings had heralded the meeting with his sister; for his spirit had been guided by strange powers from that moment until . . . But Ulrich turned away from his memories, before he formulated the thought ' yesterday ', having been abruptly and as tangibly wakened as if he had bumped against the sharp edge of a piece of furniture. *There* was something he did not want to think about yet!

He went over to his desk and looked through the letters lying there, still without taking off his coat. He was disappointed to find no telegram from his sister with the mail, and this although there was no reason to expect one. There was an immense pile of letters of condolence, with scientific journals and booksellers' catalogues jumbled among them. Two letters from Bonadea had come, both so very thick that he did not bother to open them. There was also an urgent note from Count Leinsdorf asking him to call, and two twittering *billets* from Diotima, likewise inviting him to put in an appearance as soon as he returned: on a more attentive reading, one, the later, revealed non-official overtones that were very cordial, melancholy, and almost on the verge of tenderness. He turned to the memoranda of telephone-calls that had come through during his absence: General von Stumm, Permanent Secretary Tuzzi, two from Count Leinsdorf's private secretary, several from a lady who would not leave her name (doubtless Bonadea), Director Leo Fischel, and, for the rest, various matters of business. While Ulrich was reading the list, still standing at the desk, the telephone rang, and when he lifted the receiver a voice said it was "War Ministry speaking, Cultural and Educational Section, Corporal Hirsch"; it seemed to be taken aback at actually encountering Ulrich's own voice, but went on to inform him zealously that His Excellency the General had given orders that Ulrich was to be rung up at ten o'clock every morning and that His Excellency would instantly speak to him himself.

Five minutes later Stumm was assuring Ulrich that he had to attend 'outstandingly important conferences' that same morning and must at all costs speak to Ulrich first. To Ulrich's question what it was all about and why on earth it could not be dealt with over the telephone, he sighed down the wire and hinted at having 'news, worries, problems', but it was impossible to get anything more precise out of him.

Another twenty minutes later one of the War Ministry's own carriages drew up at the gate, and General Stumm entered the house, accompanied by an orderly with a large leather despatch-case slung from his shoulder.

Ulrich, who well remembered this receptacle for the General's intellectual worries, since the days of the strategic plans and the pages for the doomsday book of great ideas, raised his eyebrows queryingly.

Stumm von Bordwehr smiled, sent the orderly out to wait in the carriage, unbuttoned his tunic in order to extract the little key that he wore on a little chain round his neck, unlocked the case and, without a word, brought to light the contents—two loaves of regulation army-bread.

" Our new bread," he exclaimed after a pause for dramatic effect. " I've brought it along for you to try."

" Well, that's very nice of you," Ulrich said, " bringing me bread after I've been travelling all night, instead of letting me get some sleep."

" If you've any schnaps in the house, which I presume you have," the General retorted, " all I can say is there's nothing like bread and schnaps for breakfast the morning after the night before. You once told me our regulation bread was the only thing you enjoyed in the Emperor's service, and I'll go to the lengths of saying that at bread-making the Austrian army can beat any other army in the world, especially since the Commissariat brought out this new loaf, Model 1914! That's why I've got it here. Or that's one of the reasons. And then, you know, I do it on principle now. Of course I don't have to spend the whole day at my office desk and I don't have to account for every step I take outside the door, that goes without saying. But you know yourself, it's not for nothing the General Staff is called the Jesuit Corps, there's always tittle-tattle if somebody's out much, and my chief, His Excellency von Frost, may not actually yet have all that clear an idea of the scope of the mind—the civilian mind, I mean—and so that's why for some time now I've always taken the bag and an orderly along with me when I go out for a bit, and so that the orderly shouldn't see the bag's obviously empty, I always pop a couple of loaves in."

Ulrich could not help laughing, and the General laughed happily too.

" You seem to have less relish for humanity's great ideas than you used to ? " Ulrich said queryingly.

" Everybody's got less relish for them," Stumm told him,

meanwhile slicing the bread with his pocket-knife. "The slogan's now 'Action!'."

"You'll have to explain that to me."

"That's just what I've come for. You're not a real man of action!"

"No?"

"No."

"Well, I don't know about that."

"I don't really know either. But it's what they say."

"Who are 'they'?"

"Arnheim for instance."

"So you get on well with Arnheim?"

"Of course I do! We get on outstandingly well. If he hadn't such a very great mind, we could really be quite chummy by now."

"Have you gone into oil now too?"

The General drank some of the rye that Ulrich had produced and munched at the bread, to gain time. "Jolly good, isn't it?" he said with his mouth full, and went on chewing.

"Of course you're mixed up in this oil business too!" Ulrich burst out in sudden illumination. "After all, it concerns your naval section because of fuel for ships, and if Arnheim means to buy up the oil-fields, he'll have to make terms and sell cheap to you. On the other hand, Galicia's strategic territory, a buffer between us and Russia, and you'll have to provide safeguards to make sure that the oil he wants to produce there will be specially protected in the event of war. And that means his arms factory will deliver you the guns you want on easy terms. Fancy not seeing all that before! The pair of you are positively born for each other!"

The General had taken the precaution of munching a second piece of bread. But now he could not contain himself any longer, and, making strenuous efforts to swallow the whole mouthful at one go, he said: "It's all very well for you to talk about easy terms: you've no idea what a skinflint he is! Sorry—I mean," he corrected himself, "with what moral dignity he conducts this sort of deal! I never dreamt that sixpence per ton per railway-mile was an ethical problem one had to read up in Goethe or in a history of philosophy."

"Are you conducting the negotiations?"

The General took another gulp of rye. " I never said any negotiations were being conducted! You can call it an exchange of views if you like."

" And that's what you've been empowered to do ? "

" Nobody's empowered to do anything! There are discussions, that's all. I suppose one's allowed to talk about something apart from the Collateral Campaign now and then, isn't one? And if anyone were empowered to do anything, it certainly wouldn't be me. That's no job for the Cultural and Educational Section. That sort of thing's a matter for the top brass, possibly roping in Ordnance. If I had anything to do with it at all, I'd only be a sort of specialist adviser on questions of the civilian mind, what you might call an interpreter, because of Arnheim's cultured style of talk."

" And because through me and Diotima you're always meeting him! My dear Stumm, if you want me to go on being your stalking-horse, you'll have to come out with the truth! "

But Stumm had meanwhile prepared himself for this. " What do you ask for if you know it all already ? " he retorted indignantly. " Do you think you can fool me ? Do you think I don't know Arnheim has taken you into his confidence ? "

" I don't know a thing! "

" But you've just been telling me that you know! "

" Well, I know about the oil-fields."

" And then you said we and Arnheim had common interests in these oil-fields. Give me your word as an officer that you do know that and then I can tell you everything." Stumm von Bordwehr seized Ulrich's reluctant hand and, gazing into his eyes, he said cannily: " All right then, since you give me your word that you knew it all already, I can give you mine that you know it all. Right? That's all there is to it. Arnheim's trying to make us serve his turn, and we're trying to make him serve ours. You know," he exclaimed, " I sometimes go through devilish compli-cated psychological conflicts over Diotima! But you mustn't say a word about that to anyone, it's a military secret." The General became very jaunty. " Do you know what a military secret is, anyway ? " he went on. " A few years ago when there was the mobilisation in Bosnia, in the War Ministry they wanted to axe me, I was still a colonel then, and they gave me the command of a Territorial battalion. I was quite capable of commanding a Regular brigade, of course, but because I'm supposed to be a cavalryman and because they were wanting to axe me, they gave me that battalion. And because you need money to fight a war with, when I got down there they also gave me the battalion pay-chest. Did you ever see one in your army days? It looks partly like a coffin and partly like a tuckbox, a great big wooden thing with iron bands round it, like the gate of a medieval castle. It has three locks, and there are three officers who carry the keys to them, one each, so that nobody can unlock it by himself. They are the commandant and the two co-chest-openers. Well then, so we gathered together as if for a prayer-meeting when I arrived, and one after the other we opened a lock and we reverently took out the bundles of bank-notes, and I felt like a priest with two altar-boys, only instead of reading out of the Gospel we read the figures from the official list. And when we'd finished we shut the box up again, put the iron bands back in place, clicked the locks, the whole thing over again in reverse order, I had to say a few words that I can't remember now, and then the ceremony was over. At least that's what I thought to myself and what you'll have been thinking to yourself, and I felt great respect for the in-domitable prudence of military administration in wartime. But in those days I had a fox-terrier, the predecessor of the one I have today, a clever little beast he was, and there wasn't any regulation against his being there too. Only as it happened he couldn't see a hole anywhere without instantly starting to dig like mad. So when I was just going, I noticed that Spot—that was his name, you know, he was an English dog—was busy over there at the box, and there was no getting him away. Well, one's often heard stories about faithful dogs leading to the discovery of deep, dark conspiracies, and we were practically at war, and so I think to myself: You just have a look and see what Spot's got hold of. And what do you think Spot had got hold of? Don't you see, what Stores provide for the Territorials isn't exactly brand-new stuff, and so of course our battalion chest was old and venerable too, but what I'd never have dreamt was that while the three of us were busily locking it up in front, there at the back, near the floor, there was a hole you could put your arm through. There'd been a big knot in the timber there, and in some previous war the

piece had fallen out. But what's a chap to do? The whole
Bosnian scare was just over when the replacement came that we
indented for, and up to then we had to go through our ceremony
every week just the same, only I had to leave Spot at home so he
wouldn't give the show away. So there you are, that's what a
military secret may very well look like."

" H'm—it strikes me you're still not being so open as that box
of yours," Ulrich commented. " Are you chaps going through
with the deal or not? "

" I don't know. I give you my solemn word as an officer and
a member of the General Staff—it hasn't reached that stage yet."

" And Leinsdorf? "

" Oh, he's got no idea of it, of course. And he can't be won
over to Arnheim either. I hear he's frightfully sick about the
demonstration—you know, the one you were still here for. He's
turned dead against the Germans."

" Tuzzi? " Ulrich asked, continuing his cross-examination.

" He's the last one who must be let discover anything! He'd
only ruin the plan at once. Naturally we all want peace, but we
military men have our way of serving peace, and the bureaucrats
have theirs."

" And Diotima? "

" Oh my dear chap, please! This is entirely men's business,
she can't think of such a thing even with gloves on! I can't bring
myself to burden her with the truth. . And I can understand
Arnheim's not telling her anything about it. You know, he talks
a lot and all very fine stuff, and it may very well be a pleasure to
keep mum about something for once. Like taking a quiet little
tot of bitters for the stomach, I can't help thinking."

" Do you realise what a scoundrel you've become? " Ulrich
asked, and raised his glass. " Here's your very good health."

" No, not a scoundrel," the General said in self-defence. " I'm
a member of a conference at ministerial level. At a conference
everyone puts forward what he'd like and thinks right, and at the
end you come out with something that nobody quite wanted: the
result, in fact. I don't know if you follow me: I can't put it any
better."

" Of course I follow you. All the same, you're all treating
Diotima quite shamefully."

" I'd be sorry to do that," Stumm said. " But you know, a hangman's a disreputable fellow, there's no denying that. Yet the rope-manufacturer who only supplies the prison with the ropes can be a member of the Ethical Society. You don't bear that sufficiently in mind."

" You've got that from Arnheim ! "

" May be. I don't know. Nowadays one's mind becomes so complicated," the General lamented sincerely.

" And what do you want me to do about it ? "

" Now look, I thought to myself, here you are, an ex-officer——"

" All right, all right. But how does that fit together with ' man of action ' ? " Ulrich asked in an affronted tone.

" Man of action ? " the General repeated in astonishment.

" It's the way you yourself started off, saying I wasn't a man of action ! "

" Oh, that ! Of course that's got nothing at all to do with it. That's only what I began with. I mean, Arnheim doesn't think you're exactly a man of action. He said so once. You've nothing to do, he says, and that puts ideas into your head. Or something of that sort."

" Mischievous ideas, you mean ? Ideas that can't be ' translated into spheres of power ' ? Ideas for their own sake ? In short, real and independent ones ! Isn't that it ? Or are they by any chance the ideas of an ' unworldly aesthete ' ? "

" Yes," Stumm von Bordwehr agreed diplomatically. " Something of that sort."

" What sort ? What is more of a menace to the mind, do you think—dreams or oil-fields ? You needn't go stuffing your mouth full of bread ! Stop it ! It's all the same to me what Arnheim thinks of me. But you started off by saying : ' Arnheim for instance '. So who else is there for whom I'm not enough of a man of action ? "

" Well, don't you know," Stumm informed him, " there are quite a few of them. Didn't I tell you the slogan now is Action ? "

" What does that mean ? "

" Frankly, I don't really know. Leinsdorf said something must be done ! That's how it started."

" And Diotima ? "

" Diotima says it's a new spirit. And there are a lot of people on the Council saying that now. I wonder if you know the feeling—one gets downright giddy round the midriff when a beautiful woman has a mind of such distinction ! ''

" I'm quite ready to believe it," Ulrich conceded, but without any intention of letting Stumm wriggle out of the situation. " Still, I'd like to hear what Diotima says about this new spirit."

" Well, *people* are saying," Stumm answered. " The people on the Council are saying that the times are getting a new spirit. Not this minute, but in a few years—if something extraordinary doesn't happen first. And this spirit won't have many ideas in it. Feelings aren't topical either. Ideas and feelings—that's more for people who haven't anything to do. To cut a long story short, it's a spirit of action, you see, I don't know any more myself. But on and off," the General added thoughtfully, " I've wondered if what it comes to isn't simply the military spirit ? ''

" Action must have a meaning ! " Ulrich insisted; and far behind this motley conversation his conscience reminded him, with deep seriousness, of the first talk he had had with Agathe about these things, on the Swedish Rampart.

And the General agreed. " That's just what I've been saying. If a chap has nothing to do and doesn't know what to do with himself, he's full of energy. He goes bawling around, boozing, duelling, and bullying horse and man. On the other hand, you'll admit: if a chap knows just what he wants, he becomes a thorough-going sneak. Look at any of these young staff wallahs, with his lips pressed right together, all taciturn, pulling a face like Moltke: in ten years he'll have grown a paunch like a bastion under his tunic-buttons, not a benevolent one like mine, but a bellyful of poison. So it's hard to decide how much sense any action ought to have." He pondered and then added: " If you set about it the right way, there's a lot you can learn in the army, that's the conclusion I come to more and more. But don't you think it'd be, as you might say, the simplest thing if we could find the Great Idea after all ? ''

" No," Ulrich disagreed. " That was all nonsense."

" I suppose so, but then there's really only Action left," Stumm said with a sigh. " That's practically what I keep on saying myself. By the way, you remember it was me who once pointed out that all these high-flown ideas would all end up in blue murder ?

That's just what we ought to prevent!" he concluded. "What's needed is someone to take over the leadership," he said cajolingly.

"And what's the job you've kindly thought up for me in all this?" Ulrich asked, now frankly yawning.

"All right, I'm just off," Stumm assured him. "But now that we've had our heart-to-heart talk, there's an important job you could do if you really felt like being a good chap: Things aren't exactly in apple-pie order between Diotima and Arnheim."

"You don't say!" His host revived slightly.

"You'll see for yourself, there's no need for me to tell you anything. Anyway, she confides in you even more than in me."

"She confides in you, does she? Since when?"

"She's got a little used to me," the General said with pride.

"Congratulations."

"H'm, thanks. But another thing, you must go and see Leinsdorf soon too. On account of the way he's taken against the Prussians."

"I won't do it."

"Now look here, I know you don't care for Arnheim. But you must do it all the same."

"That's not the reason. I'm not going to Leinsdorf at all."

"Why on earth not? He's such a grand old boy. Arrogant, of course, and I can't stand him, but towards you he's terrific!"

"I'm going to chuck the whole thing."

"But Leinsdorf won't let you. And neither will Diotima. And as for me, I don't dream of it! You won't go and leave me in the lurch?"

"I'm fed up with the whole silly thing."

"In that, as always, you're outstandingly right. But what on earth isn't silly?! Look at me, how silly I am—without you. So for my sake you will go to Leinsdorf, won't you?"

"But what's this about Diotima and Arnheim?"

"I won't tell you, otherwise you won't go to Diotima either!" The General had a sudden inspiration: "If you like, Leinsdorf can get an assistant secretary to take off your hands anything you don't want to be bothered with. Or I'll supply you with one from the War Ministry. You withdraw as far as ever you like, but you'll keep a guiding hand over me, won't you?"

"Let me get some sleep first," Ulrich suggested.

" I'm not going till you've said yes."

" All right, I'll sleep on it," Ulrich conceded. " Don't forget
to put the bread of military-mindedness back into your satchel ! "

14

Walter and Clarisse: New Developments.
An exhibitionist and his audience.

IT was his restless state of mind that made Ulrich think of going
out to see Walter and Clarisse that evening. On the way he
tried to remember the wording of the letter he had either stuffed
away somewhere in his luggage or lost; but he could not recall
any details, only the last sentence, ' I hope you'll come back soon ',
and his general impression that he must really have a talk with
Walter—an impression associated not only with regret and uneasiness, but also with some malice. This fleeting, involuntary
and quite unimportant feeling was something he now lingered over
instead of brushing it aside, and the relief was rather like that of
descending from giddy heights to a lower level.

When he turned the corner to the house, he saw Clarisse
standing in the sun by the side wall where the espalier peach was;
she had her hands behind her and was leaning back against the
yielding branches, gazing into the distance, not noticing his
approach. There was something self-oblivious and rigid in her
bearing, but at the same time something almost imperceptibly
theatrical, apparent only to this friend who knew her characteristics so well: she looked as though she were acting out a part in
the significant drama of her own ideas and as though one of those
ideas had taken hold of her and would not let go. He recollected
her saying : ' I want to have the child from you ! ' The words did
not affect him as disagreeably now as they had at the time. He
called out to her softly and waited.

But Clarisse was thinking: ' This time Meingast is having his
transformation at our house!' There had been several such
peculiar transformations in his life. Without having made any

comment on Walter's detailed answer to his letter, he had one day arrived just as he had announced he would, and Clarisse was quite sure that the work he had at once sat down to was connected with a transformation. The thought of some Indian god who takes up his abode somewhere before every new stage of purification mingled in her mind with the thought that there are creatures that choose a special place when changing into the chrysalis state; and from this notion, which impressed her as being immensely healthy and down-to-earth, she had passed on to the sensuous aroma of espalier peaches ripening on a sunny wall. The logical outcome of all this was that she was standing there under the window in the glow of the sinking sun, while the prophet had withdrawn into the shadowy cavern inside. The previous day he had explained to her and Walter that the original meaning of the word ' knight ' was boy, servant, squire, and only later became arms-bearing man, hero. Now she said to herself: ' I am his knight, his squire ! ' serving him and defending his work. There was no need of any words more, she simply stood still, dazzled, out-facing the beams of the sun.

When Ulrich spoke to her, her face slowly turned towards the unexpected voice. And he discovered that something had changed. In the eyes that looked in his direction there was a chill such as emanates from the colours in Nature after sunset, and he realised at once: ' She no longer wants anything of me ! ' In her gaze there was no longer any trace of how she had once wanted to ' force him out of the block of stone ', of his being a great devil or god, of her wanting to escape with him through ' the hole in the music ', of her wanting to kill him if he would not love her. It was all the same to him: it was no doubt a very ordinary little experience, seeing a gaze with the warmth of egoism gone out of it; and yet it was like a little rent in the veil of life, through which indifferent nothingness peered. Here the basis was laid for much that happened later.

Being told that Meingast was there, Ulrich understood.

They went quietly into the house to fetch Walter, and, still quietly, in order not to disturb the great man at his creative work, all three went out into the open air. In passing an open door, Ulrich twice had a glimpse of Meingast's back. Meingast occupied a room detached from the rest of the apartment but belonging to it. It was unfurnished, but somewhere Clarisse and Walter had got hold of an iron bedstead, and a kitchen stool and a tin basin served as wash-stand and bath; apart from this equipment, all that the uncurtained room contained was an old kitchen cupboard, now filled with books, and a small unpainted deal table. At this table Meingast sat writing, without turning his head towards them as they passed his door. All this Ulrich either saw for himself or was told by his friends, who had no scruples about having lodged the Master much more primitively than they themselves lived; they were, on the contrary, for some reason proud of the fact that he was content with what they had to offer. It was touching, and it was convenient for them. Walter declared that if one went into that room in Meingast's absence, one was aware of an indescribable aura such as there was about a threadbare old glove that had been worn on a noble and energetic hand.

And in fact Meingast was getting great enjoyment from working in this environment; the soldierly simplicity of it was flattering to him. It helped him to apprehend his will, which formed the words on the paper. And if, besides, Clarisse happened to be standing under his window, as she had been just now, or up on the landing, or even if she was only sitting in her room—' cloaked in the mantle of an invisible aurora borealis ', as she had confessed to him—, his pleasure was enhanced by the proximity of this ambitious disciple of his on whom he had such a paralysing effect. Then his pen swept the ideas on ahead of it, and those big dark eyes over the sharp, quivering nose began to glow. It was to be one of the most important sections of his new book that he planned to finish in these surroundings, a work that was not to be a mere book, but a call to arms, a summons to the spirit of a new masculinity!

When a male voice that he could not place had reached him from where Clarisse was standing, he had broken off for a moment and cautiously peered out of the window. He did not recognise Ulrich, though the man did seem vaguely familiar; anyway the footsteps coming upstairs were not sufficient reason for him either to shut his door or to turn his head from his work. Meingast, who wore a thick woollen vest under his shirt, liked to demonstrate his insensitivity to both weather and human beings.

Ulrich was taken for a walk and had the privilege of listening to enraptured praises of the Master, while the latter went on with his work.

Walter said: " It's only if one is on terms of friendship with a man like Meingast that one realises one has always suffered from one's dislike of others ! Associating with him one feels—I should like to put it this way: everything is painted in pure colours, without any grey at all."

Clarisse said: " Being together with him you have the sense of having a destiny. There you are, entirely individual, high-lighted."

Walter added: "Nowadays everything is broken up into hundreds of strata, so that it all becomes opaque and blurred. His mind is like glass ! "

Ulrich's reply to them was: " There are scapegoats and virtue-hounds. And there are, besides, sheep who have need of them."

Walter flung back: " Of course such a man couldn't meet with your approval! "

Clarisse cried out: " You once said people can't live according to their ideas ! Do you remember ? Well, Meingast can! "

Walter added circumspectly: " Not of course that I couldn't take issue with him on certain points. . . ."

Clarisse interrupted: " You feel shudders of light within you, listening to him."

Ulrich retorted: " Men with particularly fine heads are usually stupid. Particularly deep philosophers are usually shallow thinkers. In literature talents just a very little above the average are what contemporaries usually take for greatness."

What a remarkable phenomenon admiration is ! In the life of individuals it occurs only in ' fits '; in collective life it is a permanent institution. Actually Walter would have found it more satisfying if he himself could have occupied Meingast's place in his own and Clarisse's esteem, and he could not at all make out why it was not so; and yet, too, there was a slight advantage in its being the way it was. And the emotion thus saved was placed to Meingast's credit; it was rather like adopting another person's child. On the other hand, precisely this meant that his admiration for Meingast was by no means a pure and healthy emotion, and Walter knew it very well; it was rather an over-stimulated surrender to faith in him. It has something deliberate about it.

It was an emotion ' on the piano ', raging without full conviction. And Ulrich could sense this too. One of the elementary needs for passion that life nowadays breaks up into little fragments, and jumbles up until they are unrecognisable, was here seeking a way back. For Walter praised Meingast with a ferocity like that of a theatre audience applauding, far beyond the limits of its actual appreciation, commonplaces that have the function simply of stimulating its need to applaud. He praised him out of desperation, as it were, out of that need to admire which generally finds its outlet in festivals and celebrations, in the contemplation of great contemporaries or great ideas and the honours that are bestowed on them, which everyone joins in, without anyone's properly knowing for whom or for what, everyone being inwardly ready to be twice as beastly as usual the next day in order not to have anything to reproach himself with.

This is what Ulrich thought about his friends, and he kept them on their toes by means of the pointed remarks he directed at Meingast. For, like everyone who knows better, he had countless times been annoyed by his contemporaries's capacity for enthusiasm, which almost invariably fastened on the wrong object and thus destroyed even the few things not already destroyed by indifference.

Dusk had fallen by the time they returned to the house, still talking about much the same things.

" What this Meingast of yours lives on is the fact that nowadays people can't distinguish between intuition and faith," Ulrich wound up. " Almost everything that isn't science can only be understood intuitively, and that demands both passion and prudence. Hence a methodology of what one doesn't know would be practically the same as a methodology of life. But you people ' believe ' the very moment someone like Meingast puts one over on you ! And so does everyone. And this ' believing ' is pretty much the same sort of disaster as if you went and plumped yourselves down bodily in a basket of eggs in order to hatch out its unidentified contents."

They were standing at the foot of the stairs. And all at once Ulrich realised why he had come here and was talking to the two of them as he used to in earlier days. It did not surprise him that Walter answered:

" And I suppose you expect the world to stand still until you've finished working out a methodology ? "

Clearly they none of them took him seriously, because they did not understand how neglected this territory of belief was that extended between the certainty of knowledge and the haze of intuition. Old ideas began to swarm in his head; thought itself almost suffocated under their onslaught. But then he realised that now it was no longer necessary to start all over again like a carpet-weaver whose mind has been dazzled by a dream. Everything had recently become much simpler. This last fortnight had rendered all the past invalid, and had tied up the threads of inner movement in one strong knot.

Walter was waiting for Ulrich to give him answer that he could be annoyed about. Then he would pay him back twice over ! He had made up his mind to tell him that men like Meingast were bearers of salvation. ' Salvation, after all, means salving, which is healing, making whole,' he thought. And what he wanted to say was: ' Bearers of salvation may be mistaken, but they make us whole ! ' And he also wanted to say: ' I don't suppose you can imagine such a thing at all ? ' And the accompanying dislike he felt for Ulrich was similar to what he felt when he had to go to the dentist.

But Ulrich confined himself to asking vaguely what Meingast had actually been writing and doing in these last years.

" There you are ! " Walter said, disappointed. " There you are, you don't even know that, but you go on running him down ! "

" My dear chap," Ulrich said lightly, " I don't *need* to know it, it's enough to have seen a few lines ! " And he took a first step upstairs.

But Clarisse held him back, clutching at his jacket and whispering : " But his name isn't really Meingast at all ! "

" Of course it isn't. But that's no secret, is it ? "

" Once he became Meingast, and now, here in our house, he's transforming himself again ! " Clarisse whispered intensely and mysteriously, and this whispering was almost like the hissing of a blow-lamp.

Walter flung himself upon it, to put out the flame. " Clarisse ! " he implored her. " Clarisse, stop this nonsense ! "

Clarisse was silent, smiling. Ulrich went ahead up the stairs;

he wanted to take a look, now at long last, at this messenger from
Zarathustra's mountains who had descended upon Walter and
Clarisse in their domestic life.   By the time they arrived upstairs,
Walter was in a bad temper not only with him but with Meingast
as well.

Meingast received his admirers in their unlighted apartment.
He had seen them coming, from where he stood at the window,
and Clarisse at once went over to him and became, against the
grey window-pane, a small, pointed shadow beside the tall, gaunt
one that he was.   There was no introduction, or at least only a
one-sided one, Ulrich's name being recalled to the Master's
memory.   Then they were all silent.   Ulrich was curious to see
how the situation would develop; he went and stood at the other
window.   Surprisingly, Walter joined him there, probably merely
because, being equally repelled by both Ulrich and Meingast, he
responded to the stimulus of what brightness there was coming into
the twilit room through the less obstructed of the two windows.

According to the calendar it was March.   But the seasons, like
the meteorologists, are not entirely dependable and sometimes
produce a June evening long before it is due, or long after.   So
Clarisse thought, experiencing the darkness outside the window as
if it were a summer night.   Over there, in the gas-light from the
street lamps, this night was varnished bright yellow.   The nearby
bushes were a fluid mass of black.   Where they extended into the
light they were green or wan and colourless—there was actually no
word for it—, were sliced out into leaves and floated in the lamplight like pieces of washing drifting in a softly running stream.   A
narrow iron ribbon on dwarfish posts—no more than a reminiscence
and reminder of the need for order—ran some distance along the
grass where the bushes grew, and then vanished in the dark.
Clarisse knew that it simply ended there.   Once there had perhaps been a plan to embellish this district with some suggestion
of a public garden, but if so it had soon been abandoned.

Clarisse moved close up to Meingast, because from this angle
she could see farthest down the road.   Her nose was flattened
against the pane, and the two bodies were in a contact as hard and
many-cornered as if she had stretched out full-length on the stairs,
which in fact she sometimes did.   Her right arm, which had to
yield, was clasped at the elbow by Meingast's long fingers as by

the sinewy talons of an extremely absent-minded eagle crumpling, say, a silk handkerchief in its claws.

Clarisse had for some time now been looking at a man with whom there was something wrong, though she could not quite make out what: he was walking to and fro, now hesitantly, now casually. It was as though something were wrapping itself round his will to walk and each time he had torn it he walked for a while like anyone who is not exactly in a hurry but does not linger either. The rhythm of this irregular movement had taken hold of Clarisse. When the man passed a street-lamp, she tried to make out his features, and what she saw seemed to her hollow and empty. As he passed under the one before the last she decided it was a trivial, unpleasant, furtive face. But as he was coming up to the last lamp, which was almost under this window, it seemed a very pale face, and it floated about on the light as the light floated about on the darkness, so that beside it the thin iron lamp-post looked very straight and excited, impressing itself upon the eye in a sharper, paler green than actually pertained to it.

All four of them had gradually begun to watch this man, who obviously thought himself unobserved.

He now noticed the bushes bathed in light, and they reminded him of the scalloped hem of a woman's petticoat, a thicker one than he had ever seen, but the sort he would very much like to see. At this moment his decision was taken. He stepped over the low railing, he stood on the grass, which reminded him of the green wood-shavings in a toy-box, stared for a while in bewilderment at his feet, was roused by the movement of his own head turning furtively, looking around, and then hid in the shadows, as his habit was. Trippers were returning townward after spending this surprisingly warm day in the country; one could hear their loud talk and laughter some distance off. This filled the man with terror, and he sought compensation for it under the petticoat of leaves.

Clarisse still did not know what was the matter with the man. He came out each time a group of people went past, their eyes blinded to the darkness by the shine of the gas-light. Then, without lifting his feet, he shuffled towards the circle of light like someone paddling a little way into shallow water but obviously not wanting to get his ankles wet. Clarisse was struck by the man's pallor; his face was distorted and like a wan disk. She felt intense pity for him. But he was making curious little movements that she did not understand for a long time. Then suddenly, quite horrified, she had to grab hold of something; and since Meingast was still grasping her elbow, so that she could not move her arm freely, she clutched, as though in search of protection, at the stuff of his wide trousers, pulling it taut over the Master's leg as a gale tugs at a flag. So the two of them stood, not letting go.

Ulrich thought he was probably the first to have realised that the man down there outside the windows was one of those psychotics who, because of the abnormality of their sexual life, arouse the curiosity of those who are normal, and he was for a moment—unnecessarily, it turned out—anxious as to how Clarisse, unstable as she was, would react to this discovery. Then he forgot to worry about it, giving himself up to wondering what really went on in such a man. The change that took place in him (he thought), even in the moment of stepping over the railing, must be so complete as to defy detailed description. And the comparison that occurred to him as naturally as if it were relevant was with a singer who has just been eating and drinking and then goes up to the piano, clasps his hands over his abdomen and, opening his mouth to sing, is instantly in part a different man, in part not. He also found himself thinking of His Highness Count Leinsdorf, who could switch himself either into a religious-ethical circuit or into a banking-worldly-open-minded circuit. What interested him was the completeness of this transformation, which takes place inside the person but is confirmed by the obligingness of the world outside. He was not concerned with the psychological explanation of the case below the window, but he could not help imagining the man's head gradually filling with tension, like a balloon being filled with gas, a process that probably went on for days and days, the balloon still swaying on the ropes that tied it to solid ground, until an inaudible word of command, some accidental happening, or simply the expiry of the usual period, at which time any triviality would serve as a cause, loosened the ropes and the head, now severed from the human world, went floating up into the stratosphere of perversity. And there the man with the hollow, empty face stood in the shelter of the bushes, like a beast of prey, lying in wait. In order to carry out

his intentions he ought really to have waited until the holiday-
makers became less numerous and the neighbourhood became
safer for him. But the moment that, instead of a group of people,
a woman came past alone, indeed sometimes even when one came
tripping along, gaily laughing and protected by the presence of
the other people she was with, they ceased to be people for him,
they became mere dolls senselessly trimmed into shape by what
was going on inside him. What he felt towards them was the
utter callousness of a murderer, and their mortal fear would not
have mattered to him; but at the same time he himself suffered a
faint torment at the thought that they might discover him and
chase him off like a dog before he had been able to reach the peak
of abandon. His tongue quivered in his mouth with dread.
Stupefied, he waited, and gradually the last gleam of twilight
faded. Now there was a solitary woman approaching his hiding-
place, and even though she was still beyond the street-lamps, he
could already see her as something detached from these surroundings, something diving in and out of the waves of light and darkness, a black lump dripping with light, coming nearer and nearer.

Ulrich, for his part, could see it was a shapeless middle-aged
woman who was approaching. Her body was like a sack full of
gravel, and there was nothing kindly in her face, only a domineering
cantankerous look. But the gaunt pale man among the bushes
seemed to know how to get at her without her noticing until it was
too late. Her dull gaze and uncouth gait were probably already
twitching in his flesh, and he was preparing to ambush her before
she could even think of defending herself, to assault her with the
sight of himself—a sight that was to penetrate into the horrified
woman and be a violation that would remain with her always,
no matter how she might twist and turn. This excitement was
roaring and revolving in his knees, hands, and throat. At least
so it seemed to Ulrich as he watched the man groping his way
through the bushes, in a place where they were already in half-
light, and making his preparations in order to step out at the
decisive moment and exhibit himself. As though bereft of his
senses, the unfortunate man stood leaning against the last faintly
resistant twigs, his eyes fixed on the ugly face that was now bobbing
up and down towards him in the full light, and his breath seemed
to come pantingly in time with the unknown woman's tread.

' I wonder if she'll scream ? ' Ulrich thought. That coarse-grained stocky person was quite likely capable of being enraged instead of frightened, and of going over to the attack. Then the lunatic would take flight, coward that he surely was, and his frustrated lust would be like a knife plunged into his flesh, squat handle first.

But at this critical moment Ulrich heard the unrestrained talk of two men coming along the road, and just as they were audible to him through the glass, so too they seemed to penetrate the hissing of excitement in the man below the windows, for with a gingerly movement he let the veil of twigs, which he had drawn aside, fall to again and stepped back soundlessly into the darkness.

" What a swine ! " Clarisse said to her neighbour at the same moment, in a penetrating whisper, but quite without indignation.

Before Meingast had been transformed, he had often heard her utter such expressions, which were at that time directed at his own provocatively free-and-easy behaviour; the exclamation might therefore be considered an historical allusion. Clarisse was assuming that in spite of his transformation Meingast could not fail to catch the allusion, and indeed it seemed to her that his fingers stirred faintly on her arm by way of answer. There was altogether nothing accidental about this evening. It was not by chance even that that man down there had chosen the place under her window for his performance. Her conviction that she had a dreadful fascination for men with whom there was something wrong was quite firm: it had often been proved correct !

All in all, it was not so much that her ideas were confused as that connecting-links between them were dropped out or that they were drenched in emotion at various points where other people have no such inner wellspring. Her conviction that it was she who had once made it possible for Meingast to undergo a radical change was in itself not unreasonable. If, besides, one bore in mind how unrelatedly that change had gone on—unrelatedly because at a distance and in years when they had not been in touch—and how immense it had been—for it had turned a super-ficial *bon vivant* into a prophet—and finally that soon after Meingast's departure the love between herself and Walter had risen to that peak of struggle on which it still was, then her assumption that Walter and she had had to take the sins of the untransformed Meingast upon themselves in order to make his ascent possible was intrinsically no less well-founded than innumerable respectable ideas that are taken seriously nowadays. Hence arose, moreover, the relationship, as of squire to knight, in which Clarisse felt she stood to Meingast now that he had returned, and if she spoke of a new ' transformation ' he was undergoing instead of simply calling it a ' change ', she was only using an expression appropriate to the state of elevation she had been in all this time. The sense of being in a significant relationship to someone could make Clarisse feel quite literally elevated. Nobody quite knows whether to depict the saints with a cloud under their feet or merely show them standing in empty air a finger's breadth above the ground; and this was just the way it was with her since he had chosen this house to do his great work in, work that probably had a very deep background. It was not as a woman that Clarisse was in love with him, but more like a boy who admires a man and is in a state of bliss if he succeeds in wearing his hat at the same angle as the other, being filled with the secret ambition to emulate, even to surpass him.

All this Walter knew. Now he could neither hear what Clarisse was whispering to Meingast nor could his eyes distinguish more of the two of them than a heavy, coagulated mass of shadow against the grey glimmer of the window, but he knew exactly what was going on. He too had realised what was the matter with the man among the bushes, and the stillness prevailing in the room weighed most heavily upon him. He could tell that Ulrich, who was standing motionless beside him, was gazing intently out of the window, and he assumed that the two at the other window were doing the same. ' Why doesn't anyone break this silence? ' he thought. ' Why does nobody open the window and scare this monstrosity away? ' It occurred to him that it was really one's duty to call the police, but there was no telephone in the house and he had not the courage of his convictions, to enable him to do a thing that might meet with his companions' contempt. He did not really mean to behave like an outraged ' bourgeois ', it was just that he felt so exasperated! The ' knightly ' relationship in which his wife stood to Meingast was one that he could actually understand very well, for even in the realm of love Clarisse simply

could not imagine any exaltation without exertion; it was not by
sensuality that she was uplifted, but only by ambition. He well
remembered how uncannily alive she had sometimes been in his
arms in the days when he was still spending his time on art; but it
was only by such roundabout means that she could be warmed
into life. ' Perhaps all the real exaltations that people experience
come from ambition?' he thought dubiously. It had not
escaped his attention that Clarisse ' stood on guard ' while Meingast was working, defending his thoughts with her body even
though she did not know what those thoughts were. Sadly
Walter watched the solitary egoist over there in the bushes: that
unfortunate creature provided him with a warning example of the
devastation that isolation could wreck in a soul. At the same time
he was tormented by the thought that he knew exactly what Clarisse
was feeling while she looked on. ' Of course she's in a faint
state of agitation, as if she'd just taken the stairs too fast ', he
thought. He himself sensed in the picture before his eyes a
pressure as if something were about to burst out of its cocoon,
and he could feel in this mysterious pressure, which Clarisse
must be feeling too, the stirring of a will not merely to look on
but now, at once, *somehow* to act, to plunge right into what was
happening, and so to set it free. With other people ideas generally
had their origin in life, but what Clarisse experienced always
originated in ideas: that was the enviably crazy thing about her!
And Walter was more in sympathy with the extravagances of his
wife, who was perhaps mad, than with the thought-processes of
his friend Ulrich, who imagined himself to be at once prudent and
audacious. Somehow the more irrational thing was more to his
liking, it left him personally inviolate, and it appealed to his compassion; in any case there are many people who prefer crazy ideas
to difficult ones. It even afforded him a certain satisfaction to
know that Clarisse was whispering there in the dark with Meingast,
while Ulrich was condemned to remain a mute shadow at his side.
He was glad that Ulrich should be outdone by Meingast. But
from time to time he was racked by his expectation that Clarisse
would suddenly fling up the window or run downstairs and out,
across to the bushes. At such moments he loathed the two male
shadows in the room and their indecently silent looking on, which
made the situation every minute more dangerous to the poor little

Prometheus of whom he had charge and who was exposed to every temptation of the spirit.

By this time shame and frustrated lust had melted down into one feeling of disappointment in the afflicted man, who had drawn back among the bushes; and his body was like a hollow vessel filled with the bitterness of it. When he had reached the heart of the darkness, he caved in, he sank to the ground, and his head dangled from his neck like a leaf from a twig. The world stood avengingly before him, and he saw his own situation more or less as it would have appeared to the two men who had gone past, if they had caught sight of him. But after he had wept over himself for a while, dry-eyed, once again he reverted to his former state, this time indeed with an increase in defiance and vindictiveness. And once again he failed. A girl came past who was perhaps fifteen and who had obviously stayed out later than she was supposed to, and to him she seemed beautiful, a little ideal apparition hurrying along. The pervert could feel that now was the moment for him to come right out, to speak to her kindly; but the thought of it instantly plunged him into wild panic. His imagination, which was ready to conjure up before him every possibility with which a woman could be associated, grew timidly clumsy when faced with the only natural possibility, that of admiring this defenceless little creature in her beauty. It afforded the shadow side of his being all the less pleasure the more it was fitted to please his daylight side, and in vain he tried to hate her since he could not love her. So he stood there uncertainly on the border-line of shadow and light, exposing himself. By the time the little girl realised what he was revealing, she had already passed him and was some half a dozen paces further on. She had at first merely glanced at the place where there was something stirring among the leaves and she had not realised what was going on; and when it became clear to her, the distance made her feel safe enough not to be desperately frightened. True, her mouth fell open for a moment, but then though she uttered a shrill scream and began to run, the little wretch seemed to find amusement in glancing back. The man was left there alone in his humiliation. Angrily he hoped that a drop of poison had splashed into her eyes and that it would gradually eat its way through into her heart.

This comparatively harmless and comical *débâcle* was some

relief to the humane instincts of the onlookers, who would now doubtless have taken action if the affair had gone differently; and, being so much under this impression, they scarcely noticed how the scene down below subsequently finished, confirming their belief that it *had* finished only by the observation that the male ' hyena ', as Walter later called him, was suddenly no more to be seen. The man's plan at last succeeded when a woman came along who was in every sense average; she looked at him in horrified dismay and disgust; was shocked into involuntarily stopping for a moment, and then tried to pretend she had not noticed anything out of the ordinary. In this instant he felt himself, with the roof of leaves, with the whole world that was turned inside-out, the world he had sprung from, gliding deeply into the defenceless woman's reluctant gaze. Perhaps that was how it was; or perhaps different. Clarisse had not really been paying attention. Drawing a deep breath, she straightened up from where she had been leaning forward against the window; she and Meingast had let go of each other some time earlier. It seemed to her that she had suddenly landed on the wooden floor, planted on the soles of her feet, and a whirling of indescribable, horrible relish in her body now faded out. She was firmly convinced that all that had happened had a special meaning, relevant only to her; and, strange as it may sound, the feeling she got from this repulsive scene was that she was a betrothed girl who had just been serenaded. Her head was dancing with resolves that she wanted to carry out and new ones she was just forming, a wild confusion of thoughts.

" Funny ! " Ulrich suddenly said into the darkness. He was the first to break the silence between the four of them. " It's really absurdly paradoxical to think how it would spoil the fellow's game if he could know he was being watched without knowing it ! "

Meingast's shadow detached itself from the gloom and stood, an elongated concentration of darkness, as though facing the direction from which Ulrich's voice came.

" There's far too much importance attached to sex," the Master said. " The truth is—these are the caperings, the goatish gambollings, of our era's will."

That was all he said. But Clarisse, who had twitched in

annoyance at what Ulrich said, felt that, even though in this darkness of hers she did not know whither Meingast's words bore her,
they had certainly borne her onwards.

15 *The Last Will and Testament.*

WHEN Ulrich returned home, in still greater dissatisfaction than
before as a result of what he had experienced, he decided not to
put off a decision any longer and so began to recall the ' incident '
as precisely as he possibly could, this being the vaguely euphemistic
term he applied to what had taken place in the last hours of his
being together with Agathe, only a few days after their big
discussion.

He had packed and was ready to leave to get the *wagon-lit* train
that came through the town late in the night, and Agathe and he
were dining together for the last time. It was already arranged that
Agathe was to follow him before long, and they roughly estimated
this period of separation at anything from just under a week to
perhaps a fortnight.

At dinner Agathe said: " But there's something we must do
before you go."

" What ? " Ulrich asked.

" We must alter the Will."

Ulrich remembered having glanced up at his sister without
surprise: in spite of all the previous talk about it he assumed she
was leading up to a joke. But Agathe was gazing at her plate,
with the familiar thoughtful frown between her eyebrows.

Slowly she said: " He shan't keep anything of me between his
fingers, not even so much as if a woollen thread had burnt away
between them ! "

Something must have been working intensively in her during
the last few days. Ulrich was about to tell her that he regarded
these notions about ways of damaging Hagauer as quite beyond the
pale and that he did not want to talk about it again. But at that

moment their father's old servant came in with the next course and they could only go on talking in veiled allusions.

"Aunt Malvina"—Agathe said, smiling at her brother—"you remember how Aunt Malvina meant all her property to go to one of our cousins; it was all definitely fixed and everyone knew about it. And so all this girl was to get under her parents' Will was the share she was legally entitled to as her parents' child, while her brother got the rest, so that neither of the children, whose father had been equally fond of them both, should be better off than the other. I'm *sure* you remember about it ! The annuity that cousin Agathe—Alexandra, I mean of course," she corrected herself, laughing, " had been getting since her marriage was henceforth discounted against the legal share—it was all very complicated, to leave Aunt Malvina plenty of time to die in . . ."

" I don't follow," Ulrich had muttered.

" Oh, but it's perfectly simple ! Before Aunt Malvina died she lost all her money, in fact she had to be supported. Now Papa only needs to have forgotten to revoke the change in his own Will and Alexandra gets nothing at all ! And so even if her marriage-contract stipulates that her property is held jointly——"

" I don't know about that. I think that would be far from certain," Ulrich could not help saying. " And then there are sure to have been definite assurances given by their father. Father can't possibly have made such provisions without discussing it with his son-in-law ! "

Yes, Ulrich distinctly remembered having replied in those terms, being quite unable to listen in silence to his sister's dangerously wrong-headed ideas. And the smile with which she had looked at him then was still very clear in his mind. ' Isn't that just like him ! ' she had obviously been thinking. ' One only needs to put a case to him as if it weren't flesh and blood, but merely a generalisation, and one can lead him by the nose ! '

And then she had asked briefly: " Was any such arrangement made in writing ? " and had herself answered: " I've never heard of it, anyway, and after all, if anyone knew of it, I should ! But Papa was always very odd."

At this moment the servant came round to Ulrich with a dish: and she took advantage of her brother's helplessness to add: " Verbal agreements can always be gone back on. But if the

Will was changed again after Aunt Malvina lost her money, everything suggests that that new codicil was lost!"

And once again Ulrich let himself be lured into correcting her. "Still," he said, "there's still a not inconsiderable bequest that goes to the person concerned automatically, which the 'child of one's body' can't be deprived of!"

"But I've just told you it was paid over in the father's lifetime! Alexandra was married twice, don't forget that!" The servant left the room for a moment and Agathe hastened to add: "I've looked at the passage very carefully. It's only a few words that need altering, and then it'll look as if my legitimate portion had been paid out already. There's nobody left to prove anything to the contrary! When Aunt had lost her money and Father went back to leaving us equal shares, it was put in a codicil, which can be destroyed. Anyway there's nothing to stop me having renounced the share I'm legally bound to get, say for some reason or other in your favour!"

Ulrich looked at his sister in amazement, and so missed his chance to deal with her fantasies in the way he felt obliged to: by the time he was ready to speak, they were no longer alone and he had to resort to roundabout expressions.

"Really," he began hesitantly, "one oughtn't even to think of such things!"

"Why on earth not?" Agathe retorted.

Such questions are very easy to deal with so long as they are left alone; but as soon as they are touched they rear up like a monstrous serpent that has been curled up into a harmless-looking ball. Ulrich could remember the answer he had given: "Even Nietzsche insists that 'free spirits have got to respect certain outer rules for the sake of inner freedom'!" He had said it with a smile, but at the same time with the feeling that it was rather cowardly to hide behind another man's words.

"That's a lame principle!" Agathe decided out-of-hand. "That's the principle I was married on!"

And Ulrich thought to himself: 'Yes, it really is a lame principle.' It seems that people who have wholly new and revolutionary answers to give to specific questions compensate for that by making a compromise with everything else and leaving worthy, respectable morality to go on slopping about in slippers: the more so since this method, which aims at keeping all conditions constant except the one that is to be changed, entirely corresponds to the creative intellectual economy they feel at home with. Even Ulrich had always regarded this rather as a strict than as a slack way of going about things. But when that conversation took place between himself and his sister, he realised that it hit him in a sore spot: he could no longer endure the state of indecision that had been so dear to him, and it seemed to him it was precisely Agathe who had been ordained to bring him to this point. And as he nevertheless went on holding up the Rule of the Free Spirits to her, she laughed and then asked him if he was not aware that the moment he tried to formulate general rules a different man stepped into his place.

" And although I'm sure you admire him, and rightly, fundamentally you don't care tuppence for him ! " she asserted. She looked at her brother wilfully and challengingly.

Once again he found it difficult to answer her. He remained silent, expecting an interruption at any moment, yet he could not quite make up his mind to stop this talk.

This emboldened her. " In this short time we've been together," she went on, " you've given me all sorts of wonderful advice about how I should live, things I'd never have dared to think out for myself. But afterwards you've always asked whether what you'd said was really true ! It seems to me that the truth, for you, is just some force that's there to ill-treat people !—h'm ? "

It was not that she felt she had any right to reproach him in this way; her own life was surely so worthless that she had better have kept silence. But she drew her courage from Ulrich himself. He was struck by how weirdly feminine it was of her to borrow her attitude from him even while she attacked him.

" You just don't understand the urge to organise ideas in large, articulated patterns," Ulrich said. " For you the mind's fighting experiences are simply passing columns all keeping in step, the impersonality of a great many feet stirring up truth like a cloud of dust ! "

" But didn't you yourself describe to me the two states you can live in," she answered, " and describe them far more precisely and clearly than I could ever do ? "

A glow passed over her face, like a swift-floating cloud with changing outlines. She wanted to get her brother to a point where he could not turn back. She was quite feverish with the thought of it, though still without knowing whether she would have the courage; and so she lingered over the meal.

All this Ulrich knew, or at least guessed. But now he had given himself a shaking and begun to argue with her. Sitting opposite her, with an absent gaze, he forced his mouth to form words, and all the time he could not help feeling he was not really in himself but, rather, left somewhere behind himself and calling out to himself what he was saying.

" Say I'm travelling," he said, " and I want to steal a stranger's gold cigarette-case. I ask you: isn't it simply unthinkable ? And so I don't even mean to discuss whether any loftier freedom of the mind can or cannot justify the sort of action you seem to have in mind. It may even be right to do Hagauer an injury. But imagine me, in a hotel somewhere, neither penniless nor a professional thief, nor a mental defective with an outsize head or a deformed body, nor having had an hysteric for a mother nor an alcoholic for a father, myself not unbalanced or afflicted by any other kind of misfortune either, and yet I steal—well, I repeat, it's a situation that doesn't occur anywhere in the world ! It simply doesn't occur ! It can be ruled out with positively scientific certainty."

Agathe burst out laughing. " But Uli, what if one does do it all the same ? "

At this answer, which he had not foreseen, Ulrich could not help laughing too. He leapt to his feet and resolutely pushed his chair back into place, for he did not want to encourage her by falling in with her mood.

Agathe also rose and left the table.

" You mustn't do it ! " he implored her.

" But Uli," she retorted, " are you yourself thinking in a dream or are you dreaming something that's happening ? "

This question recalled an assertion he had made only a few days earlier: that all morality's demands referred to a sort of dream-state that had evaporated out of them by the time they became concrete.

After that question of hers Agathe had gone into their father's study, which now appeared, lamp-lit, beyond two open doors, and Ulrich, who had not followed her, saw her standing there as in a frame. She was holding a sheet of paper to the light, reading something. 'Has she no notion what she's committing herself to?' he wondered. But in all that bunch of key-concepts in use nowadays, such as inferiority complex, mental deficiency, arrested development, and the like, there was none that would fit; and the graceful picture Agathe presented while committing her offence seemed devoid of any trace of greed or vengefulness or any other spiritual ugliness. And although Ulrich could have used such concepts to see even the actions of a criminal or a semi-demented person as comparatively controlled and civilised, since somewhere at the back of them, distorted and displaced, the motives of normal life still gleam, he was at this moment left completely dumbfounded by his sister's resolution, at once fierce and mild, an indistinguishable blend of purity and criminality. He simply could not find room for the thought that this person, who was quite openly engaged in performing a bad action, could be a bad person; and all this time he was helplessly watching Agathe taking one paper after another out of the desk, reading it, laying it aside, and quite seriously looking for a specific document. Her decisiveness had the air of having descended out of another world on to the plane of everyday decisions.

While he watched, Ulrich was also perturbed by the question why he had talked Hagauer into going away, believing all was well. It seemed to him that he had from the very beginning acted as his sister's tool, and to the very last all the answers he had given her, even when disagreeing with her, had encouraged her to behave as she was doing. Truth ill-treated people, she had said. 'Nicely put, but she has absolutely no idea what truth means!' Ulrich mused. 'With the passing of the years it leaves one stiff and gouty, but in one's youth it's like a life of wine, women, and song!' He had sat down again. Now it suddenly struck him that not only had Agathe somehow got from him what she had said about truth, but what she was doing in the other room was also something he had outlined. It was after all he who had said that in the highest state a human being could reach there was no longer any such thing as Good and Evil, only faith or doubt; that definite rules were contrary to the essential nature of morality, and that faith must never be more than at the most an hour old; that when acting in a state of faith one could not do anything beastly; and that intuition was a more passionate state than truth. And now here was Agathe on the point of leaving the confines of the moral territory, about to venture out upon those limitless deeps where there is no other criterion than whether a thing will lift one up or let one down. She was carrying it out in the same way as, that other time, she had taken the decorations out of his hesitant hand, in order to exchange them. And at this moment, regardless of her lack of conscience, he loved her, with the strange feeling that it was his own thoughts that had gone from him to her and were now returning from her to him, now poorer in reasoning but, like a creature of the wild, with an elusive odour of freedom about them. And while he trembled with the effort of fighting down his feelings, he suggested cautiously:

" I'll put off going for a day, and go and get some information from the notary or a solicitor. What you're doing may be frightfully obvious ! "

But Agathe had already found out that the notary her father had employed was no longer alive. " There's nobody left who knows anything about it," she said. " Don't stir anything up ! "

Ulrich watched her take a sheet of paper and begin making attempts to imitate her father's handwriting.

Fascinated by this, he went into the other room and stood behind her. There, in a pile, lay the sheets of paper on which their father's living hand had moved—one could still almost sense the movement of it—and here, with positively theatrical ability to project herself into another personality, Agathe was conjuring up the very image of it. It was an odd thing to watch. The purpose for which it was being done, the thought of the intended forgery, vanished. And indeed Agathe had simply not thought about that at all. There was an aura about her as of justice all in flames, a justice not of logic. For her, goodness, decency, and law-abidingness, as she had encountered these virtues in people she knew, and particularly in Professor Hagauer, had always been somehow like removing a stain from a dress; but the wrong that hovered around her at this moment was like when the world is drowning in the light of the rising sun. It seemed to her that right and wrong were no longer general terms, a compromise arranged for the benefit of millions of human beings, but a magical encounter of I and Thou, the madness of a primal, still incomparable, and incommensurable creation. Actually she was making Ulrich the gift of a crime by putting herself into his hands, entirely trusting him to understand her rashness, just as children have the most astonishing inspirations when they want to give a present and have nothing to give. And Ulrich guessed most of this.

As his eyes followed her movements, he felt a pleasure he had never experienced before, for there was something of the nonsensical quality of fairy-tale in for once entirely yielding, and without misgiving, to what another being did. And even when he now and then recalled that at the same time harm was being done to a third person, it flashed up only for a second, like the blade of an axe, and he swiftly put his mind at rest by thinking that what his sister was doing here was actually nobody's concern; there was no need to assume that these experiments in imitating another person's handwriting would really be turned to account, and what Agathe did between their own four walls remained her own affair so long as it had no consequence outside the house.

Now she called out to him and, turning round, was surprised to see him standing close behind her. She woke up. She had written all that she wanted to write and now resolutely yellowed it at a candleflame, to give paper and ink a suitable aged look. She held out her free hand to Ulrich. He did not take it, but neither could he manage to withdraw entirely behind a sombre frown.

" Listen ! " she said. " When something's a contradiction and you love both sides of it—really love it!—doesn't it mean you cancel it out, whether you want to or not ? "

" The question is much too frivolously posed," Ulrich said gruffly.

But Agathe knew what he would think about it in his ' other mode of thinking '. She took a clean sheet of paper and light-heartedly wrote, in the old-fashioned hand that she was so good at imitating: " My bad daughter Agathe gives no occasion to alter the above instructions to the disadvantage of my good son Ulo ! " And, not satisfied with this, she wrote on a second sheet: " My daughter Agathe is for some time longer to be educated by my good son Uli."

And so that was how it had been. But after Ulrich had recalled all the details of it, he ended up by knowing just as little what to do about it as he had at the beginning.

He ought not to have left without straightening out the situation: there was no doubt of that! And clearly the modern superstition that one must not take anything too seriously had played him a trick when it prompted him to withdraw from the scene of action for the time being and not over-emphasize the importance of that controversial episode by putting up any emotional resistance. One always went on the assumption that 'it'll all come out in the wash'; what comes of the most violent exaggerations, if they are left to themselves, is, in due course, a new average. One could not ever take a train, one would always have to carry a pistol, with the safety-catch off, when walking along the street, if one could not trust the law of averages, which automatically makes high-falutin possibilities improbable: it was this European empiricism that Ulrich was obeying when, despite all scruples, he returned home. At bottom he was actually glad that Agathe had turned out to be so different.

All the same, the end of the matter could not properly be any other than that Ulrich should now, and without delay, make good what he had neglected. He ought instantly to have sent his sister an express letter or a telegram, the wording of which, he imagined, would have been approximately: 'I won't have anything to do with you unless you promise . . .' But he had absolutely no intention of writing anything of the kind; for the moment he was simply incapable of it.

Besides, before that fateful incident they had already decided that in the next few weeks they would try to set up house together or at least that Agathe should stay with him for some time; and in the brief period between making this decision and his departure they had of necessity talked chiefly of that. They had agreed provisionally on 'the period that divorce proceedings would take', so that Agathe should have advice and protection. But now, as Ulrich went over this in his mind, he remembered a remark his sister had made earlier, that she wanted to 'kill Hagauer'; obviously this 'plan' had been working in her and had taken on a new form. She had vehemently insisted on selling the family property with all speed, and even that might have had the purpose of making the inheritance disappear, although it might very well seem advisable on other grounds; however this might be, they had decided to put the sale in the hands of an estate-agent, and they had laid down their terms. And so Ulrich had to give some thought to what was really to be done about his sister, now that he had returned to his negligently 'provisional' life, which he himself had never acknowledged to be a life at all. Her present situation could not possibly continue. However surprisingly close they had drawn to each other in that short time—it had all the appearance, Ulrich thought, of a linking of two destinies, even though it had probably been brought about by all sorts of irrelevant factors too; while Agathe perhaps had a more romantic view of it—they knew very little of each other in the many and various superficial respects that count for so much when two people live together. When he thought about his sister objectively Ulrich found, indeed, that there were many unsolved problems, and he could not even arrive at any certainty about her past; what seemed to offer most enlightenment was the surmise that she had a very careless way of treating everything that happened either through her or to her, that she lived very vaguely and perhaps romantically, in expectations that ran alongside her real life: such a view was made all the more plausible by the fact that she had gone on living with Hagauer for so long and had broken with him so suddenly. And the thoughtlessness with which she treated the future also fitted in with this: she had left home, and that seemed to suffice her for the present; questions about what was to happen next she simply dodged. And Ulrich himself was unable either to picture her remaining without a husband, leading the indeterminate existence of a young girl, or to imagine the sort of man for whom she would be the right woman. He had indeed said as much to her shortly before his departure.

But she had looked him in the face with a startled expression—probably it was a slight piece of clowning, an affectation of being startled—and had then calmly countered with the question: " Can't I just stay with you for the present? We don't have to settle everything at once, do we? "

It was in this way—no more definitely than this—that the idea of setting up house together had taken shape. But Ulrich realised that this experiment necessarily meant the end of his experiment in ' living on vacation '. He did not want to consider what it might lead to. At least it was not unwelcome to him to know that henceforth his life would be subject to certain modifications, and for the first time he thought again of the circles, and especially of the women, associated with the Collateral Campaign. The notion of cutting himself off, which was inherent in the intended change, was wonderful. Just as it often takes only a small alteration in a room to turn its dreary booming acoustics into a glorious resonance, so now in his imagination his little house was transformed into a shell in which the roaring of the city was audible only as the far-off murmur of a great tide.

And then, after all—and it must have been towards the end of their talk—there had been a minor exchange of a special kind.

"We'll live like hermits," Agathe had said with a gay smile. "But as for love-affairs, of course each of us will be free. At any rate there's no impediment in your way!" she assured him.

"Do you realise," Ulrich said by way of answer, "that we shall be entering into the Millennium?"

"What does that mean?"

"We've talked so much about the sort of love that has no goal, that isn't like a flowing stream, but like the sea—a state of existence! Now tell me honestly: When they told you at school that the angels in Paradise did nothing but behold the countenance of the Lord and glorify Him, were you able to imagine that bliss of doing nothing and thinking nothing?"

"I always thought it must be a bit boring—though I'm sure I've only my own imperfection to blame," Agathe had replied.

"But bearing in mind all we've agreed about," Ulrich declared, "imagine that sea as a state of immobility and detachment filled to the brim with everlasting crystal-clear eventfulness. In past ages people have tried to imagine such a life upon earth: that's the Millennium, the Kingdom of a Thousand Years, formed in our own image and yet not among any of the kingdoms that we know. Well, that's the way we'll live! We shall cast off all egoism, we shall not accumulate possessions or knowledge or lovers or friends or principles, not even ourselves. Accordingly our spirit will open up, becoming fluid in relation to man and beast, opening out till we're no longer ourselves and maintain ourselves solely by being interwoven with the whole world!"

This little interlude had been a joke. He had been sitting with paper and pencil, making some notes and desultorily talking with his sister about what she could expect from the sale of the house and furniture. He was, incidentally, in rather an ill humour and did not even know whether he was blaspheming or being fanciful. And with all this they had had no time left to argue out seriously the matter of the Will.

It was doubtless because of the complicated and ambiguous way it had all come about that even today Ulrich was far from having arrived at active contrition. There was a good deal about his sister's piece of mischief that appealed to him, even though it meant he himself was defeated. He had to confess that it brought the person living along ' according to the Rule of Free Spirits ', the person in himself to whom he had granted far too much indulgence, straight into dangerous conflict with that profoundly undefined person from whom real seriousness emanated. Nor did he want to dodge the consequences of such an act by quickly making it good in some conventional way. But this meant there was no rule, and one had to let things take their own course.

16   *Another encounter with Diotima's diplomatic husband.*

MORNING found Ulrich no clearer, and late in the afternoon he resolved—with the intention of lightening the serious mood that was weighing on him—to go and see how his cousin was getting on with liberating the soul from civilisation.

To his surprise he was appropriated, before Rachel had time to return from Diotima's room, by Permanent Secretary Tuzzi, who came in to greet him.

" My wife's not feeling very well today," he said in the well-versed husband's tone of unthinking tenderness, which regular monthly use develops into a formula exposing the domestic secret to public knowledge. " I don't know whether she'll feel up to seeing you." He was dressed to go out, but seemed very willing to stay and talk to Ulrich.

Ulrich took the opportunity of enquiring about Arnheim.

"Arnheim's been in England and is now in St. Petersburg," Tuzzi told him.

The effect of this trivial and quite natural piece of news on Ulrich, oppressed as he was by his own affairs, was to make him feel as though the world, in all its plenitude and activity, were rushing in upon him.

"It has its points," the diplomat remarked. "Let him travel to and fro as much as he likes. One can make one's observations, one picks up all sorts of information."

"So you still think," Ulrich asked with amusement, "that he travels about on a pacifist mission from the Czar?"

"I'm surer of it than ever," was the plain answer given by the man officially responsible for the workings of Austro-Hungarian foreign policy.

But suddenly Ulrich was assailed by doubt whether Tuzzi was really so unsuspecting or was only pretending to be and making a fool of him. In some vexation he dropped the subject of Arnheim and asked: "Am I right in believing that while I've been away the slogan here has become 'Action!'?"

As always in relation to the Collateral Campaign, Tuzzi seemed to enjoy playing at once the simpleton and the shrewd politician. He shrugged his shoulders and grinned. "I don't want to anticipate what my wife will tell you—she'll tell you all about it as soon as she feels able to see you." But after a moment his little moustache began to twitch and the big dark eyes in his tan face shone with a vague look of suffering. "Look," he said hesitantly, "you're a bookish sort of chap, aren't you? Perhaps you can tell me what it means when a man is said to have 'soul'?"

It seemed that Tuzzi really wanted to talk about this problem, and it was clearly some uncertainty of his that created the impression of suffering. When Ulrich did not instantly answer, he went on: "If we talk of 'a good soul', what we mean is an honest, decent, conscientious person—I have a principal in my office who is one. But there you are, you see: it amounts to a sum total of subaltern qualities! Or there's 'soul' as a quality women have —which means pretty much the same as that they cry more easily than men, blush more easily. . . ."

" Soul is something your wife has," Ulrich rectified, as gravely as if he were stating that she had midnight-blue hair.

A faint pallor passed over Tuzzi's face. " My wife has a mind," he said slowly. " She is rightly regarded as an intellectual woman. I sometimes tease her about it and tell her she's *une femme bel esprit*. It makes her rather cross. But that's not quite the same as ' soul '. . . ." He reflected for a moment. " Did you ever go to one of those mysticist women ? " he then asked. " The sort that reads the future from your hand or a hair—astoundingly correct sometimes. Well, special gifts, you know, or trickery. But can you make any sense of it if someone says, for instance, that there are signs of the approach of a time when our souls will see each other so to speak without the mediation of the senses ? Let me say at once," he added quickly, " that this isn't meant to be understood just figuratively, but it's like this : if you're not a good person, try as you may nowadays, since we've already entered the age of the awakening soul, everyone can sense what you are much more clearly than in earlier centuries. Do you believe that ? "

With Tuzzi one never knew when his barbs were directed against himself and when against his listener, and Ulrich answered for all eventualities : " In your place I should just let it come to the test."

" Don't make jokes about it, my dear fellow—it's not fair if one's in safety oneself," Tuzzi said plaintively. " The thing is, my wife expects me to take such propositions seriously, even if I can't agree with them, and I have to give in without any chance of defending myself. And in this extremity it occurred to me that since you're a bookish sort of chap yourself——? "

" Both the assertions come from Maeterlinck, if I'm not mistaken," Ulrich said helpfully.

" Oh ? Do they ? Yes, that might very well be. That's the chap who——? H'm yes, I see, I see. Then I suppose it's he too who says there's no such thing as truth ? Except for the person who loves ! he says. If I love a person, the idea is I participate directly in a mysterious sort of truth that's deeper than the ordinary kind. On the other hand, if we formulate an idea because we've a thorough knowledge of human nature, because we've made our observations, that, of course, is supposed to be just worthless. Does that also come from what's-his-name ? "

" I'm afraid I don't know. It may. It's just the sort of thing you'd expect from him."

" Actually, I'd assumed the last bit was Arnheim."

" Arnheim's taken over a lot from him, and he's taken a lot over from others. They're both gifted eclectics."

" Oh, really? So this is quite old stuff, is it? But then can you explain to me, for heaven's sake, how people can get such things printed nowadays? " Tuzzi asked. " If my wife retorts: ' Reason proves nothing, ideas can't reach to where the soul is,' or: ' Above exactitude there is a realm of wisdom and love that one only desecrates by uttering reasoned statements! ' I can understand what makes her talk like that: she's simply a woman, it's her way of defending herself against male logic. But how can a man talk like that?! " Tuzzi edged his chair nearer and, putting his hand on Ulrich's knee, he said: " Truth swims like a fish in an invisible principle. As soon as one lifts it out, it's dead. What do you say to *that*? Would you say it's connected with the difference between an ' eroticist ' and a ' sexualist '? "

Ulrich smiled. " You really want me to say? "

" I'm dying to hear! "

" I don't quite know how to begin."

" There you are, you see! Men can't bring themselves to talk about such things. But if you had a soul, you'd simply be contemplating my soul and admiring it. We'd land up at an altitude where there are no such things as thoughts, words, and deeds, but mysterious powers and an overwhelming silence. May a soul smoke? " he asked and absent-mindedly lit a cigarette. Then he suddenly reawoke to his obligations as host and held out his cigarette-case to Ulrich. At bottom he was rather proud of now having read Arnheim's books, and precisely because he found them insufferable, it flattered his vanity that he had privately discovered how useful their high-falutin style might be to the inscrutable workings of diplomacy. And indeed no one would have wanted to do all that hard work for nothing; anyone else in his place, after making fun of it for a while according to taste, would soon have yielded to the temptation to try out one or other quotation or to put something that anyway cannot be expressed exactly into the garb of one of those irritatingly unclear new sayings. This sort of thing is done reluctantly, because one feels there is something ridiculous about the new garb, but one soon gets used to it, and so the spirit of the time changes imperceptibly with its changing modes of expression. And in this particular case Arnheim might have gained a new admirer. Even Tuzzi now admitted that the demand that soul and commerce should be united could, despite all opposition on principle, be regarded as something like a psychology of economics; and all that kept him immune from Arnheim's influence was actually Diotima herself. For between her and Arnheim there had—unknown to anyone else—already begun to be a certain cooling, which attached to all that Arnheim had ever said about ' soul ' the suspicion of its being only a screen for something else; and the consequence was that Tuzzi got these dicta flung in his face with ever greater exasperation. It was understandable that in these circumstances he assumed his wife's relationship to the other man to be still growing in intensity— this relationship that was not a love-affair (which a husband could take appropriate steps to deal with), but a ' state of love ' and a ' loving state of mind ' and so far exalted above all base suspicion that Diotima herself openly talked of the ideas with which it inspired her and had indeed recently begun somewhat insistently demanding that Tuzzi should spiritually partake of it.

He felt extremely bewildered and vulnerable, surrounded as he was by something that dazzled him like sunlight coming from all sides, without the sun's being in any definite position so that one could seek shade and relief from it.

And he heard Ulrich talking. " But I should like to put forward the following for your consideration. We generally have a constant influx and efflux of experience. The stimuli set up within us originate outside us and flow out of us again as actions or words. Think of it as a mechanism. And then suppose it gets out of order. There must be a blockage, mustn't there? Some sort of inundation? In some cases it may be merely a kind of flatulence . . ."

" At least you talk sensibly, even if it's all nonsense," Tuzzi remarked approvingly. He did not yet see that this was really developing into an explanation, but he remained outwardly imperturbable, and while inwardly he was lost in misery, on his lips the little malicious smile still proudly lingered, ready for him to slip back into it at any moment.

" I believe the physiologists say," Ulrich continued, " that what we call conscious action originates in the fact that a stimulus does not simply flow in and out through a reflex arc, but is forced to take a roundabout course. From this it follows that although the world we experience and the world in which we act appear to us to be one and the same, they really resemble the water above and below a mill, they're connected by a sort of reservoir of consciousness with a sluice-gate to regulate the level, pressure, and so forth, on which the influx and efflux depend. In other words, if a disturbance occurs on either side—if the world seems to become alien, or if there is marked disinclination to action—surely one may very well assume that in this way a second and higher consciousness can be formed? Or don't you think so?"

" Me?" Tuzzi said. " I'm afraid it leaves me pretty cold. That's something for the professors to make up their minds about if they think it's important. But speaking practically—" he thoughtfully stubbed out his cigarette in the ash-tray and then looked up irritably—" is it the two-reservoir people or those with only one reservoir of consciousness that decide things in the world?"

" Oh, I thought all you wanted was to know how I imagine such ideas arise . . ."

" If that's what you've been telling me, I'm afraid I didn't quite follow you," Tuzzi said.

" Look, it's quite simple: you don't have the second reservoir, so you don't possess the principle of wisdom and you don't understand a word of what the people who have a soul say. And I must say I congratulate you!"

Ulrich had gradually become aware that in ignominious terms and in very strange company he was uttering ideas that might serve to explain the feelings by which his own heart had been obscurely stirred. The surmise that in a state of much enhanced receptivity one's experiences might overbrim and flood out into a limitless, fluid union of one's senses with all things, so that it was all like a single sheet of water, recalled to him his long talks with Agathe, and unconsciously his face took on an expression that was partly grim, partly forlorn. Tuzzi looked at him from under indolently drooping eyelids, and from the particular tinge of Ulrich's sarcasm gathered that he himself was perhaps not the only person here in whom things were ' dammed up ' in a way not in keeping with his wishes.

Both of them scarcely noticed how long Rachel was taking. She had been kept by Diotima, who wanted her help in quickly giving both herself and the room a decent air of malady that would be at once informal and decorous. Now the maid came to say Ulrich would be received, if he would wait just a little longer; whereupon she hurried back to her mistress.

"All the quotations you have produced are, of course, allegories," Ulrich went on after this interruption, doing his best to make up to his host for being kind enough to keep him company. " A sort of butterfly language ! And the impression I get from people like Arnheim is pretty much that they become quite inflated with all this vaporously thin nectar they drink in ! I mean," he added hastily, as it struck him just in time that he must not seem to be including Diotima in his offensive remarks, " it's Arnheim in particular who gives me this feeling, just as I also get the rather paradoxical feeling that he carries his soul in his breast-pocket like a wallet."

Putting down the despatch-case and gloves he had picked up when Rachel came in, Tuzzi answered with some force: " Do you know what it is ? I mean, what you've just explained so interestingly. It's simply the spirit of pacifism ! " He paused to let this revelation sink in, and then added significantly: " In the hands of amateurs, you know, pacifism can be extremely dangerous."

Ulrich felt like laughing, but Tuzzi was in deadly earnest and he had, moreover, linked two things that really were remotely related to each other, however droll it might seem that he connected love and pacifism solely because both affected him as being a dilettante form of debauchery. So, not knowing what to answer, Ulrich fell back on the Collateral Campaign, objecting that it had, after all, just issued the slogan of ' Action ! '.

" That's a typical Leinsdorf idea ! " Tuzzi commented disdainfully. " Do you recollect the last discussion we had here shortly before you went away ? Leinsdorf said: ' Something must be done ! ' That's all it amounts to, that's what's being called the call to action ! And of course Arnheim's trying to work his Russian pacifism into it. Do you remember I warned them against it ? I'm afraid they'll have cause to remember that some day.

There's nowhere where foreign policy is as difficult as it is here, and even then I said: Anyone nowadays who takes it upon himself to put fundamental political ideas into practice must have a fair slice of the gambler and the criminal in him ! " This time Tuzzi was really opening up, no doubt because at any moment Ulrich might be summoned to see his wife, or perhaps because he did not want the conversation to end leaving him the only one who had had things explained to him. " The Collateral Campaign is arousing international mistrust," he announced, " and the effect it's having at home, where it's regarded both as anti-German and as anti-Slav, has its repercussions in foreign relations as well. But to give you a proper idea of the difference between amateur and expert pacifism, let me tell you just this: Austria could prevent any war for a good thirty years by joining the Entente Cordiale ! And on the occasion of the Emperor's Jubilee she could of course do that with an incomparably fine pacifist gesture, at the same time assuring Germany of her sisterly affection whether she followed suit or not. The bulk of our national minorities would be delighted. With cheap French and English credits we could make our army so strong that Germany couldn't intimidate us. We'd be rid of Italy. France couldn't do anything without us. In short, we'd be the key to peace and war, we'd swing all the big political deals. I'm not betraying any secrets to you in saying this: it's an elementary sum in diplomacy that any commercial attaché can work out for himself. So why can't it be done ? Imponderables at Court, where hearty dislike of H.M. goes to such lengths that it'd be considered almost indecent to fall in with such projects. Monarchies are at a disadvantage nowadays, weighed down as they are with considerations of decency ! Then there are the imponderables of what's called public opinion—and here I come to the Collateral Campaign. Why doesn't it educate public opinion ? Why doesn't it teach the public to see things objectively ? Look "— but here Tuzzi's exposition lost something of its plausibility and began to sound more like an effort to conceal certain difficulties —" this fellow Arnheim and his writing really amuse me ! He's not the first person to go in for that sort of thing. The other night, not being able to get to sleep for a while, I had the time to give it a little thought. There've always been politicians who wrote novels or plays. There's Clemenceau for instance, not to speak of Disraeli. Not Bismarck, but then Bismarck was a destroyer. And look at these French lawyers who're in power today! Enviable! Gerrymandering frauds, but with a first-rate professional diplomatic corps to advise them, to lay down the main lines of policy for them—and every one of them has at some time or other flung off plays or novels, at least in his youth, and they're still writing away at books today. Do you suppose those books are worth anything? I don't suppose so for a moment. But upon my word, last night I was thinking to myself: our own diplomats are a little deficient in so far as they don't produce any books. And why? First of all, it's just as true of a diplomat as it is of an athlete that he must sweat off his superfluous fat. Secondly, it increases public security. You know what the European balance of power is?"

Their talk was brought to an end by the reappearance of Rachel, coming to conduct Ulrich to Diotima. Tuzzi looked to her for his hat and coat. "If you were a patriot——" he said, slipping his arms into his coat-sleeves, while Rachel held the coat.

"What would I do then?" Ulrich asked, glancing into Rachel's black starry eyes.

"If you were a patriot, you'd do something to make my wife or Count Leinsdorf aware of these difficulties. I can't do it—coming from a husband it would easily seem rather narrow-minded."

"But nobody here takes me seriously," Ulrich retorted calmly.

"Oh, don't say that!" Tuzzi exclaimed with some vigour. "They don't take you seriously in the same way as they do other people, but for a long time now they've all been very frightened of you. They're afraid you might give Leinsdorf some quite crazy advice. You know what the European balance of power is?" he repeated searchingly.

"I suppose I do, more or less," Ulrich said.

"Then you're to be congratulated!" Tuzzi replied fiercely and unhappily. "We professional diplomats don't know—the whole lot of us. It's what mustn't be disturbed if everyone isn't to be at everyone else's throat. But what it is that mustn't be disturbed nobody quite knows. Just cast your mind back a little over what's been going on around you in these last few years and still is going on: the Italo-Turkish war, Poincaré in Moscow, the Baghdad question, armed intervention in Libya, Austro-Serbian tension, the Adriatic problem. . . . Is that a balance? Our never-to-be-forgotten Baron Aehrenthal—but I mustn't keep you."

" I'm sorry we can't go on talking about this," Ulrich declared. " If that's what the European balance of power comes to, then it's the best possible expression of the European spirit."

" Yes, that's what's so interesting," Tuzzi replied from the door, with an indulgent smile. " And from that point of view our Campaign's spiritual achievement mustn't be underestimated."

" Why don't you put a stop to it all? "

Tuzzi shrugged his shoulders. " In this country, when a man in His Highness's position wants something, one can't get up and oppose it. All one can do is keep a weather-eye open."

" And how have *you* been getting on? " Ulrich asked his little black-and-white-clad guide as, on Tuzzi's departure, she conducted him to Diotima.

17 *A change in Diotima's reading habits.*

" *Mon cher*," Diotima said when Ulrich came in, " I didn't want to send you away without saying a word to you, but you must forgive the state in which I receive you." She was wearing a négligé in which, by some chance of the position she had adopted, her majestic form took on a slight contour as of pregnancy, lending that proud body, which had never given birth, something of the gracious complacency that often goes with the sufferings of maternity. Beside her on the sofa lay a fur tippet, which she had obviously been using to keep her abdomen warm, and on her forehead she had a compress against migraine which had been allowed to remain where it was because she knew it gave her the look of wearing a Greek headdress. Although it was late, no lamp had been lit, and the aroma of medicaments, eau-de-cologne, and smelling-salts brought into play against some undefined malaise, mingled in the air to form one strong aromatic odour that was like a blanket over all the individual odours.

Ulrich bent low as he kissed Diotima's hand, as though to identify, from the scent of her arm, what changes had taken place during his absence. But her skin exuded only the same rich, saturated, well-bathed aroma as on all other days.

" Ah, *mon cher*," Diotima repeated, " how good it is to have you back!—Oh!" she suddenly moaned, but smiling. " I have such awful stomach-cramps!"

This information, which, had it been given by a natural person, would have been as natural as a comment on the weather, on Diotima's lips took on all the emphasis of a breakdown and a confession.

" Dear cousin!" Ulrich exclaimed, bending forward with a smile, to look into her face. At this moment Tuzzi's delicate hints as to his wife's indisposition became confused, in Ulrich's mind, with the conjecture that Diotima was pregnant and that the fate of this ménage was therefore decided.

Half guessing his surmise, she made a languid gesture of denial. The truth was that formerly she had never had menstrual cramps of this kind, and their obscure connection with her wavering between Arnheim and her husband was apparent in the fact that they had only come on in the last few months. When she heard of Ulrich's return, it gave her some comfort, and she welcomed him as her confidant in her struggles. This was why she had received him. There she reclined, only half pretending to sit up and, abandoned to the pains that raged in her, let herself be, in his company, simply a piece of untrammelled nature without surrounding fences or notices warning off the potential trespasser: a rare state of things with her. She had vaguely assumed it would be plausible if she pretended to have a nervous stomach-ache, and that it was even a sign of a sensitive constitution. Otherwise she would not have let him see her.

" Isn't there something you can take?" Ulrich asked her.

" Ah," Diotima sighed, " it's just all this agitation, you know. My nerves won't stand it much longer!"

There was a little pause, because now Ulrich ought really to have asked after Arnheim; but he was more curious to hear something about events that concerned himself, and he did not instantly find a way of combining the two questions. Finally he asked:
" I suppose the soul's liberation from civilisation is causing some

trouble?" and added: "I'm afraid I can't resist boasting that I told you long in advance that your efforts to blaze a trail for the spirit's entry into the world would end in pitiful failure."

Diotima remembered how she had fled from her drawing-room and sat on the little chest in the hall together with Ulrich. Her depression then had been almost the same as today, and yet between then and now there had been innumerable flood-tides and ebbings of hope.

"Oh, how glorious it was, *mon cher*," she said, "when we still believed in the great idea! Today I feel I can say the world harkened. But how deeply disappointed I am in myself!"

"And why?" Ulrich asked.

"I don't know. I suppose it's something in me."

She was on the point of saying something about Arnheim, but Ulrich now asked what people had made of the demonstration. His own experiences went only as far as having been sent by Count Leinsdorf to call on Diotima and prepare her for some resolute measure and at the same time to put her mind at rest, and not having found her at home.

Diotima made a disdainful gesture. "The police arrested a few young men and then let them go again. Leinsdorf is very cross—but what else could have been done? It's just made him back up Wisnietzky more than ever and keep on saying that something must be done. But Wisnietzky can't organise any propaganda if nobody knows what for!"

"I've heard it said the slogan's 'Action!'," Ulrich put in. Mention of Baron Wisnietzky, who as a Cabinet Minister had been shipwrecked on the rocks of the German parties' resistance and whose name among the leaders of the committee trying to work up enthusiasm for the Collateral Campaign's undefined great patriotic idea therefore inevitably aroused intense suspicion in all quarters, vividly recalled to Ulrich's mind His Highness's political operations, of which this was the result. It seemed as though the unembarrassed progression of Count Leinsdorf's ideas—perhaps aided by the expected failure of all efforts to use the concerted influence of Austria's most distinguished men in order to rouse the spirit of the homeland and, beyond that, the spirit of Europe— had now led him to the conclusion that the best thing to do was to give that spirit a vigorous push, no matter what the direction.

Possibly His Highness also based his argument to some extent
on the fact that in cases of diabolic possession the sufferer sometimes benefited from being shouted at or violently shaken.   But
no sooner did this surmise flash through Ulrich's mind than
Diotima began to speak again, once more addressing him as
'mon cher'.

" Mon cher," the invalid said, " it's true in a way !   Our century
thirsts for some sort of action.   Some act——"

" But what action ?   What kind of action ? " Ulrich interrupted.

" It doesn't matter !   In action, as contrasted with words, there's
a magnificent pessimism.   Let us not deny that in the past there
has never been anything but talk.   We have been living for great
and eternal words and ideals: for a heightening of human values:
for our quintessential individuality: for an increasing total plenitude of being.   We have been striving towards a synthesis, we
have been living for new aesthetic delights and new standards of
happiness, and I will not deny that the search for truth is child's-
play compared with the immense gravity of becoming a truth
oneself.   But it was all over-intensity in the face of the present-day
low reality-content of the soul, and we have been living in a dream-
like yearning, as it were for nothing."   Diotima had risen im-
pressively on one elbow.   " It's a healthy sign if we now renounce
the search for the buried entrance to the soul, and strive rather to
come to terms with life as it is," she concluded.

And so now Ulrich had besides his conjectural Leinsdorfian
interpretation of the slogan of ' Action! ' another, authorised one.
Diotima seemed to have taken to different reading.   It had struck
him as he came in that she was surrounded by a great many
books, but it had already been too dark to make out the titles.
Indeed, this thoughtful young woman was lying on some of them
—he could see this now that she reared up, like a magnificent great
serpent, gazing at him expectantly.

From girlhood Diotima had had a preference for fine sentiment
and the subjective in her reading, but now, as Ulrich clearly
concluded from her talk, she must have been seized by that
spiritual urge for renewal which is always at work, striving in vain
to find in the ideas of the coming decade all it has already failed
to find in the previous decade's ideas: this may indeed even be
the reason for history's great changes of mood, which alternate

between humanitarianism and cruelty, passion and indifference, and all sorts of other contradictions for which there is no completely adequate explanation. It passed through Ulrich's mind that the little unresolved residue of uncertainty in every moral experience, the thing he had talked about so much with Agathe, must surely be the cause of this human instability; but because he would not allow himself the happiness that lay in remembering those talks, he forced his thoughts away, directing them instead to the General, who had been the first to tell him that the time was acquiring a new spirit, and had told it indeed in a tone of healthy vexation that left no room for the enjoyment of alluring doubts. And since he had begun thinking of the General, he also recalled the latter's plea that he should look into the disruption of harmonious relations between his cousin and Arnheim. This was why Ulrich finally answered Diotima's farewell speech to the soul by saying bluntly: " So ' limitless love ' didn't agree with you very well ? "

" Oh, you're incorrigible ! " his cousin sighed, letting herself sink back into the pillows, whereupon she closed her eyes. For, having become unused, in Ulrich's absence, to such straightforward questions, she had first of all to recall how much she had confided in him. And all at once his proximity stirred up what had been forgotten. Obscurely she remembered a discussion with Ulrich about ' loving immeasurably ', which had been continued at their last or second-last meeting—a discussion in which she had declared that souls could step forth from the prison of the body, or at least lean out, as it were head and shoulders; and Ulrich's answer had been that these were the delirious ravings of starved sex and that she should let herself go, should grant some favours to Arnheim or himself or anyone at all. He had even suggested Tuzzi, as she now recalled. It was probably easier to remember suggestions of that sort than the rest of what a man like Ulrich talked about. And she had probably been right at the time in regarding it as an impertinence; but since a past distress is a harmless old friend by contrast with present distress, it now had all the advantage of being a memory she was at least thoroughly at home with. So Diotima opened her eyes again and said: " Probably there's no such thing as perfect love on this earth ! "

She smiled as she spoke, but under her compress her brow was furrowed with care, which gave her face a strangely twisted expression in the twilight.   In problems that affected her personally Diotima was not disinclined to believe in supernatural possibilities.   General von Stumm's unheralded appearance at the Council meeting that time had startled her as though it were the work of spirits, and as a child she had often prayed that she might never die.   This had made it easier for her to attach a supernatural belief to her relationship with Arnheim or, to put it more correctly, to attach to it some of that incomplete unbelief, that thinking-it-not-quite-impossible, which has nowadays become people's fundamental attitude in matters of faith.   If Arnheim had been capable of more than drawing out of her and his soul something invisible that, at a distance of five yards from both of them, communed upon the air, or if their eyes had been capable of communing in such a way as to leave behind something as tangible as a coffee-bean, a grain of tapioca, an ink-blot, any visible trace of something's having gone on, even any sign of progress at all, then the next thing Diotima would have expected was that some day it would go higher still, becoming one or other of those supernatural relationships of which one can form just as little of a picture as one can of most natural ones.   She bore it patiently, too, that recently Arnheim had been away more often and for longer periods and that even when he was there he was surprisingly taken up with his own affairs.   She permitted herself no doubt that his love for her was still the great event of his life, and when now and then they met alone the rise in the spiritual level was instantly so great and their contact so quintessential that emotions grew mute in awe; indeed if there was no occasion to talk about anything impersonal, a vacuum arose, leaving behind it a sense of bitter exhaustion. However little one could exclude the possibility that this was passion, she could just as little bring herself—accustomed as she was, from living in the age in which she lived, to the idea that everything not practical is anyway merely an object of belief, of precisely that uncertain unbelief—to exclude the possibility that something else was yet to come, which would fly in the face of all rational premises.   But in this minute, having opened her eyes to look straight at Ulrich—who was now no more than a dark, silent shadow —she wondered: ' What am I waiting for ?   What really ought to be done ? '

At length Ulrich spoke: " But Arnheim wanted to marry you, didn't he? "

Diotima propped herself up on her arm again and said: " Can one really solve the problem of love by getting divorced or married ? "

' So I was wrong, at any rate she isn't pregnant,' Ulrich noted privately. He could not think of any answer to his cousin's exclamation. But then all at once he said abruptly: " I warned you against Arnheim ! "

Perhaps at this moment he felt an obligation to tell her what he knew about the millionaire who had linked her soul, like his, with his business deals, but if so he instantly dropped the idea again; for it struck him that in this conversation every word had its old allotted place, just like the things in his study, on which, returning home, he had found no speck of dust, as though he had merely been one instant dead and oblivious of them.

Diotima reproved him: " You mustn't take it so lightly. There's a deep friendship between Arnheim and me. And if at times there's also something between us that I might call a great fear, that comes from our sincerity. I don't know whether you've ever experienced this or are capable of it: between two people who've reached a certain level of feeling, any sort of falsehood becomes so impossible that they practically can't speak to each other any more ! "

Ulrich's ear was so delicately attuned that from this reproof he perceived the entry to his cousin's soul stood wider open to him than at other times, and because he was exceedingly amused by her involuntarily confessing to him that she could not talk to Arnheim without being insincere, he commended his own sincerity to her for a while by not saying anything either. Then, since Diotima had meanwhile lain back again, he bent over her arm and gently kissed her hand, like an old friend. Light as the marrow of elder-twigs it lay in his, remaining there after the kiss. Her pulse throbbed between his fingertips. The powdery delicate scent of her nearness hung about his face like a puff of cloud. And although his kissing of her hand had been merely a little jesting bit of gallantry, it was like infidelity in leaving that bitter aftertaste of erotic pleasure, the bitterness of having leaned right over, drinking from another person deeply as an animal drinks, so that one no longer saw one's own reflection on the blurred water.

" What are you thinking of ? " Diotima asked.

Ulrich merely shook his head, thus—in the darkness, which was relieved by no more than a last velvety glimmer—giving her another opportunity to make comparative studies in silence.

A wonderful saying came to her memory: ' There are people with whom not even the greatest hero would dare to remain silent.' Somehow like that it went. It was a quotation, she seemed to remember; Arnheim had used it, and she had taken it as referring to herself. And with the exception of Arnheim's hand, since the days of her honeymoon she had not held any man's hand in hers for more than an instant; and here it was happening with Ulrich's hand now. Wrapped up in herself as she was, she scarcely noticed what was happening, but a moment later she found herself agreeably convinced that she had been utterly right in not idly waiting for the hour of sublimest love, for that was perhaps still to come or perhaps impossible, but in using the time of indecision to devote herself somewhat more to her husband. Married people have a very easy time of it: in situations where other people would be breaking faith with a lover, they can say they are recalling themselves to their duty; and because Diotima told herself that come what might she must for the present do her duty in the place to which destiny had called her, she had begun trying to counterbalance her husband's defects by infusing somewhat more ' soul ' into him. Again a poet's words came to her mind: they were more or less to the effect that there was no greater cause for despair than being involved in one destiny with a human being one did not love; and this was more evidence that she must make an effort to feel something for Tuzzi so long as destiny had not divided them. In rational contrast with the incalculable activities of the soul, which she did not want to make him go on paying for, she had set about this systematically; and it was with pride that she felt the books on which she was lying, for they treated of the physiology and psychology of marriage. And somehow the situation was rounded out by the fact that it was dark, that she had these books by her, that Ulrich was holding her hand, and that she had conveyed to him the magnificent pessimism that she would now perhaps soon express in her public activities by renouncing her ideals. And as she thought these things Diotima pressed Ulrich's hand from time to time, as though the suit-cases were already packed for her goodbye to all the past. Then she moaned softly, and a very faint wave of pain coursed through her body as though to supply the reason. Ulrich meanwhile soothingly returned the pressure with his fingertips, and after this had happened a few times, Diotima was inclined to think it was perhaps too much, yet she did not dare to withdraw her hand now, because it lay so light and dry in his, at times even trembling, so that it seemed to her like an impermissible piece of evidence of the physiology of love, evidence she was utterly resolved not to betray by any awkward gesture of attempted escape.

It was 'Rachelle', busying herself in the next room, who (having recently become remarkably impertinent) put an end to this scene by suddenly turning on the light on the other side of the connecting door, which was ajar. Diotima hastily pulled her hand away from Ulrich's—in which a sense of that weightless presence continued to repose for a moment longer.

"Rachelle!" Diotima called in a hushed voice. "Turn the light on here too!"

When this had been done their lamplit heads had the look of something just emerged from the depths, as though the darkness had not yet quite dripped off them. Shadows lay about Diotima's mouth, making it seem moist and full. The pearly little rolls of flesh on her neck and under her chin, which at other times seemed as though made for connoisseurs of voluptuous delicacies, were hard as in a lino-cut, fiercely shaded as with ink. Ulrich's head also rose into the sudden light painted black and white like that of a savage on the war-path. Blinking, he tried to decipher the titles of the books surrounding Diotima, and he was astonished by what his cousin's choice of reading-matter revealed of her thirst for knowledge in matters of the soul's and the body's hygiene.

'Some day he *will* do something to me!' she felt suddenly, having followed his gaze and being disturbed by it. She did not actually formulate the thought; it was rather that she simply felt herself too helplessly at his mercy, lying there in the light under his gaze, and she felt the need to adopt an air of self-assurance. With a gesture that was meant to be thoroughly superior, such as befitted a woman 'free of prejudice' in every respect, she waved her hand over her reading-matter, and said in the most objective tone possible: " Believe it or not, adultery sometimes strikes me as a much too easy solution of marital conflicts ! "

" It's certainly the mildest remedy," Ulrich replied, with a note of mockery that annoyed her. " I'd go so far as to say it can't do any harm anyway."

Diotima cast him a look of reproach, at the same time making a sign to warn him that Rachel in the next room could hear what they were saying. Then she said aloud: " That's certainly not what I meant ! " She called to her maid, who appeared, looking sullen, and, being sent away, obeyed with an expression of bitter jealousy.

This interlude had however given the emotions time to settle down tidily. The darkness-inspired illusion that they were committing a tiny act of unfaithfulness, even if one that was so to speak nondescript and to nobody in particular, evaporated in the bright light. Ulrich now endeavoured to bring their talk round to the business they had to discuss before he could take his leave.

" I haven't yet told you that I'm resigning the secretaryship," he began.

Diotima, however, turned out to be already informed and simply declared that he must stay on, there was nothing else for it. " The work we have to get through is still really immense," she said pleadingly. " Have patience just a little while, it can't be long till we find the solution ! You'll be provided with a proper secretary."

This impersonal ' be provided with ' struck Ulrich, and he asked for further details.

" Arnheim has offered to lend you his secretary."

" No thanks," Ulrich replied. " I can't help feeling that wouldn't be entirely altruistic." At this moment he once again felt heartily inclined to tell Diotima the bald facts about the oil-fields.

But she paid no attention at all to the dubious phrasing of his refusal; she simply went on:

" Apart from that, my husband has said he'd be prepared to let you have one of the clerks from his office."

" Wouldn't you mind ? "

" Candidly, I wouldn't altogether care for it," Diotima this time said more definitely. " Especially since there's no shortage of offers: your friend the General has also told me he'd gladly supply you with clerical help from his own department."

" And what about Leinsdorf? "

" These three possibilities were spontaneous offers, so I had no cause to ask Leinsdorf. But I'm sure he wouldn't shrink from a sacrifice."

" I *am* being spoilt," Ulrich commented, summing up Arnheim's, Tuzzi's, and Stumm's astounding readiness to assure themselves cheaply of a source of information as to all that went on inside the Collateral Campaign. " But perhaps after all it would be wisest if I took on your husband's clerk."

" *Mon cher*——" Diotima said in vague protest, but without quite knowing how to go on, which was probably the reason why what came out next was rather obscure. She propped herself up on her elbow again and said vehemently: " I reject adultery as an excessively crude solution of marital conflicts: that's what I told you! But for all that: there's nothing so hard as being linked in one destiny with a human being whom one does not love sufficiently! "

This was a highly unnatural cry wrung from Nature. But Ulrich stuck imperturbably to his resolve. " There's no question that the Permanent Secretary would like such a way of acquiring influence on what you're doing. But that's just what the others want too! " he expounded to her. " All three of them are in love with you, and each of them somehow has to reconcile that with his duty." He was really astonished that Diotima did not appear to understand either the language of facts or that of the comments he made on them, and, rising to take his leave, he added with even heavier irony: " The only one who loves you unselfishly is myself—because I've absolutely nothing to do and no duties of any sort. But emotions without distraction only destroy. *That* you've meanwhile discovered for yourself. And you've always regarded me with justifiable, even if only instinctive, mistrust."

Although Diotima did not know it, this was perhaps precisely and rather delightfully the reason why she was pleased to see Ulrich siding with her husband in this matter of the secretary, and she kept hold of the hand he had held out to her.

" And how does this fit in with your affair with ' that woman '? " she asked, ebulliently taking her cue from his remarks—in so far as

Diotima was capable of ebullience, which had pretty much the same effect as the sight of a professional strong man exercising with a feather.

Ulrich pretended not to know whom she meant.

" That judge's wife you introduced to me ! "

" So you noticed that, cousin ? "

" Herr Dr. Arnheim drew my attention to it."

" Oh, did he ? Very flattering that he should think it's a way of damaging me in your eyes. But of course my relations with the lady are entirely innocent ! " Ulrich declared, in conventional defence of Bonadea's honour.

" She was at your house only twice in your absence ! " Diotima said, laughing. " The first time we happened to be passing, and the second time it came to our knowledge in another way. So your discretion is a waste of time. On the other hand, I wish I could understand you ! I simply cannot."

" Good heavens, how could one explain it to you of all people ? "

" Explain ! " Diotima commanded. She had adopted her pose of ' official unchastity ', a sort of bespectacled expression that she put on when her mind bade her listen to or say things that were actually taboo for her lady-like soul.

But Ulrich refused, saying that he could only resort to conjectures about Bonadea's character.

" Very well," Diotima granted. " Though your lady friend has not been sparing of hints herself! In speaking to me she seems to feel bound to justify some wrong-doing. But if that's what you prefer, talk as if you were merely conjecturing."

Now Ulrich's curiosity was aroused and he discovered that Bonadea had several times been to see Diotima, and not only in matters connected with the Collateral Campaign and her husband's position.

" I must admit," Diotima said generously, " I find her beautiful. And she's of an unusually idealistic turn of mind. I'm rather cross with you for claiming my confidences and always keeping your own from me."

What Ulrich felt at this was approximately: ' The devil take the lot of you ! ' He wanted to give Diotima a fright and pay Bonadea out for her intrusiveness—or was it that he momentarily felt all the distance that lay between himself and the life he had been allowing himself to lead? " Well then, listen," he said, yielding the point. And with a contrived air of gloom he went on: " The woman's a nymphomaniac, and that's something I can't resist."

Diotima knew ' officially ' what nymphomania was. There was a pause, which she ended by drawling: " Poor woman! And that's the sort of thing you enjoy? "

" It's so idiotic! " Ulrich said.

Diotima wanted to know ' details '; he must explain this ' deplorable phenomenon ' to her and ' show it in a human light '. He did not do so at much length, yet as he talked she was gradually overtaken by a sense of satisfaction, the basis of which was doubtless the standard thanks to the Lord that she was not as that other woman was, and the apex of which tapered off into dismay and curiosity—which was not to be without its influence on her later relations with Ulrich. Pensively she said: " But it must be simply dreadful to embrace a person without being inwardly convinced by that person."

" You find it so? " her cousin retorted genially.

At this piece of offensiveness Diotima felt indignation and injured innocence going to her head; but she refused to show it. She contented herself with letting go of his hand and sinking back into her pillows with a gesture bidding him goodbye.

" You never ought to have told me! " she said from where she lay. " You've just been behaving very badly towards that poor woman, committing such an indiscretion."

" I never commit indiscretions! " Ulrich objected, unable to help laughing at his cousin. " You really are unfair. You're the first woman to whom I've ever told anything in confidence about another woman, and it was you who dragged it out of me."

Diotima felt flattered. She wanted to say something to the effect that without a spiritual transformation one only cheated oneself of the best in life; but she could not manage to get it out, because it suddenly seemed too personal to herself. However, in the end the thought of one of the books surrounding her prompted her to a non-committal reply that was, as it were, fortified by the barricades of her ' office '. " You make the mistake all men make," she said disapprovingly. " You don't treat your partner in love as an equal, but merely as a supplement to yourself, and then you're disappointed. Have you never faced the question whether a lofty, harmonious erotic life may not be achieved only through stricter self-discipline ? "

Ulrich just stopped himself from gaping at her. But he answered in involuntary self-defence against this text-bookish onslaught: " You know, I've already been asked about the problems of the soul's discipline and development today—by your husband."

Diotima started up. " What ? " she said in astonishment. " He's been discussing the soul with you ? "

" Yes, of course. He's trying to find out what it is," Ulrich declared. But he would not let himself be kept any longer; all he would do was promise that another time he might betray another confidence and tell her about that too.

18   *A moralist in difficulties over writing a letter.*

WITH this visit to Diotima there was an end of the restive state Ulrich had been in since his return. The very next day, towards evening, he sat down at his desk again, and, feeling at home there simply by virtue of having done so, began writing a letter to Agathe.

It was clear to him—as simple and clear as sometimes a windless day may be—that her wild scheme was extremely dangerous; what she had done so far might amount to no more than a risky joke involving only the two of them, but that depended entirely on its being undone before it became in any way an established fact in the real world around them; and the danger of that increased with every passing day. This was the point Ulrich had reached in writing when he paused, beset by qualms about entrusting to the mail a letter that discussed this matter in unveiled language. He told himself it would be more suitable from every point of view if he took the next train himself, instead of merely sending a letter; but this naturally struck him as an equally unreasonable course to follow, seeing that he had, after all, done nothing whatsoever about the matter for days on end. And he knew he would not go.

He realised that behind this there was something practically amounting to a resolve: what he felt like was simply letting it go at that and seeing what, if anything, came of the episode. So the problem he had set himself was merely that of how far he could really, clearly, *want* to let it go at that; and as he faced this problem all sorts of random thoughts went through his mind.

Right at the start, for instance, he observed that up to now, whenever he took a ' moral ' attitude, he had always found himself in a worse intellectual position than when it was a matter of actions or ideas of the sort one would normally call ' immoral '. This is a general state of affairs: for in situations that bring them into conflict with their environment people always deploy all their resources, whereas whenever they are only doing what is proper they naturally enough behave no differently from the way they do when paying their taxes—from which it can be concluded that all Evil is enacted with more or less imagination and passion, whereas the Good is characterised by an unmistakable pitifulness and poverty of emotion. Ulrich recalled that his sister had expressed this moral dilemma in a very uninhibited way by asking whether what it came to was that being good was no longer a good thing. It ought to be difficult and breath-taking, she had asserted, marvelling at the fact that moral people were almost always bores.

He smiled contentedly and proceeded from this thought to the reflection that Agathe and he were united in a special sort of opposition to Hagauer—roughly that of people who were bad in a good way to a man who was good in a bad way. And if one leaves out of account the wide middle stratum of life, which is, quite properly, occupied by people in whose way of thinking the general terms ' good ' and ' bad ' simply have not occurred since they let go of their mothers' apronstrings, what one is left with is the marginal strata where deliberately moral endeavours are still made, and nowadays these strata are indeed left to the bad-good and the good-bad people. The former have never seen the Good flying nor heard it singing and therefore expect all their fellow-men to share their enthusiasm for a landscape of morality in which stuffed birds perch on dummy trees; whereupon the second group, the good-bad people, being exasperated by their antagonists, at least in their own minds zealously cultivate a taste for the wrong, as though they were convinced that it is only in bad acts, which to them seem not quite so threadbare as the good ones, that a trace of moral life still twitches. And so—of course without Ulrich's being quite conscious of the further implications —the world at that time had the choice between perishing of its paralysed morality and being destroyed by its mobile immoralists, and probably even to this day it does not know which of the two it finally decided for with all the overwhelming consequences, unless it may be that the majority of people, who never have time to pay any attention to morals in general, this time paid attention to a particular case because they had lost confidence in their prevailing condition and consequently, of course, had lost a number of other things as well. For bad-bad people, who can so easily be blamed for everything, were as rare then as today, and the good-good existed only as a far-off ideal still to be achieved, remote as the spiral nebulae. But it was precisely of them that Ulrich was thinking, while everything else of which he seemed to be thinking was a matter of the utmost indifference to him.

And he gave his thoughts a still more general and impersonal form by putting the relationship that exists between the imperatives 'Do!' and 'Do not!' in the place of Good and Bad. For so long as a morality is in ascension—and this applies to the spirit of love for one's neighbour as to the spirit of a horde of Vandals —'Do not!' is only the reverse and the natural corollary of 'Do!'; then both the doing and the leaving undone are red-hot, and whatever they cover in the way of faults does not matter much, for the faults are those of heroes and martyrs. In this state of things Good and Bad are equivalent to the whole man's happiness and unhappiness. Yet as soon as one of these two elements wins, expands, and begins to run its course smoothly, the relationship between positive and negative injunctions necessarily goes through a decisive phase: then duty is no longer born alive and new every day, but has to be kept on hand, drained of its strength and dissected into ifs and buts, always available for every kind of use. Here then a process begins in the further course of which virtue and vice, because of their common origin in the same rules, laws, exceptions, and limitations, become ever more like each other, until the final result is that weird, fundamentally unbearable, self-contradictory state of things which Ulrich had begun by thinking about: namely that the distinction between Good and Bad loses all meaning when compared with the pleasure to be got from any pure, deep, and spontaneous mode of action—a pleasure that can leap, like a spark, both from permissible and from prohibited actions. Indeed, anyone who enquires into this impartially will probably find that the prohibitive field of morality is more highly charged with this tension than the hortatory. Whereas it seems comparatively natural that certain actions, referred to as ' bad ', such as appropriation of other people's property or excessive sensual enjoyment, must not be performed or, if they are, at any rate ought not to be, the corresponding positive moral principles—in this case, that is, unqualified generosity in giving or the urge to mortify the flesh—have almost entirely disappeared, and where they are still put into practice are the preserve of cranks, lunatics, or bloodless prigs. And in such a state of things, when virtue is decrepit and the moral attitude consists chiefly in the restriction of the immoral one, it may easily come about that the latter appears not only more spontaneous and vigorous than the former, but positively more moral—if one may use that term not with connotation of law and justice but to indicate whatever passion can still be aroused by problems of conscience. But could anything possibly be more perverse than inwardly giving preference to the Bad because with whatever one still possesses by way of a soul one is in search of the Good ?

This was a contradiction Ulrich had never felt so strongly as in the moment when the rising arc that his reflections had followed led him back to Agathe. Her innate readiness to make use of a scale of values that was (and here he again resorted to the term they had casually coined) good-bad, which materialised significantly in her act of interference with their father's Will, offended his own similar innate readiness, which had assumed a merely abstract pattern (something extremely like a spiritual pastor's admiration for the Devil), while he himself, as an individual, yet not only contrived to get along perfectly well in life as he was but also objected to being disturbed in that way of getting along. With as much melancholy satisfaction as ironical lucidity he concluded that his whole theoretical concern with the Bad amounted in the end to a preference he had for taking the side of the bad things that happened as against the bad people who set out to deal with them; and he suddenly felt a longing for goodness, just as a man who has been wasting time roaming about in foreign parts will imagine coming home some day and going straight to drink the water from the well in his native village. But if this comparison had not occurred to him first, he might have noticed that his whole attempt to form a mental image of Agathe in terms of a morally hybrid person—such as the present age produces in great quantities—was merely a screen to prevent himself from seeing a vista that frightened him a great deal more. For, oddly enough, his sister's attitude, which one could not help disapproving of if one examined it rationally, did become fascinating and alluring the moment one let oneself fall under its spell; for then all that was controversial and dualistic vanished, and the impression that took its place was one of a passionate, affirmative, activating goodness that, juxtaposed with the debilitated everyday forms of goodness, could easily look like some very ancient vice.

It did not come easily to Ulrich to indulge in such an exaltation of his feelings, and the last thing he wanted to do was to let it happen when he had to write this letter; and so he now directed his musings out into generalities again. These musings would have been incomplete if he had not remembered how easily and often, in these times through which he had lived, the desire for some obligation having its source in existential completeness had led to now one and now another virtue being extracted from the available stock of virtues and made the focus of noisy veneration. National, Christian, humanistic virtues, all had had their turn. One time it was the virtue of chromium steel and another time the virtue of goodness, now individuality and now fellowship, and one day the virtue of the split second, when the day before it had been the detachment of a broad historical view: the variable climate of public life derives fundamentally from the principle of exchanging one such ideal for another. But this had always left Ulrich cold; it had merely meant that he felt himself an outsider. Even now it meant no more to him than a completion of the general picture; for it is only half-understanding that makes one believe it possible to tackle the moral indecipherability of life, which becomes apparent whenever the complications have grown too great, by means of ciphers already contained in the given situation. Such attempts merely resemble a sick person's restless shifting and tossing in bed while the paralysis that ties him to that bed takes its inexorable course. Ulrich was convinced that the state of affairs in which these attempts occurred was an inevitable one and that it characterised the level from which every civilisation goes into decline, because no civilisation has yet been capable of replacing its lost inner elasticity. He was also convinced that what had happened to every moral system in the past was bound to happen to every future one. For slackening of moral energy has nothing to do with the Commandments or the keeping of them; it is independent of nuances in the moral code; it is not affected by external severity; it is an entirely interior process, equivalent to a diminution in the significance of all actions and a diminution in people's belief in their own integral responsibility for their actions.

And so, without his having intended it, Ulrich's thoughts returned to the idea he had sardonically presented to Count Leinsdorf, calling it the ' World Secretariat for Precision and the Spirit '; and although he had never spoken of it otherwise than flippantly, he now realised that all his adult life he had consistently behaved as if such a World Secretariat lay within the realm of possibility. Perhaps—this he could say in self-defence—perhaps every thinking person goes around with some such idea of order, just as grown-up men still wear next their skin the holy medal that their mothers hung round their necks when they were small. And this mental medallion, which nobody can nerve himself either to take seriously or to discard, looks pretty much as follows: on one side there is a blurred image of the longing for a law of right living, a law both iron and natural, allowing of no exceptions and dealing with all objections, a law both as liberating as an intoxicating drink and as sober as truth itself; on the other side, however, what is depicted is the conviction that one's own eyes will never behold such a law, that one's own thoughts will never think it out, that it cannot be promulgated by any one man's gospel and authority, but only by the exertions of all mankind—if, indeed, it is not simply a phantasm of the mind.

For an instant Ulrich hesitated. Without doubt he was a man of faith, though one who believed in nothing: his greatest dedication to science had never succeeded in making him forget that the beauty and goodness of people comes from what they believe and not from what they know. But belief has always been bound up with knowledge, even if with what was only thought to be knowledge, and this since the primordial days of its magical foundation. And that ancient knowledge-element has long crumbled, pulling belief down with it into the same ruin: so what has to be done now is to establish the connection anew. And this of course not simply by means of, say, raising faith ' to the level of knowledge '; yet in some way, certainly, so that it takes flight upwards from that high level. The art of rising above knowledge must be learnt anew. And since this cannot be done by any one man, it becomes necessary for all men to put their minds to it, whatever else they may have in their minds. And if in this moment Ulrich thought of a ten-year plan, a centennial or even a millennial plan, by which mankind might direct its exertions towards the goal that it cannot actually know yet, it did not take him long to realise that this was what he had often imagined, under all sorts of names, as the truly experimental life. For what he meant by the word ' faith ' was not that debilitated *wanting* to know, that credulous not knowing, which is what people generally understand by it. What he meant was rather a consciously apprehending insight, something that is neither knowledge nor delusion nor yet belief either, but precisely that ' quite other ' experience which eludes all these terms.

With a swift movement he drew the letter to him. But at once he pushed it away again.

His face, which just now had been alight with austere fervour, grew blank again, and his dangerous pet idea struck him as preposterous. As though glancing through a suddenly opened window, he was aware of what really surrounded him: Europe with its guns and its traffickings. The notion that people who lived like that could ever get together for the rationally planned navigation of their intellectual and spiritual destiny was simply unrealistic; it was preposterous. Ulrich could not fail to see that historical developments had never come about by means of any such planned association of ideas as is just possible in the mind of an individual, but always as squanderingly and wastefully as if some uncouth gambler had flung them like cards upon the table. He even felt a little embarrassed. All he had thought in this last hour was suspiciously reminiscent of a certain Enquiry as to the Drafting of a Guiding Resolution and the Ascertaining of the Wishes of all Participant Sections of the Population; indeed the very fact that he was moralising at all, this theoretical mode of thinking, which surveys Nature by candlelight, appeared to him utterly unnatural in contrast with the way the plain man, accustomed to having everything clear as daylight, always reaches out only for whatever is nearest to him and never bothers about any question but the immediate one whether he can make, whether he can at all risk, that gesture of reaching out.

Now suddenly Ulrich's thoughts flowed back from generalities to himself, and he felt what meaning his sister held for him. It was to her he had revealed that strange, unqualified, incredible and unforgettable state of mind in which all is affirmation: the state in which one is capable of no stirring of the spirit that is not moral—that is to say, the only state in which uninterrupted morality prevails, even though that may consist only in the fact that all actions hover in it without foundation. And all Agathe did was to stretch out her hand for this. She was the person who stretched out her hand. And into the place of Ulrich's reflections there now entered the bodies and patterns of the real world.

All he had been thinking now seemed to him mere delaying and transition. He decided to ' take a chance ' and see what came of Agathe's notion, and it was a matter of complete indifference to him at the moment that the mysterious promise it held had begun with what by ordinary standards was an infamous act. One could only wait and see whether the morality of ' being lifted up or let down ' would turn out to be as applicable to this as the simple morality of honesty. And he remembered his sister's impassioned question whether he himself believed what he had been telling her; but even now he could not answer ' yes ' any more than he had been able to then. He admitted to himself that he was waiting for Agathe in order to be able to answer this question.

At this instant the telephone rang, and Walter, at the other end of the wire, suddenly began talking into his ear with a rush of flustered explanations, in hasty, random words. Ulrich listened negligently and amicably, and when he had put the receiver down and straightened up again, it was as though only now the ringing of the bell began to ebb away out of him. Depth and darkness came flowing back soothingly, but he could not have said whether it was in his ears or in his eyes; it was simply like a deepening of all his senses.

Smiling, he took the sheet of paper on which he had begun writing to his sister and, before leaving the room, slowly tore the letter to shreds.

19   *Onward to Moosbrugger.*

DURING that same time Walter, Clarisse and the prophet Meingast had been sitting round a tray loaded with radishes, mandarins, almonds, big Turkish prunes, and cream cheese, engaged in eating this delicious and wholesome evening meal. The prophet, whose somewhat scraggy torso was covered by nothing but a woollen cardigan, from time to time lauded the simple, natural nutriment set before him, while Clarisse's brother Siegmund sat, his hat and gloves on his knee, at a little distance from the table, giving an account of a further conversation he had had with Dr. Friedenthal, the assistant medical officer at the mental hospital, with a view to enabling his ' utterly crazy ' sister to see Moosbrugger.

" Friedenthal insists he can do it only with a permit from the *Landesgericht*," he wound up in his off-hand way, " and at the *Landesgericht* they won't be satisfied with the application I got you from the ' Last Hour ' Welfare Society, they demand a letter of recommendation from the Embassy, since unfortunately we trumped up that story about Clarisse being a foreigner. Now there's nothing else for it: tomorrow Herr Dr. Meingast must go to the Swiss Embassy."

Siegmund resembled his sister in appearance, except that his face had less character, although he was the elder. If brother and sister were looked at side by side, in Clarisse's pallid face the nose, mouth, and eyes were like cracks in dry earth, while the same features in Siegmund's face had the soft, somewhat blurred con-

tours of rolling grassland, even though except for a little moustache
he was clean-shaven. The middle-class respectability had not
worn away from his looks to nearly the same extent as it had from
his sister's, and this gave him an ingenuous, natural air even at
the moment when he was so brazenly disposing of a philosopher's
valuable time. Neither of the other two would have been surprised if, after his words, thunder and lighning had burst from
the bowl of radishes. But the great man himself took the im-
position quite amiably—which his admirers noted as the makings
of a good story—and nodded, blinking an eye at Siegmund like
an eagle tolerating a sparrow on the perch beside him.

Nevertheless, the tension, which had arisen so suddenly and
not been adequately discharged, made it impossible for Walter to
control his feelings any longer. He pushed his plate back, turning
red as a little cloud at dawn, and vehemently asserted that no sane
person, unless he was a doctor or a warder, had any business inside
a lunatic asylum. On him too the sage bestowed a scarcely perceptible nod of assent. Noticing this, Siegmund, who saw more
than one would have given him credit for, added a remark
meant to clear the air: " I'm afraid the well-off middle class have
a disgusting way of regarding lunatics and criminals as somehow
demonic."

" But for heaven's sake then tell me," Walter exclaimed, " why
you're all trying to help Clarisse to do something you don't
approve of and which can only work her up more than ever ? "

His wife herself did not think this worth commenting on. Her
face now had an unpleasant look of remoteness from reality that
was quite frightening; a long haughty line formed on each side
of her nose, and her chin ran to a hard point.

Siegmund did not feel obliged or authorised to speak for the
others. So Walter's question was followed by a short silence.

At last Meingast said quietly and equably: " Clarisse has had a
shock that was too much for her. It can't be left at that."

" When did she get a shock ? " Walter asked, raising his voice.

" The other day—that evening at the window."

Walter turned pale, because he was the only one who had not
been told before, whereas Clarisse had obviously confided in
Meingast and even in her brother. But that was just like her !
he thought.

And although it really had nothing at all to do with it, suddenly
—as it were across the barrier formed by the trayload of fruit and
nuts—he had the feeling they were all about ten years younger
again. That was the time when Meingast, still the old, untransformed Meingast, had taken leave of them and Clarisse had
decided on Walter. Later she had confessed to him that in those
days, although he had already renounced her, Meingast had sometimes kissed and caressed her. In his memory it was all like
the wide movement of a swing. Higher and higher Walter had
soared: he had succeeded in everything in those days, even though
many an abyss had lain between his successes. Yet even then
Clarisse had been unable to talk to Walter if Meingast was about;
he had often had to wait to hear from others what she was thinking
and doing. In his proximity she became rigid. 'When *you*
touch me, I go all rigid!' she had said to him. 'My body
becomes serious—that's quite different from the way it is with
Meingast.' And when he kissed her for the first time, she said
to him: 'I promised Mamma never to do anything like this.'
Later, though, she confessed to him that in those days Meingast
had been in the habit of playing footy-footy with her under the
table. Such was Walter's influence: the richness of inner development that he had brought about in her was—thus he explained
it to himself—what prevented her from behaving without
restraint.

And he thought of the letters Clarisse and he had written to each
other at that time: he still believed it would be difficult to find
anything to equal them for passion and originality, even if one
hunted all through literature. In those stormy days he used to
punish Clarisse by rushing away whenever she let Meingast be
with her; and then he would write her a letter; and she would
write him letters, assuring him of her constancy and candidly
telling him whenever Meingast had once again kissed her on the
knee through her stocking. Walter had thought of publishing
these letters in book form, and he still now and then thought he
would do it some day. But unfortunately nothing had ever come
of it except for a misunderstanding right at the beginning with
Clarisse's governess, a misunderstanding that had great consequences. One day Walter had said to this governess: " You'll
see, before long I shall make up for everything." He had meant

this in his own way, thinking of the great success and justification he would enjoy in the family's eyes as soon as the publication of the ' Letters ' had made him famous. For, to make no bones about it, in those days the relation between Clarisse and himself was not entirely conventional. Clarisse's governess—an heirloom, so to speak, kept on in the honourable capacity of a sort of assistant mother—misunderstood him in her own way, as a result of which the rumour soon arose in the family that Walter was about to do something that would put him in a position to ask for Clarisse's hand; and once this proposal had been framed it gave rise to all sorts of peculiar delights and compulsions. Real life had, as it were, suddenly waked up. Walter's father suddenly refused to go on doing anything for his son unless he earned something himself. Walter's prospective father-in-law called him into his studio and there talked to him about the frustrations and disappointments involved in serving in the sanctuary of pure art, whether it be visual art or music or literature. And finally both Walter and Clarisse began to itch with the thought, which had all at once become tangible, of setting up house for themselves, of having children, of openly sharing a bedroom; it itched like a sore that cannot heal because one cannot stop scratching at it all the time. So it came about that only a few weeks after this impulsive statement Walter really became engaged to Clarisse, which made them both very happy and also very excited; for now began that search for a permanent place in life which loaded them with the whole predicament of western man, since the job that Walter was in desultory, wavering quest of was determined not only by the salary it would bring but also by the six repercussions it would have—namely on Clarisse, on himself, on their sex-life, on literature, on music, and on painting. Actually it was only a short time later—as they emerged from the whirl of complications that had started with the moment when he had been overcome by loquacity in the old mademoiselle's company—that he accepted the appointment in the Ministry of Works and Ancient Monuments and, with Clarisse, moved to this modest house where fate must decide the rest.

And at the bottom of his heart Walter thought it would do very nicely if fate were now to call it a day. True, the end would then not be precisely what the beginning had promised—but, after all, when apples are ripe they do not fall up the tree either, they fall to the ground.

That was what Walter thought, and while he thought it, opposite him, above the other end of the bright-coloured tray of wholesome vegetarian food, there floated his wife's small head. There Clarisse was, trying to complete Meingast's explanation as objectively as possible, indeed just as objectively as Meingast had put it himself.

" I've got to do something to break down the shock.   The shock was too much for me, Meingast says," she expounded, adding off her own bat: " And it was certainly no mere accident that the man stopped in the bushes right under my window ! "

" Nonsense ! "   Walter waved that away like a sleeper brushing off a fly.   " After all, it was just as much my window."

" All right then, our window," Clarisse emended, with her tight-lipped smile, which was pointed without its being clear whether it expressed bitterness or merely scorn.   " We attracted him. But shall I tell you what one can call the thing that man was doing ? He was stealing sexual pleasure ! "

That went through Walter's head like pain.   His head was crammed full of the past, and here was a wedge of the present being driven in, without any convincing difference being there between present and past.   There were still bushes there in Walter's head, forming bright patches of foliage, with cyclists' tracks winding between them.   The bold adventure of long trips and walks was like something experienced only this morning. Girls' skirts swung again as in those years when for the first time ankles had been daringly revealed and the hems of white petti-coats had frothed in the new movements of sport.   It was putting it rather mildly to say Walter had thought the relation between himself and Clarisse in those days was ' not entirely conventional ' for—not to put too fine a point upon it—on those cycling trips in the spring of the year when they became engaged everything had happened that can happen and yet leave a girl technically a virgin. ' Almost unbelievable of a decent girl,' Walter thought, raptur-ously recalling it all.   Clarisse had called it ' taking Meingast's sins upon ourselves '—the sins of Meingast who at that time had not even had that name and who had only just gone abroad. ' It would be cowardly not to be sensual now just because he was ! '

This was how Clarisse explained it, announcing: ' But *we* mean it spiritually ! ' True, Walter had at times had misgivings that these incidents were perhaps after all too closely connected with the only recently vanished Meingast, but Clarisse retorted: ' If people want something great, say as we do in art, they simply mustn't worry about anything else.' And Walter could recollect the eagerness with which they destroyed the past by repeating it in a new spirit, and the intense relish with which they discovered the magical possibility of making excuses for illicit physical pleasures by attributing a suprapersonal function to them. Walter admitted to himself that at that period Clarisse had shown the same energy in her eroticism as she had shown later in her rejection of everything erotic. And he lost the thread for a moment as an obstinate thought told him that her breasts were still as tense as in those days. Everyone could see it, even through her clothes. Meingast was indeed looking straight at her breasts now; perhaps he did not know it. Her breasts are mute ! Walter inwardly proclaimed, and it seemed as significant as a dream or a poem. And it was almost with the same significance that the present penetrated to him through the padding of his emotion.

" Come along, tell us what you're thinking, Clarisse ! " he heard Meingast saying encouragingly, like a doctor or a teacher; he sometimes spoke to her in that polite and distant tone.

Walter also noticed that Clarisse looked at Meingast enquiringly.

" You were telling me about one Moosbrugger—a carpenter, you said . . ."

Clarisse simply gazed at him.

" And who else was a carpenter ? The Saviour ! Isn't that what you said ? In fact, you even told me you'd written a letter about it to some influential personage, didn't you ? "

" Stop it, all of you ! " Walter burst out imploringly. Everything was whirling inside his head. But he had hardly uttered the angry exclamation when he realised that this letter was another thing he had never heard about before and, weakening, he asked: " What letter ? "

He got no answer from anyone. Ignoring the question, Meingast said: " It's one of the most modern ideas there are. We're incapable of liberating ourselves by our own efforts, there can be no doubt about that.   We call it democracy, but that's merely the political expression of the spiritual state of affairs, the ' It can be done this way, or, of course, the other way '.   This is the age of the voting-slip.   Look at how every year we set up our sexual ideal, the beauty queen, by means of a voting-slip, and our having made empirical science our intellectual ideal means nothing more or less than pressing the voting-slip into the hands of what we call facts so that they can vote in our stead.   The age is un- philosophic and cowardly.   It hasn't the courage to decide what is of worth and what is worthless, and democracy, reduced to basic terms, signifies: *Do* whatever *happens* !   Incidentally, that is one of the most infamous vicious circles in thought that has ever occurred in the history of our race."

The prophet, having irritably cracked a nut and peeled it, now thrust the broken pieces into his mouth.   Nobody had understood him.   He broke off his speech in order to use his jaws in slow masticatory movement, in which the up-turned tip of his nose also participated, while the rest of his face remained ascetically immobile; but he did not avert his gaze from Clarisse—it stayed fixed somewhere in the region of her breasts.   Involuntarily both the other men's eyes left the Master's face and followed his abstracted gaze.   Clarisse felt a suction, as of a vacuum, as though if they went on gazing at her much longer she would be lifted right out of herself by these six eyes.   But, gulping down the remains of the nut, the Master proceeded with his instruction:

" Clarisse has dicovered that Christian tradition makes of the Saviour a carpenter.   Not entirely accurate—only his foster- father.   Nor is it, of course, at all accurate for her to draw any conclusion from the fact that a criminal who has attracted her attention also happens to be a carpenter.   Intellectually that is simply beneath criticism.   Morally it is frivolous.   But it is courageous of her—that's what it is ! "   Meingast paused to let the harshly uttered word ' courageous ' take its effect.   Then he went on calmly: " Recently, like the rest of us, she saw a psycho- path at his exhibitionism.   She attaches too much importance to it.   Altogether too much importance is attached to sex nowadays. But Clarisse says: It is no accident that the man stopped under my window.   Now let us understand this rightly !   She's wrong, of course, for from the causal point of view it was the merest coincidence. Nevertheless she says to herself: If I regard everything as being already explained, human beings will never change anything in the world. She regards it as inexplicable that a murderer who, if I'm not mistaken, is called Moosbrugger, should be precisely a carpenter. She regards it as inexplicable that an unknown psychopath, suffering from sexual disturbances, should stop precisely under her window. And in the same way she has got into the habit of regarding many other things that happen to her as being inexplicable, and——" once again Meingast kept his audience waiting a moment; his voice had begun to suggest a resolute but wary approach, a tip-toeing up to something, and now came the pounce. "And so," he sprang it on them, "she will do something!"

Clarisse felt her blood run cold.

"I repeat," Meingast said, "that intellectually this is beneath criticism. But intellectuality is, as we know, only the expression or the tool of a life that has dried up. On the other hand, what Clarisse expresses probably has its source in another sphere: that of the will. One can assume that Clarisse will never be able to explain what happens to her, but she may very well be able to solve it, resolve it. And for that reason she is quite right in calling it 'salving' or 'saving'. Instinctively she is using the right word for it: 'salvation'. Now it might easily be that one of us might say these seem to him to be delusions, or that Clarisse is neurotic. But that would make no sense. The world is at present so undeluded that there's nothing it knows whether to love or hate, and because all values are ambivalent it follows that people are all neurasthenics and weaklings. In a word," the prophet concluded abruptly, "though it is not easy for the philosopher to renounce understanding, this is probably the great thing that the twentieth century is gradually beginning to understand: that one must do precisely that. For me, in Geneva, it is today spiritually more important that there is a French teacher of boxing there now than that Rousseau's destructive analytic mind was at work there once!"

Meingast could easily have gone on talking, now that he had got going. First of all about the fact that the notion of salvation had always been anti-intellectual. 'And so there is nothing more devoutly to be wished for in the world today than a strong healthy delusion ': he had actually had the statement on the tip of his tongue, but swallowed it down in favour of the other conclusion. Secondly, about the concomitant physical significance of the notion of salvation, implied in the word's etymology, with its connotations of the hale and hearty and of safety: so that the inference was that only action could ' save ' one—only experiences, that is, that involved the ' whole ' person, neck and crop. Thirdly, he had meant to speak of how the over-intellectualisation of the male might well mean that women would take over the instinctive leadership towards action, Clarisse being one of the first representatives of this trend. Finally, about the shifting significance of the ' salvation ' idea in the history of nations in general and about how in the present stage of that evolution the centuries-old predominance of the belief that salvation was a concept created solely by religious feeling was giving way to the realisation that salvation was something that must be achieved by firmness of will, even indeed, if necessary, by force. For the salvation of the world by force was at present the central point of Meingast's thought.

Meanwhile however Clarisse had found the suction of the eyes fixed on her was growing intolerable and she blocked the Master's further discourse by turning to Siegmund, as the point of least resistance, and saying to him, rather too loudly:

" There you are. I told you so: one can only understand what one experiences oneself. That's why we must go to the lunatic asylum ourselves."

Walter, who was peeling a tangerine simply as a way of keeping a hold on himself, at this instant cut too deep, and a jet of acid juice spurted into his eyes, making him start back and grope for his handkerchief. Siegmund—well dressed as ever—surveyed with an expert's loving interest first the effect of the irritation on his brother-in-law's eye, then the hogskin gloves that reposed on his knee together with his bowler hat, forming a still-life study in respectability; and it was only when his sister's gaze would not shift from his face and no one spoke up to save him the trouble, that, glancing up again, he nodded gravely, and, with composure, murmured:

" I've never doubted that the madhouse was the place for us all."

Clarisse at once turned to Meingast and said: " Well, I told you about the Collateral Campaign. That would probably be another tremendous chance—and it would be a duty—to clear away this laissez-faire of ' this way and just as easily any other way ', which is the sin of our century ! "

The Master smilingly waved this off.

Brimming over with enthusiasm in the sense of her own importance, Clarisse cried out abruptly and obstinately: " A woman who lets a man have his way when it weakens his spirit is just another kind of sex-murderer ! "

" Let us keep to generalities ! " Meingast admonished. " Incidentally, I can set your mind at rest on one question: in those somewhat ludicrous councils, where dying democracy is trying to bring forth yet one more great achievement, I've long had my observers, my confidential agents."

Clarisse simply felt icicles forming at the roots of her hair.

In vain did Walter try once more to put a stop to what this was working up to. Opposing Meingast with all respect, in a tone utterly different from what he would have used in speaking to, for instance, Ulrich, he said to him: " What you're saying probably amounts to the same as what I've been meaning for a long time when I say one ought to paint only in pure colours. We must make an end of all that's broken and blurred, make an end of concessions to empty air and to a cowardliness of vision that no longer dares to see every object with a firm outline and its own colour. I put it in pictorial terms, you in philosophic terms. But even though we are of the same opinion. . . ." He suddenly became embarrassed, feeling that in the others' presence he could not say in so many words why he dreaded Clarisse's contact with the insane. " No, I don't wish Clarisse to do it ! " he exclaimed. " And it certainly won't be done with my agreement ! "

The Master had listened pleasantly, and he answered Walter just as pleasantly as if not one of these weightily uttered words had reached his ear: " Come to think of it, there's another thing Clarisse has expressed very finely. She maintains that apart from our ' body of sin ', in which we live, we all have yet another form, the ' body of innocence '. One might, I think, take this beautifully to mean that, independently of the miserable so-called empirical world, our perceptions have an entry into a world of majesty where, in lucid moments, we feel our image moved by dynamics of an infinitely different kind! How did you put it, Clarisse?" he asked at once formally and encouragingly, turning to her. "Did you not maintain that if you succeeded in making a stand for that worthless creature without feeling revulsion, going into his cell and there playing the piano day and night, without wearying, you could not but, as it were, draw his sins out of him, taking them upon yourself and then ascending with them? Naturally," he remarked, turning again to Walter, "that is not to be taken literally. It is a subliminal process in the soul of the age, a process that here assumes the guise of a parable about this man and in this guise inspires her will . . ."

He was uncertain whether he should not after all add something about Clarisse's relationship to the history of the 'salvation' idea or whether it would be more interesting to explain her mission of leadership to her once again *tête-à-tête*. But at this point Clarisse jumped up from her chair like an over-excited child, flung up her arm, her fist clenched, and, with a smile that was at once abashed and ferocious, cut short all further praise of herself with the shrill cry:

"Onward to Moosbrugger!"

"But we still haven't got anyone to get us permission to go there," Siegmund put in.

"I won't go with you!" Walter assured them firmly.

"I myself cannot accept any favours from a State in which freedom and equality are to be had in every style and at every price," Meingast declared.

"Then Ulrich must get us the permit!" Clarisse exclaimed.

Meingast and Siegmund gladly approved this decision, which for the present relieved them of responsibility; for they felt they had already gone to enough trouble in the matter. So it came about that, albeit reluctantly, Walter finally had to give in and go down to the grocer's shop, where the nearest telephone was, to ring up the friend who they had decided should help.

His doing so was what put a final stop to Ulrich's attempt at writing the letter he meant to write to Agathe. Both Walter's telephone-call itself and what Walter had to say surprised Ulrich. There was plenty of room for differences of opinion about the matter, Walter told him, but it certainly could not be discounted as a mere whim. Perhaps a beginning ought really to be made

somewhere, and it did not much matter where. Of course it was
no more than a coincidence that she should have picked on
Moosbrugger. But Clarisse was so weirdly direct, wasn't she?
Her way of thinking was always like those modern paintings that
were done in unmixed pure colours, harsh and formally un-
wieldy—but if one tried to enter into the spirit of it, it often turned
out to be astonishingly true. He could not explain it adequately
on the telephone, he said, imploring Ulrich not to let him down.

Ulrich was quite glad to be called away, and he agreed to come,
although it was a long way to go for the sake of talking to Clarisse
for a mere quarter of an hour, which was all she could spare,
since she was expected to dine at her parents' house together with
Walter and Siegmund. On the way he realised with some surprise that it was quite a while since he had thought of Moosbrugger
and that time and again he had had to be reminded of him by
Clarisse, whereas in the past the man had constantly been in his
thoughts.

Even the darkness was no longer haunted by that ghoulish
apparition, Ulrich realised as he walked along through the late
evening towards his friends' house. A void in which that used to
loom up no longer existed. He observed this with satisfaction
and also with a faint uncertainty about himself, such as one may
feel when there has been a change and the extent of the change is
clearer than its cause. He was enjoying the sense of cutting through
the loose darkness with the more solid darkness of his own body
when he encountered Walter, who came towards him with faltering
steps, being nervous out at night in this lonely district but anxious
to say a few words to Ulrich before they joined the others.

Eagerly Walter continued from where he had broken off on the
telephone. He seemed to want to protect himself, and Clarisse
as well, from possible misunderstandings. Of course, he said,
her notions might strike one as being without rhyme or reason,
but wherever one went right into them, one found behind them a
symptom of disease that was in fact fermenting in the whole
epoch; this, he said, was the most amazing faculty she had. She
was like a hazel-twig twitching over underground water. In this
case the hidden element was the necessity of replacing modern
man's passive, merely intellectual and rational, attitude by new
' values '; the intellect of this age had left no solid point anywhere,

and so now it was only the will—indeed, if it could not be done otherwise, then it was only violence that could create a new hierarchy of values in which man would find an alpha and omega for his inner life. . . . He was repeating, hesitantly and yet enthusiastically, what he had heard Meingast say.

Guessing this, Ulrich asked with some exasperation: " What on earth are you talking in this high-falutin way for ? I suppose that's your prophet's doing ? In the old days it seems to me you could never get enough of simplicity and naturalness."

Walter put up with this for Clarisse's sake, lest their friend should refuse his aid; but if there had been so much as a ray of light in the moonless gloom the flash of his teeth would have been visible as he bared them in impotent anger. He did not answer; but suppressed vexation enfeebled him and the proximity of his muscular companion, shielding him from the somewhat intimidating solitude of the place, made him soft. Suddenly he said: " Imagine loving a woman and then meeting a man whom you admire and realising that your wife also admires and loves him and now both of you in love, jealousy, and admiration, feel this man's inaccessible superiority . . ."

Ulrich ought to have let him have his say, but, squaring his shoulders and bursting out into laughter, he interrupted him: " I haven't the faintest wish to imagine anything of the sort ! "

Walter shot a venomous glance in his direction. He had wanted to ask: ' What would you do in such a case ? ' But here was a repetition of the old game that had been played between them ever since they were boys.

As they entered the house and crossed the dimly lighted hall to the stairs, he exclaimed: " Don't put on that act of yours ! You're not nearly so callously conceited as you try to make out ! " And then he had to hurry to catch up with Ulrich on the stairs and tell him, in a whisper, the rest of what he needed to know.

" What has Walter been telling you ? " Clarisse asked when they entered the room.

" I can do it all right," Ulrich said, going straight to the point, " but I have my doubts about its being reasonable."

" There you are, the first word he utters is ' reasonable ' ! " Clarisse called out laughingly to Meingast. She was rushing to and fro between wardrobe, wash-basin, looking-glass, and the half-open door connecting her room with the room in which the men were. From time to time there was a glimpse of her: with wet face and hair hanging over her eyes; then with her hair done, but bare-legged; then in stockings but shoeless; then in her long-skirted evening dress but with a peignoir over her shoulders, which looked like the kind of white overalls worn in institutions. This popping in and out did her good. Since she had got her way, all her feelings were dipped in a faint sensuality. " I'm walking on tight-ropes, light-ropes ! " she called into the room.

The men smiled. Only Siegmund glanced at his watch and matter-of-factly urged haste. He regarded the whole thing as a form of gymnastics.

Now on a ' light-rope ' Clarisse went gliding across to the far corner of the room, looking for a brooch and then shutting the drawer of the night-table with a bang.

" I change faster than a man ! " she called through the open door to Siegmund, but then suddenly paused, realising the ambiguity of the word ' change ', which for her at this moment held the meaning both of dressing for dinner and of becoming involved in mysterious destiny. Quickly she did the finishing-touches and then, putting her head round the door, gravely looked at the men one after the other. Anyone not regarding this as ' fun ' might have been taken aback by a blankness in this grave face, as though some light had gone out that contributed to the expression of a normal, sane face. She bowed to her friends and said ceremonially: " And so now I have changed my destiny ! " But by the time she straightened up again her face once more looked normal, indeed quite charming.

" Onward—march ! " her brother Siegmund cried. " Papa doesn't like people to be late for dinner."

When the four of them walked to the tram, Meingast having vanished before they left the house, Ulrich fell back a few steps with Siegmund and asked him if he had not been a little worried about his sister recently. Siegmund's glowing cigarette sketched a flat arc in the darkness.

" She's quite certainly abnormal," he replied. " But is Meingast normal ? Is Walter, even ? Is it normal to play the piano ? It's an unusual state of excitement associated with a tremor in wrists and ankles. For a doctor there's no such thing as ' normal '.

Still, if you want my serious opinion, here it is: my sister is some-what over-wrought. In my view that'll pass off when ever the arch-sage takes his departure."

He gave a slight malicious emphasis to the words ' when ever '.

" What do you make of him? "

" He's a gas-bag," Ulrich declared.

" Isn't he just? " Siegmund exclaimed, delighted. " Loath-some, loathsome! Still," he added after a moment's pause, " an interesting thinker—I wouldn't go to the lengths of denying that."

20 Count Leinsdorf has qualms about Capital and Culture.

SO it came about that Ulrich went to see Count Leinsdorf again.

He found His Highness in an atmosphere of tranquillity, devotion, solemnity and beauty, at his writing-desk, reading a newspaper spread out over a high pile of documents.

Reiterating his condolences to Ulrich, the Imperial Liege-Count shook his head mournfully.

" Your distinguished father was one of the last true champions of Capital and Culture," he said. " I well remember the days when he and I were both members of the Bohemian Diet. He richly deserved the confidence we always reposed in him ! "

Out of mere punctilio Ulrich asked what progress the Collateral Campaign had made during his absence.

" Well now, because of that hullabaloo in the street outside here that afternoon you were with me, we've set up a Commission of Enquiry into the Wishes of the Relevant Sections of Society with regard to the Reform of Administration in Home Affairs," Count Leinsdorf recounted. " It was the Premier's own wish that we should relieve him of that matter for the time being, seeing that as a patriotic enterprise we enjoy, so to speak, the confidence of the public."

With perfect gravity Ulrich assured him that at any rate the Commission was felicitously named; the name alone would surely create a certain amount of effect.

"Yes, the right way of putting things counts for a great deal," His Highness said thoughtfully and then suddenly asked: "And what do you say to this business of the municipal employees in Trieste? To my mind it's high time for the Government to pull itself together and take a firm stand." He seemed about to hand Ulrich the newspaper, which he had folded up on his visitor's entry, but at the last moment decided to open it again himself and to read aloud, with much zeal, a long-winded article in it. "Can you imagine," he asked when he had finished, "such things happening in any other State in the world? There you have what the Austrian city of Trieste has been doing for years now, employing only Italians, owing allegiance to the Italian Crown, in their official service, in order to make a point of demonstrating that they feel allegiance not to us but to Italy. I was there once on His Majesty's birthday, and not a single flag did I see anywhere in all Trieste except on the Governor's house, the tax office, the prison, and the various barracks! On the other hand, if you have an errand in an office in Trieste on the King of Italy's birthday, you won't find a clerk anywhere without a flower in his buttonhole!"

"But why has this been tolerated up to now?" Ulrich enquired.

"Why on earth shouldn't it be tolerated?" Count Leinsdorf answered in a disgruntled tone. "If the Government forces the city authorities to dismiss their foreign clerks, everyone will instantly start saying we're 'Germanising'. And that's just the reproach every government dreads. As a matter of fact, His Majesty doesn't care to hear it either. After all, we're not Prussians!"

Ulrich seemed to remember that the port of Trieste had been founded there on the Slavonic coast by the Venetian Republic and today included a large Slovenian population; and so, even if, in spite of its being also the gateway to the Empire's eastern trade and in every way dependent on the Empire for its prosperity, one regarded it as merely the private concern of its own population, there was no getting round the fact that its numerous Slavonic lower-middle-class passionately contested the favoured Italian-speaking upper-class's right to regard the city as its own property. Ulrich said as much.

" That's true enough," Count Leinsdorf said and he continued didactically: " But as soon as the word goes round that we're ' Germanising ', the Slovenes immediately side with the Italians, even if at other times they're doing their best to tear each other's hair out. In that event the Italians get the support of all the other minorities as well. We've been through all that often enough. If one sets out to think in terms of practical politics, don't you know, willy-nilly one has to see it's the Germans that are the menace to harmony in the Empire ! " Thus, very thoughtfully, did Count Leinsdorf conclude, and he remained thoughtful for a while, for he had touched on the great political concept that he had so much at heart, even if it had not yet become really clear to his mind. Suddenly he took comfort and went on cheerfully: " Anyway, those chaps have been taken down a peg or two this time ! " But then, with a movement quite tremulously impatient, he replaced his *pince-nez* and with much relish read over again to Ulrich all the particularly satisfactory passages in the edict issued by His Imperial-Royal Majesty's Governor in Trieste.

" ' Repeated warnings from the authorities have been issued, without avail . . . harmful effect on our peoples. . . . In view of obstinate persistence in this antagonistic attitude to governmental decisions the Governor of Trieste is now faced with the necessity of taking action to ensure observance of existing regulations for the maintenance of law and order . . .' That's a dignified tone. don't you agree ? " he said, breaking off. He raised his head, but instantly lowered it again, for he was all eagerness to get to the concluding paragraph, which he read aloud with an aesthetic satisfaction that underlined its portentous official dignity: " ' Furthermore,' " he read, " ' the Governor has, of course, the right to give careful and sympathetic consideration to each individual case in which application for naturalisation may be made by such public officials, in cases where especially long public service, with an unblemished record, justifies such consideration, and indeed the trend in such cases is for His Majesty's Governor to avoid any immediate enforcement of these regulations while reserving his full right to do so at any such time and in any such circumstances as he may think fit.' That's the tone the Government ought to have taken all along ! " Count Leinsdorf exclaimed.

" Don't you think, sir, this final paragraph suggests that in the end it'll all just stay the way it's always been ? " Ulrich asked after a little pause, when the tail-end of the officialese serpentine sentence had finally vanished inside his ear.

" Yes, that's just it," His Highness replied, beginning to twiddle his thumbs the way he always did when some difficult speculative process was going on within him. Then he gave Ulrich a searching look and opened his heart to him. " You remember, at the opening of the Police Exhibition, the Minister of the Interior spoke of the imminence of a spirit of collaboration and severity ? Well, I'm not asking them to go so far as to take all those agitators who made that rumpus on my doorstep and lock them up, but," he said in a pained tone, " the Minister ought at least to have found it in himself to speak a few dignified words in Parliament in condemnation of such behaviour."

" I thought that had been done while I was away ? " Ulrich exclaimed with feigned astonishment, for he perceived that his benign paternal friend was suffering genuine distress.

" Nothing's been done ! " His Highness said. Once again he fixed his worried, protuberant eyes on Ulrich's face with a searching look and then opened his heart further: " But something is going to be done ! " He straightened up and leaned back in his chair, shutting his eyes as he relapsed into silence.

When he opened his eyes again, he began in a calmer tone to explain: " You see, my dear fellow, our Constitution of 1861 entrusted the leadership in the new, experimental political scheme of things to the German minority and, within that minority, to the sections representing Capital and Culture. That was a munificent gift of His Majesty's, a proof of his generosity and confidence . . . But perhaps not quite in keeping with the times. For what has become of Capital and Culture since then ? " Count Leinsdorf raised one hand and then dropped it with a resigned air on the other. " When His Majesty ascended the throne in 1848, at Olmütz, which is to say, practically in exile—" he went on slowly, but he suddenly grew impatient or uncertain, with trembling fingers fished a sheet of notes out of his pocket, struggled in some agitation to get his *pince-nez* settled on his nose, and read aloud, his voice sometimes quavering with emotion, while he strenuously endeavoured to decipher his own handwriting, as follows: "—he was surrounded by the uproar of the nations' wild urge for freedom. He succeeded in quenching this exuberance. Finally, even if only after some concessions to the wishes of his peoples, he stood triumphant, not only the victor but a victor who was merciful and gracious, forgiving his subjects for the error of their ways and stretching out his hand to them with the offer of a peace equally honourable to them. Though the Constitution and the other rights and liberties were granted by him under the pressure of circumstances, it was nevertheless an act of free will on His Majesty's part, the fruit of his wisdom and compassion and hope in the progressive civilisation of his peoples. But in recent years this fair relationship between Emperor and people has been tarnished by the activities of rebellious, demagogic elements——" Count Leinsdorf at this point broke off the reading of his exposition of political history, in which every word had been scrupulously weighed and every phrase polished, and gazed pensively at the portrait of his ancestor, the Marshal, Knight of the Order of Maria Theresa, on the wall facing him. And when at last he felt Ulrich's expectant gaze, he turned back to him and said: " That's as far as it goes for the present."

" But you can see," he went on, " I have been carefully pondering these problems recently. What I have just read to you is the beginning of the answer that the Minister would have given to Parliament in the matter of the demonstration directed against me if he had properly fulfilled his function. I've been gradually working it out for myself, and I don't mind telling you that I shall have the opportunity to put it before His Majesty as soon as I have it finished. For, you see, it was not for nothing that the Constitution of 1861 entrusted the leadership to Capital and Culture. That was intended as a guarantee for the future. But where are Capital and Culture now ? "

He seemed to be very angry with the Minister of the Interior, and in order to take his mind off that Ulrich remarked ingenuously that one could at least say of Capital that nowadays it was not only in the hands of the bankers but also in the well-tried hands of the landed aristocracy.

" I've nothing at all against the Jews," Count Leinsdorf declared suddenly, as though Ulrich had said something requiring this *démenti*. "They're intelligent, industrious, and reliable. But it was a great mistake to give them unsuitable names. Rosenberg and Rosenthal, for instance, are aristocratic names. Lyon and Wolfe and similar creatures are originally heraldic beasts. Meyer comes from land-owning. Silver and Gold are armorial colours. The whole of these Jewish names," His Highness disclosed rather surprisingly "were nothing but a piece of impertinence on the part of our bureaucracy, aimed at the nobility. It was the nobility that was being got at and not the Jews, and that's why the Jews were given other names as well, like Bloom, Popper, and Finkelstein. This animus our bureaucracy has always had against the old nobility is something you would observe by no means seldom even today, if you went behind the scenes," he said oracularly, with a gloomy and stubborn expression, as if the central administration's fight against feudalism had not long been overtaken by history and completely vanished from the sight of the living. And in fact there was nothing His Highness could feel such pure and impersonal annoyance about as the social privileges that high civil servants enjoyed by virtue of their position, even when they were no more than plain Herr Schmidt or Herr Müller. Far from being a die-hard backwoodsman, Count Leinsdorf endeavoured to move with the times, and such names caused him no distress when they belonged to a member of Parliament, even a Cabinet Minister, or to an influential gentleman of independent means; nor did he ever object to the political and economic weight carried by the middle classes; it was the high-ranking civil servants with middle-class names that roused him to ire, this reaction being a last vestige of ancient and venerable traditions.

Ulrich wondered whether what was at the bottom of Count Leinsdorf's remarks was not perhaps his own cousin's husband; indeed, it was not impossible. However, Count Leinsdorf went on talking and was, as always happened, soon carried away above all personal feelings by an idea, one which had obviously been preoccupying him for some time.

"The whole so-called Jewish question would disappear in a twinkling if the Jews would only make up their minds to speak Hebrew, go back to their old Hebrew names, and wear Oriental garb," he declared. "Frankly, a Galician Jew who has just come and made a fortune in Vienna doesn't look quite the thing, on the Esplanade at Ischl, got up in Tyrolean costume, with a chamois-tuft in his hat. But just put him in a long flowing robe, as costly as you like so long as it covers the legs, and you'll see how admirably his face and the great sweep of his temperamental gestures go with such a style of dress ! All the things that people make jokes about now would be in their proper place—including the expensive rings they like to wear. I am opposed to assimilation of the kind the English nobility practise. It's a tedious and uncertain process. But give the Jews back their true character, and you'll see what a gem they turn out to be, positively an aristocracy of a rare and different kind among the peoples gratefully thronging round His Majesty's throne—or if you'd rather picture the thing in everyday terms, quite clearly, pacing along our Ringstrasse, which is unique in the world because there in the midst of the highest degree of west-European elegance one may also see a Mohammedan in his red fez, a Slovak in his sheepskin, or a bare-legged Tyrolean."

At this point Ulrich could not help expressing his admiration for His Highness's perspicacity, saying that it had also been reserved for him to discover the ' true Jew '.

" Yes, you know, the true Catholic Faith educates one to see things as they really are," the Imperial Liege-Count benevolently explained. " But you would never guess what put me on the track of it. It wasn't von Arnheim—I'm not concerned with the Prussians for the moment. But I have a banker, of the Mosaic faith of course, whom I've been seeing regularly for years. And at first his intonation always used to bother me a bit, so that I couldn't quite keep my mind on the business in hand. The fact is, the way he talks is exactly as if he were trying to convince me he's my uncle. I mean it's just as if he'd only got out of the saddle a moment earlier or had just come in from a day's grouse-shooting, exactly the way our own sort of people talk, if I may put it that way. Well, to cut a long story short, now and then when he's carried away he can't keep it up, and then, to make no bones about it, he falls into a very marked Jewish sing-song. It used to bother me a great deal, as I think I said before, because, the point is, it always happened at the most important moments from the business point of view, so that I couldn't help waiting for it, and

finally I became quite incapable of paying attention to what he
was saying or else simply believed I was listening to something
important the whole time. But then I found the way to get
round it. Every time he began to talk like that, I simply said to
myself: Now he's talking Hebrew. And I only wish you could
have heard how attractive it sounded! Positively enchanting.
The point is, it's a liturgical language. Such a melodious chant-
ing—I'm very musical, you know—in a word, from then on he
had me lapping up complicated calculations in compound interest or discount positively as if he were at the piano singing it
to me."

And for some reason Count Leinsdorf smiled in a melancholy
manner.

Ulrich permitted himself the remark that those distinguished
by this benign and sympathetic interest on His Highness's side
would in all probability reject his suggestion.

" Oh, of course they won't want to ! " the Imperial Liege-Count
said. " But then they'd just have to be made to, for their own
good ! It would amount to no less than a world mission for the
Empire, and in such a case whether at first the other chap *wants*
it isn't the point. You know, people have often had to be forced
at the beginning for their own good. But just think what it
would mean if later on we had an alliance with a grateful Jewish
State instead of with Germany and the Prussians ! Especially
seeing that our Trieste is, in a manner of speaking, the Hamburg
of the Mediterranean, apart from the fact that it would make us
diplomatically invincible to have not only the Pope on our side but
the Jews as well ! "

Unexpectedly he added: " The fact is, I'm now looking into
currency questions too." Once more he smiled, a strangely
mournful and absent-minded smile.

It was remarkable that His Highness had repeatedly urged
Ulrich to call on him and now, when Ulrich had at last come, did
not touch on the problems of the day, but was extravagantly
strewing his ideas before him. However, the explanation was
probably that while he had been deprived of his confidant a great
many ideas had sprung up in his mind; and they seemed to be as
restless as bees, which go buzzing out a long way but are sure to
return in their own good time laden with their honey.

" You would be quite justified in reminding me," Count Leinsdorf admitted, although Ulrich had said nothing, " that on previous occasions I've often expressed downright dislike of finance.
I'm not going to deny it. For too much of a thing is of course
always a bad thing, and we have too much finance in modern life.
But that's the very reason why we must take an interest in it !
You know, Culture hasn't been pulling its weight alongside
Capital—there you have the whole secret of developments since
eighteen-sixty-one. And that's why we must take an interest
in Capital." He made an almost imperceptible pause, just long
enough to convey to his listener that now he was coming to the
mysteries of Capital; but then he went on in a sombrely confidential
tone: " The most important thing about a liberal education, you
see, is what it makes impossible: certain things don't go with it,
and that's that. A man of education, a man of culture, will for
instance never eat gravy with his knife. Heaven knows why !
It's not as though he learnt it at school. That's where breeding
comes in, and that's based on the existence of a privileged class
to which what we call Culture looks up—an example to Culture—
in short, if I may say so: an aristocracy. I admit that our own
aristocracy hasn't always lived up to this. And here we come to
the meaning of the downright revolutionary experiment of the
1861 Constitution: Capital and Culture were meant to make
common cause with the aristocracy. But were they capable of
doing it ? Were they able to make good use of the great opportunity that His Majesty, in his graciousness, held out to them?
And I'm sure you won't assert that our experiences, arising week
by week out of your cousin's great experiment, are in keeping
with such hopes ! " His voice became livelier again as he exclaimed: " You know, it's really very interesting what sets up to
be the mind these days ! I was talking to His Eminence the Cardinal about it recently, out with the guns at Mürzsteg—no, it was
at Mürzbruck, at Hostnitz's girl's wedding—and he clapped his
hands together and just laughed. ' Always ringing the changes ! '
that's what he said to me. ' There you see how unassuming we
are,' he said, ' telling people the same old thing for nearly two
thousand years ! ' Now that's very true. The main thing about
faith is to keep on believing the same thing all the time—that's the
way I'd put it even if it is heresy. ' You know,' he said, ' I always

go out with the guns because my predecessor in the days of Leopold of Babenberg always followed the chase too. But I never kill,' he said—he's a by-word for never firing a shot when he's out for a day's shooting—' because there's an inner repugnance tells me it's not in keeping with my cloth. And I don't mind saying that to you, my dear boy, because we've known each other since we went to dancing-class together as little chaps. But I'm not going to get up in public and say: Thou shalt not shoot when out shooting! The Lord alone knows whether it would be right, and anyway it's no part of the Church's doctrine. But the people who forgather at your charming friend's place make a public pronouncement about a thing like that the very instant it pops into their heads—and there you have what's called the mind nowadays!' It's all very well for him," Count Leinsdorf went on, now speaking for himself, "his office is perpetual and unchanging. But we laymen have the onerous office of finding good even in perpetual change. I said as much to him. I asked him: ' Why has God permitted literature and painting and all that sort of thing to exist at all, when we find them such a bore?' And he gave me a very interesting explanation. ' You've heard about psychoanalysis, haven't you?' he said to me. I didn't quite know what I was supposed to say. ' Well,' he said, ' you may be going to say it's all just piggery. We needn't argue about that. It's what everyone says. And yet they all go rushing off to these new-fangled doctors, far more than they come to our Catholic confessional. Take it from me, they rush after it in throngs because the flesh is weak. They go in for talking over their secret sins because they thoroughly enjoy it, and if they run it all down—well, you know the saying, you always pick holes in the thing you mean to buy. But I could easily prove to you that what their atheistical doctors think they've invented is nothing but what the Church has been doing from her very beginning. You can see how it corresponds to the ritual of exorcism right down to the details, for instance when with their own methods they get the possessed person to start and talk about what's there inside him. According to the Church, too, that's precisely the turning-point when the Devil first shows signs of rushing out. It's only that we haven't kept up with the changing needs of the time, instead of talking about filthiness and the Devil we ought to have been calling it psychosis, the unconscious, and all that sort of up-to-date claptrap.' That's very interesting, don't you think?" Count Leinsdorf asked.

"But what comes next is perhaps even more interesting. ' Still,' the Cardinal said, ' don't let's talk about the flesh being weak, the point is the spirit is weak too, the mind is weak! And that's where the Church was clever enough to look out for herself. You see, people aren't half as frightened of the Devil that enters their body—even if they make a show of fighting against him— as of the illumination that comes to them from the spirit. You haven't studied theology,' he said to me, ' but at least you feel respect for it, and that's more than any secular philosopher in his blindness succeeds in doing. Take it from me, theology is a very difficult thing. It's so difficult that when someone has put in fifteen years at it, and nothing less, he only begins to realise that he doesn't really understand a single word of it! And of course nobody'd have faith if they knew how difficult it is really. They'd all just run us down. They'd start picking holes in us—you see what I'm getting at?' he said slyly, ' exactly the way they pick holes in the others now, the ones that write their books and paint their pictures and trot out theories. And it's with a joyful heart that we leave them plenty of rope in their presumption, for, let me tell you: the more seriously one of those fellows sets about things—the less he provides mere entertainment, just looking after his own pocket, the more, in other words, he serves God in his erring way, the more of a bore he is to people and the more they pick holes in him. That's not what life is like! they say. But *we* know, after all, what true life is, and we'll show them, too, and because we don't mind waiting, you may still see the day when they come tearing back to us, in a rage at all that futile cleverness. You can see it going on in our own families even now. And in our parents' day, God knows, they thought they were going to turn Heaven itself into a university! '

"I wouldn't go so far," Count Leinsdorf said, concluding this part of his exposition and starting on a new one, " as to say he meant it all literally. The Hostnitzes at Mürzbruck happen to have a celebrated Rhine wine that General Marmont left behind and forgot in eighteen-five when he had to march on Vienna in such a hurry, and they brought some of it out for the wedding. But in the main I'm sure the Cardinal hit the nail on the head. And when I ask myself now how I ought to look at it, all I can say is: it's undoubtedly right, but it doesn't quite seem to work out. That's to say, there can't be any doubt that these people we've been asking to our meetings all the time, because we're told they represent the spirit of our age, have nothing to do with real life, and as for the Church, she can well afford to wait. But we civilian politicians can't wait, we must get on and squeeze the good out of life as we find it. After all, man doesn't live by bread alone, but by the soul as well. The soul is, as it were, what he needs in order to digest the bread properly. So what must be done is——" and here Count Leinsdorf declared his opinion that politics must spur the soul on.

"What I mean——" he said, "something must be done. The times cry out for it. That's the feeling that, as you might say, everyone has nowadays, not only the politically-minded. The times have a sort of interim character that nobody can stand indefinitely."

He had formed the theory that the tremulous balance of ideas, on which the no less tremulous balance of European power rested, must be given a push.

"It's almost irrelevant what sort of a push!" he assured Ulrich, who declared in mock dismay that since they had seen each other last His Highness had practically become a revolutionary.

"And why not?" Count Leinsdorf retorted, somewhat flattered. "His Eminence was naturally also of the opinion that it would be at least a small step forward if His Majesty could be persuaded to put somebody else into the Ministry of the Interior. But in the long run such small reforms don't have much effect, however necessary they may be. Sometimes, do you know, in the course of my present reflections, I actually find my thoughts turning to the Socialists!" He gave his companion time to recover from the amazement he assumed to be inevitable, and then went on resolutely: "Believe me, real Socialism wouldn't be nearly as terrible as most people seem to think. I dare say you will object that the Socialists are republicans. True, one simply mustn't listen to the things they say, but if one looks at it in the light of practical politics, one almost feels that a social-democratic republic with a strong monarch at its head might be a far from impossible form of government. For my own part, I'm sure that if one were to go just a little way to meet them, they'd gladly give up the idea of using brute force and all the rest of their objectionable principles. As it is, they're already inclined to modify their idea of the class struggle and their hostility to private property. And there really are men among them who still put Country before party, whereas since the last elections the middle-classes have become completely radicalised in their conflicting national interests. Which brings us to the Emperor," he went on, lowering his voice confidentially. " As I was trying to show you just now, we must learn to think in economic terms. The one-sided policies of our various national minorities have brought the Empire to the brink of ruin. Now, so far as the Emperor himself is concerned, all this tuppenny-ha'penny liberty-mongering of the Czechs and the Poles and the Italians and the Germans—well, I don't know quite how to put it—you might say: he doesn't care tuppence. What His Majesty does care about is that the defence estimate should go through without reduction so that the Empire may be strong, and apart from that he has a hearty dislike of all the pretensions of the middle-class intelligentsia, a dislike that probably goes back to 'forty-eight. But with these two feelings His Majesty is of course simply in a manner of speaking the First Socialist in the land. I dare say by now you see for yourself the magnificent vista I have in mind! Which leaves us only with the question of religion, where there's still an unbridgeable gap, and that's something I need to have another talk about with His Eminence."

His Highness sank into silence, absorbed in his conviction that history, and particularly that of his own country, having got bogged down in barren nationalism, would soon be compelled to take a step forward into the future—whereby he pictured the spirit of history as being to that extent two-legged, though for the rest as a philosophic necessity. So it was understandable that when he surfaced again it was suddenly and with bleary eyes, like a diver who has gone down too deep.

" Be that as it may, we must be prepared to do our duty ! " he said.

" And where do you see our duty as lying at the present moment, sir ? " Ulrich asked.

" Where do I see our duty as lying ? Simply in doing our duty !
That is the only thing one can always do ! But, to talk of something else——" Count Leinsdorf seemed only now to remember
the pile of newspapers and files on which he had brought his fist to
rest. " It's like this; what the people want today is a strong hand.
But a strong hand needs a sweet voice, or else the people won't put
up with it these days. Now you, you yourself, are I think very
gifted in that respect. What you were saying for instance that last
time, before you went away, when we were all gathered together
at your cousin's, if you recollect, about how what we really ought
to do now is set up a central committee for salvation to bring it
into line with our temporal accuracy in rational thinking—well, of
course it wouldn't be all that easy to manage, but His Eminence
laughed heartily when I told him about it. Fact is, I rubbed it in
a bit, as they say, and even if he always does make fun of things, I
can always tell whether his mockery comes from the spleen or from
the heart. What it comes to is that we absolutely can't do without
you, my dear fellow . . ."

Whereas all Count Leinsdorf's other pronouncements that day
had had the character of complicated dreams, the wish he now
expressed—that Ulrich should make an ' at least provisionally
definitive ' renunciation of his intention of resigning the honorary
secretaryship of the Collateral Campaign—was so definite, and so
directly aimed, and Count Leinsdorf laid his hand on Ulrich's
arm in a way so suggestive of a surprise manoeuvre that Ulrich
could not help getting the slightly disturbing feeling that the
previous elaborate harangues had been far more cunningly contrived than he had surmised, and intended solely to put him off his
guard. At this moment he was rather annoyed with Clarisse, who
had got him into this situation. But since he had on her behalf
appealed to Count Leinsdorf's kind-heartedness at the first
instant when there was a lull in the conversation, and since the
benevolent nobleman, who only wanted to go on talking, had
immediately and most kindly fallen in with his wishes, he had no
choice now but, however reluctantly, to repay one good turn with
another.

" And by the way, I've heard from Tuzzi," Count Leinsdorf
said, pleased with his success, " that you may decide to have a man
from his office to take all the tiresome work off your hands.

'Excellent,' I said to him, 'so long as he himself stays on!'
After all, the man you'll be supplied with is under official oath,
so that's all right.   My own secretary, whom I'd gladly have put
at your disposal, is, I'm sorry to say, a perfect fool.   It's only
strictly confidential matters that I think we shouldn't let him see,
don't you agree?   After all, he'll be Tuzzi's man, and that has
got its slight drawbacks, hasn't it?   For the rest, do take it easy
from now on, be sure to take it easy!" His Highness said in
gracious conclusion of this successful interview.

21   *Cast all thou hast into the fire, even thy very shoes.*

DURING all this time, from the moment when she had remained
behind alone, Agathe had been living in a state of utter relaxation,
without any sort of social contact, her will as it were suspended in
unworldly melancholy: it was like being at a great height, where
there was nothing to be seen but the wide blue sky.   Every day
she went for a stroll through the town, just for the pleasure of it;
when she was at home, she read; she attended to her affairs; and
this mild and trivial business of living was something she experienced with grateful enjoyment.   There was nothing pressing upon
her, no clinging to the past, no straining for the future.   Whenever
her glance fell on one of the objects around her, it was as though she
were trying to coax a young lamb to her: either it came gently
nearer and nearer to her, or it simply took no notice of her at all;
but at no time did she consciously set her mind to trying to grasp
it with that inner movement of mere cold understanding which
has something of violence in it and something of futility as well,
since it scares off the happiness that lies in the things.   And so it
seemed to Agathe that everything around her was much more
intelligible than usual.   But what mainly occupied her mind was
still her talks with her brother.   Having an unusually exact
memory, which did not deform its contents by any sort of prejudice

or wishful thinking, she was able to conjure up again the living words, the little surprising cadences of the voice and the gestures accompanying the talk; but they came to her more or less at random, more or less as they had been before she had quite understood them and realised what they were driving towards. Nevertheless it was all in the highest degree meaningful. Her memory, which had so often been troubled by remorse, was now full of quiet affection, and in a caressing way the time that had just passed clung close to the body's warmth, instead of being lost, as so often happened, in the freezing darkness that waits for what has been lived in vain.

And, thus veiled in invisible light, Agathe also dealt with the lawyers, notaries, brokers and agents who now played a part in her affairs. She met with no difficulties anywhere; everyone was glad to oblige the charming young woman whose father's name was in itself a recommendation. In all this she acted, fundamentally, with as much sureness as detachment; what she had determined on was clear to her, but, as it were, outside herself, and the experience she had accumulated in the course of her life—likewise something distinct from her own personality—went on working away at that resolution like a steady labourer who knows how to make his job easy for himself. That she was on the way to committing a felony—the aspect of her actions which would have been the most apparent to any outsider—simply did not impinge on her mind at all during this period. The integrity of her conscience excluded it. The radiance of conscience outshone that dark point, which nevertheless lay at the centre of it like the darker nucleus in a flame. Agathe herself did not know how to express it, but it was somehow like this: as a result of her intention she was in a state as aloof from that ugly intention as sky is aloof from earth.

The morning after her brother had left Agathe spent a long time considering her appearance: she had begun studying her face, her gaze having become fixed on her reflection in the looking-glass. She was seized as though by a compulsion, the way that sometimes, though one has not the least wish to walk on, one does walk another and yet another hundred paces towards some object that barely became visible from the point where one had really meant to turn back and where, after all, one did not turn. In this way she succumbed, quite without vanity, to the fascination of this landscape that was her own person there before her, separated from her not by distance but by a vapour of glass.   She considered her hair, which was still like bright velvet.   She opened the collar of her reflection's dress and slipped the dress off her reflection's shoulders.   In the end she undressed her reflection completely, surveying it right down to the rosy nails where the body tapers off into fingers and toes and scarcely belongs to itself any more. It was still all like the twinkling day that is only approaching its high noon: in the ascendant, pure, poised, and infused with that radiant morning energy which manifests itself in human beings or in young animals as ineffably as in a bouncing ball that has almost, but not quite, reached the highest point it will reach in the air.   'Perhaps it is passing through that point this very moment,' Agathe thought to herself.   The thought startled her.   But there was plenty of time ahead of her yet: she was only twenty-seven. Her body, never subjected to athletics or massage any more than to child-bearing and maternal cares, had been formed by nothing except its own organic growth.   If it could have been set down naked in some grand lonely scenery where Alpine ranges rear into the sky, the vast, infertile, billowing swell of those heights would have borne it like the statue of some pagan goddess.   In such a landscape noon does not pour down streamers of light and heat; it merely seems for a while to rise a little higher above its zenith and then to pass over imperceptibly into the sinking, floating beauty of the afternoon.   What came out of the looking-glass was the uncanny sense of that indefinable hour.

Now Agathe was struck by the thought that Ulrich too was letting his life go by as though it would last for ever.   'Perhaps it was a mistake that we didn't get to know each other only when we were old, old people,' she said to herself, with a melancholy picture of two banks of cloud mistily sinking earthwards at evening. 'They're not as splendid as the blazing noon,' she thought, 'but what do those two formless grey things care what human beings make of them!   Their hour has come, and it's just as soft as the most glowing hour there is.'   By now she had almost quite turned her back on the looking-glass, but some extravagant tendency in her mood all at once provoked her to turn round again, and she could not help laughing at the memory of two fat people taking the waters at Marienbad years ago, whom she had watched, sitting on one of those green benches and billing and cooing with what were obviously the tenderest and most exquisite of feelings. 'Their hearts are slim too, beating under all that fat, and being lost in their inner vision they have no notion what a joke they are to the outside world,' Agathe mused in self-reproach. Then she twisted her face into an ecstatic expression while she tried to swell her body out into stoutness and squash it into podgy folds. When this fit of exuberance had passed off, it looked just as if a few tiny tears of anger had risen to her eyes, and pulling herself together, she returned to a cool and exact scrutiny of her appearance.

Although she was slim she observed with some fascination the shade of a possibility that in time she might grow heavy. Perhaps the thorax was too deep. In the face the very white skin was dimmed by the golden hair, as though by candles burning in bright daylight; the nose stood out a little too far, and on one side its almost classical line was dented at the tip. Indeed it might well be that everywhere in the flame-like primal form a second form lay hidden, one that was broader and more melancholy, like a linden-leaf among twigs of laurel. Agathe became curious about herself, as though she were looking at herself properly for the first time. So it might well be that the men with whom she had had affairs had seen her, and she herself had known nothing at all of it. There was something slightly eerie about this feeling. But before she could call her memories to account for this, by some trick of the imagination she heard, behind all that she had experienced, the long-drawn, hankering love-call of the donkey, a cry that had always set up a strange excitement in her: it sounds infinitely foolish and ugly, but that is just the reason why there is perhaps no other heroism of love as disconsolately sweet as his. She shrugged her shoulders at life and turned back to her reflection with the firm intention of finding a point in it where it was already yielding to age. There were the little recesses by the eyes and ears that are the first to change, at first looking as though something had been using them to sleep on, or the inner curve under the breasts, which so easily loses its definition: at this moment it would have been a satisfaction to her, and a promise of peace to come, if she could have observed any such change, but there was still none to be perceived anywhere, and the loveliness of the body floated almost uncannily in the depths of the mirror.

At this moment it struck Agathe as really strange that she was Frau Hagauer. The difference between the distinct and dense relationship implicit in being that and the vagueness of inner relation between that and herself was so marked that she seemed to herself to be standing there bodiless while her body belonged to the Frau Hagauer in the looking-glass; and it seemed that it was up to *her*, Frau Hagauer, to cope with the body now, since it had bound itself to circumstances beneath its dignity. Even in this there was something of that flickering enjoyment of simply being alive which one is sometimes recalled to with a shock, and it reminded Agathe of something: the moment she was dressed again she went into her bedroom and began to look for a capsule that must be somewhere among her things. This little air-tight capsule which she had had almost as long as she had been married to Hagauer, and from which she was never parted, contained a minute quantity of a dun-coloured substance that she had been assured was a deadly poison. She recalled certain sacrifices she had had to make in order to obtain possession of this forbidden substance, but all she knew of the stuff itself was what she had been told of its effect and what it was called—one of those chemical names that sound like a magic formula and which the non-initiate are supposed to remember even though they do not know the meaning. Now obviously all the means of bringing one's end within easy reach, such as possession of poison or weapons or the seeking of dangerous adventures, go together with the romanticism of *joie de vivre*; and it may be that for most people life runs its course under such a sense of oppression, so waveringly, with so much darkness in the light, and altogether so topsy-turvily that the only way they can release the latent joy in it is by having at least the possibility of putting an end to it. So Agathe felt easier when her gaze lit upon the small metal object that appeared to her, in all the uncertainty now lying ahead of her, as a talisman and a token of luck.

Now this certainly did not mean that at this period Agathe already had the intention of killing herself. On the contrary, she feared death in exactly the way all young people do, as when, before falling asleep in bed at night, after a wholesomely spent day, it occurs to them: some day there'll be a day just as beautiful as this was, but I shall be dead—there's no escaping it. Nor does it by any means heightens one's desire to die if one has to watch someone else dying, and her father's death had left her with tormenting impressions, which returned with fresh horror since she had been left alone in the house after her brother's departure. But ' I am a little dead ' was a feeling that Agathe often had; and above all in moments like this, when she had just been so conscious of her young body's shapeliness and health, of this taut beauty that in its mysterious composition was just as groundless as the decomposition of its elements would be in death, she tended to slip out of a state of happy confidence into one of awe, amazement and silence: it was like leaving a noisy, crowded room and suddenly coming out under the glimmer of the stars. Despite a stirring within her of resolves for the future, and despite her satisfaction at having extricated herself from a life that had been a mistake, she now felt a little detached from herself. She was linked with herself only in some realm where all was obscure. Quite coolly she thought of death as of a state in which one was rid of all toils and delusions. She pictured it as a sort of being gently rocked to sleep: one lies in God's Hand, and this Hand is like a cradle or a hammock slung between two tall trees faintly swaying in the wind. She imagined death as being very tranquil and very tired, with no more willing or wanting, no more effort, free from any awareness and any thought: it must be like the pleasant slackness in fingers that have been clutching some last thing of this world, when sleep gently loosens their hold. This notion she had of death was of course a rather facile and casual one, typical of someone who did not much care for the exertions of living. After a while she noticed with amusement how reminiscent it was of having had the divan moved into her father's austere drawing-room to lie on, reading—the only change in the house that she had made on her own initiative.

Nevertheless, the thought of giving life up was far from being one that Agathe merely toyed with. It seemed to her profoundly credible that all this frustrating upheaval should be followed by a state of blissful repose, which she could not help imagining in rather corporeal terms. She felt it this way because she had none of that thrilling illusion that the world is something to be improved. Even now she was ready to dispose of her share in it, so long as this could be done pleasantly. Besides, in that extraordinary illness she had had on the border-line between childhood and girlhood, she had already had a peculiar encounter with death. Then there had been a scarcely measurable failing of her strength, a failure that seemed to infiltrate into every tiniest particle of time and yet as a whole to go on with irresistible rapidity, with more and more of her body apparently becoming detached from her and being annihilated. Yet keeping pace with this decline, this slipping away from life, there had been an unforgettable new striving towards some unknown goal, banishing from her illness all its unrest and anxiety. It had been a peculiarly rich state in which she was even able to exert a certain domination over the adults around her, while they became increasingly unsure of themselves. Possibly this advantage, which she had come to know under such impressive conditions, was the nucleus of her later faculty for spiritually withdrawing from a life in which, for some reason or other, the stimuli did not correspond to her expectations. But it is more probable that the reverse was the case. Probably that illness, which enabled her to escape the demands of school and home, was the first manifestation of her attitude to the world— an attitude that was, as it were, translucent, irradiated by the light of a feeling she had never identified. For Agathe felt herself to be of a spontaneous, simple temperament, warm, lively, and even gay and easily satisfied. She had indeed adapted herself good-naturedly to many very different kinds of circumstances; nor had she ever gone through that collapse into indifference that befalls women who cannot go on bearing their own disillusion. But even in the midst of laughter, or in the tumult of some sensual adventure that continued nonetheless, there lay the disenchantment that made every fibre of her body tired and nostalgic for something else, something that might best be described as nothingness.

This nothingness had a definite, even if indefinable, content. For a long time she had been in the habit of repeating to herself, on all sorts of occasions, Novalis's words: " What then can I do for my soul, which dwells within me like an unsolved riddle, granting the visible man the utmost licence because there is no way it can check him ? " But the flickering light of this utterance always went out as swiftly as it had come, like a flash of lightning that had illumined her only to leave her in darkness again. For she did not believe in the existence of a soul. To her such a belief seemed arrogant, as well as much too definite for her own indefinite being. But neither could she believe in the earthly Here and Now. To understand this rightly one must only bear in mind that this aversion from the earthly order, without compensating belief in a heavenly order, is something quintessentially natural. In every mind there is not only logical thought going on, with its austere and simple orderliness, which is a reflection of conditions in the external world; alongside it there is also affective thought going on, with a logic—if one can call it logic at all—of its own, which is appropriate to the peculiarities of the feelings, the passions, and the moods. The laws governing these two bear roughly the same relationship to each other as the laws of a timber-yard, where chunks of wood are hewn into rectangular shape and stacked ready for transport, bear to the dark interlacing laws of the forest with all their mysterious workings and rustlings. And since the objects of our thinking are far from being independent of the state our thinking is in, in every man these two modes of thought get mixed up with each other. And not only that: to a certain extent they can confront a man with two worlds—at least immediately before and after that ' first mysterious and indescribable instant ' which, as a celebrated religious thinker asserts, occurs in every sensory perception before vision and feeling separate and fall into the places we are accustomed to find them in: one of them a function extending into space and the other a mental attitude within the observer.

Anyway, whatever exactly the relationship may be between civilised man's experience of things and his feelings about things, everyone knows those exalted moments when that differentiation has not yet occurred: it is as though the waters had not yet been divided from the dry land, and the rippling waves of the emotions still ran out to the same horizon as the hills and dales forming the panorama of the objective world. It need not even be assumed that Agathe experienced such moments more often or more intensely than most people. But she did perceive them more vividly or—if one prefers it that way—more superstitiously; for she was always ready to believe in and yet of course not believe in the world, just as she had done ever since her schooldays, not giving up the habit even when she came into closer contact with masculine logic. In this sense, which has nothing to do with wildly irrational behaviour and whims, Agathe could, had she had more self-confidence, have claimed to be the most illogical of all women. But it had never occurred to her to see the ' averted ' feelings that she experienced as anything more than a private eccentricity of her own. It was only the encounter with her brother that brought about a transformation in her.

In these empty rooms, all hollowed out by the shadowiness of solitude, rooms that only a short time ago had been filled with talk and fellowship, penetrating to the innermost core of the soul, the distinction between physical separation and mental presence was gradually lost. And as the days glided by without anything to mark them, Agathe felt, more intensely than ever before, the peculiar stimulus of that sense of omnipresence and omnipotence which arises when the world of feelings begins to overlap that of sensory perceptions. Her attention now seemed to be not with the senses, but wide open somewhere deep within her heart, and nothing penetrated there but what was as luminous as the heart itself; and in spite of the ignorance of which she generally accused herself, it seemed to her now, remembering things that her brother had said, that she understood everything that mattered without having to reflect on it. And as in this way her spirit was so filled with itself that even the liveliest thought was tinged with the soundless floating quality of a memory, everything that came her way expanded into a limitless Now. Even when she did anything, all that happened was that a dividing-line disappeared from between herself the doer and the thing done, and the movement she made seemed to be the path along which the things came towards her of their own accord when she stretched out her arms to them. This mild power, this knowledge of hers, and the speaking presence of the world yet turned out, when she smilingly asked herself what she *was* doing, to be scarcely distinguishable from absence, helplessness, and a profound muteness of the spirit. With only a faint exaggeration of her sensations Agathe might well have said that now she had ceased to know where she was. On all sides she was in some kind of suspension where she felt at once exalted and as though vanished. She might have said: I am in love, but I don't know with whom. She was filled with a clear will that was just what she had always felt she lacked; but she did not know what to set about doing in this clarity of will, for all her life had held of good and evil was now meaningless.

So it was not only while she gazed at the capsule containing the poison, but every day, that Agathe thought of how she would like to die or that the bliss of death must be like the bliss in which she was passing these days, waiting to go and join her brother and meanwhile doing precisely what, before leaving, he had besought her not to do. She could not picture what it would be like when she arrived at her brother's place in the capital. Almost reproachfully she recalled that he had from time to time nonchalantly given signs of assuming that she would be a social success there and would soon find a new husband or at least a lover. And if there was one thing she knew, it was that it would not be like that! Love, children, happy days, light-hearted sociability, travelling, and a bit of artistic appreciation—the good life was so very easy, and she understood its appeal, and was not unsusceptible to it. But prepared though she was to regard herself as entirely useless, she nevertheless had all the born rebel's innate contempt for that sort of straightforward simplicity. She recognised the deception of it. The sort of life that is supposed to be a life lived to the full is in fact ' without rhyme or reason ': at the end—and truly at its real end, at death—it always lacks something. It is—she searched for an expression for it—like a jumble of things left in a pile, which no higher desire has put in order: in its fullness unfulfilled, the opposite of simplicity, merely a tangle that is accepted with the cheerfulness of habit. And suddenly going off at a tangent she thought: ' It's like a gang of strange children that you look at with conventional friendliness, filled with growing anxiety because you can't catch sight of your own anywhere among them.'

It calmed her to reflect that she had resolved to put an end to her life if after this last turn, which was now imminent, it should still not have become different. Like the fermentation in wine the expectation seethed in her that death and terror would not be the ultimate word of truth. She felt no need to think about this. Ulrich did feel such a need, and yielded to it gladly; but she was afraid of that, and her fear was aggressive. For she was never quite free of a haunting sense that everything that took such an intense hold on her was perhaps mere illusion. Yet even if it was illusion, there was a reality in it, however fluid and dissolved: or, perhaps, she thought, a sort of reality that had not yet become solid earth; and in one of those wonderful moments when the place where she stood seemed to melt into vagueness, it seemed possible to believe that somewhere behind her, in the space one could never see, God might be standing. She was startled by this excess. An awe-inspiring immensity and emptiness suddenly flooded her, a shoreless radiance obscured her spirit and set her heart pounding with fear. Her youth—readily given to such anxiety as inexperience makes natural—told her insinuatingly that she was in danger of encouraging the first symptoms of madness. She struggled to get away from that. Fiercely she reminded herself that of course she did not believe in God! And in fact she had not done so since she had been taught to do so: this was typical of the mistrust she felt for all she had been taught. There was nothing she was further from than that solidity of religious belief which gives people a sense of the supernatural or at least a moral conviction. But after a while, exhausted and trembling, she had to admit to herself once more that she had felt 'God' just as distinctly as a man standing behind her and laying a coat round her shoulders.

After she had thought about this enough and grown bold again, she discovered that the meaning of what she had experienced did not lie in that 'solar eclipse' which had befallen her physical sensations; its meaning was chiefly a moral one. A sudden change of her inmost condition and hence of all her relations to the world had for a moment given her that 'unity of the conscience with the senses' which she had hitherto known only in hints so faint that all it left in ordinary life was a trace of something disconsolate and mournfully passionate—and this regardless of whether she tried to act in a way that was good or in a way that was bad. It seemed to her this change had been an incomparable outpouring, which had emanated both from her surroundings and from herself, pouring into her surroundings, a simultaneity of some utmost significance apprehended and of the mind's almost complete passivity—for her mind scarcely detached itself from the material things around her. The things were penetrated by the sensations, and the sensations by the things, in a way so convincing that Agathe felt she had never before been touched by anything to

which she had applied the word 'conviction'. And this had
happened in circumstances that most people would think excluded
the possibility of being convinced.

So the significance of what she experienced in her solitude did
not really lie in the role that might be attributed to it psychologically, as some sort of indication of an excitable or dangerously
unstable personality. For it did not lie in the person at all, but
in something general, or perhaps rather in the association of the
person with that something general, an association that Agathe
not unjustifiably regarded as a moral one, in the sense that it struck
her—a young woman disappointed with herself—as though if she
could always live as in those exceptional moments, if she were not
too weak to endure their continuation, she would be able to love
the world and to accept her own part in it sympathetically: and
that this was the only way in which she could do it! Now she was
filled with passionate longing to get back into that state. But such
moments of greatest exaltation cannot be forced. And with the
clarity that a pale day takes on after the sun has gone down, as she
perceived the futility of her tempestuous efforts she realised that the
only thing she *could* expect, the thing indeed that she was waiting
for with an impatience that had merely been in hiding during
these solitary days of her, was the strange prospect that her
brother had once, half jokingly, defined as the Millennium. Probably he could just as easily have called it something else. What
counted, for Agathe, was simply the convincing and confident ring
of something that was on its way. She would not have gone so
far as to say this. Nor did she even know for sure whether it was
truly possible. She did not even know what it was. At this
moment she had again forgotten all the words her brother had
used to prove that behind what filled her spirit with sheer shining
mists there was a possibility extending far away to infinity. But
so long as she had been in his company she had simply felt as though
his words were conjuring up a land, not only in her mind, but
actually under her feet. The very fact that he often spoke of it
with irony, and indeed his alternating between coolness and
emotion—an alternation that had at first often confused her—
now in her loneliness gladdened her because it was a sort of pledge
that he really meant it—and this is an advantage that all unamiable
emotional states have over states of rapture. 'Probably I was

only thinking about death because I'm afraid he doesn't quite mean it ', she confessed to herself.

The last day that she had to spend on her own took her by surprise. All at once everything in the house was cleared out and tidied up, and all that remained was to hand over the keys to the old couple who were being pensioned off under the provisions of her father's Will; they were to go on living in the servants' lodge until the property was sold. She had decided not to go to a hotel; she meant to remain at her post until the time when her train left in the small hours. Everything in the house was packed and shrouded. One naked bulb was burning. A few crates were pushed together to serve as table and chair. She had had the cloth laid for dinner on the brink of an abyss, on a terrace of crates. Her father's old man-servant juggled his loaded tray through light and shadow; he and his wife had insisted on cooking a dinner in their own kitchen so that ' the young mistress ' should be properly looked after when she was having her last meal in her old home. And suddenly Agathe thought, slipping right out of the state of mind she had been in for the last few days: ' Can they possibly have noticed anything? ' It could well be that she had not destroyed all the sheets of paper on which she had practised imitating her father's handwriting in order to make changes in the Will. She felt cold terror, an awful nightmarish oppression weighing down her limbs, the mean terror of real life, which gives the spirit nothing but only takes away from it. At this moment she became passionately, intensely aware of her newly awakened desire to live. It rebelled violently against the possibility of her being prevented from doing so. Keenly she tried to read the servant's face when he came in again. But the old man, with his gingerly smile, went unsuspectingly to and fro, in a special silence and solemnity. She could not see into him any more than into a wall and did not know whether there was anything in him behind this blank silveriness. She too now felt an atmosphere of silence, solemnity, and mournfulness. The old man had always been her father's henchman, always ready to betray every one of the children's secrets to him as he discovered them. But Agathe had been born in this house, and all that had happened since was coming to an end today, and it moved her that she and he were here so solemnly and alone. She resolved to give him a small extra present of money, in sudden weakness deciding to say it was from Professor Hagauer, and she thought of this not out of cunning but rather as an act of atonement, in the hope of not omitting anything, although it was clear to her that it was as unnecessary as it was superstitious.   And before the old man came back again she took out her two tiny receptacles.   The one, the locket containing the portrait of her never-forgotten young beloved, she gazed at for the last time, wrinkling her brow, and then pushed it under the loosely nailed lid of a crate that was to go into storage indefinitely; it probably contained kitchen utensils or lamps, for she heard the clinking of metal upon metal as the locket fell as though from branch to branch of a tree.   And then she put the capsule containing the poison in the place where she had always worn the portrait.

'How old-fashioned I am!' she thought, smiling, as she did so.   'I'm sure there are things more important than love-affairs!' But she did not believe it.

At this moment it could just as little be said that she rejected the thought of entering into illicit relations with her brother as that she wished for it.   That was for the future to decide; and nothing in her present state of mind was definite enough to formulate such a question.

The bare boards of the crates, by which she sat surrounded, in the unshaded light seemed painted glaring white and deepest black, as though with greasepaint.   And there was, as it were, a similar tragic mask, lending something uncanny to an otherwise quite plain meaning, over the thought that here she was spending her last evening in the house where she had been born of a woman she had never been able to remember and of whom Ulrich had also been born.   An old, old memory crept upon her—clowns with dead-serious faces and weird instruments standing round her.   They began to play.   Agathe recognised it as a waking dream of her childhood.   She could not hear that music, but all the clowns were looking at her.   She told herself that at this moment her death would be no loss to anyone or anything, and indeed for herself it might mean no more than the outward con-clusion of an inner dying.   So she thought while the clowns sent their music high up to the ceiling, and she seemed to be sitting on a circus floor strewn with sawdust, and the tears trickled through her fingers. It was a feeling of utter fuility she had often known as a girl, and she thought: ' I suppose I'm still quite childish even to this day?' Yet that did not prevent her from also thinking, as of something looming immeasurably great through her tears, of how at their first reunion she and her brother had come face to face in clownish attire. ' What does it mean that whatever there is in me should have attached itself to my own brother, of all people?' she wondered. And suddenly she was really weeping. She could not have given any reason but that it was for the sheer pleasure of it, and she shook her head violently as though there were something inside that she could neither undo nor put together.

Still, she reflected in natural simplicity, Ulrich would certainly have the answer to all her questions. And she was still thinking of that when the old man came back into the room and was moved at beholding her emotion.

" Ah, dear dear, the young mistress . . . ! " he said, likewise shaking his head.

Agathe looked at him in bewilderment. But as soon as she realised the misunderstanding in this compassion—which was aroused by her appearance of childlike grief—her youthful high spirits returned.

" Cast all thou hast into the fire, even thy very shoes. When thou hast nought left, think not even of thy shroud, but cast thyself naked into the fire ! " she said to him.

They were ancient words that Ulrich had read aloud to her with enthusiasm. And the old man smiled over the grave and mellow lilt of the words that she uttered, her eyes sparkling through her tears—and, following the movement of his mistress's hand, which was intended to lighten his understanding by misleading him, looked at the high-piled crates, which formed something almost like a pyre. At the word ' shroud ' the old man had nodded comprehendingly, all readiness to follow even if the way that the words led seemed a little hard. But at the word ' naked ' he stiffened and when Agathe repeated her maxim his face petrified into the mask of the well-trained servant, conveying the assurance of neither seeing nor hearing nor judging.

In all the time he had served his old master, this word had never been uttered in his hearing; at the most the word had been ' undressed '. But young people were different nowadays, and he thought to himself that with them he would probably not be able to give satisfaction. With the peacefulness of evening, when work is done, he realised that his days of service were at an end.

But Agathe's last thought before leaving was: ' Would Ulrich really cast everything into the fire ? '

22 *From Koniatowski's critique of Danielli's theorem to the Fall of Man. From the Fall of Man to the emotional conundrum of the Sister.*

THE mental state in which Ulrich came out into the street, on leaving the Palais Leinsdorf, was rather like the down-to-earth sensation of hunger. He stopped in front of a placarded hoarding and satiated his hunger for bourgeois normality by taking in the announcements and advertisements. The hoarding was several yards square and covered with words. ' One would surely be justified in supposing,' it occurred to him, ' that precisely words like these, turning up everywhere all over the town, must have cognitive value.' They seemed akin to the clichés that the characters in popular novels utter in moments of crisis and high drama. ' You have never worn anything at once so flattering to the skin and so durable as your Topinam silk stockings ', he read. ' The Prince Goes Gay '. ' Saint Bartholomew's Night: Entirely New Production '. ' For Good Fun and Good Food: Come to THE LITTLE BLACK HORSE '. ' For Dashing Daring and Dancing: Come to THE LITTLE RED HORSE '. Next to this last he was struck by a party-political proclamation: ' Iniquitious Machinations ! ' It referred, however, not to the Collateral Campaign, but to the price of bread. He turned away and, a few steps farther on, looked into a bookshop window. ' The Great Writer's Latest Work ' he read on a cardboard notice placed by a row of fifteen copies of the one book. Opposite this notice, in the other corner of the window, was a companion-piece to it, drawing attention to another

work: ' Men and women readers alike are fascinated by LOVE'S
TOWER OF BABEL, by . . .'

' The " great " writer? ' Ulrich thought. He remembered
having read one book of his and having seen no reason why he
should ever read a second one; since then, however, the man had
become famous. And as Ulrich considered the shop-window of
the German intellect, he recalled an old joke dating from his army
days: ' Mortadella ' had been their nickname for an unpopular
general, after the popular Italian sausage, and if anyone asked the
reason, he got the answer: ' Half pig, half ass.'

Ulrich was just groping for a variant of this witticism when his
thoughts were interrupted by a woman's voice asking him:

" Are you also waiting for the tram? "

Only then did he become aware that he was no longer standing
at the bookshop window.

He had not realised that he had somehow moved on and then
paused again, this time at a tram-stop. The lady who made him
aware of this wore spectacles and was carrying a rucksack. She was
an acquaintance of his, one of the staff at the Astronomical
Institute and one of the few women who did important work in
this very masculine subject. He looked at her nose and at the
bags under her eyes, which the strain of unremitting intellectual
work had made look rather like gutta-percha dress-protectors.
Glancing down, he saw her short tweed skirt; glancing up, he
saw a black-cock feather in the green hat that shaded her learned
face. He smiled.

" Off into the mountains? " he asked.

Yes, Fräulein Dr. Strastil was going into the mountains for
the weekend ' to get right away from things '.

" What do you think of Koniatowski's paper? " she asked
Ulrich.

Ulrich offered no opinion.

" Kneppler'll be furious," she remarked. " But Koniatowski's
critique of Kneppler's deduction from Danielli's theorem is
interesting, don't you agree? What do you think of Kneppler's
deduction? "

Ulrich shrugged his shoulders dubiously. He was one of those
mathematicians, called logicians, for whom nothing was ever
' correct ' and who were constructing new foundations for their

science. But for him not even the logic of the logicians was entirely correct. If he had gone on with his work, he would have gone right back to Aristotle; he had his own views about that.

" Still, it seems to me Kneppler's deduction is not mistaken, but merely false," Fräulein Dr. Strastil pronounced. She might just as well have said that she considered the deduction mistaken, but nevertheless in its essential principles not false; she knew what she meant, but everyday language, in which words are not defined, is a medium in which nobody can express himself unequivocally. While she was making use of this holiday language, something seemed to be stirring under her countrified hat, something comparable to the timid haughtiness that must be aroused in a cloistered monk if he is incautious enough to come into contact with the sensual world of the laity.

Ulrich got into the tram together with Fräulein Dr. Strastil. He did not know why. Perhaps it was because Koniatowski's criticism of Kneppler was so important to her. Perhaps he wanted to talk to her about literature, of which she knew nothing.

" What are you going to do in the mountains ? " he asked.

She was going up the Hochschwab, she said.

" There'll still be too much snow up there," he cavilled. He knew the mountains. " It's too late to go up on skis, and too early to go up without."

" Then I'll stay down," Fräulein Dr. Strastil declared. " I once spent a weekend at the hostel on the Farsenalm, at the foot of the mountains. All I want is to get out into the country a bit."

The expression on the worthy astronomer's face as she uttered the word ' country ' provoked Ulrich to ask what she expected of the country.

Fräulein Dr. Strastil was sincerely indignant. She was capable of spending the whole weekend lying on the grass, without stirring. ' Just like a boulder ', she declared.

" That's only because you're a scientist," Ulrich objected. " A peasant would be bored."

Fräulein Dr. Strastil did not see that. She spoke of the thousands who poured out into the country every weekend, on foot, on wheel, or by boat.

Ulrich spoke of the flight from the land, of the way the peasants were attracted to the towns.

Fräulein Dr. Strastil cast doubt upon the naturalness of his feelings.

Ulrich asserted that apart from eating and making love the only natural thing was being comfortable—not going up mountains. The allegedly natural feeling that drove people to do such things was actually a sort of modern Rousseauism, a complicated and sentimental attitude.

He had not the feeling that he was putting it at all well. He did not really care what he was saying. He only went on talking because he had still not got to whatever it was that he wanted to get out of his system.

Fräulein Dr. Strastil cast a mistrustful glance at him. She could not make him out. Her great experience in thinking in abstract terms was not of the slightest use to her here; the ideas he seemed to treat as merely something to juggle with she could neither keep clear of each other nor really fit together; she surmised that he talked without thinking. The thought of the cock's feather in her hat was the one thing that gave her satisfaction as she listened, and she looked forward all the more to the solitude she was going out to seek.

At this moment Ulrich's glance lighted upon the newspaper held by the man sitting opposite him. In heavy type an advertisement began: " Questions of Our Time—Answers of Our Time." It might have been boosting a new orthopaedic arch-support or announcing a lecture: nowadays there was no way of telling. But Ulrich's thoughts suddenly jumped straight into the groove he had been wanting.

His companion was endeavouring to be objective. " I'm afraid," she said hesitantly, " I don't know much about literature. After all, how much time do people like us get for reading ? And perhaps I don't read the right things, either. But— for instance," she said, mentioning a popular name, " means a great deal to me. It seems to me if a writer can make us feel so intensely that's what one means by greatness."

However, since Ulrich had by now got all he needed from Fräulein Dr. Strastil's combination of an extraordinarily highly developed capacity for abstract thought with a notably retarded development of emotional understanding, he rose with alacrity, made a pointedly flattering remark to his semi-colleague and, adding that he had already gone two stops too far, quickly got out of the tram.

When he was down in the street, raising his hat to her once more, Fräulein Dr. Strastil remembered having recently heard disparaging remarks about the progress of his work, but she also felt some normal human emotion, at his parting words of flattery, and blushed—which, to her intellectual way of thinking, did not exactly raise him in her esteem.

But Ulrich now knew, though without knowing it quite consciously yet, why his thoughts were revolving round the subject of literature and what they had been after from the interrupted 'mortadella' association to his unconscious leading on of poor dear Dr. Strastil to confidences about her literary taste. After all, literature had ceased to be any business of his since he had written his last poem at the age of twenty. All the same, at that time he had written, in secret, fairly regularly, and had given it up not just because he had grown older or had realised that he was not sufficiently gifted, but for reasons that now, under the influence of immediate impressions, he would have liked to describe by some word that would convey a great deal of effort pouring out into emptiness.

For Ulrich was one of those book-lovers who do not want to read any more, because they feel that the whole business of writing and reading is a blight. 'If that rational woman Strastil wants to be " made to feel " ', he thought—'and she's quite right too! If I'd disagreed with her, she'd only have produced music as her ace of trumps ! ' (and as it often happens, this was partly a thinking in words, partly a musing that worked as a wordless argument in his mind), well then, if that rational woman Strastil wanted to be made to feel, it amounted to the same as what everyone wanted: what man wants is that art should move, overwhelm, entertain, and surprise him, that it should give him a whiff of noble thoughts, and, in short, really make him ' live ' something and itself be ' alive ', a living ' experience '. And Ulrich was far from rejecting that point of view. Somewhere at the back of his mind there was a thought that ended in a mingling of faint sentimentality and stubborn irony: ' Feeling is rare enough, anyway. To keep feeling at a certain temperature, to prevent it from cooling down, probably means safeguarding the warmth needed if any intellectual life is to be hatched out. And whenever a man is momentarily raised above the tangle of his rational intentions, which involve him with innumerable alien objects, whenever he is raised into a state entirely free from purpose—for instance, whenever he is listening to music—he is almost in the same biological state as a flower on which the rain and the sunlight fall.' He was ready to admit that there was a more eternal eternity in the mind's pauses and quiescence than in its activity; but here he had been thinking now ' feeling ', now ' experiencing ', and that implied a contradiction. For there were after all experiences of the will! There were experiences of action at the peak of intensity! True, one could probably assume that by the time each of them reached its highest point of radiant bitterness it had become sheer feeling. But didn't that bring one straight up against the contradiction that in its absolute purity the state of feeling was a quiescence, a dying away of all activity ? Or was it not a contradiction after all ? Was there some strange pattern in which the intensest activity was motionless at the core ? Here however it became apparent that this sequence of ideas was not so much a train of thought merely at the back of his mind as one that was actually unwelcome; for with a sudden stiffening of resistance to its sentimental turn Ulrich repudiated the whole attitude into which he had slipped. He was not at all minded to go in for musing on certain states of mind and, when he reflected on the subject of feeling, himself to fall a prey to feeling.

It instantly struck him that what he was getting at would best be described, without more ado, as the futile actuality or eternal momentariness of literature. Does literature get one anywhere at all ? Either it is an immensely long way round from experience to experience, leading back to its point of origin, or it is a quintessence of stimuli producing nothing definite of any kind. ' There's no one,' he went on thinking, ' who hasn't at some time or other got much greater sense of depth from a duck-pond than from the ocean, and for the simple reason that one has more opportunities of experiencing duck-ponds than oceans.' And it seemed to him it was the same in matters of feeling; and this was the plain reason why ordinary feelings were accounted the deep ones. For the preference given to the activity of feeling over the feeling itself, which is characteristic of all ' feeling ' people, like the wish to make feel and to be made to feel, a wish that is common to all those institutions that serve the cause of feeling, amounts to a demotion of the feelings, a depreciation of their essential nature in contrast with their fleeting existence as a state in the person affected, and hence to that shallowness, stunted development, and utter irrelevance for which there is no lack of example in the life of our time. ' Of course such a view must be repugnant,' Ulrich mentally continued, ' to all those people who feel as cosy in their feelings as a rooster in his feathers and even preen themselves in the thought that eternity starts all over again with every single " personality ".' He had a clear mental picture of an enormous topsy-turviness, one of positively universal human dimensions, yet he could not quite manage to express it in any way that would satisfy him— probably because it was all far too complex.

While he was occupied with these thoughts he was watching the trams going past, and waiting for one that would bring him back as near as possible to the centre of town. As he watched the people getting out and in, his trained eye played abstractedly with the technical patterns produced by welding and casting, rolling and bolting, processes of engineering and hand-finishing, of historical development and present-day achievement, out of which there had arisen the invention of this wheeled and mobile hut that was people's mode of transport. ' Then in the end a commission from the public transport corporation comes down to the tram-car factory and decides on the sort of wood to be used for the veneer, the colour of paint, the upholstery, the arrangement of arms on the seats and strap-hangers for the standing passengers, and the ash-trays, and all the rest of it,' he thought idly, ' and it's precisely these trivial details, and the red or the green colour of the box, and the way they can swing themselves up the step and on board, that for tens of thousands of people makes up what it means to them, all that is left, so far as they are concerned, of the genius that has gone into it—*that's* all they experience of it. This is what, for them, constitutes the tram's character, this is what makes it a fast or a dawdling tram, this is what makes them feel red trams mean home and blue ones are abroad. Such is the unmistakable odour of countless tiny facts which clings about the clothes the centuries wear.' So it was undeniable (and this suddenly hinged right on to what had been Ulrich's main current of thought) that to a very large extent even life itself simply poured away into trivial, meaningless actuality—or, to put it technically, that life's co-efficient of spiritual effectiveness was a very small one.

And suddenly, as he felt himself swinging aboard a tram, he said to himself: ' I must make Agathe really see that morality means subordinating every momentary state in our life to one single permanent state ! '

This idea had all at once presented itself to him in the form of a definition. But the highly polished, bevel-edged thought had been preceded and was followed by other notions, not fully developed and articulated, that set off its comprehensibility. What it amounted to was associating with the harmless occupation of feeling an austere conception and discipline—a severe hierarchy of values that appeared, vaguely foreshortened, in the far distance: feelings must either be functional or refer to a state of being (never yet adequately described) extending right to the last horizon and immense as the open sea. Should one call that an idea? Or should one call it a longing? Ulrich had to leave it at that, for from the moment his sister's name had occurred to him, her shadow had darkened his thoughts. As always when he thought of her, he could not shake off a sense of having shown himself, while in her company, in a frame of mind different from usual. He knew too that he passionately wanted to get back into that frame of mind. But what he remembered of it also filled him with shame at having been overstrung, having behaved ludicrously, frantically, no better than a man who in his drunken frenzy goes down on his knees in the presence of people whom he will not be able to look in the face next day. Considering how balanced and controlled the intellectual relationship between brother and sister was, this was a wild exaggeration, and if it was not completely unfounded, then probably it was no more than a reaction to feelings that had not yet taken on shape. He knew Agathe was bound to arrive in a few days, and he did nothing. Had she actually done anything wrong? One could of course assume that as her mood cooled off she would have gone back on it all. Yet a very vivid premonition told him that Agathe had not abandoned her intention. He could have tried to find out from her. Once again he felt he ought to write and warn her off it. But instead of taking the thought seriously even for an instant, he began to work out for himself

what might have brought about this extraordinary attitude of
Agathe's: it seemed to him it was an incredibly vehement gesture
meant to show her trust in him by putting herself in his power.
'She has very little sense of reality,' he thought, 'but a splendid
way of doing what she wants. Unpremeditated, one might say.
But just for that reason: un-cooled-off too. When she's angry,
she sees ruby-red!' He smiled indulgently and glanced around
at the other people in the tram. Every single one of them had
wicked thoughts, that was certain, and every single one of them
suppressed them, and none of them reproached himself unduly;
but no one else had those thoughts outside himself, in another
human being, so that they took on the enchanting inaccessibility of
a dream experience.

This was the first time since he had left his letter unfinished that
Ulrich faced the fact of no longer having to choose: he was already
in the state that he had been hesitating to enter. According to
its laws—he indulged himself in the overweening ambiguity of
calling them 'holy'—Agathe's error could not be repented of,
but only *made good* by things done afterwards—which, incidentally,
seemed to be in keeping with the original meaning of 'repentance',
which is after all not a traumatic state of mind but a purifying fire.
To make reparation to Agathe's inconvenient husband, or in-
demnify him, would mean nothing but undoing damage done, in
other words, merely that double and paralysing negation of which
ordinary good behaviour consists, which inwardly cancels itself out
into nothing. But reducing to nothing the hovering load of what
was to be done to Hagauer was only possible, on the other hand,
if one mustered up great feeling for him, and that could not be
thought of without dismay. So according to the logic that Ulrich
was trying to adjust himself to, all that could ever be made good
was something other than the damage, and he did not for a moment
doubt that this other was to be his and his sister's whole life.

'Putting it presumptuously,' he thought, 'this means: Saul did
not make good each single consequence of his earlier sins, he
simply became Paul!' To this peculiar logic, however, feeling
and conviction raised their habitual objection that it would in any
case be more civilised—and no detriment to later exaltations—if one
were first of all to straighten out accounts with one's brother-in-
law and only then give one's mind to the new life. The kind of

morality that so attracted him was after all not in the least suited
to the settling of money-affairs and the conflicts that arise out of
them.   On the border-line between that other life and every-day
life there must therefore necessarily arise contradictory and insoluble problems, which it was probably wiser not to let develop
even into border-line cases: it was best to clear them away from the
very start in the normal unimpassioned way that was the way of
decency.   But here again Ulrich felt it was impossible to take
one's bearings from the normal rules and conditions of goodness
if one wanted to press on into the realm of unconditional goodness.
The task imposed on him, that of taking the first step into the
uncharted country, apparently would not suffer any abatement of
effort.

His last line of defence was held by a strong aversion to the
fact that concepts such as ' ego ', ' feeling ', ' goodness ', ' the
other kind of goodness ', ' evil ', of which he had made a great
deal of use, were so subjective and at the same time such high-
falutin and rarefied generalisations that they actually befitted none
but the moral speculations of very much younger people.   He
fared as doubtless many of those who follow his story will fare:
he irritably picked out words and phrases, asking himself such
questions as: ' " Production and results of feelings " ?   What a
mechanical, rationalistic, psychologically unrealistic concept !
" Morality as the problem of a permanent state to which all
individual states are subordinate "—is that all ?   The inhumanity
of it ! '   If one looked at it with the eyes of a reasonable man, it
all seemed fantastically topsy-turvy.   ' The very essence of morality
rests on the important feelings always remaining constant,' Ulrich
thought, ' and all the individual has to do is to act in harmony with
them ! '

But just at this point the moving box that enclosed him, this
geometrical construction designed by the aid of set-square and
compass, stopped at a place where his eye, peering out of the body
of this modern means of transport and still involuntarily partici-
pating in its décor, lit on a stone column that had been standing at
the edge of the street since Baroque times; and the engineered
comfort of the rational artifact, all unconsciously taken for granted,
suddenly clashed with the invading passion emanating from the
statue's antiquated pose, which rather suggested a petrified belly-

ache. The effect of this optical collision was an uncommonly vehement confirmation of the ideas from which Ulrich had just been trying to escape. Could anything have demonstrated life's aimlessness more clearly than this chance spectacle? Without letting his taste take sides with either the Now or the Then, as is usual when such juxtapositions occur, his mind instantly felt that it was left high and dry by both the modern and the bygone age, and saw only the great demonstration of a problem that at bottom was probably a moral one. He could not doubt that the transience of whatever is regarded as style, culture, the trend of the time or attitude to life, and is admired as such, was a symptom of moral frailty. For all this, in the great framework of the ages, amounts to the same as, in the smaller framework of one's own life, developing one's faculties one-sidedly, dissipating oneself in diffuse extravagances, never getting the measure of one's own will, never achieving a complete personal form, and living in disjointed passions, doing now this, now that. And thus even what is called the changing or sometimes the progress of the ages seemed to him only a term for the fact that none of these experiments ever arrives at the rallying-point where all of them would unite and move on towards one all-comprehending conviction, which would be the precondition for steady development, permanent enjoyment, and the gravity that lies in great beauty, that gravity of which nowadays scarcely more than a shadow falls across life.

Naturally it struck Ulrich as preposterous arrogance to assume that everything should simply have amounted to nothing. And yet it was nothing. Existentially it was immeasurable, meaningfully it was confusion. At least, measured by its result, it was no more than that from which the spirit of the present day had evolved: in other words, precious little. While Ulrich was thinking all this, he nevertheless surrendered to this ' little ' with the sort of relish he might have felt if this had been the last meal from the table of life that his intentions permitted him.

He had left the tram-car and set off down a street that quickly brought him back to the centre of town. He felt as if he were coming up out of a basement. The streets were a-scream with gaiety and unseasonably ripe and full as though with the warmth of a summer day. The sweet toxic taste of soliloquy was no longer in his mouth; everything was communicative, right out in the sunlight. He paused at almost every shop-window. Those little bottles in so many colours, stoppered fragrances, those countless versions of nail-scissors: what a sum-total of genius there was to be found even in a beauty-parlour window! A glove-shop: what intricate processes, what inventions before a goat's skin was drawn on to a lady's hand, the beast's hide becoming more lady-like than her own hide! He marvelled at all the little things that people could not get on without, at the innumerable exquisite little trappings of good living, as though he were seeing them all for the first time. What a fascinating word that was, too: 'trappings'—the delightful little luxuries that ensnared one! And what happiness—this tremendous co-operative effort in living together! Not a trace was there now to be seen of the earth-crust of life, the unmetalled roads of passion, the—as he positively felt—*uncivilised* thing that the soul is! A bright and narrow beam, one's attention glided over a pleasure-garden of fruits, precious stones, fabrics, forms, allurements that opened their sweetly penetrating eyes in all the colours of the rainbow. Since at that period whiteness of skin was much prized and to be protected from the sun, there were already here and there some bright-coloured parasols hovering over heads in the crowd, laying silky shadows on pale feminine faces. And Ulrich's gaze was delighted even by the opaque golden beer of which he caught a glimpse in passing a glass-fronted restaurant, where the table-cloths were so white that in the angle of shadow they formed blue planes. Then the archbishop drove past: a gently rocking, heavy carriage with red and purple in its darkness; it must certainly be the archbishop's carriage, for this horse-drawn vehicle that Ulrich followed with his gaze was entirely ecclesiastical to behold and two policemen sprang to attention, saluting that minister of Christ without giving a thought to their own predecessor who had run a lance into His side.

He gave himself up to these impressions, which he had only a short while earlier been calling 'life's futile actuality', with such enthusiasm that little by little, as he satiated himself with the world, he began to react against it again and his earlier antagonism reasserted itself. Now Ulrich saw precisely where the weakness of his speculations lay. 'What on earth,' he wondered, ' in the face of all this self-glorification, is the point of looking for any other answer above, behind, or underlying it?! What sort of philosophy is that? An all-embracing conviction, a law? Or the Finger of God? Or, rather, the assumption that morality has hitherto lacked an 'inductive approach', that it's much more difficult to be good than has generally been thought, and that it will call for an immense co-operative effort similar to that in every kind of research? I assume there is no morality because it can't be deduced from anything stable, that there are only rules for the useless maintenance of transitory conditions; and I assume there is no profound happiness without a profound morality. At the same time it seems to me that thinking about it is an unnatural, pallid state of mind, and not at all what I want.' Indeed he might well have asked himself, much more simply: 'What have I taken upon myself?' And this was what he now did. But this question touched his sensibility more than his intellect, indeed, it stopped his thoughts and destroyed his characteristically keen delight in strategic plan-making before he had even quite formulated it. This question had been like a deep note resounding close to his ear, accompanying him; and then the note was ringing within him, only an octave deeper than everything else, and then in the end Ulrich was one with his question and seemed to himself like a strangely deep sound in the bright, hard, treble world, a sound with a wide interval on each side of it. And what then had he really taken on himself, what had he promised?

He thought hard. He knew that, even though it had been metaphorical, he had not been merely joking when he spoke of 'the Millennium'. If that promise was taken seriously, what it amounted to was the wish to live, by means of mutual love, in a secular condition so exalted that one could only feel and do whatever heightened and maintained that condition. That there were at any rate hints of such a disposition in human beings had been a certainty for him so long as he could remember. It had begun for him with 'the affair with the Major's wife', and though his subsequent experiences of it had not been many or great, they had always been the same in kind. If one summed it all up, what it more or less came to was that Ulrich believed in the 'Fall' of man and in 'Original Sin'. That is to say, he could just as easily have assumed that at some time or other there had been a fundamental change in man's basic attitude, a change somewhat similar to that which takes place in a person falling out of love: that person then doubtless sees the whole truth, but something greater has been torn to shreds, and truth is everywhere no more than, as it were, a fragment that has been left over and then patched together again. Perhaps it was indeed really the apple of ' knowledge ' that brought about this change in the spirit and thrust the human race out of its primal state, into which it could make its way back only after endless experiments and when it had grown wise through sin. However, Ulrich did not believe in such stories in their traditional form, but in the form in which he had discovered them for himself: he believed in them like a man doing calculations with the system of his feelings spread out before him and concluding, from the fact that not a single one of them could be justified, the necessity of introducing a fantastic hypothesis of a kind he could glimpse only vaguely, intuitively. That was no small matter ! He had turned over similar thoughts often enough before, but never yet had he been in a situation where he had to decide within a few days whether to take it in life-and-death earnest or not.

A faint sweat was breaking out under his hat and his collar, and the proximity of all these people jostling past him excited him. What he was thinking amounted to taking leave of most living relationships; he had no illusions about that. For nowadays one lives divided, with parts of oneself interlocked with other people; what one dreams is connected with dreaming as a thing in itself and with what others dream; what one does coheres in itself but is still more intimately connected with what other people do; and what one is convinced of is connected with convictions of which one personally holds only a very small part: so it is quite unrealistic to demand that one should try to act out of the fullness of one's personal reality. And he was the very man who all his life long had been penetrated with the belief that one must divide one's convictions, that one must have the courage to live in the midst of moral contradictions, because that is the price of all great achievement. Was he at least convinced of what he had just been thinking about the possibility and significance of another way of living ? By no means ! Still, he could not help his feelings going over to this, rather as though they now saw the unmistakable outlines of a fact for which they had been waiting for years.

Now, however, he had to ask himself what, if anything, entitled him to act like one who had fallen in love with himself and resolve never again to do anything that left the soul indifferent. It goes against the whole approach of the active life, the approach that comes naturally to everyone nowadays; and even though former ages, convinced of God's existence, were able to pursue such endeavours, it all subsequently passed away like the half-light of dawn when the sun grows stronger. Ulrich noticed an aura of seclusion and cloying sweetness about himself that was becoming steadily more repugnant to him. And so he strove to restrain his intemperate thoughts as fast as possible and told himself, though not quite sincerely, that the promise of a Millennium he had so oddly held out to his sister amounted, if regarded rationally, to no more than a sort of welfare work; for no doubt living with Agathe would require of him an effort of tenderness and selflessness that had hitherto been all too lacking in his life. He recalled, in the way one recalls seeing an unusually transparent cloud flitting across the sky, certain moments of their recent time together that had already been of such a character. ' Perhaps the substance of the Millennium is simply the increase of that force—which at first manifests itself only when two are together—into a sonorous communion of all?' he speculated in some embarrassment. Once again he sought his bearings in his own ' affair with the Major's wife ', which he now began thinking about. Leaving aside the delusions, the youthful infatuation in which the whole mistaken affair had originated, he concentrated all his attention on the compassionate sensations of goodness and adoration that he had been capable of at that time, in his solitude; and it seemed to him now that feeling trust and affection, or living for another person, must be a happiness such as would move one to tears, as beautiful as the lambent glow of day sinking into the peace of evening, and rather in the same way spiritually dim and reducing one to tears of boredom. For at moments his plan really began to seem rather comical, a bit like two elderly bachelors agreeing to set up house together, and such twitchings of the imagination made him feel how little the notion of a life of service and brotherly love was likely to offer him complete fulfilment. With a fair degree of objectivity he admitted to himself that from the very beginning there had been a large measure of the a-social in the relationship between Agathe and himself. Not only the business with Hagauer and the Will, but the whole emotional tone of their association was a pointer to something violent and there was no doubt that in their brother-and-sisterliness there was implicit not more love for each other than distaste for the rest of the world. 'No!' Ulrich thought. 'Trying to live for another person is nothing more or less than the bankruptcy of egoism, which then goes and opens a new shop next door, but this time with a partner!'

In fact, despite this brilliantly rounded observation, his inner exertion had already passed its highest point at the moment when he had been tempted to take the light vaguely filling him and contain it in a small earthly lamp; and now that it was apparent that this had been a mistake, his thoughts had already lost any urge to seek for a decision, and he readily let himself be distracted.

Not far from him two men had just collided, and they were shouting disagreeable remarks at each other as though on the verge of fisticuffs. He observed this with a revival of interest in his surroundings. And scarcely had he turned away from this when his glance collided with a woman's glance, which was like a luscious flower nodding on its stem. In that pleasant mood which is an equal mixture of feeling and extraverted attention, he noted that the ideal obligation to love one's neighbour was something to which real people had two ways of reacting: the first consisted of not being able to endure the human race, and the second made up for that by entering into sexual relations with one half of it. Without stopping to think, after a few paces he turned and followed the woman; it was no more than an automatic reaction to having met her gaze. Ahead of him he saw her figure under her dress like a big white fish quite close to the surface. He felt the masculine urge to harpoon that white fish and see it flap and struggle, and the urge was an equal blend of repugnance and desire. Various scarcely perceptible tokens made him certain that this woman knew he was prowling along after her, and that she approved of it. He tried to work out what stratum of society she belonged to, and guessed at the sort of middle-class milieu where it is difficult to define the exact position. 'Wholesale business? Civil Service?' he wondered. Several images arbitrarily loomed up, including even a chemist's shop: he almost sensed the pungently sweet smell that the husband brought home with him, the compact atmosphere of the home itself, now betraying nothing of the twitching gleam of a burglar's flash-light, which had only a short time earlier moved right through it. It was undoubtedly revolting, yet also dis-honourably alluring.

And while Ulrich continued to stroll along after the woman, rather afraid that she might stop at some shop-window and force him either to stumble stupidly past her or speak to her, there was still something undistracted and wide awake in him. ' I wonder what it actually is Agathe wants of *me* ? ' he said to himself for the first time. He did not know the answer. He vaguely assumed it must be rather like what he wanted of her, but his reasons for thinking so were purely emotional. Was it not really astounding how swiftly and unexpectedly it had all come about? She had been, for him, scarcely more than a childhood memory: the little else that he had known of her—for instance, the fact that she was Hagauer's wife—was on the whole not to his taste. Now too he recalled the peculiar hesitation, almost reluctance, with which he had approached his old home on arrival there. And suddenly an idea lodged in his mind: ' My feeling for Agathe is just imagina-tion ! ' In a man who consistently wanted something other than what he found around him—he began to think again seriously—in a man who constantly feels nothing but misliking and never attains to liking, the habitual benevolence and the lukewarm goodness of humankindness must have a tendency to disintegrate into a cold hardness and a mist of impersonal love floating above it. Seraphic love he had once called it. One might also (he thought) say: love without a partner. Or just as well: love without sex. People nowadays loved exclusively in sexual terms: like and like could not endure each other, and in the sexual conjunction people loved each other with growing resistance to the over-importance attached to that compulsion. But seraphic love was free from both of these defects. It was the love that was liberated from the counter-currents of social and sexual aversions. It could be sensed everywhere side by side with the cruelty of modern life, and one could truly call it the sisterly love of an age that had no room for brotherly love—so he said to himself, with a little jerk of irritation.

But although he had now come to this conclusion, alongside this and intermittently with it he went on dreaming of a woman who could never be attained at all. She floated in his mind like the late autumn days in the mountains where the air is almost as though drained of blood and dying, while the colours burn in the

highest intensity of passion. His inner eye saw the blue distances
vistas mysteriously without an end. He entirely forgot the real
woman who was walking in front of him; he was remote from all
desire and perhaps near to love.

He was distracted only by the prolonged gaze of another woman,
which was similar to the first woman's yet not so impudent and
voluptuous, but well-bred and delicate as a pastel stroke even while
making itself felt in that fraction of a second. He focused his
eyes and, in utter inner exhaustion, beheld a very beautiful lady
in whom he recognised Bonadea.

The glorious day had lured her out for a walk. Ulrich glanced
at his watch: he had been strolling along for only a quarter of an
hour, and no more than forty-five minutes had passed since he
had left the Palais Leinsdorf.

Bonadea said: " I'm busy today."

Ulrich thought: ' And so how long a whole day is, how long a
year—and what then of a resolution made for life ! '

It was beyond calculation.

23 *Bonadea or the relapse.*

SO it came about that Ulrich was soon afterwards visited by his
forsaken mistress. Their meeting in the street had neither given
him adequate opportunity to reproach her in the way he wanted
to for misusing his name in order to make Diotima's acquaintance,
nor given Bonadea enough time to reproach him for his long silence
and not only defend herself against the charge of indiscretion and
call Diotima a ' tactless, treacherous snake ', but also make up a
story to prove it. And so it was hurriedly agreed between her and
her ex-lover that they must meet once again to have it all out.

The woman who appeared was no longer the Bonadea who
coiled her hair until, gazing into the looking-glass with narrowed
eyes, she considered it gave her head a sufficiently Grecian look
and resolved to be just as pure and noble as Diotima; nor was she

the Bonadea who, in raving nights, shamelessly and with feminine ingenuity cursed her exemplar for this course of treatment intended to break an addiction; but it was once again the beguiling Bonadea of old, whose curls hung down over her not very intellectual brow or were swept back from it just as she felt fashion demanded, and in whose eyes there was always something reminiscent of the tremulous air above a fire. While Ulrich set about calling her to account for having betrayed their relationship to his cousin, she was at a looking-glass carefully removing her hat, and when he tried to find out exactly how much she had said, she described complacently and in detail how she had told Diotima a whole story about having had a letter from him asking her to see that Moosbrugger was not forgotten and how she had thought the best thing she could do was to go to the woman of whose high-mindedness the writer of the letter had often talked. Then she seated herself on the arm of Ulrich's chair, kissed his forehead, and meekly assured him that all this was quite true, after all, except for the bit about the letter.

A great warmth radiated from her bosom.

" And why then did you call my cousin a snake ? You've been one yourself ! " Ulrich said.

Bonadea thoughtfully turned her eyes away from him and looked at the wall. " Oh, I don't know," she answered. " She's so nice to me. She takes such an interest in me."

" What does that mean ? " Ulrich asked. " Are you now involved in her endeavours on behalf of the Good, the True, and the Beautiful ? "

" She explained to me," Bonadea replied, " that no woman can live for her love up to the limit of her resources, she just as little as I. And that is why every woman must do her duty in the place to which destiny has called her. You know, she's so frightfully decent," Bonadea went on, still more thoughtfully. " She keeps telling me I should be tolerant with my husband, and she says that a superior woman finds considerable happiness in mastering her marriage. She rates that far above any adultery. And actually, you know, it's what I've always thought myself."

And this really happened to be true: Bonadea had never thought otherwise, it was only that she had always acted otherwise. So she could with a good conscience agree. When Ulrich said as much to her, this earned him yet another kiss, this time somewhat lower than the brow.

" You're just disturbing my polygamous balance ! " she said with a little sigh of apology for the discrepancy between her ideas and her actions.

A fair amount of cross-questioning led to the discovery that what she had meant was ' polyglandular balance ', this being a physiological term that had recently come into currency among the initiate and which might be translated as balance of the secretions, on the hypothesis that there were certain glands having an effect on the blood whose stimulating or inhibiting action had an influence on the character and more especially on the temperament, above all the kind of temperament of which Bonadea in certain conditions had so much that it was a trial to her.

Ulrich raised his eyebrows in curiosity.

" Well, something to do with glands, anyway," Bonadea said. " It *is* a sort of relief to know one can't help it." She smiled wistfully upon her lover, now lost to her: " And if one loses one's balance easily, it just leads to unfortunate sexual experiences ! "

" My dear Bonadea," Ulrich said, marvelling, " what sort of talk is this ? "

" It's the way I've been learning to talk.   You are an unfortunate sexual experience, your cousin says.   But she also says a person can escape the shattering physical and emotional results by bearing in mind that nothing we do is just our own personal affair.   She's very nice to me.   What she says about me is that it's my personal defect to have clung too much to an individual detail in matters of love instead of considering sexual experience as a whole.   Do you see, what she means by the detail is what she also calls ' the crude experience ': it's often very interesting to see what that sort of thing looks like in the light she throws on it.   But there's one thing about her that I don't care for.   Because, though she does say that a strong woman seeks her life-work in monogamy and should love it as an artist loves his work, there's no getting away from it that she has three—and with you perhaps four—men in tow, and I'm not lucky enough to have even one any more ! "

The gaze she bent on her erstwhile lover was warm and dubious. Ulrich did his best to ignore it.

" So the two of you talk about me ? " he asked with some forboding.

" Oh, only on and off," Bonadea replied.   " When your cousin wants an example, or when your friend the General is there."

" I suppose Arnheim's there pretty often too ? "

" He inclines a dignified ear to the conversation of noble women," Bonadea mocked, not without a glint of talent for unostentatious mimicry, but she immediately added gravely: " I don't like it a bit the way he treats your cousin.   Mostly he's away.   And when he is there, he talks too much to everyone, and when she quotes the example of Frau von Stern and——"

" Frau von Stein, you mean ? " Ulrich corrected interrogatively.

" Yes of course that's the one I mean, it isn't as if Diotima didn't talk about her enough.   Well, when she talks about the relationship between Frau von Stein and Goethe's other woman, the Vul—goodness, what's the woman's name ? Something slightly indecent, isn't it ? "

" Vulpius."

" Of course.   Do you see, I hear so many long words and foreign names there that I'm beginning to forget the obvious ones! Well, so when she compares Frau von Stein with that woman, Arnheim keeps on looking at me, as if compared with his adored one I were just about good enough to be the—whatever you said the woman's name was ! "

Now Ulrich began probing for an explanation of these changes. It turned out that since Bonadea had claimed the status of Ulrich's confidante, she had made great progress in her intimacy with Diotima.

Her alleged nymphomania, which Ulrich had been frivolous enough to denounce to Diotima in a moment of annoyance, had had a far-reaching effect on his cousin.   Having begun inviting the newcomer to her gatherings in the role of a lady who in some not precisely definable way was active in welfare work, she had for some time studied her covertly; and this intruder with eyes that were as soft as blotting-paper, soaking up the picture of her household, had not merely disturbed her in some quite uncanny way, but had aroused in her as much feminine curiosity as horror. To make no bones about it, when Diotima uttered the expression ' venereal disease ', she experienced vague sensations like those she felt when she imagined her new acquaintance's goings-on, and from one occasion to the next she was expecting, with an uneasy conscience, to encounter some impossible behaviour and shame and disgrace. However, Bonadea succeeded in allaying this mistrust by her sheer ambition, which resembled the particularly well-brought-up behaviour of naughty children in surroundings that arouse their impulse to moral emulation. This even made her forget that she was jealous of Diotima, and the latter noticed in astonishment that her perturbing *protégée* was just as taken with ' the ideal ' as she was herself. For very soon this ' sister fallen by the wayside ', as she thought of her, had become a *protégée*, and before long Diotima was taking an especially active interest in her because she felt that her own situation was making her see in the ignoble mystery of nymphomania a kind of feminine sword of Damocles, which, she said, might hang by a thin thread even over the head of a Genoveva. " I know, my child," she said consolingly, imparting instruction to Bonadea (who was about the same age as herself), " there is nothing so tragic as embracing a person of whom one is not inwardly convinced ! " and kissed her on her unchaste mouth with an upsurge of courage that would have sufficed to make her press her lips among the bloodthirsty prickles of a lion's beard.

The position in which Diotima found herself at the time was, as a matter of fact, simply that between Arnheim and Tuzzi: a see-saw, one might symbolically say, on which one of them put too much weight, the other too little. On his return Ulrich himself had found his cousin with a towel round her head and a hot-water bottle and rugs over her; but these female torments, the intensity of which she intuitively felt to be her body's protest against the contradictory instructions it was receiving from her soul, had also awakened in Diotima that noble determination which was characteristic of her as soon as she began refusing to be just like every other woman. Admittedly, at first it had been questionable whether this task should be tackled from the psychological or the physical side, whether it was better dealt with by a change of attitude towards Arnheim or towards Tuzzi; but this was settled with the world's help, for while the soul, with all the enigmas of love, was slipping away from her like a fish one tries to hold in one's bare hand, this seeker and sufferer to her surprise found plenty of advice in the books written in the spirit of the age. These works of the *Zeitgeist* she came to when for the first time she resolved to tackle her fate from the other, the physical end, namely that represented by her husband. She had not known that our era, from which the notion of passionate love seems to have withdrawn because it is a religious rather than a sexual notion, scornfully regards it as childish to pay any further attention to love and makes up for this by applying its exertions to the institution of marriage, the natural operations of which it investigates with energetic thoroughness in all their gradations. Even at that time there had already come into existence many of those books that talk, with the pure-mindedness of a gymnastics instructor, of ' revolutions in sexual life' and which set out to help people to be happy though married. In these books man and woman were referred to only as ' the sexual partner', and the boredom between them, which was to be obviated by means of all sorts of mental and physical variations, was termed ' the sexual problem'. When Diotima worked her way into this literature, at first her brow wrinkled, but in due course it became smooth again; for here was, so to speak, a prod in the ribs of ambition, in so far as an incipiently great movement of the *Zeitgeist* had hitherto escaped her attention. And finally, drawn ever further on by the fascination of it, she clasped her brow in astonishment over the fact that, although she had been capable of giving the world a goal (even though it was not yet decided *what* goal), she had never before realised that even the nerve-racking vexations of the married state might be treated with intellectual superiority. This possibility fitted in very well with her inclinations and suddenly gave her a prospect of managing her relationship with her husband, which she had been experiencing only as a cause of suffering, in terms of a science or an art.

" Why go so far a-roving when the good lies close at hand? " Bonadea remarked, confirmed in this attitude by her own taste for platitudes and quotations. For it soon came about that Diotima, ever ready to be a guardian angel, took her as a pupil in such matters, and treated her as such. This was done on the paedo-gogic principle of learning by teaching, and on the one hand it helped Diotima to keep on extracting from the still thoroughly unregulated and unclear impressions gained from her new reading something of which she was quite firmly convinced—guided as she was by the felicitous mystery of 'intuition', which means hitting the bull's eye as a result of talking at random. On the other hand, it was also to Bonadea's advantage in that it brought about that response without which the pupil remains barren soil even for the best teacher: for though she was cautious enough to maintain a certain reserve about her wealth of practical experience, for the pure theoretician Diotima she had nevertheless been an anxiously studied source of information ever since she, Diotima, had set about putting her marriage in order with the aid of textbooks.

" Look, it's like this," Bonadea explained. " I'm sure I'm not nearly as clever as she is, but there are lots of things in her books that even I never had any notion of—sometimes it makes her so downhearted that she says quite sadly: ' The fact is, that can't be decided at the conference-table of matrimonial life, I'm afraid it calls for immense sexual experience, the result of sexual practice on the living material.' "

" But for heaven's sake," Ulrich exclaimed, overcome with mirth at the mere idea of his chaste cousin's straying into ' sexual science ', " what on earth is she after ? "

Bonadea collected her memories of that happy association between the scientific interests of the time and an unthinking mode of expression. " It's a matter," she retorted at length in the spirit of her instructresss, " of attaining the best development and management of her sexual instinct. And she's convinced that the road to a joyful and harmonious erotic relationship must lead through very harsh self-education."

" Are the two of you deliberately educating yourselves ? And very harshly, what's more ? Really, it's superb the way you talk ! " Ulrich exclaimed. " But now kindly explain what Diotima's educating herself for."

" In the first place, of course, she's educating her husband," Bonadea corrected him.

' Poor chap ! ' Ulrich could not help thinking. " Well then," he said, " I'd like to know how she does it. Don't go and be so reserved all of a sudden ! "

At this interrogation Bonadea did indeed feel inhibited by ambition, like a ' top ' pupil in an examination. " Her sexual atmosphere is poisoned," she began cautiously explaining.

" And if she's to save that atmosphere, it can only be done if Tuzzi and she test their way of behaving as carefully as possible. There aren't any general rules for it. Each has to do his best to observe how the other reacts to life. And in order to observe properly, a person has to have a certain insight into sex-life. One has to be able to compare practical experience with the results of theoretical research, Diotima says. The thing is, nowadays women have a new, different approach to the sex problem: a woman doesn't just want the man to act, what she wants is for him to act with proper understanding of feminine psychology ! " And either in order to distract Ulrich or because it amused her, she added merrily: " Just imagine what it must be like for a man who hasn't the slightest inkling of these new things and gets to hear most of it at bedtime, when they're undressing—imagine Diotima, for instance, taking her hair down and hunting around for hairpins to pull out, and with her petticoat tucked between her knees, and suddenly she starts talking about all that. I've tried it out on my husband, and it made him nearly apoplectic. So there's one thing that can be admitted, anyway,—if there's to be ' permanent marriage ', then at least it has the advantage of dragging all the erotic possibilities out of a person's husband or wife. And that's what Diotima's trying to do with Tuzzi, who's just a teeny-weeny bit crude."

" It's the dawn of a hard time for your various husbands," Ulrich said, teasing her.

Bonadea laughed, and from the way she did so he realised how gladly she would sometimes play truant from the oppressive seriousness of her school of love.

But Ulrich's scientific blood was up and he refused to abandon the investigation. He could sense that his much-changed mistress was hushing up something she would really much rather have talked about. He made the intimate objection that judging by all he had heard the error of the two husbands now being involved in all this had hitherto lain rather in an excess of ' erotic possibilities '.

" Oh yes, that's all you ever think of ! " Bonadea said reprovingly, accompanying the remark with a long, pointed glance that had a little hook on the end of it—something that might very well have been interpreted as regret for her newly won innocence. " You're

just as bad yourself, taking unfair advantage of women's physiological feeble-mindedness."

" Of *what* do I take unfair advantage ? That's a magnificent
expression you've got hold of to describe the history of our love ! "

Bonadea lightly cuffed his ear and went to the looking-glass,
where she nervously rearranged her hair. Gazing at him in the
mirror, she said: " It's out of a book."

" Of course. A very well-known book."

" But Diotima says it isn't true. There's something she found
in another book, which is ' the physiological inferiority of the
male '. It's a book written by a woman. Do you think it's really
so important ? "

" Since I've no idea what is or isn't so important, how can I
answer ? "

" Well, listen ! Diotima starts out from a discovery of hers
that she calls ' woman's constant readiness for sexual excitement '.
Does that make any sense to you ? "

" Not with Diotima ! "

" Don't be so crude ! " she rebuked him. " It's a very delicate
theory, and I'll have to see how I can explain it to you without
your drawing any false conclusions from the fact that at the same
time I'm alone with you in your house. Well, the theory is
fundamentally that a woman can be made love to even when she
doesn't want to be. Do you understand now ? "

" Yes."

" I'm afraid it can't be denied. On the other hand, they say
that very often when a man wants to make love he can't. Diotima
says that's scientifically proved. Do you believe it ? "

" It's said to happen."

" Well, I don't know," Bonadea said doubtfully. " But
Diotima says if you look at it scientifically it's a matter of course.
For in contrast with a woman's constant readiness to be made love
to, a man—well, I don't know how to put it—the manliest part of
a man—is very easily discouraged." Her face was a deeper pink
as she averted it from the looking-glass.

" I'm surprised to hear that about Tuzzi," Ulrich remarked,
trying to divert her attention.

" Oh, I don't think it used to be like that," Bonadea said. " It
just comes along afterwards to confirm the theory because she

keeps on lecturing him about it, day in, day out. She calls it the theory of the fiasco. It's like this—because the male sex-partner is so prone to this fiasco, he only feels sexually safe if he doesn't have to be afraid of any sort of spiritual superiority in the woman, and that's why men almost never have the courage to have rela- tions with a woman who's their human equal. Or at any rate they at once start trying to get the upper hand over her. Diotima says that's the guiding principle in all male eroticism, and especially in male arrogance, which comes from fear. Even great men have it—she means Arnheim, of course. Smaller men hide it behind brutal physical bullying and misuse the woman's spiritual life— and I mean you! And she means Tuzzi. That sort of ' This very moment—or never ! ' that you men often bring us down with is only a sort of over-compensation. That's the way you men escape the thought of your physical inferiority."

" And what have you two decided to do ? " Ulrich asked meekly.

" A person has to try to be nice to men ! And that's just why I've come to see you. We'll see how you take it."

" But what about Diotima ? "

" Heavens, what do you care about Diotima ! Arnheim's eyes pop out like a snail's when she tells him that intellectually exalted men unfortunately only seem to find full satisfaction with inferior women, whereas they fail with women who are their spiritual equals—which is scientifically proved by the case of Frau von Stein and the Vulpius woman. (You see, I've got her name right now. But of course I always did know she was the celebrated sexual partner of the aging Olympian.)"

Ulrich tried to get the conversation back to Tuzzi, in order to steer it away from himself. Bonadea began to laugh; she was not devoid of understanding for the diplomat's miserable situation— she rather liked the man—and she quite maliciously enjoyed ganging up with Diotima in the thought of how he was suffering under the corrective rod of the soul. She recounted that Diotima's point of departure in her treatment of her husband was the idea that she must free him from fear of herself, and in this way she had also somewhat reconciled herself to his ' sexual brutality '. Diotima admitted, she said, having recognised her great mistake was not to have seen that her own significance was too much for her marriage-partner's naïve need to feel superior, and had set about diminishing this by now hiding her spiritual superiority under erotic coquetry suited to his needs.

Ulrich interrupted to ask, with lively interest, what Diotima understood by this.

Bonadea gave him a solemn, searching look. "For instance, she says to him: 'Up to now our life has been spoilt by competition to see which of us matters more.' And then she grants that the poisonous effect of men's striving to assert themselves does also dominate the whole of public life . . ."

"But surely that's neither coquettish nor erotic?" Ulrich objected.

"Oh yes it is! You've got to bear in mind that when a man's really passionate he treats a woman the way an executioner treats his victim. That's part of his striving for self-assertion, as it's called nowadays. On the other hand, you won't deny that the sexual instinct's important to women as well?"

"Of course not!"

"Right. But if the sexual relationship is to work out successfully it needs an even balance between both partners. If one wants to get a rapturous embrace out of one's sexual partner, one has to grant him or her equality of status, not merely regard him or her as a complement to oneself, without any will of his or her own," she went on, dropping so entirely into her mentor's mode of expression that she was like someone on a smooth surface who is carried forward involuntarily and frighteningly by her own movements. "For if no other human relationship will stand constant pressure and oppression, how much less the sexual relationship will!"

"Oho!" Ulrich said, disagreeing.

Bonadea squeezed his arm, and her eyes flashed like falling stars. "You be quiet!" she exclaimed. "All you men are devoid of any first-hand knowledge of the feminine psyche! And if you want me to go on telling you about your cousin——" but here she had reached the end of her tether, and her eyes were now glittering like those of a tigress watching meat being carried past her cage. "No, I can't stand the sound of it any more myself!" she cried.

"Does she really talk like that?" Ulrich asked. "Did she really say that?"

"Good heavens, every single day I hear of nothing but sexual practice, embrace brought to a successful conclusion, erotic stimuli, glands, secretions, repressed urges, erotic training, and regulation of the sexual instinct! Probably everyone has the sexuality he deserves, at least that's what your cousin claims, but do *I* have to go all out to acquire such a lofty one?"

Her gaze held his.

"I don't think you have to," Ulrich said slowly.

"After all, couldn't one just as easily say that my strong capacity for experience implies a physiological supervalue?" Bonadea asked with a happily ambiguous burst of laughter.

There was no more discussion. When, some considerable time later, Ulrich became aware of a sort of resistance in himself, the living day was sprinkling through chinks in the curtains, and when he glanced that way the darkened room resembled the sepulchre of an emotion that had shrivelled away until it was no longer recognisable. Bonadea lay there with closed eyes, giving no sign of life. The sense she now had of her body was not unlike that of a child whose defiance had been broken by a whipping. Every inch of her body, which was both satiated and battered, cried out for the tenderness of moral forgiveness. From whom? Certainly not from the man in whose bed she lay and whom she had implored to kill her because her lust could not be broken by any repetition or intensification. She kept her eyes shut in order not to see him. In a merely experimental way she thought: 'I'm in his bed!' This, and likewise: 'I'll never let myself be driven away from here again!', was what she had been inwardly crying out only a short time earlier; now it merely expressed a situation from which there was no escaping without the embarrassment of going through a number of operations still to be performed. Slowly and indolently Bonadea picked up her thoughts where she had dropped them.

She thought of Diotima. Gradually she began to recall words, sometimes whole sentences, sometimes only fragments, but mainly just the feeling of satisfaction at being there while words as incomprehensible and difficult to remember as hormones, lymphatic glands, chromosomes, zygotes or internal secretion went rushing past her ear in the cascade of talk. For her mentor's chastity knew no bounds as soon as those bounds disappeared in the glare of scientific illumination.   Diotima was capable of saying to a mixed company: " Sex-life is not a craft to be acquired, but something we should always regard as the highest of arts that it's given to us to learn in this life ! " at the same time feeling as little unscientific emotion as when in her zeal she spoke of a ' point of reference ' or a ' point of gravity '.   And her pupil now recalled such expressions quite accurately.   Critical analysis of the embrace —clarification of the physical aspects of the situation—erotogenous zones—woman's way to complete fulfilment—well-disciplined husbands always considerate to their partners . . .   Approximately an hour earlier Bonadea had felt foully cheated by these scientific, intellectual, and highly refined expressions, which at other times she admired.   That this jargon had a meaning not only for science but also for the emotions was something she realised with surprise only when the flames were already lashing forth from the unattended emotional side.   At that moment she had hated Diotima.   ' Talking about such things like that is enough to spoil it for anyone ! ' she had thought to herself, and amid horribly vengeful feelings it had seemed to her that Diotima, who herself had four men at her disposal, would not allow her anything at all and so was tricking her.   Yes, Bonadea had really believed that the enlightenment by means of which sexual science settled accounts with the dark operations of sex was nothing but a plot on Diotima's part.   Now she could not understand that any more than her passionate yearning for Ulrich.   She tried to recall the moments when all her thoughts and sensations had become deranged : just as incomprehensible could it seem to a man bleeding to death when he remembers the rage that made him tear off the protective bandage.   Bonadea thought of Count Leinsdorf, who had called marriage a high office and who compared Diotima's books on the subject to a ' new method of rationalising procedure '. She thought of Arnheim, who was a multi-millionaire and who had described the revival of connubial faithfulness, which arose from the idea of the body, as an authentic need of the time.   And she thought of the many other famous men whom she had got to know recently, without quite remembering whether they had short or long legs or were portly or gaunt: all she saw in them was the radiance of celebrity, rounded out by a vague corporeal mass, rather the way a delicate young roasting pigeon is padded out with a solid mass of herbal stuffing. Remembering all this, Bonadea swore to herself that she would never again fall a prey to one of those swiftly looming storms that brought the higher and the lower self into collision, and she swore it so fervently that she already saw herself, if she could only stick firmly to her resolutions, as being in the spirit and without physical commitment the beloved of the rarest of all the men she could choose from among her great friend's admirers. But since for the present it could not be denied that she was still lying flimsily clad in Ulrich's bed, without wanting to open her eyes, this rich feeling of willing contrition failed to develop into a mood of consolation and, instead, turned into wretched annoyance and exasperation.

The passion whose effects divided Bonadea's life into such opposites had its basic origin not in sensuality but in ambition. This was what Ulrich, who knew his *chère amie* so well, was thinking about; he kept silence in order not to arouse her reproaches, while he surveyed her face, as she lay there with her eyes shut. The basis of all her desires seemed to him to be a desire for distinction that had got on to the wrong track, indeed literally into the wrong nerve-track. And why should an ambition to break social records—ambition of the kind that may for instance see its triumphs in drinking more beer than anyone else or wearing the biggest possible jewels—not really be capable for once of manifesting itself, as it did with Bonadea, as nymphomania? Now that it was over, she had revoked this form of expression with regret—that he could see for himself—and he could also appreciate the fact that Diotima's painstaking unnaturalness must be quite paradisically impressive to one, like Bonadea, whom the devil had always ridden as it were bare-back. He contemplated the balls of her eyes, which lay heavy and exhausted in their sockets; he saw the freckled nose that turned up briskly at the tip, and the pink, pointed nostrils; in some bewilderment he contemplated the various lines of this body: the large round breasts lying on the arched cage of the ribs; the bulbous curve of the buttocks and, rising from there, the long, hollow sweep of the back; the stiff keyboard of the pointed nails over the soft fingertips. And while he finally spent a long time gazing in revulsion at a few tiny hairs sprouting in his mistresses's nostrils, he was also preoccupied with the memory of how seductively this same human being had affected his desires only a little while earlier. The animated and equivocal smile with which Bonadea had appeared for their ' discussion ', the natural way in which she had fended off all reproaches or retailed some amusing new anecdote about Arnheim, indeed the for once almost witty accuracy of her observations: all this pointed to her really having changed for the better. She seemed to have grown more independent; the forces drawing her upwards and those drawing her downwards seemed to be more evenly balanced. This lack of moral ponderousness had been delightfully refreshing to Ulrich, who had for some time been suffering severely under his own seriousness; even now he could feel how he had enjoyed listening to her and watching the play of expression on her face, like sunlight on the waves. And suddenly it occurred to him, while his gaze was still fixed on Bonadea's face (now turned sulky), that actually it was only serious people who could be wicked. ' One might really go so far,' he thought, ' as to say that cheerful people are proof against it. It's the same as the way the operatic villain's always a bass ! ' In some rather uncannily disturbing way this implied also in his own case that ' profound ' and ' gloomy ' were connected. For it seems that guilt is mitigated if it is incurred ' lightly ' by a cheerful person; or perhaps this applies only to love, in which the heavy-blooded seducers wreak much worse and much more unforgivable havoc than the frivolous ones, even if they both only do the same thing. So Ulrich's thoughts went this way and that, and instead of being merely disappointed that the lightly begun hour of love had ended in melancholy, he was also unexpectedly stimulated.

Over all this he somehow forgot that Bonadea was still there: resting his head on his arm and thoughtfully gazing through the walls at things far away, he had turned his back on her. His complete silence finally provoked her to open her eyes. At that moment, all unsuspectingly, he was thinking about a time once when he had been travelling and had never arrived at his destination: a transparently clear day had mysteriously and panderously skimmed the veils off the countryside and lured him into simply setting off on foot from a wayside station, so that at nightfall he found himself, luggageless, in a hamlet many miles away from where he had been going. Indeed it seemed to him that he had always had a tendency to go for incalculably long walks and never to take the same road home. And now suddenly a very remote memory, from an earlier period of his childhood than he normally got back to, cast a ray of light upon his life.

Through an immeasurably small chink in time he seemed to feel again the mysterious yearning by which a child is drawn towards an object that it sees—drawn to touch it or even to put it in its mouth, at which point the magic then stops, as in a blind-alley. In the next instant it seemed to him probably that adults' yearning was in no wise better or worse than this, drawing them on towards every far distance in order to transform it into the near-at-hand—the same sort of yearning that governed him and which, being almost without rational content, even though its emptiness was masked by curiosity, was probably no more than a compulsion. And finally this fundamental image modified into a third aspect, emerging as this impatient and disappointing episode, unwished for by both of them, in which this latest encounter with Bonadea had culminated. Lying side by side in bed like this struck him now as infantile in the extreme. ' But what then does the opposite thing mean—that motionless, airy, hushed, long-distance love that's as incorporeal as an early autumn day ? ' he wondered. ' It's probably only the transformation of some child's-play too,' he thought doubtfully, recalling the brightly painted pictures of animals that he had loved, as a child, more rapturously than nowadays he could love his mistress.

But now Bonadea had seen enough of his back to give her the measure of her unhappiness, and she said: " It's all your fault."

Ulrich turned to her, smilingly, and answered unreflectingly: " In a few days my sister'll be coming to live with me. Did I tell you ? After that we'll scarcely be able to meet."

" How long for ? " Bonadea asked.

" Permanently," Ulrich replied, smiling again.

" Well ? " Bonadea commented. " Why should that change anything ? You're surely not going to try and make me believe your sister won't let you have a mistress ? "

" That's exactly what I do want you to believe," Ulrich said.

Bonadea laughed. " I came to see you today quite innocently, and you didn't even let me get to the end of my story," she reproached him.

" My nature is designed as a machine for the continuous

devaluation of life! I want to be different for once," Ulrich countered.

Although this was of course quite beyond her, she now rebelliously remembered that she loved Ulrich. All at once she was no longer the irresolute, phantom prey of her own nerves, but was suddenly capable of behaving in a convincingly natural way, and she said downrightly: " You're having an affair with her ! "

Ulrich told her not to say such things; he spoke more seriously than he had intended. " I've resolved that for a long time I won't love any woman otherwise than as if she were my sister," he declared. And then he was silent.

The length of this silence was such as to give Bonadea the impression of greater determination than was perhaps justified.

" Heavens, you *are* perverse ! " she suddenly exclaimed in a tone of warning prophecy and leapt out of bed in order to hasten back to Diotima's academy of love, whose portals stood all un-suspectingly wide open to receive the pupil returning repentant and refreshed.

24 Agathe is really there.

THAT evening a telegram arrived, and the next afternoon Agathe.

Ulrich's sister came with only a few suit-cases, just as she had pictured leaving everything behind—not that the quantity of her luggage was wholly in keeping with the principle ' Cast all thou hast into the fire, even thy very shoes '. When Ulrich heard of that resolution, he laughed: two hat-boxes were included in what had escaped the fire.

Agathe's brow took on its delicious furrow of umbrage and vain speculation about it.

Whether Ulrich was right in finding fault with the incomplete expression of a feeling that had been grand and sweeping was left undiscussed, for Agathe refused to raise that question. The merriment and disorder inevitably brought about by her arrival made a roaring in her ears, a swirling before her eyes, like a crowd dancing round a brass band. She was very cheerful and yet faintly disappointed, although she had not been expecting anything definite and on the journey had even been telling herself not to expect anything. Only she suddenly became very tired, remembering the past night, in which she had not been to bed at all. She was quite glad when after some time Ulrich was obliged to tell her that when her telegram came it had been too late to postpone an appointment he had for that afternoon. Promising to be back in an hour, he settled his sister down, with an elaborate carefulness that set them both laughing, on the divan in his study.

When Agathe woke the one hour was long over and Ulrich was nowhere to be seen. The room was sunk in the almost complete obscurity of dusk and seemed so strange that she was suddenly dismayed by the thought of being now irrevocably in the midst of the new life to which she had been looking forward. So far as she could make out, the walls were lined with books, just like her father's study, and the tables were covered with papers. Inquisitively she opened a door and went into the adjacent room: here she found wardrobes, boot-cupboards, the punching-ball, dumb-bells, and the parallel bars. Exploring further, she found more books. She came to the bathroom, with its bottles of eau-de-cologne and bath-salts, its brushes and combs, then to her brother's bedroom, and finally to the hall, with its trophy of the chase. Her passage through the house was marked by the flashing on and off of lights; but as chance would have it, Ulrich noticed nothing of this even though he had returned home. He had put off waking her in order to let her have a longer rest, and now he ran into her on the landing, as he was coming up from the little-used basement kitchen. He had been down there in the hope of providing her with a little snack, since owing to his lack of organisation there was no one there to wait on them. It was only when they were standing side by side that Agathe became capable of summarising the random impressions she had been receiving, and the result disconcerted and disheartened her, making her feel it would be best to clear out without delay. There was something impersonally, even callously, hotchpotch about this house that daunted her.

Noticing this, Ulrich became apologetic and offered some light-hearted explanations.   He told her how he had come to live here, recounting it all in detail, beginning with the antlers he had come to own without ever going out deer-stalking and ending with the punching-ball, which he set bobbing for Agathe's benefit.   Agathe looked at all of it this second time with perturbing gravity, and each time they left one of the rooms she would even turn her head and look back searchingly.   Ulrich tried to make a joke of this examination, but as it went on it began to make him embarrassed about his house.   It now became apparent—what habit otherwise glossed over—that he used only the few rooms he really needed, leaving the rest as it were dangling like useless gauds.   When they were sitting down together after this survey, Agathe asked: " But why did you do it, if you don't like it ? "

Her brother was giving her tea and offering her whatever the house could provide, making a point of some sort of formal welcome, however belated, so that in its material aspect this second reunion should not be inferior to the first.   Dashing back and forth, he conceded: " Oh, I know, it was all frivolous and wrong, I did the place up in a way that makes it have nothing at all to do with me."

" Still, it's very nice," Agathe said now, consolingly.

Now Ulrich remarked that if he had tried to do it differently it would probably have been worse.   " I can't stand houses made to spiritual measure," he declared.   " It would give me the feeling of having ordered myself as well from an interior decorator."

And Agathe said: " Houses like that frighten me too."

" All the same, it can't stay the way it is," Ulrich said encouragingly.

He had sat down at the table too, and the very fact that they would now always be having their meals together raised a number of problems.   He was really astonished at his discovery that all sorts of things must be changed; he felt what was being expected of him was a quite extraordinary effort, and he had an upsurge of beginner's keenness.

" Someone by himself," he said, countering his sister's readiness to leave everything the way it was, " can afford a weakness: it'll merge with his other qualities and disappear among them.   But when two people share a weakness, in comparison with the qualities that they don't share its weight doubles and it becomes something like a deliberate profession of faith."

Agathe could not agree.

" In other words, as brother and sister we can't do a number of things that each of us could do on our own. After all, that's why we've decided to join forces."

This appealed to Agathe. Nevertheless his negative way of putting it—that they had come together merely in order not to do something—did not seem adequate, and after a while, returning to the subject of how his house had been arbitrarily furnished by a congeries of high-class firms, she said: " No, I still don't quite understand. Why *did* you have the place done like this if you didn't think it was right? "

Ulrich met her cheerful gaze and began to consider her face, which—over the rather crumpled travelling-costume she was still wearing—suddenly to him looked silvery smooth and so marvellously present that it was just as near as it was remote, or rather that nearness and remoteness cancelled each other out in this presence, just as out of the infinite distances of the sky the moon suddenly appears from behind the roof of the house opposite.

" Yes, why did I? " he retorted, smiling. " I've quite forgotten. Probably because it could just as easily have been done differently. I felt no responsibility. I'd be on less certain ground if I were to tell you that the irresponsibility with which we conduct our lives nowadays may very well be the first step towards a new sense of responsibility."

" In what way? "

" Oh, in all sorts of ways. You know yourself: each single person's life is perhaps only a slight divergence, this way or that, from the most probable average value in a series. And so on and so forth."

Of this Agathe heard only what made sense to her. She said: " The result of it all is ' Rather nice ' and ' Very nice indeed '. Soon one stops realising how appallingly one lives. But sometimes it gives one the creeps, as if one woke up to find oneself on a slab in the mortuary! "

" What was your place like? " Ulrich asked.

" Middle-class respectability. *À la* Hagauer. ' Quite nice '. Just as much a fake as this."

Meanwhile Ulrich had taken a pencil and was sketching out the plan of the house on the table-cloth, re-allotting the rooms. It was so easy to do, and he did it so quickly, that Agathe's house-wifely gesture in defence of the table-cloth came too late and ended with her hand coming ineffectively to rest on his. Difficulties arose again only over the principles on which the place should be furnished.

" Well now, here we have this house," Ulrich said argument-atively, " and we have to fix it up differently for the two of us. But by and large this problem is an idle one nowadays, it's ob-solete. ' Setting up house ' suggests a mere façade with nothing more behind it. Social conditions and personal relations are no longer solid enough for houses. It no longer gives anyone genuine pleasure to keep up a front of durability and permanence. In the old days people used to do it, showing who they were by the number of their rooms and servants and guests. Nowadays almost every-one feels that formlessness is the only form of life in keeping with the multiple purposes and possibilities that life is packed with, and the younger generation either go in for unadorned simplicity, like a stage without props, or what they dream of is wardrobe-trunks and bobsleigh-championships, tennis-cups and luxury hotels on the great motor-highways, with a golf-course for scenery and hot and cold music laid on in every room." He spoke in a light conversational tone, as if entertaining a stranger; what he was actually doing was talking himself up to the surface, because he was made uneasy by something about their being together that suggested both finality and a new beginning.

But after she had let him have his say out, she asked: " Are you proposing, then, that we ought to live in hotels ? "

" Good heavens no ! " Ulrich hastened to assure her. " Except when we travel, of course."

" And for the rest of the time are we going to build ourselves a wattle hut on an island or a log-cabin in the mountains ? "

" We'll re-furnish this place for ourselves, of course," Ulrich answered, more seriously than their talk warranted.

There was a brief lull in the conversation. He had got up and was pacing up and down the room. Agathe pretended to be picking a thread out of the hem of her dress, bending her head below the line on which all this time their eyes had met. Suddenly Ulrich stopped and said with some difficulty, but going straight to the point: " Dear Agathe, there is a circle of questions with a very large circumference and no centre. And what all these questions come to is: ' How am I to live ? ' "

Agathe had also risen, but still without looking at him. She shrugged her shoulders.

" One has to try," she said. Her face was flushed from bending; but when she lifted her head, her eyes were shining and bright with exhilaration.

" If we're going to stay together," she declared, the flush still lingering on her cheeks for a moment like a passing cloud, " you'll have to start by helping me to unpack and put my things away and change—since there's no sign of a maid anywhere ! "

Ulrich's bad conscience now became active, galvanising his arms and legs into an endeavour to make good, under Agathe's direction and with her aid, for all his inattentiveness. He cleared out cupboards in the manner of a hunter eviscerating a dead animal, and left his bedroom with the solemn asseveration that it was now all Agathe's and that he would make up a bed for himself on a divan somewhere. Eagerly he carried to and fro all the objects of daily use that had hitherto stood in their places as quietly as flowers in a flower-bed, the only intervention in their fate the hand of their owner reaching out to choose one or the other. Suits piled up on chairs; on the glass shelves in the bathroom careful reorganisation made room for division between masculine and feminine cosmetic paraphernalia. By the time order had been more or less transformed into disorder, the only thing left in its old place was Ulrich's gleaming leather slippers, abandoned there on the floor, looking like an offended lapdog that has been evicted from its basket—these pleasant, trifling objects, by their very nature a pitiful symbol of disrupted comfort. But there was no time to sentimentalise over this, for now it was the turn of Agathe's suit-cases, and however few of them there had seemed to be, yet they were inexhaustible as regards exquisitely folded things that floated open as they were lifted out, blossoming upon the air like hundreds of roses conjured out of a magician's hat. All this had to be shaken out and hung up or laid in neat piles in drawers and on shelves, and since Ulrich lent a hand in this task, it was accompanied by all sorts of little accidents and laughter.

But in the midst of all this activity he could not really think of anything but one thing, always the same thing: that all his life long, until just a few hours ago, he had been alone. And now here was Agathe. This little statement: ' Now Agathe is here ' kept on coming into his mind, coming in waves, bringing with it something like the startled sensation of a small boy who had just been given a toy; there was something about it too that inhibited the mind, but on the other hand there was also an utterly incomprehensible plenitude of presence, and all in all it kept on coming back to the little statement: ' Now Agathe is here.'

' So she's tall and slim ? ' Ulrich thought, secretly observing her. But in fact she was not like that at all: she was shorter than himself and trimly broad of shoulder. ' Is she attractive ? ' he wondered. That was hard to say. Her proud nose, for instance, when seen from one side turned out to be slightly tip-tilted; there was far more potent charm in that than in mere good looks. ' Is she actually beautiful ? ' Ulrich wondered rather oddly. For the question did not come easily although, if one left convention entirely aside, this woman was actually a stranger to him. There is after all no such thing as an inner taboo on gazing upon a blood-relation with sexual desire; the taboo, such as it is, is merely a matter of custom or based on arbitrary notions of morality and eugenics. Besides, the fact that Ulrich and Agathe had not grown up together had prevented their developing that sterilised brother-and-sister relationship which prevails in European families. On the other hand, awareness of being siblings was enough to deprive their feeling for each other—even the harmless feeling of merely imagined beauty in the other—of its finer point, a lack that Ulrich sensed at this moment in his own distinct astonishment. For finding something beautiful doubtless means above all *finding* it: whether it is a landscape or a woman one falls in love with, there it is, gazing back on its complacent finder and appearing to have been waiting simply and solely for him. And thus, with this delight in the fact of her now belonging to him and being there for him to discover, he was immeasurably pleased with his sister; and yet he thought: ' One's own sister is someone one can't find truly beautiful, at the most one can be complacent about it if others admire her.' But then where a moment earlier there had been a hush, he heard her speaking voice, and heard it continuing—

and what was her voice like? Waves of fragrance floated from the stirring of her clothes—and what was this fragrance like? Her movements were high-lighted now as knee, now as delicate finger, now as the stubbornness of a stray curl. The only thing that could be said about it was: that it was there. It was here, where up to now there had been nothing. The difference between the most concentrated moment of Ulrich's thinking of the sister he had left behind and the emptiest of the present moments was still so great and distinct in its pleasantness that it was like a shady place filling up with warm sunlight and the scent of wild herbs unfurling . . .

Agathe herself was aware that her brother was studying her, but she behaved as if she did not notice. In the lulls in their talk, when she felt his gaze following her movements, in the silences between one remark and the response to it, which were not so much a coming to a halt as like coasting along in a motor-car with the engine switched off, a sort of gliding on a precarious surface over unknown depths, she too was enjoying the superreality of this present moment, the tranquil intensity of this re-union.

And when all the unpacking and tidying away was done and she had retired to have a bath, what came about was an adventure, threatening to break wolfishly in upon these peaceful pastures: for she had undressed, down to her underclothes, in a room where Ulrich was now sitting, smoking a cigarette and keeping vigil over her belongings. Soaking in the water, she mused what she should do. Since there was no maid there was no sense in ringing or calling out, and apparently there was nothing to be done but to wrap herself in Ulrich's bath-robe, which was hanging on the wall, put her head round the door and send him out of the room. But Agathe blithely doubted whether, in view of the grave intimacy that was, if not already fully established between them, at least there by implication, it was suitable to behave so much like an average young lady and ask Ulrich to withdraw; so she decided not to acknowledge any sort of equivocal femininity, but simply to appear before him as the natural and familiar companion that she must be for him even when scantily clad.

Yet when she resolutely entered the room, both of them felt an unexpected quickening of the heart. Both tried not to be embarrassed. For an instant neither could shake off the conventional sense of inconsequence there was in knowing that while semi-nakedness is permissible at the sea-side, indoors the hem of a petticoat or the frills of panties become a smugglers' path to romantic fancies. Ulrich smiled awkwardly as, with the light of the anteroom behind her, Agathe appeared in the doorway like a silver statue mistily veiled in delicate batiste; and her voice was a little too elaborately casual as she asked where she had left her stockings and dress—which turned out to be in the room beyond. Ulrich showed her where they were and saw to his secret delight that she strode a little too boyishly, almost defiantly enjoying it, as women tend to do when they no longer have the protection of their skirts. Then there was again a new turn, a little later, when Agathe was half in her dress, half caught in it, and had to call Ulrich to her aid. As he disentangled fastenings at her back, she discerned—without sisterly jealousy, even with a sort of complacency—that he was expert in dealing with women's clothes, and she herself shifted this way and that responsively as the nature of the operation required.

Bending over close to the live, delicate and yet satiated skin of her shoulders, and all attention to his unaccustomed occupation, which raised a flush on his brow, Ulrich felt himself lapped by a pleasing sensation that it was hard to put into words, unless one were to say that his body was assaulted by a sense of equally having a woman and of having no woman very close to him; one could just as well say that though he stood there solidly with both feet on the ground he felt himself being drawn out of himself and over to her, as though he had here been given for his own a second and far more beautiful body.

Straightening up again, the first thing he said to his sister was therefore: " Now I know what you are: you're my self-love ! " Perhaps it sounded odd, but it did really describe what moved him. " In a certain sense," he explained, " I've always been devoid of any proper self-love such as other people have so strongly. And now," he added abruptly, " by mistake or by an act of fate, it has evidently been embodied in you instead of in myself ! "

It was his first attempt that evening to make a clear pronouncement on what his sister's arrival meant.

25   *The Siamese Twins.*

LATER that evening he came back to this.

"It's like this," he began telling his sister, "there's a sort of self-love that I don't know, a certain tender relationship to oneself that seems to come naturally to most other people. I don't know how best to describe it. I might say, for instance, that I've always had mistresses with whom I had a false relationship. They've always been illustrations of sudden notions that occurred to me, caricatures of a mood I had: in other words, just examples of my incapacity to be on natural terms with other people. Even that's connected with one's relationship to oneself. At bottom I've always landed myself with having affairs with women I didn't like . . ."

"Oh, but you're quite right!" Agathe interrupted. "If I were a man, I shouldn't have any qualms about treating women quite irresponsibly. And I'd desire them only out of distraction and astonishment!"

"Oh? Would you? That's nice of you!"

"Women are ridiculous parasites. Women share a man's life together with his dog!" Agathe made this assertion with anything but moral indignation. She was agreeably tired and kept her eyes closed, having gone to bed early, and Ulrich, who had come to say goodnight to her, looked at her lying in his place in his bed.

But it was also the bed in which Bonadea had lain only thirty-six hours earlier. That was probably what brought Ulrich back to the subject of his mistresses.

"All I was trying to get at," he went on, smiling, "was my incapacity to have a mildly reasoned relationship with myself. If I'm to experience anything with real interest, it must be something that happens as part of a coherent complex, it must be under the aegis of an idea. The experience itself is something I'd really rather have got over and done with, already in my memory. The actual expenditure of emotion involved strikes me as unpleasant and ludicrously out of place. That's how it is if I try to describe myself to you ruthlessly. The simplest and most spontaneous idea one has, at least in one's youth, is that one's a hell of a chap, of a new kind that the world's been waiting for. But after one's thirtieth year that gives out!" He reflected for a moment and then said: "No! It's so hard to talk about oneself. Really I ought to say right out that I've never been ruled by any one permanent idea. There never *was* one. An idea's something one ought to love like a woman. In raptures when one's returning to her. And having her always inside oneself! And looking for her in everything outside oneself! I never found any such ideas. I've always had a man-to-man relationship to what are called the great ideas: perhaps even to those that are rightly so called. I never believed I was born to subordinate myself, they provoked me into knocking them down and setting up others in their stead. Yes, perhaps it was just this jealousy that drove me into science, the laws of which are established by team-work and are not re-garded as immutable either!" He paused again and laughed, either at himself or at his argument. "But however that may be," he went on earnestly, "there it is: by having this way of associ-ating no idea or every idea with myself, I got out of the habit of taking life seriously. I really find it much more exciting when I read about life in a novel where it's wrapped up in a particular view of things. But whenever I ought to experience it in all its detailed elaboration, I always find it already obsolete, over-elaborate in an old-fashioned way, and the intellectual substance of it out of date. And I don't think it's peculiar to me. Most people are pretty much like that nowadays. Many of them do work themselves up into an artificial state of intense delight in life, rather the way schoolchildren are taught to skip along merrily among the pretty little flowers, but there's always something rather deliberate about it, and they feel that. In reality they're just as capable of cold-bloodedly murdering each other as of getting on together with the utmost cordiality. It really does seem that our time doesn't take the happenings and adventures it's full of seriously. If things happen, they cause a stir. So then they instantly bring about more happenings, even a sort of vendetta among happenings, an alphabet that has to be compulsively gone through from B right to Z because one's said A. But these things that happen in our life have less life in them than a book because they have no coherent meaning."

That was how Ulrich talked—somewhat at random, his mood shifting.

Agathe did not answer. She still had her eyes shut, but she smiled.

" I've forgotten what I was talking about," Ulrich said. " I don't think I can get back to the beginning."

They were silent for a time. He was able to scrutinise his sister's face at leisure, since it was not defended by the gaze of open eyes. It lay there, simply a piece of naked body, as women are when they are together in a public bath for women only. The feminine, unguarded, natural cynicism of this sight, not intended for masculine eyes, still had an unusual effect on Ulrich, even though this was no longer as intense as in the first days when they had been together and Agathe had at once claimed her sisterly right to talk to him without the least emotional beating round the bush, since for her he was not a man as others were. He remembered the disconcerted amazement he had always felt as a boy whenever he had seen a pregnant woman in the street, or a woman suckling her baby : secrets carefully kept from the boy then suddenly bulged, full-blown and unembarrassed, in the light of day. And perhaps he had carried vestiges of such impressions about with him for a long time, for suddenly now it seemed to him that he was all at once quite free of them. It seemed pleasant and comfortable to think that Agathe was a woman and must have been through all sorts of experiences ; talking to her, there was no need to be as much on one's guard as with a young girl, indeed it struck him as touchingly natural that with a mature woman everything should be morally laxer. He felt the need, too, to protect her and to be good to her in some way in order to make up for something, he did not know how or what. He resolved to do everything he could for her. He even resolved to look for another husband for her. And this need for goodness imperceptibly gave him back the lost thread of his talk.

" Our self-love probably undergoes a change during adolescence," he said without transition. " For in that phase a meadow of tenderness that one has always played about in is mowed to provide fodder for one particular instinct."

" To make the cow give milk ! " Agathe supplemented, after the slightest pause, pertly and yet with dignity, though still without opening her eyes.

" Yes, I suppose it's all connected," Ulrich agreed, and went on: " So there's a moment when our life loses almost all its tenderness, which concentrates on that one particular operation, and this then remains over-charged. Doesn't that seem to you too like a horrible drought prevailing all over the earth except in one place, where it keeps on raining, unceasingly ? "

Agathe said: " It seems to me as a child I loved my dolls more than I've ever loved a man. After you'd left I found a trunkful of my old dolls in the attic."

" What did you do with them ? " Ulrich asked. " Did you give them away ? "

" Who could I have given them to ? I cremated them in the stove," she said.

Ulrich took this up with animation: " When I remember as far back as I can, my impression is that in those days inside and out-side were scarcely distinguishable. When I crawled towards anything, it came on wings to meet me. And whenever anything happened that mattered to us, it wasn't just we that were excited, but the things themselves began to seethe. I won't go so far as to say that we were happier then than later. After all, we didn't yet possess ourselves. In fact we didn't yet really exist, our personal states were not yet distinctly separated from those of the world. It sounds strange, but it's true: our emotions, our volitions, even our very selves, were not yet entirely inside us. What's still stranger is that I might just as well say: they were not yet removed to a distance from us. Today, when you think your-self entirely in possession of your self, if you were to ask yourself for once who you actually are—you'd make the same discovery. You'll always see yourself from outside, like an object. You'll notice that one thing makes you angry and another makes you sad, just as one time your coat is wet and another time it's too heavy. However carefully you observe, at the most you'll get to ' what's behind you ', but you'll never get inside yourself. You remain outside yourself, you stand beside yourself, whatever you try to do about it, and the only exceptions are precisely those rare moments when somebody else would say you were ' beside yourself '. Admittedly we've managed to make up for this, as adults, by being able to think ' I am ' on every conceivable occasion, for what that may be worth. You see a motor-car, and in some shadowy way at the same time you also see: ' I am seeing a motor-car.' You're in love or you're sad, and you see yourself being it. But in a full sense neither the motor-car nor your sadness nor your love, nor even yourself, is entirely there. Nothing is any longer entirely there the way it was once upon a time in childhood. Everything you touch, right into your innermost self, is more or less petrified from the moment you have attained to being a ' personality ', and what's left over, enveloped in an out-and-out external existence, is a spectral misty thread of self-certainty and murky self-love. What has gone wrong? One has the feeling there's some process that could still be reversed ! One surely can't maintain that a child experiences quite differently from a man ! I don't know any definite answer, even if there may be this or that theory about it. But for a long time I've answered it by saying that I've lost all love for this sort of being ' myself ' and for this sort of world."

Ulrich found it pleasant that Agathe listened without interrupting him, for he did not expect an answer from her any more than from himself and he was convinced that for the present nobody could give an answer such as he was looking for. On the other hand, he was not for an instant afraid that anything he said might be above her head. He did not regard it as philosophising and did not even think it was an unusual subject to talk about, any more than a very young man—which was, in this situation, what he resembled—is prevented by difficulties of terminology from treating everything as simple and straightforward when someone else has stimulated him to exchange views on the eternal problems : ' Who are you? This what I am.' His certainty that his sister could follow his words was based not on reflection but on her very existence here and now. His gaze rested on her face, and there was something there that made him happy. This face with the closed eyes was entirely without any power of repulsion. It had some indefinable attraction for him; and it was as though it drew him into never-ending depths. Submerging himself in contemplation of this face, he nowhere found that muddy bottom of dissolved resistances which one who has dived deep down into love suddenly kicks off from, so that, being repelled, he rises to the surface and comes to dry land again. But since he was in the habit of experiencing every inclination towards a woman as a violently reversed disinclination towards the human being—which, even though he disapproved of it, did offer some guarantee of not losing himself in her—he was now scared by his own pure inclining, this bending searchingly ever deeper, almost with a loss of equilibrium, so that he soon drew back and from sheer happiness took refuge in a rather boyish little trick, to recall Agathe into everyday life: with the most circumspect touch he was capable of he tried to raise her eyelids.

Agathe opened her eyes, laughing, and exclaimed: " Considering that I'm supposed to be your self-love, you treat me pretty roughly ! "

This response was as boyish as his trespass, and their eyes met, gaze exuberantly pushing against gaze, like two little boys who want to have a tussle but who are laughing too much to begin. But suddenly Agathe dropped this and asked seriously:

" You know the story Plato tells, derived from some ancient myth, about how the gods divided the original human being, who was a whole, into two halves, man and woman ? " She had propped herself up on her elbow and all at once blushed, as it struck her too late that it was rather foolish to ask Ulrich if he knew a story probably familiar to everybody. Then, making up her mind to go through with it, she added: " Now the two pathetic halves do all sorts of silly things, trying to join up again into a single whole. It's in all the school-books ' for older children '. Unfortunately they never say why the attempt doesn't succeed ! "

" I can tell you that," Ulrich said instantly, delighted to realise how exactly she had understood what he meant. " The point is that nobody knows which of all the halves at large in the world is his own missing half. He grabs hold of one that seems to be the right one and makes wildly futile efforts to unite with it, until in the long run it turns out to be no good. If a child happens to result, for some years of their youth both halves believe they've at least combined in the child. But that's merely a third half, which soon shows signs of endeavouring to get as far away from the other two as it possibly can, going off in search of a fourth. So humanity keeps on physiologically halving itself, and the essential union remains remote as the moon outside the bedroom window."

"It seems reasonable to think that brothers and sisters, anyway, must have gone half the way!" Agathe interjected, her voice all at once husky.

"Twins perhaps."

"Aren't we twins?"

"Certainly!" Ulrich suddenly slid away from this: "Twins are rare. Twins of different sex are very rare indeed. But when, into the bargain, they're of different ages and have scarcely known each other for a very long time, the result is a remarkable phenomenon—really worthy of us!" he declared, struggling back into the shallows of gaiety.

"But we met as twins!" Agathe said challengingly, unaffected by his tone.

"Because we happened to be dressed almost the same?"

"Perhaps. And in all sorts of ways! You may say it was chance. But what is chance? I think just what's called 'chance' is fate or destiny or whatever you may like to call it. Haven't you ever thought what chance it was that you were born precisely as you? Our being brother and sister is the same twice over!" That was how Agathe put it, and Ulrich submitted to this wisdom.

"So we declare ourselves twins!" he agreed. "Symmetrical creature of Nature's whim, henceforth we're the same age, the same height, have the same hair, walk through the highways and byways of humanity in identical striped clothes and with identical scarves tied under our chins. But I must point out to you that they'll turn round to stare at us, finding us rather touching and also rather absurd, as always happens when something reminds them of the mysteries of how they themselves came into life."

"Oh well, we can do the other thing and dress in strict contrast to each other," Agathe retorted in amusement. "One yellow when the other's blue, or red next to green, and we can dye our hair purple or scarlet, and I'll adopt a hump and you a paunch. And for all that, we're twins!"

But the joke was exhausted, the pretext worn out, and they fell silent for a while.

"Do you realise," Ulrich at last said suddenly, "this is a very serious matter we're talking about?"

No sooner had he said this than his sister again dropped her eyelids, and, so concealing her readiness to follow as though behind a fan, left the talking to him.   Or perhaps it only looked as if she had shut her eyes.   The room was dark; such light as there was did not so much make anything distinct as pour out in patches of brightness on the outlines of things.

What Ulrich said was: "There's not only the myth of the human being divided into two.   We might also take Pygmalion, or Hermaphroditus, or Isis and Osiris: with slight variations it's always the same thing.   It goes back a very long way, this desire for a *doppelgänger* of the opposite sex, this craving for the love of a being that will be entirely the same as oneself and yet another, distinct from oneself, a magical figure that is oneself and that does nevertheless remain a magical figure as well and is more than any figment of the imagination in that it has the life-breath of self-sufficiency and independence.   This old, old dream of the essence of love meeting, unhampered by the limitations of the corporeal world, in two identical-distinct figures—it's conjured up innumerable times through the ages by the solitary alchemistic processes that go on inside the alembic of the human skull . . ."

Here he came to a stop.   Something had obviously occurred to him that disturbed him, and he concluded with the almost unfriendly words:

"Even under the most ordinary everyday conditions in which love occurs one does still find traces of this: one finds it in the stimulus associated with every change and every disguise, and in the significance of correspondences between oneself and the other, the repetition of oneself in the other.   The flicker of magic is always the same, whether one's seeing 'a lady' undressed for the first time or the girl one is used to seeing undressed now for the first time in a ladylike dress buttoned right up to the neck, and the great ruthless erotic passions are all connected with the fact that everyone thinks it is his own most secret self peering out at him from behind the curtains in other eyes."

It sounded as though he were pleading with her not to attach too much importance to what they had been saying.   But Agathe thought once again of the lightning-flash of surprise she had felt when they first met, both as though disguised in their lounging-suits.   And she replied:

"So this has been going on for thousands of years.   Does it

make it any easier to understand if one explains it as a result of
two delusions ? "

Ulrich was silent.

And after a while Agathe said delightedly: " But in sleep it's like
that ! In sleep one does sometimes see oneself turned into something else. Or meets oneself as a man. You'll probably say
those are sexual dreams. But it seems to me they go much
further back."

" Do you often have that sort of dream ? " Ulrich asked.

" Sometimes. Not often."

" I almost never do," he confessed. " It's ages since I had a
dream like that."

" All the same, you once explained to me," Agathe said, " —I
think it must have been right at the beginning, back there in the
old house—that human beings really had other experiences
thousands of years ago ! "

" Oh, you mean the ' giving ' and the ' receiving ' vision ? "
Ulrich replied and smiled at her, even though she could not see
him. " The ' being embraced ' and ' embracing ' of the spirit ?
Yes, of course I ought to have talked about that mysterious dual
sexuality of the soul too ! And, for that matter, about how much
else besides ! There's a trace of it haunting everything. You
know, even in every analogy there's a residue of that magic of
being identical and yet not identical. But haven't you noticed ?
—in all these aspects of things that we've been talking about, in
dreams, in myth, in poetry, childhood, even in love, the great
share of emotion is bought at the cost of intelligent understanding,
and that means: by a reduction in reality."

" So you don't really believe in it ? " Agathe asked.

To this Ulrich gave no answer. But after a while he said: " If
one translates it into the disastrous modern mode of expression,
one can call this thing, of which there's so terrifyingly little available for everyone today, the individual's percentual participation
in his experiences and actions. In dreams it seems to be a hundred
per cent: in waking life it doesn't even amount to a half ! You
noticed it at once today in everything about this house: didn't
you ? But my relations to the people you'll come to know are just
the same. Once—and as a matter of fact it was in conversation
with a woman, where it was very relevant—I called it the acoustics

of the void. If a pin falls on the floor in an empty room, a room entirely stripped of furniture, the sound it makes is somehow disproportionate, even incommensurable. But it's just the same if there's emptiness between and among people. Then there's no way of knowing: is one shouting or is it deathly quiet? For everything out-of-place and crooked takes on the magnetic force of a tremendous temptation as soon as one has ultimately nothing to oppose it with. Don't you agree? But look, I'm sorry," he said, breaking off, " you must be tired, and I don't give you any peace. I'm rather afraid there's a good deal about my milieu and my way of doing things that won't be to your liking."

Agathe had opened her eyes. After being hidden so long, her gaze expressed something extremely hard to define, and in it Ulrich felt a sort of sympathy that seemed to extend over his whole body.

Suddenly he began to talk again: " When I was younger, I tried to see a strength precisely in that. So one hasn't anything to set against life? All right, so life flies away from man and into his works! That was more or less the way I thought of it. And I suppose there's something rather formidable about the lovelessness and irresponsibility of the world today. At any rate there's something of a hobble-de-hoy about the century—for why shouldn't that apply to centuries just as to the years of human growth? And like every young man I started by plunging into work, adventure, and amusement. It seemed to me it didn't matter what one set about doing so long as one gave it all one had. You remember we once talked about ' the morality of achievement '? That's the inherent image in us by which we set our course. But the older one gets, the more clearly one discovers that this apparent exuberance, this independence and mobility in everything one does, this sovereignty of the driving parts and the partial drives—both that of your own against yourself and yours over against the world—in short, everything that we, as ' people of the present day ', have regarded as a force and a peculiarity of the species conferring distinction upon us—is all fundamentally nothing but a weakness of the totality in relation to its parts. Passion and will-power won't help one to do anything about it. The moment you want to get right to the bottom, to the centre, of something, you find yourself washed up on to the edge of it again : that's the experience nowadays in all experiences ! "

Agathe, with her eyes now open, was waiting for something to happen to his voice. When it did not happen, when her brother's talk simply came to an end like a path that diverges from a road and does not lead anywhere, she said: " So judging by your experience one can never really act from conviction and never will be able to. By conviction I mean," she emended, " not some science or other, nor even the moral *dressage* that's been drilled into us, but feeling entirely at home with oneself and also feeling oneself in everything else, I mean the feeling that something that otherwise stays empty is filled to the brim, I mean something one always starts out from and always comes back to. Oh, I don't really know *what* I mean ! "—she broke off vehemently. " I was hoping you'd explain it to me ! "

" You mean just what we've been talking about," Ulrich answered gently. " And you're the only person I can talk to about it like this. But there wouldn't be any sense in my beginning all over again just for the sake of adding a few tantalising words. On the contrary, it seems to me that ' being right at the centre ', a state of undisturbed ' inwardness ' of life—if the expression isn't taken in some woolly sentimental sense, but in the sort of way we've just been implying—is probably something that can't be demanded in a rational frame of mind." He had leaned forward and was touching her arm and gazing into her eyes. " Perhaps it's not *in* human nature," he said in a low voice. " What is real, though, is that we painfully feel the lack of it ! For this must be what the desire for brother-and-sisterliness comes from—this desire that's a complement to ordinary love, moving in the imaginary direction towards a love unadulterated with estrangement and not-love." And after a while he added: " You know how in bed people go in for Babes-in-the-Wood stuff. People who could murder their real brothers or sisters play in the silliest way at being brother and sister, a sort of conspiracy, under the blankets."

In the half-darkness his face twitched with self-mockery. But Agathe's trust was in this face and not in the confused words. She had seen faces quivering like this a moment before they came plunging downwards; but this one did not come nearer: it seemed to be moving at infinitely great speed over infinitely great distances. Abruptly she answered:

" Being brother and sister isn't enough, that's all."

" Well, we've already made it ' twin ' brother and sister," Ulrich retorted, now quietly rising, since it seemed to him that her fatigue was at last getting the better of her.

" It ought to be ' Siamese twins '," was the last thing Agathe said.

" Then Siamese twins it is ! " her brother concurred. Warily he let go of her hand, laying it softly on the quilt, and his own last words sounded imponderable: weightless and volatile, expanding ever further even after he had left the room.

Agathe smiled. Slowly she sank into a solitary mournfulness, and gradually, imperceptibly to her weariness, the darkness of it merged into the darkness of sleep.

But Ulrich tip-toed into his study and there, till he too grew tired, he stayed for two hours, unable to work, making his first acquaintance with the experience of being cramped and confined by consideration for another person. He was amazed to realise how many things he would normally have done in this time that might make a noise and therefore had to be left undone. This was new to him. And it almost irritated him, although he did his utmost to feel his way sympathetically into imagining what it would be like really to be bodily attached to another human being. He had little information about the workings of two such nervous systems, which are like two leaves on a single stalk, united not only through having one blood-stream but still more through their complete interdependence. He conjectured that every agitation in the one psyche must also be felt by the other, while the process that evoked it went on in a body that was, in the main, not one's own. ' An embrace, for instance: you are embraced in the other,' and he thought. ' You may not even want it, but your other self floods you with an over-powering wave of acceptance ! What concern is it of yours who kisses your sister ? But her response to it is something you must love together with her ! Or say it's you who love, and now you must somehow give her a share in it—for surely you can't go flooding her with merely senseless physiological processes . . . ? ! ' Ulrich felt an intense stimulus and a great uneasiness in these speculations. It seemed difficult to draw the border-line here between new views of things and distortion of the usual views.

26 *Spring in the vegetable garden.*

THE praise that Meingast had bestowed on her, and the new ideas she was getting from him, had made a deep impression on Clarisse.

Her mental unrest and excitability, which sometimes rather perturbed even her, had eased off; yet this time it did not pass over, as at other times, into dejection, frustration, and hopelessness, but into an extraordinarily taut lucidity and an inner atmosphere that was quite transparent. Once again she surveyed herself, making a critical summary. Without any doubt of it, and even with a certain satisfaction, she noted that she was not particularly clever: the fact was she had had too little education. Ulrich, on the other hand—and this was how it seemed to her whenever she happened to think of him during such comparative scrutinies—Ulrich was like a skater on intellectual ice, coming nearer and going off into the distance again just as he felt inclined. There was never any understanding where it came from whenever he said anything, or when he laughed, when he was annoyed, when his eyes flashed, simply when he was there, with his broad shoulders taking up room between their four walls, taking it away from Walter. Even when he simply turned his head in curiosity, the sinews of his neck tightened like the rigging of a sailing-boat cutting swiftly through the waves on its wind-bright voyage. There was always something about him that reached beyond what was accessible to her and which kept at full stretch her desire to fling herself bodily upon him in order to catch hold of it. But the tumult in which this sometimes occurred—and which had once gone so far as to leave nothing solid in the world but the wish to have a child by Ulrich—had now receded into the distance, and this time it had not left behind even that flotsam and jetsam with which memory is incomprehensibly strewn after the tide of passion has ebbed. At the most Clarisse felt cross whenever she thought of her failure that time at Ulrich's house, in so far as she ever thought of it any more at all. Her self-confidence turned out to be unscathed; it was fresh and immaculate. This was the effect of the new notions she had been supplied with by her philosophic visitor—apart from the immediate excitement of again seeing this old friend who had undergone such a transformation into magnificence. Thus many days passed in a state of multiple tension, while everyone in the little house that now lay bathed in spring sunshine was waiting to see whether Ulrich would or would not bring the permit to visit Moosbrugger in his sinister abode.

And in this connection there was one idea that struck Clarisse as chiefly important: the Master had said the world was ' free of illusions in such measure ' that there was no longer anything that one knew whether to love or to hate. Since then Clarisse was convinced that one must abandon oneself to illusion once one had been given the grace to feel it. For an illusion is an act of grace. If one came to think of it, who was there who still knew whether to turn right or left when he left his house ?—unless he had a job, like Walter, and that again was something that constrained him, or unless, like herself, one were going to keep an appointment with one's parents or brothers and sisters, who were a bore ! How different things were under illusion ! Then life fell into shape and was as practical as a modern kitchen: one sat in the middle of it, scarcely needing to stir, able to set all the gadgets going at a touch of one's hand. This was the sort of thing of which Clarisse had always had a real appreciation. And besides, what she meant by ' illusion ' was nothing more or less than what was called ' the will ', only with a special intensification. Up to now Clarisse had always been discouraged by the fact that there were very few things going on in the world that she could really explain to herself; but since the re-union with Meingast she saw this as positively an asset, enabling her to love, hate, and act as seemed best to her. For according to the Master there was nothing mankind was so much in need of as will-power, and this capacity to will intensely was something she had always possessed ! When Clarisse thought of this she grew cold with happiness and hot with a sense of responsibility. Of course ' will ' in this sense did not mean anything like the sombre struggle to learn a piece of piano-music or to win in an argument; it meant being tremendously steered by life itself, being seized by one's self, and swept away in a flash of happiness.

And in the end she could not help telling Walter something about this. She told him that her conscience was growing stronger day by day.

However, in spite of his admiration for Meingast, the presumable originator of this state of affairs, Walter answered very irritably: " It's probably a very good thing that Ulrich evidently isn't managing to get that permit ! "

Clarisse's lips merely tightened with a flicker of grimness, but it was also a sign of pity for his hopeless innocence and his resistance.

" And what," Walter asked excitedly, " what is it you really want of this criminal, who isn't of the slightest concern to any of us ? "

" I shall know that when I get there," Clarisse answered.

" It seems to me you ought to know it now ! " was Walter's manly comment.

His little wife smiled the way she always did when she was on the point of hurting him deeply. But then she merely said: " I shall do something."

" Clarisse ! " Walter remonstrated firmly. " You are not to do anything without my permission. I am your lawful husband and guardian ! "

This tone was new to her. She turned away from him and began to walk off in some confusion.

" Clarisse ! " Walter called after her, getting up to follow her. " I shall take steps to deal with the madness that's going round in this house ! "

At this point she realised that the healing power of her resolve was already making itself felt, even in Walter's increase in strength. She span round, asking him: " What steps ? " and a lightning-flash from her narrowed eyes struck into the moist, wide-open brown of his.

" Look," he said, trying to mollify her, retreating a step or two in surprise at the concreteness of her retort, " we've all got this in us, after all—this intellectual taste for the unhealthy, ghastly, and problematic—all of us intellectuals have it. But——"

" But we let the Philistines have it their way ! " Clarisse interrupted him in a flare of triumph. Now she was advancing upon him, not taking her eyes off him; she felt her healing power holding him in its strong embrace, overpowering him. Her heart was suddenly filled with an indescribable strange joy.

"But we don't make so much fuss about it," Walter muttered crossly, finishing what he had been going to say. Behind him, at the hem of his jacket, he felt some impediment; and, reaching backwards, he vaguely identified it as the edge of one of the light, thin-legged little tables that stood about all over their house and which all at once struck him as spectral. He realised that if he were to retreat any further it would mean pushing the table along behind him, which would be ludicrous. So he resisted the suddenly awakening desire to get right away from this warfare, to be somewhere on a lush green meadow, under blossoming fruit-trees, and among people whose healthy cheerfulness would cleanse and purify his wounds. It was a quiet, obese desire, embellished with women hanging on his words and paying their toll of grateful admiration. And in the moment of reality when Clarisse came close up to him, her presence affected him as a sordid, dream-like molestation. But then, to his surprise, Clarisse did not say: 'You're a coward!'

What she said was: "Walter? Why are we unhappy?"

At the sound of this alluring, clairvoyant voice he felt overwhelmingly that no happiness with any other woman could ever mean as much to him as his unhappiness with Clarisse. "We have to be!" he answered on an equally noble upsurge of emotion.

"No, we oughtn't to be!" Clarisse declared mildly. She let her head droop to one side as she searched for something to convince him. At bottom it ought not to make any difference what it was: they stood facing each other like a day without an evening, its fieriness pouring out hour after hour without ever growing less. "You'll admit," she began at last, at once shyly and stubbornly, "that the really great crimes don't come about because they're committed, but because they're tolerated!"

Now indeed Walter knew what was coming: he felt a shock of disappointment.

"Oh God!" he exclaimed impatiently. "I know as well as you do that far more people's lives are ruined by indifference and the easiness of squaring one's conscience nowadays than by the evil intentions of individuals! And I know what you're going to say now: that that's why everyone must quicken his conscience and evaluate every single step before he takes it. And that's admirable."

At this point Clarisse opened her mouth to say something, but thought better of it and remained silent.

"And do you suppose *I* don't think about the poverty and hunger and corruption of every sort that's allowed to go on in the world, or about the catastrophes that happen in mines because the management wouldn't spend the money on safety-devices?" Walter went on dejectedly. "And what's more, I've agreed with you about it many a time already."

"But then two lovers mustn't love each other, either, so long as they're not in a state of 'pure happiness'," Clarisse said. "And the world will never get any better until there are such lovers!"

Walter clasped his hands in exasperation. "Don't you see how unrealistic, how untrue to life, such great, dazzling, unalloyed demands are?" he exclaimed. "And it's exactly the same thing with this fellow Moosbrugger who keeps turning up in your head like something on a revolving-stage! Of course you're quite right to say one mustn't rest so long as such unfortunate human beasts are being simply killed off because society doesn't know what to do with them. But it's even more obvious that the healthy normal conscience is right in simply refusing to bother with such over-refined scruples. The fact is there are certain ultimate criteria of healthy thinking that one can't prove, one has to have them in one's blood!"

Clarisse retorted: "Only according to *your* blood 'of course' is always 'of course not'!"

Walter was nettled and shook his head to show her that he was not going to answer this. He was thoroughly tired of always being the one who had to utter warnings against the danger of living on a diet of one-sided ideas, and perhaps by now it was even making him unsure of himself.

But, with that nervous sensitivity which never failed to amaze him, Clarisse read his thoughts. Lifting her head high, she took one of her mental leaps over all the intervening stages and landed beside him on the peak of the argument, softly and urgently asking: "Can you imagine Jesus as the manager of a coal-mine?"

Her face betrayed that what she really meant by 'Jesus' was he himself; it was one of those extravagances in which love becomes indistinguishable from madness.

He waved this off with a gesture that was at once indignant and discouraged. " Not so direct, Clarisse ! " he implored. " One mustn't say things so directly ! "

" Oh yes, one must ! " Clarisse contradicted. " Direct is just what one must be ! If we haven't the strength to save him, we won't have the strength to save ourselves ! "

" And what the hell does it matter if they do string him up ? " Walter burst out. The savour of this brutal answer was so strong that it was like rolling round his tongue the liberating taste of life, gloriously blended with the taste of death and of the entangled doom that Clarisse was obscurely conjuring up.

Clarisse looked at him expectantly. But Walter was silent, either in relief after his outburst or in indecision.

And, like one whose turn it is now to play her irresistible final trump, she said: " I have been sent a sign ! "

" You and your fantasies ! " Walter shouted ceilingwards, as if to high heaven.

But after those last imponderable words of hers Clarisse left him alone, giving him no chance to say any more.

However, it was not very long afterwards that Walter saw her eagerly talking to Meingast, who was evidently made uneasy, short-sighted as he was, by a feeling of their both being watched. And indeed Walter was not taking any share in the gardening so energetically being done by his brother-in-law. Siegmund, who had arrived a little while earlier, was kneeling at the edge of a bed, in his shirt-sleeves, doing something or other that Walter had insisted must be done in the garden in spring if one was serious about being a human being and not merely a marker lying flat between the pages of the textbook of life. Yet all Walter himself was doing was glancing furtively over at the two others who were in the far corner of this rather bare, exposed kitchen-garden.

He did not really think there was anything going on over there to which he could have taken exception. Still, his hands felt unnaturally cold in the spring air; his legs were cold too, for there were wet patches on his trousers as a result of his kneeling down occasionally, giving Siegmund instructions. He took a high tone with him, as weak, downtrodden people will do whenever they get a chance to work off their bad temper on someone. He knew that Siegmund, having taken it into his head to think highly of him, would not easily be put off. Yet it was positively an after-sunset solitariness, a graveyard chill, that he seemed to feel as he watched Clarisse, who never cast a glance in his direction but kept her gaze on Meingast with every sign of intense interest. And he actually took pride in this. Since Meingast had come to stay in his house, he had been just as proud of the chasms that suddenly gaped wide everywhere in it as he had been anxiously trying to fill them in again. Standing over the kneeling Siegmund, he had just said to him: " Of course we all feel and are familiar with that sort of thing—that hankering for the problematic and morbid." *He* was no cringer and crawler, no hypocrite. In the short time since he had said the same thing to Clarisse and she had practically called him a Philistine, he had formulated a new dictum, on ' the petty dishonesty of life '.

" A small act of dishonesty adds a taste to things, like sweetness or sourness," he now held forth to his brother-in-law. " But it is our duty to refine it within ourselves until it does credit to healthy life. And what I mean by a small act of dishonesty," he went on, " is both the nostalgic compact we make with death when we listen to ' Tristan ' and the secret fascination that most sexual crimes have for us even though we don't yield to it. For there's something dishonest and anti-human, you see, both about elemental life when it overpowers us with want and disease *and* about ex-aggerated scruples of intellect and conscience trying to do violence to life. Whatever tries to overstep the limits set us is dishonest ! Mysticism is just as dishonest as the delusion that Nature can be reduced to a mathematical formula. And the project of going to see Moosbrugger is just as dishonest as——" here Walter paused for a moment in order to hit the nail on the head the more effectively, and concluded: " as if you were to invoke God at a patient's bedside ! "

There was certainly something in what he had said, and he had even managed to take Siegmund by surprise with this appeal to his automatic, professional humanitarianism as a doctor, which ought to make him agree that Clarisse's scheme and her over-wrought reasons for it did overstep the limits of what was permissible. But in relation to Siegmund Walter was a genius, and this was manifest in the fact that Walter's healthy-mindedness had led him to confess to such ideas, whereas his brother-in-law's even healthier healthy-mindedness expressed itself in his remaining doggedly silent in the face of this dubious world of ideas. Siegmund was patting the loosened earth firm with his fingers and, at the same time, still without uttering a word, was tilting his head now to one side, now to the other, as though observing the contents of a test-tube before proceeding further with the test, or perhaps merely as if he were shaking the talk out of his ears.

And when Walter had thus relieved his feelings, there was a deadly deep silence. And he now heard words that Clarisse must once have called out to him; for though it was by no means as vivid as a hallucination, these words gaped like holes in the solid silence: ' Nietzsche and Christ perished of their half-heartedness ! ' And in some faintly uncanny way, reminiscent of the ' manager of a coal-mine ', he felt flattered. It was indeed a queer situation, to be standing here, normality personified, here in the cool garden between a man on whom he looked down condescendingly and two unnaturally excited people, gesticulating just out of earshot, at whom he gazed with an air of superiority and yet in yearning. For what it came to was that Clarisse was the petty dishonesty that his normality needed if it was not to grow sluggish, and a secret voice told him that Meingast was at this very moment engaged in boundlessly enlarging the permissible pettiness of that dishonesty. He admired him the way an unfamous man admires a famous relative, and seeing Clarisse conspiratorially whispering with him aroused his envy more than his jealousy—a feeling, that is, that ate into him even more deeply than jealousy would have: and yet it also somehow elevated him, making him conscious of his own dignity and so preventing him from growing angry. And he refused to let himself go over and disturb the two of them; over against their excitement he felt superior, and what all this gave rise to—he himself did not know how—was a hybrid obscure thought born outside the realm of logic: the thought that the two of them over there were calling upon God in some uninhibited and reprehensible way.

If such a queerly complicated state of mind could be called thinking at all, then it was a kind of thinking that cannot be formulated in words because the chemical constitution of its obscurity is instantly destroyed when exposed to the light of language. Besides, as he had revealed to Siegmund, Walter did not associate any belief with the word ' God ', and after it had occurred to him an abashed void rose all around it. So the first thing that he said to his brother-in-law after a long silence was very remote from that subject. " You're a silly ass," he said reproachfully, " if you think you have no right to warn her off this visit, in the strongest possible terms. What are you a doctor for anyway ? "

Siegmund did not take this in the least amiss either. " It's up to you to have it out with her," he replied, looking up calmly for a moment and then turning back to what he was doing.

Walter sighed. " Of course, Clarisse is an unusual person ! " he began all over again. " I can well understand her. I even grant you there's something in the austerity of her views. You've only got to think of all the poverty, hunger, and misery of every kind that the world's full of—just take for instance the disasters in coal-mines, roofs falling in because the management wouldn't spend enough on proper scaffolding——! "

Siegmund gave no indication that he ever gave a thought to it.

" Well, she does think of these things ! " Walter went on sternly. " And I regard it as very fine indeed that she does so. The rest of us find it much too easy to put our conscience to sleep. And she's better than we are for insisting that we should all *change* and acquire a more active conscience, so to speak a conscience with no limit to it, an infinite one. But what I want to know from you is : mustn't this necessarily lead to a pathological state of moral scruples, if indeed it isn't already something of the sort ? Surely you can give an authoritative opinion on that ? ! "

Thus vigorously challenged, Siegmund rose up on one knee and gave his brother-in-law a searching look. " Crazy ! " he declared. " Still, not in a medical sense, you know."

" And what do you say to this ? " Walter continued, unmindful now of his superior position. " She claims to get signs sent to her."

" She says she gets signs sent her ? " Siegmund asked dubiously.

" Signs, I tell you ! This mad murderer's one of them. And then just recently that filthy mad pig outside our windows ! "

" *Pig ?* "

" No, no, not literally.   A sort of exhibitionist."

" H'm, I see," Siegmund said, turning it over in his mind.
" You get signs sent to you too, when you find something to paint.
The only difference," he finally decided, " is that she expresses
herself in a more high-strung way than you do."

" And," Walter exclaimed fiercely, " what about her assertion
that she's got to take these people's sins on herself, and mine too,
and yours, and I don't know whose besides ? "

Siegmund had got to his feet and was brushing earth from his
hands. " She feels oppressed by sins, does she ? " he asked,
somewhat rhetorically, and he seemed glad to be able now at last
to do his brother-in-law the courtesy of agreeing with him, as he
said : " That's symptomatic."

" Symptomatic ? " Walter asked, all at once utterly cast
down.

" Fixed ideas about sin are a symptom," Siegmund assured him
with professional detachment.

" But look, it's like this," Walter objected, instantly bringing
up the idea of ' vocation ' against the expert opinion he had gone
to the trouble of extracting.   " First of all, surely, you have to ask
yourself : Is there such a thing as sin ?   Of course there is.   But
then there's no reason why a fixed idea about sin should be a
delusion.   I dare say you don't understand that—it's supra-
empirical, you see !   It's man's injured sense of responsibility
towards a higher life ! "

" But you say she claims to get signs sent her ! " Siegmund
persisted.

" But you yourself say I get signs too ! " Walter furiously
exclaimed.   " And I can tell you there's many a time when I could
easily go down on my knees and implore my destiny to leave me
in peace !   But it keeps on sending signs, and the most magnificent
of them are sent through Clarisse ! "   Then, more calmly, he
went on : " For instance, what she's saying now is that this Moosbrugger chap stands for herself and me in our ' body of sin ' and
is sent to us by way of admonition.   But this can be understood
as a symbol of the way we neglect the higher potentialities in our
lives, which might be called our ' body of light '.   Many years
ago, when Meingast left us——"

" But fixed ideas about sin *are* symptomatic of certain disorders ! " Siegmund reminded him, with maddening professional calm.

" Symptoms—of course that's all you can understand ! " Walter said in animated defence of his Clarisse. " The other side of things is outside your scope. But perhaps this superstition, which regards anything as a disturbance or a disorder if it doesn't fit in with the most deadly commonplace experience, is the very thing I mean—sin and our life's sinful form. What Clarisse calls out for is a spiritual campaign against that. It was actually many years ago, at the time Meingast left us, that we first ——" He stopped, thinking of how Clarisse and he had ' taken Meingast's sins on themselves '. But it was hopeless to try explaining the process of a spiritual awakening to Siegmund. So he concluded rather vaguely with the words: " Anyway, I don't suppose you'll deny there've always been people who have done what might be called drawing everyone's sins on themselves or even concentrating them in themselves ? "

His brother-in-law gave him a placid look. " There you are then ! " he responded amiably. " Now you've yourself proved what I began by saying. Thinking oneself weighed down by sins, the way she does, is a characteristic of certain disorders. On the other hand, there are also non-typical attitudes and modes of behaviour to be found in life. That's all I ever maintained."

" And what about this exaggerated stringency of hers in all she does ? " Walter asked after a while, sighing. " Surely it isn't quite normal to be as rigorous as all that ? "

Meanwhile Clarisse was having an important conversation with Meingast.

" You said," she reminded him, " that the people who pride themselves on being able to explain and understand the world will never change anything in it—isn't that it ? "

" Yes," the Master replied. " ' True ' and ' false ' are the excuses made by those who never want to reach any decision. For truth is something without an end."

" And so that's why you said one must have the courage to decide between ' value ' and ' non-value ' ? " Clarisse pressed on.

" Yes," the Master said, somewhat bored.

" And that was a marvellously contemptuous formula of yours,"

Clarisse exclaimed, " about how in modern life people only *do* what *happens* ! "

Meingast stood still, looking at the ground. One might have thought he was inclining an ear, or equally that he was contemplating a pebble on the path, a little to his right. But Clarisse did not go on paying tribute with the honey of praise. She too had now bent her head, so that her chin nearly rested in the hollow of her neck, and her gaze bored into the earth between the toecaps of Meingast's boots. Her pallid face flushed slightly as she went on, warily lowering her voice: " You said all sexuality was nothing but goatish caperings."

" Yes, I said that in a particular context. Whatever our age lacks in will-power it makes up for, apart from its so-called scientific activities, in sexuality."

Clarisse hesitated for a while, and then she said: " I have a great deal of will-power myself, but Walter capers ! "

" What's actually the trouble between you two ? " the Master asked with sudden curiosity. But he instantly added in a tone of disgust: " I can imagine, of course."

They were in a corner of the treeless garden, which was full of the spring sunlight, and in another corner, almost diametrically opposite to them, there was Siegmund squatting on the ground, with Walter standing over him, apparently haranguing him. The garden was a rectangle running along the length of the house, with one gravel path leading between vegetable-beds and flower-beds and two other gravel paths forming a light-coloured cross upon the still bare earth. Warily glancing over in the direction of the other two, Clarisse replied: " Perhaps he can't help it, but the fact is I attract Walter in a way that isn't right."

" I can well imagine it," the Master answered, this time with a sympathetic glance. " There is something boyish about you."

At this praise Clarisse felt happiness bouncing through her veins like hailstones. " Did you notice," she swiftly asked, " ' that time ', that I can change faster than a man ? " Seeing the blank expression that came over the sage's benevolently furrowed face, she giggled. " ' Change ' is a double word," she declared. " There are more of them, too. ' Sex-murder ' for instance."

The Master now seemed to think it well to show no surprise at anything. " Oh yes, yes indeed," he replied, " I know. I re-

member your once maintaining it was ' sex-murder ' to quench
love in the usual embrace." But what, he asked then, did she
mean about ' changing ' ?

" Letting things take their course is murder," Clarisse explained
with the speed of someone going through his paces on slippery
ground and taking a tumble as a result of too much nimbleness.

" You know," Meingast confessed, " now I've completely lost
track. I suppose you're again talking about that fellow the
carpenter. What do you want with him ? "

Clarisse pensively scraped the gravel with the tip of her shoe.
" It's all the same thing," she said. And suddenly she glanced
up at the Master. " I think Walter ought to learn to deny me,"
she said very abruptly.

" I can't judge that," Meingast remarked, after vainly waiting
for her to go on. " But certainly the radical solutions are always
the better ones."

He said that merely for all eventualities. But now Clarisse
lowered her head again, so that her gaze buried itself somewhere
in Meingast's suit, and after a while her hand slowly approached
his forearm. She suddenly felt a wild desire to grasp that hard,
lean arm under the loose sleeve and touch the Master, who was
pretending to have forgotten the illuminating words he had
himself uttered concerning the carpenter. While this was going
on she felt she was pushing some part of herself across to him,
and in the slowness of her hand's disappearance into his sleeve,
slow as the movement of a tide, there eddied flotsam and jetsam
of some incomprehensible voluptuous pleasure, emanating from
her perception of the Master's staying quite still and letting himself
be touched by her.

Meingast however for some reason looked down aghast at the
hand clutching his arm in this way and moving up it like a many-
legged creature thrusting itself upon the female of its species.
Looking down at this small woman's lowered eyelids, he caught a
flash of something unusual and suddenly understood a dubious
process that, because of the public way in which it was going on,
was quite affecting.

" Come along," he proposed, removing her hand with all
friendliness. " If we stand here like this, we're too noticeable.
Let's go on walking up and down."

And while they once again strolled up and down, Clarisse re-counted: " I change very quickly, faster than a man, if need be. My clothes simply fly on to my body when I'm—I don't know how to put it—when I'm like *that*! Perhaps it's a sort of electricity. What belongs to me gets drawn on to me, *at-tracted* to me.   But usually it's a sinister sort of attraction."

Meingast bestowed a smile on these puns, which he still failed to understand, and made a random attempt at giving an impressive answer.   " So you clothe yourself in your clothes rather the way a hero clothes himself in his destiny ? "

To his surprise Clarisse stopped short, exclaiming: " Yes, that's exactly it !   If you live like that you feel it even in clothes, shoes, knives and forks ! "

" There's some truth in that," the Master said in confirmation of this obscurely convincing assertion.   Then he asked point-blank: " How do you actually manage with Walter ? "

Clarisse did not understand.   Looking at him, she saw his eyes suddenly filled with yellow clouds, like sand blown on a desert wind.

" You said," Meingast went on with some hesitation, " that you attract him in a way that ' isn't right '.   You mean, I suppose, not right for a woman ?   How's that ?   Are you entirely frigid with men ? "

Clarisse did not know what ' frigid ' meant.

" A frigid woman," the Master explained, " is one who gets no pleasure from sexual intercourse with men."

" But the only man I've had any experience of is Walter," Clarisse objected, crestfallen.

" Well yes, but from all you've said it does seem reasonable to assume it, doesn't it ? "

Clarisse was nonplussed.   She had to reflect on this.   She did not know.   " Me ?   But I mustn't.   I've actually got to prevent it ! " she said.   " I mustn't let it come to that ! "

" You don't say ! "   Now the Master uttered a ribald laugh. " You mean you've got to prevent yourself feeling anything? Or prevent Walter from having his way ? "

Clarisse blushed.   But at the same moment she also saw more clearly what she meant.   " If you give way," she answered gravely, " everything gets drowned in pleasure.   I won't allow men's pleasure to go from them to me and become my pleasure. That's why I've attracted them ever since I was a little girl: I ' change ' them. There's something about men's pleasure that isn't right."

There were various reasons why Meingast preferred not to take up this point. " And can you control yourself to that extent ? " he asked.

" Well, it depends," Clarisse candidly admitted. " But I've told you: I'd be a sex-murderer if I let him have his way ! " She became more intense as she went on: " My women friends talk of ' passing out ' in a man's arms. I've never experienced that. I've never passed out in a man's arms. But I know what it is to ' pass out ' when I *wasn't* being made love to. I'm sure you've had the same experience. After all, didn't you say the world's much too free of illusion ? "

Meingast waved his hand deprecatingly, apparently to indicate that she had not properly understood him.

But by now it had become almost too clear to her. " If for instance you say," she exclaimed, " that one has to decide against what's inferior and in favour of the higher values, what that comes to is: there is a life of voluptuous ecstasy that's tremendous, with no limits to it ! That's not the lust of sex, it's the lust of genius ! And that's what Walter's a traitor to the moment I don't stop him ! "

Meingast shook his head. He dissociated himself from this impassioned variation on what he had said: his rejection of it was startled, almost frightened, and he responded only to the most random and trivial element in what she had said: " But it's very doubtful whether he *could* do anything else ! "

Clarisse again pulled up short, as though lightning had rooted her to the ground. " He must ! " she cried out. " And it's you yourself who taught us that one must ! "

" That's true," the Master reluctantly granted. He vainly tried to get her to walk on with him. " But precisely *what* is it you want ? "

" Look, I didn't want anything until you came," Clarisse said softly. " But it's so awful, this life that scoops no more than the wretched bit of sexual pleasure out of the whole ocean of life's pleasures ! And now I do want something."

" That's what I'm asking you about," Meingast prompted her.

" A person must be in the world for some purpose. One must be ' good ' for something. Otherwise everything's just a frightful muddle," Clarisse replied.

" Is what you're after connected with Moosbrugger ? " Meingast probed.

" That can't be explained. We'll have to see what comes of that," Clarisse retorted. Then she added thoughtfully: " I shall carry him off, I'll create a scandal ! " Her expression had changed, becoming mysterious. " I've been watching you," she said suddenly. " Mysterious people keep coming to see you. You ask them to come when you think we're not at home. They're boys and young men ! You don't say what they want ! "

Meingast stared at her blankly.

" You're working up to something," Clarisse went on. " You're setting it going ! But I—" she gasped it out, whispering, " I'm so strong too that I can be friends with several people at the same time ! I've acquired a man's character and a man's duties ! Living with Walter I've learnt to have a man's feelings ! " Once again her hand groped for Meingast's arm, obviously without her being conscious of it herself. Her fingers crept out of her sleeve, curved like claws. " I'm a double being," she whispered. " I want you to know that ! But it isn't easy. You're right, that's something where a person mustn't be afraid to use force."

Meingast was still looking at her with dismay. He had not met these states of hers before. It was unintelligible to him what she was getting at. Obviously for Clarisse herself at the moment nothing was plainer than the idea of a ' double being ', but Meingast was wondering whether she had guessed something of his secret life and was alluding to that. There was not yet much to guess; it was only recently, in accord with his exclusively masculine philosophy, that he had begun to observe a shift in his feelings and to surround himself with young men who amounted to something more than disciples. But perhaps that was why he had moved and come here, where he felt safe from observation. He had never before thought of such a possibility, and here was this little creature, who had become quite uncanny, now seemingly capable of guessing at what was going on in him. Somehow more and more of her arm was emerging from the sleeve of her dress, longer and barer, though without any reduction of the distance between the two bodies linked by her touch; and this bare, skinny forearm and the hand clutching at Meingast seemed at this moment to make such an extraordinary pattern that in the man's imagination there was now a wild confusion of all that had previously been separate and distinct.

But Clarisse was no longer able to get out what she had been on the way to saying, and this even though it was inwardly clear to her. What she called 'double words' were tokens of it, scattered about in language like twigs one breaks or leaves one strews on the ground in order to mark a secret way one has gone. There were 'sex-murder' and 'change', and then too there was 'quick', and there were many other words; in fact perhaps all words had two meanings, one of which was secret and private. But a double language signified a double life. Ordinary life is obviously that of sin, the secret one that of the body of light. So for instance 'quick' in its sinful form meant ordinary, every-day, fatiguing haste, but in its light-form everything was a swift bouncing out of it, bounding and deliciously rebounding. But then instead of 'pleasure-form' one can equally well say 'power-form' or 'innocence-form', and on the other hand one can refer to the sinful form by all the words that imply anything of ordinary life's depression, dullness and irresolution. Here there were remarkable connections between things and the self, so that any-thing one did had an effect where one would never have expected it; and the less Clarisse was able to formulate this idea, the more vividly the words sprang up within her, coming faster than she could collect them. But there was one conviction she had had for some time now: the duty, the privilege, the mission of what is called conscience, illusion, will-power, is to find the strong form the form that is light. And this is to be found wherever there is nothing random or accidental, where there is no room to waver, where happiness and necessity coincide. Other people have called this 'living essentially', have spoken of the 'intelligible character', have equated instinct with innocence and intellect with sin. Clarisse could not think that way, but she had made the discovery that one could set events in motion, and sometimes then particles of the body of light spontaneously attached them-selves to the event and became assimilated into it. For reasons that were primarily connected with Walter's over-sensitive inactivity, but also for reasons of a heroic longing for glory, which she had never had the means of satisfying, she had finally come to the conclusion that every person could set up a memorial ahead of himself, by resolving to do something by sheer force, and that this memorial would then automatically draw him on towards it. For this reason too she was quite in the dark about what she meant to do with Moosbrugger, and she could not give Meingast any answer to his question.

Nor did she want to. Although Walter had told her she was not to say that the Master was having another transformation, there was no doubt that his spirit was moving towards secret preparation for some act of which she knew nothing, but which must surely be as glorious as his spirit was. And so he could not but understand her, even if he pretended not to. The less she said, the more she showed him how much she knew. It was also permissible for her to take hold of him, and he could not forbid it. Thus he accorded recognition to her enterprise, and she penetrated into his and partook of it. This likewise was a sort of double being, and one so strong that it remained obscure to her. Through her arm there flowed all the strength she had, this strength she did not know the measure of, an utterly inexhaustible current flowing from her to her mysterious friend and leaving her hollow, the very marrow drained from her bones, in a state of sheer weakness far surpassing any sensation caused by physical love. She could not do anything but gaze smilingly at her hand, or shift her gaze to his face. Nor did Meingast do anything but gaze now at her, now at her hand.

And all at once something happened that took Clarisse by surprise and then threw her into a whirl of bacchantic ecstasy.

Meingast had been trying to keep a superior smile fixed on his face, lest his uncertainty should betray itself to her. At the same time this uncertainty was increasing from minute to minute, as she continued to say things that seemed incomprehensible.

For preceding every act performed with doubtful conviction there is a period of weakness, corresponding to the moments of remorse after the act, though in the natural course of events it may scarcely be noticeable. The convictions and intense mental images that protect and approve the accomplished act have at this stage not yet reached their highest pitch: they are still wavering in the steadily mounting tide of passion, vague and amorphous as they will probably be later when they tremble and disintegrate in the outgoing tide of passionate remorse. It was on just this phase of evolving intentions that Meingast had been surprised. It was doubly distressing to him, because of the past and because of the regard in which he was now held by Walter and Clarisse. And then, every intense excitement alters one's picture of reality, shifting it into its own key so that it can draw new stimulation from it. Thus the uncanny state that Meingast was in made Clarisse uncanny to him; fear lent her a touch of the frightful; and all attempts to come down to earth and the truth were such a failure as merely to increase bewilderment. So it was that, instead of suggesting superior calm, the smile on Meingast's face stiffened with every passing moment; indeed it became a sort of stiff floating, and finally seemed about to float away as stiffly as on stilts. By then the Master found it impossible to behave otherwise than as a big dog does when faced with some much smaller creature that he does not quite dare to attack, such as a caterpillar, a toad, or a snake: he reared up higher and higher on his long legs, drew back his lips and arched his back—and suddenly felt the currents of discomfort sweeping him away from the place where they had their source, himself unable to cover his flight by any word or gesture.

Clarisse did not let go of him. As he took the first, still hesitant steps, it might have been taken for ingenuous eagerness; but then it became obvious that he was tugging her along with him. With an effort he explained, stammeringly and briefly, that he was in a hurry to get up to his room and work. It was only inside the house that he managed to disentangle himself from her completely, and up to that point he had been driven only by the urge to get away, paying no attention to what Clarisse was saying and almost choking with eagerness not to be noticed by Walter and Siegmund.

Indeed Walter had guessed the general pattern of what had been going on. He could see that Clarisse was passionately trying to get out of Meingast something that Meingast was refusing her, and jealousy was boring into his breast like a double-threaded screw. For although he suffered agonies at the thought that Clarisse was offering her favours to their friend, he was perhaps even more intensely insulted at seeing her, as he believed, disdained. If that feeling were carried to its logical conclusion, then he would force Meingast to take Clarisse to himself; and then he, Walter, would be plunged into despair by the sweep of the same inner impulse. He was stirred, wistfully and heroically. He could not bear it that while Clarisse was poised on the knife-edge of her destiny he should have to be listening to Siegmund asking whether the seedlings should have the earth left loose around them or patted down firmly. He had to say something, and he felt like a pianoforte in that hundredth of a second between the moment when the ten-fingered lightning is tremendously about to strike and the next moment when the great crash comes. There was light in his throat: words that would surely explain everything differently from ever before. But somehow the only thing he could get out was not that at all.

"I won't put up with it! I won't allow it!" he repeated, speaking more to the garden than to Siegmund.

But it turned out that though Siegmund had seemed intent on seedlings, dibber and trowel, he had also been observing what was going on and having his own ideas about it. For now he rose to his feet, brushed the earth off his knees, and gave his brother-in-law some advice.

"If you think she's going too far, then it's up to you to start her thinking about something else," he said in a tone that implied he had, as a matter of course, all this time been considering, with physicianly conscientiousness, what Walter had confided to him.

"And how on earth am I to do that?" Walter blankly asked.

"Just as any man does," Siegmund said. "'All a woman's fret and fuss has but one point of cure', or however it goes."

Siegmund put up with a great deal from Walter, and indeed life is full of such relationships, in which one elbows and overpowers the other and the other does not rebel. In fact—and this was Siegmund's own belief—this is just the way that normal healthy life is. For the world would probably have come to an end round about the Bronze Age if everyone had stood up for himself to the last drop of his blood. Instead, the weaker have always meekly knuckled under, looking round for other neighbours whom they themselves will be able to elbow out: this is the pattern on which most human relationship are based to this day, and time cures all ills. In the family circle, where Walter passed for a genius, Siegmund had always been treated as rather a booby; he had accepted that, and even today he would have been the yielding and respectful one wherever it was a matter of precedence within the family hierarchy. For years now that old structure of relationships had been unimportant compared with the new status they had each of them acquired in life; and just for that reason it had been left in its traditional form. Siegmund not only had a very respectable practice as a physician—and the doctor, unlike the civil servant, rules not by means of extraneous power but through his individual ability, coming to people who look to him for help and are docile in accepting what he offers—but he also had a wealthy wife, who had within a short period bestowed three children on him and whom he betrayed, if not often, at least fairly regularly, whenever it suited him, with other women. Thus Siegmund was, if he chose, well equipped to give Walter confident and reliable advice.

At this moment Clarisse came out of the house again.

She could not remember now what had been said during their tempestuous rush indoors. In a way she realised very well that the Master had fled from her, but the details had faded from that memory, leaving it to fold up into something closed and compact. Something had happened! With this one notion in her mind Clarisse felt like someone emerging from a thunderstorm, still charged from top to toe with sensual force. A few yards in front of her, beyond the bottom of the small stone steps outside the door where she had come out, she saw a cock blackbird, in its flame-yellow beak a fat caterpillar that it was devouring. There was tremendous energy in the bird—or was it in the two contrasting colours? It was not exactly that Clarisse was thinking anything about this; it was rather that something was answering her from everywhere behind her. The jet-feathered bird was a body of sin in the moment of doing violence. The caterpillar was a butterfly's body of sin. Both creatures had been put in her path by destiny, as a sign that she must act. One could actually see the blackbird absorbing the caterpillar's sins through its blazing orange beak. Was the blackbird not the ' black genius '? Just as the dove is the ' white spirit '? Did the signs not form a chain? The exhibitionist a link with the carpenter, with the Master's light . . .? None of these notions took such clear form in her, they lodged invisibly in the walls of the house, summoned but still keeping their answer to themselves; but what Clarisse really felt, as she came out on to the steps and saw the bird eating the caterpillar, was an ineffable correspondence of interior and exterior experience.

She conveyed this in a peculiar way to Walter. The impression he got was instantly something very like what he referred to as ' calling upon God ': this time he diagnosed it unerringly. He could not tell, at this distance, what was actually going on in Clarisse: but there was something non-accidental that he perceived in her bearing; the way she stood facing the world into which the small flight of steps descended, like the steps leading down into the water of a swimming-pool. It was something exalted. It was not the attitude of ordinary, normal life. And he suddenly realised it was this very state of being non-accidental that Clarisse meant when he said: ' This man is not by chance under my window ! ' Gazing at his wife, he himself felt everything becoming charged and flooded with the current of some other kind of force. Even the fact that he was standing here and Clarisse over there, at such an angle to him that he had to turn his eyes away from the direction they had been involuntarily taking, along the length of the garden, if he wanted to see her clearly—even this simple fact suddenly proved how the mute emphasis of life itself outweighed all natural chance, randomness, the accidental. Out of the fullness of images thrusting themselves upon the eye there now reared up something geometrically linear and extraordinary. That was probably how it was for Clarisse when she found a meaning in almost insubstantial correspondences, such as the fact that one man stopped under her window and another was a carpenter. Then, surely, events had a way of composing themselves that was different from the ordinary way, manifesting themselves as elements in some other totality that revealed other aspects of them; and because this brought these aspects out of their obscure hiding-places, it entitled Clarisse to assert that it was she herself who attracted whatever it might be. It was hard to formulate this without sounding fanciful, but it did finally occur to Walter that it was in fact closely akin to something he himself knew very well, namely what happened when one was painting a picture. For a painting has its own inexplicable way of excluding any colour or line that does not correspond to its fundamental form and style and scale of colour, while it draws out of the hand whatever it needs, and this by virtue of the laws of genius, which are not the ordinary laws of Nature. At this moment he no longer felt any of that rounded wellbeing in health and sanity which scrutinises life's excrescences to see what might turn out useful. That was what he had been lauding only a short while earlier; what he felt now was more like the woefulness of a little boy who does not dare to join in a game he is watching.

But Siegmund was not the man to drop something once he had taken it in hand.

" Clarisse is overstrung," he declared. " She's always been one to run her head against brick walls, and now she's got that head of hers stuck in one of them. You'll have to make a dead set at her, no matter what sort of fight she puts up."

" You doctors don't understand the slightest thing about psychological processes ! " Walter exclaimed. He sought a second point of attack, and found it. " You talk about ' signs '," he went on, his irritation overlaid, however, by his delight in being able to talk about Clarisse, " and you worry about when signs indicate a disorder and when they don't. But I tell you: the true state of man is that in which everything is a sign ! Absolutely everything ! You may be able to look Truth in the eye, but Truth will never look you in the eye. That's a divinely uncertain feeling you'll never know ! "

" You're both as mad as hatters," Siegmund remarked dryly.

" Yes, yes, of course we are ! " Walter exclaimed. " After all, you're the uncreative type. You've never known what ' expressing oneself ' means—that for an artist it's simply the basic equivalent of ' understanding '. It's only the expression we give to things that evolves our capacity to perceive them aright. I understand what I mean, or someone else means, only by carrying it out ! That's our living experience, as distinct from your experience, which is dead ! Of course you'll say that's paradoxical, a confusion of cause and effect—you with your medical causality ! "

However, Siegmund did not say that. He merely went on, with dogged persistence: " It's definitely only for her own good if you don't put up with too much nonsense from her. Neurotic people need a certain amount of strict discipline."

" And when I play the piano at the open window, what am I doing ? " Walter demanded, apparently not even hearing his brother-in-law's warning. "People go by, some of them girls I dare say, and anyone who feels like it stops and listens. I play for young lovers and lonely old people. There are the clever ones. What I give them isn't anything rational, anyway. What I play isn't rational. I'm communing with them, it's myself I'm giving them. I sit there unseen in my room, giving them signs: a few notes, and it's their life, and it's my life. You might tell me if that's mad too ! " He broke off abruptly. The feeling of ' Oh, I could tell you all a thing or two ! ', that basic ambitious urge of every dweller upon earth who feels impelled to communicate something and who has only a moderate capacity to create anything, had petered out. Every time that Walter sat in the soft emptiness of that room of his with the open window, sending forth his music with the lofty sense of being the artist who gives happiness to anonymous thousands, this feeling was like an open umbrella; and then, the instant he stopped playing, it was a sloppily closed one. Then all the lightness was gone, all that had happened might just as well never have happened at all, and he could only say such things as that art had lost touch with ' the people ' and that everything had gone to the dogs. Recalling this, he became dejected. He tried not to be. After all, Clarisse had said one must play the music ' right through to the end '. Clarisse had said one understood a thing only so long as one was joining in, doing it oneself. But Clarisse had also said: That is why we must go to the lunatic asylum ourselves ! Walter's interior umbrella flapped, half down, in irregular stormy gusts.

Siegmund said: " Neurotic or high-strung people need a certain amount of discipline, it's for their own good. You said yourself you won't put up with any more of it. Professionally and personally I can only give you the same advice: show her you're a man. I know she jibs at that, but she'll come round all right ! " Siegmund was like a reliable machine indefatigably repeating the ' answer ' it had arrived at.

In one of his interior storm-gusts Walter replied: " You know, all this medical emphasis on a well-adjusted sex-life is simply out of date ! When I play, or paint, or think, I act upon those around me and those out of reach, without depriving the ones of what I

give the others. On the contrary! Take it from me, there's
probably no sphere where one's any longer justified in living only
for oneself—not even in marriage!"

But the intenser pressure was on Siegmund's side, and Walter
went sailing before the wind across to Clarisse, whom he had not
lost sight of all during this talk. He did not at all like to think of
anyone's suggesting he was unmanly: he turned his back on the
suggestion by letting it waft him towards Clarisse. And halfway
there he felt the certainty, as his lips drew back nervously to show
his teeth, that he was going to start by saying: ' What do you mean
by this talk about signs?!'

But Clarisse saw him coming. She had even seen him beginning to waver towards her while he was still standing there. Then
his feet had been drawn from the earth, had borne him her way.
She participated in this with a furious delight. Startled, the
blackbird flew away with its caterpillar. Now the way was quite
clear for the attraction, the magnetic change. But suddenly
Clarisse thought better of it and eluded the encounter for the time
being by slipping slowly along the side of the house into the open,
not turning away from Walter, yet moving faster than he, hesitant
as he was, could move out of the realm of remote control into that
of argument and counter-argument.

27   *Agathe soon discovered by General Stumm as an asset to society.*

SINCE Agathe had joined forces with him, Ulrich's relations
with the extensive social circle centred on the Tuzzi household had
been making great demands on his time. For although the year
was advancing, there was as yet no slackening in the intense
sociability of the winter season, and the sympathetic interest
bestowed on Ulrich at the time of his father's death required some
return: he had, in fact, to produce Agathe, even though their
mourning relieved them of the obligation of appearing at large

functions. Indeed, if Ulrich had fully exploited the advantage that mourning offered, it would have been an adequate pretext for avoiding any social intercourse for some time and he could have dropped out of a circle that he had only got into by a strange constellation of circumstances. However, since Agathe had put herself into his charge he had begun acting in a way contrary to the way his feelings bade him act; to a part of himself that he housed in the traditional concept ' duties of an elder brother ' he referred many decisions from which his whole self would have held aloof, if it had not actually disapproved. The first of these elder-brotherly duties was to see that Agathe's flight from under her husband's roof should end solely under the roof of a better husband.

" If things go on the way they are going," he would say when-ever she suggested that this or that should be done if they were to continue living together, " you will soon be getting offers of mar-riage—or if not of hand, certainly of heart." And if Agathe drew up schemes reaching more than a few weeks ahead, he would object: " Oh, by that time everything'll be different."

This would have wounded her still more had she not observed the conflict in her brother, and this for the present kept her from putting up any strong resistance when he chose to extend their social explorations to the farthest extent. And so indeed it was that from soon after Agathe's arrival they were both far more involved in social obligations than Ulrich would have been on his own.

This unfailing appearance of two people together, after such a long period when everyone had been acquainted only with Ulrich and had never heard a word from him about his sister, caused no slight sensation. It had begun one day when General Stumm von Bordwehr, arriving at Ulrich's house with his orderly, his despatch-case and his loaf of bread, had scented something suspicious in the atmosphere. There was actually a trace of scent in the air. Then Stumm discovered a woman's stocking hanging over the arm of a chair and said reprovingly: " Ah, these young chaps ! "

" My sister," Ulrich declared.

" Get along with you ! You haven't got a sister ! " the General protested. " Here we are, all up to the eyes in all sorts of serious problems, and you go and shut yourself up with some wench ! "

At that moment Agathe came into the room, and her appearance thoroughly rattled the General. Apart from the family resemblance he saw, the casualness of her entry suggested that Ulrich had spoken the truth; on the other hand he could not shake off the feeling that this was a woman that Ulrich was having an affair with, though why she should look so bewilderingly like him he could not understand.

'I really don't know what came over me, dear lady,' he said later, giving Diotima an account of it, 'but I couldn't have been more amazed if he'd suddenly been there in front of me as an ensign again!' For at the sight of Agathe, to whom he was instantly attracted, Stumm became flustered, as he always did when he was profoundly stirred. The pudgy little General's sensibility made him wish to retreat from a tactically impossible position, and in spite of all the trouble Ulrich went to to make him feel at ease, little more was this time heard of the serious problems that had brought the War Ministry's culture-laden emissary to the house.

"No, no," Stumm demurred. "Nothing's so important as to justify my butting in like this."

"But you're not butting in!" Ulrich assured him, smiling. "What is there to butt in on?"

"Well no, of course not," Stumm agreed, losing his head entirely. "Of course, in a certain sense not. But all the same —look, I'll drop in some other time."

"But at least tell me what you came for before you dash away again," Ulrich demanded.

"Oh nothing, nothing at *all*! A mere trifle!" the General exclaimed in his eagerness to get away. "I think the 'Great Event' is just beginning."

"A horse! A horse! Aboard for France!" Ulrich nonsensically exclaimed, in high amusement.

Agathe looked at him in astonishment.

"I do apologise," the General said to her. "You can't know what this is about."

"The Collateral Campaign has found a crowning idea," Ulrich interposed.

"No," the General modified, "I didn't say that. I only meant: the great event that everyone's been waiting for is now on its way."

" Oh, I see," Ulrich said. " Well, it's been on its way since the very start."

" No," the General gravely assured him. " Not just like that, I mean. Now there's a very definite nobody-knows-quite-what in the air. In a short time your cousin's having a decisive gathering. Frau Drangsal——"

" Who's she ? " Ulrich interrupted, not having heard the name before.

" There you are, you're out of touch with things ! " the General reproached him sadly. He turned to Agathe the next instant to make up for it. " Frau Drangsal is the patroness of the poet Feuermaul. I suppose," he said, revolving again towards Ulrich, from whom no comment came, " you don't know him either ? "

" Yes I do. Lyrical stuff."

" Poems," the General remarked, keeping his distance from unfamiliar territory.

" Even some good ones. And plays as well."

" I don't know about plays. Fact is I haven't got my notes with me. But he's the one that says ' man is good '. Cut a long story short, what Frau Drangsal's extending patronage to is the idea that man is good. They say it's a European idea, and Feuermaul's supposed to have a great future. Husband she had was a doctor, world-famous, and probably she wants to make a famous man out of Feuermaul too. Anyway there's a risk of your cousin losing the leadership, it might go to Frau Drangsal's *salon*, where all the famous people go anyway."

The General wiped sweat from his brow. Ulrich, however, regarded this prospect with equanimity.

" Now, look here ! " Stumm scolded. " You've got a great respect for your cousin, haven't you, same as me ? How can you talk like that ! Don't you agree," he said, appealing to Agathe, " it's outstandingly faithless of him, an ungrateful way to treat a woman we all rave about ? "

" I've never met my cousin," she confessed to him.

" Oh," Stumm said, and with rather back-handed chivalry in which there was an obscure tribute to Agathe, he added: " As a matter of fact, she has been going off rather."

Neither Ulrich nor Agathe responded to this, and the General got the feeling that he must elucidate. " And you know very well

what it is, too," he said meaningfully to Ulrich. He disapproved
of the interest in sexual science that was diverting Diotima's mind
from the Collateral Campaign, and he was worried because her
relations with Arnheim were not improving; but he did not know
how far he might speak of such matters in front of Agathe, whose
expression had been growing steadily cooler.

However, Ulrich replied calmly: " I suppose you can't make
headway with your oil-fields if our Diotima no longer has her old
influence on Arnheim ? "

Stumm made a pathetically imploring gesture, as though to stop
Ulrich from making a joke not fit for a lady to hear; at the same
time he looked him straight in the eye, warning him off. With an
effort he bounced himself to his feet, in all his rotundity, at quite
youthful speed, and tugged his tunic straight. There was still
enough of his original doubt in his mind as to who Agathe really
was to prevent him from exposing the mysteries of the War
Ministry in her presence.

Only in the hall, whither Ulrich accompanied him, did he clutch
his host's arm and hoarsely whisper: " For heaven's sake, don't
go openly talking high treason ! " He impressed it on Ulrich
that no word about the oil-fields must be uttered in front of any
third person, even if she were one's own sister.

" Oh, all right," Ulrich reassured him. " But she's my *twin*
sister ! "

" Not even in front of a twin sister ! " the General expostulated,
still so incredulous of the sister that ' twin sister ' could not
astonish him further. " Promise ! "

" It's no use," Ulrich said with some extravagance, " your
making me promise any such thing. The fact is we're Siamese
twins. D'you see what I mean ? "

At least Stumm did see now that Ulrich, whose way was never
to give a straight ' yes ' to anything, was making fun of him. " I
must say," he said disapprovingly, " I've known you make jokes
in better taste—what an indecent fancy to think of such a delightful
woman, even supposing she was your sister ten times over, being
grown together with you ! " But then because his agitated mistrust of Ulrich's reclusion had been reawakened, he appended a
few more questions, to get at the bottom of what was going on
here. " Has the new secretary turned up yet ? Have you been

to see Diotima? Have you kept your promise to go and see Leinsdorf? Have you found out what's going on between your cousin and Arnheim?" Since this rotund sceptic was of course well informed on all these points, he was merely testing Ulrich's truthfulness. He was satisfied with the result. "Well then, be a good chap and for my sake don't be late at the fateful session," he begged while buttoning up his great-coat, still a little breathless from struggling into it. "Tell you what, I'll ring you up first and fetch you in my carriage."

"And when is this dreary occasion to be?" Ulrich asked, not very encouragingly.

"Well, in a couple of weeks, I should think," the General said. "Fact is we want to get the other party to Diotima's, but we also want Arnheim there, and he's still away." With one finger he tapped the golden sword-knot dangling over his great-coat pocket. "'We' don't feel quite happy without him: I don't have to tell you that. But believe me," he said with a sigh, "there's nothing I personally want more than that your cousin should keep the spiritual leadership. It'd be awful if I had to adapt myself to an entirely new situation."

And so it was this visit that brought Ulrich, now accompanied by his sister, back into the social life from which he had vanished when he was still alone. Now he would indeed have had to resume his social obligations, even if he had not wanted to, because he could not possibly hide away with Agathe even one day longer on the assumption that Stumm would keep to himself a discovery so ripe for gossip.

When the 'Siamese' called on Diotima, it was evident that she was already aware of this unusual and somewhat dubious epithet, even if she was not yet ready to be delighted. For the divine Diotima, celebrated on account of the distinguished and remarkable people who were constantly to be met under her roof, had at first taken Agathe's unheralded debut very ill: a kinswoman who might not meet with unanimous approval would be much more damaging to her own position than any mere male cousin, and she knew precisely as little of this new female cousin as she had once known about Ulrich. This alone caused the universally informed Diotima annoyance when she had to admit her ignorance to the General. She had therefore decided to refer to Agathe as 'the orphan sister ', partly to relieve her own ill-humour, partly as an anticipatory measure in wider circles. It was more or less in this spirit that she received brother and sister when they first called. She was agreeably surprised by the impression of social sophistication that Agathe knew how to convey, and Agathe—mindful of her convent education and always guided by her mocking wonder at life, her readiness to take it as it came, the very thing she accused herself of to Ulrich—from this moment on managed, almost without meaning it, to win the gracious sympathies of the stupendous young woman whose ambition, turning as it did on ' greatness ', left her completely cold and uncomprehending. She considered Diotima with the same innocent astonishment she would have felt if she were being shown over a gigantic power-station: one simply did not meddle in its incomprehensible function of spreading light. Once Diotima had been won over, and all the more since she was soon convinced that Agathe was generally liked, she laid herself out to extend Agathe's social success, enlarging it, as it were, also to redound to her own credit. The ' orphan sister ' aroused sympathetic interest, which among Diotima's intimates began on a note of frank amazement at their never having heard of her before and in wider circles manifested itself as that indefinable enjoyment of the new and surprising which is common to princes and the daily press.

So it was then that Diotima—who had the *bel esprit*'s traditional capacity for instinctively choosing, from among several possibilities, that which was at once the intrinsically worst and the most promising of public success—made the move that assured Ulrich and Agathe of their permanent place in the memory of that distinguished circle of society. For what their patroness did, having suddenly herself found it charming, was to pass on as charming to everyone else the story she had originally heard, namely that her two cousins, having met again in romantic circumstances after an almost life-long separation, had decided to call themselves henceforth the Siamese Twins—and this though the blind will of Destiny had hitherto made them practically the opposite of that. It would be hard to say why first Diotima and subsequently everyone else was so taken with this and why it made the Twins' resolve to live together appear both extraordinary and natural. But such was Diotima's gift for leadership. Anyway, there were both these reactions, and it was evidence that despite all the manœuvres of her rivals she still exerted her gentle sway. When Arnheim heard of it, on his return, he delivered an elaborate address to a select circle, rounding it off on a note of homage to aristocratic and folk-traditional values. In some way or other a rumour even began to circulate that Agathe had taken refuge with her brother from an unhappy marriage to a celebrated foreign *savant*. And since at that period those who ordained what was good form had the land-owner's traditional dislike of divorce and made do with adultery, many older persons positively saw Agathe's decision in that double light, a blend of will-power and edification, which was the aura of an exalted life—a light that Count Leinsdorf, who was especially gracious to the Twins, once evaluated in the following words: " When you go to the theatre, you always see plays about such horrible passions. It'd be a good thing for the Burgtheater if they took an example from the like of this ! "

Diotima, in whose presence these words were uttered, replied: " It has become the fashion to say that man is naturally good. But anyone who has come to know something of the tortuous ways of sex, as I have through my studies, well knows how rare such examples are ! " Did she wish to modify His Highness's praise, or to give it emphasis ? She had not yet forgiven Ulrich what—on account of his not having told her of his sister's imminent arrival—she called his lack of trust; but she was proud of a success in which she herself shared, and there was a trace of that pride in her answer.

28   *Excess of high spirits.*

AGATHE showed innate good taste in her use of whatever advantages these social contacts brought her, and her brother was pleased with her serene bearing in circles where the highest demands were made. The years she had spent as the wife of a grammar-school master in the provinces seemed to have dropped off her as though they had never been. For the present, however, Ulrich summed up the situation with a shrug, saying: " The high nobility find it amusing that we should be called the Siamese Twins. They've always gone in for menageries more than for, say, art."

By tacit agreement they treated all that went on as a mere interlude. There was a good deal that needed to be reorganised or altered in the house they now lived in together. This had indeed been clear to them for the very first day, but they did nothing about it, shying off a discussion—such as they had had before—to which they could not see the limits. Having given up his bedroom to Agathe, Ulrich had settled himself in the dressing-room, separated from his sister by the bathroom, and bit by bit he had made over most of his wardrobe-space to her. An offer of sympathy for these hardships he declined with an allusion to St. Lawrence and his grill. However, it did not seriously occur to Agathe that she might have disorganised her brother's bachelor existence, because he assured her that he was very happy and because she had only a very shadowy notion of whatever degrees of happiness he could have enjoyed previously. She had come to like this house with its non-bourgeois arrangements, its numerous reception-rooms and ante-chambers useless and unused around the few habitable rooms, which were now over-crowded: it somehow suggested the elaborate ceremonial of a bygone age, defenceless against the self-indulgent and churlish high-handedness of the present ages. Yet sometimes, too, the beautiful rooms' mute protest against this disorderly invasion was mournful, like broken and tangled strings on the exquisitely curving wood of a viola da gamba. Then Agathe realised that her brother had chosen this secluded house by no means without interest and feeling, even though he pretended it was not so, and its old walls communicated a passion that was neither quite mute nor quite audible. But neither she nor Ulrich admitted to anything more than enjoying the casualness of it all. They lived in some disarray, having their meals sent in from a nearby hotel, and finding in everything a pretext for the sort of excessive high spirits generated by a picnic, when one has a meal on the grass more uncomfortably than one would need to at a table.

Nor did they have proper domestic service under these conditions. The well-trained servant whom Ulrich had taken on for a short time when he moved into the house was an old man—he wanted to retire and was only waiting for some technicality to be settled—and they could not ask much of him; Ulrich gave him as little as possible to do. The part of lady's maid fell to Ulrich himself, since the room where a trained maid-servant might have been put was in as merely potential a condition as much else besides, and some experiments in getting over this difficulty had not produced good results. Thus Ulrich made great progress in the squire's duties of arming his lady knight to set forth on her conquests. Then too Agathe had done some shopping to supplement her wardrobe, and these additions were strewn all round the house. Built as it was, with so many rooms opening out of each other, and none of them furnished for a woman's needs, it had got her into the habit of haphazardly using any part of it for trying on her clothes: and so whether or no he wished to, Ulrich made acquaintance with her acquisitions. The doors between the rooms were left open, Ulrich's gymnastic equipment was turned into clothes-horses and coat-racks, and he would be called away from his desk like Cincinnatus from his plough. This crossing of his at least potential will to continue working was something he put up with not merely because he assumed it was temporary; it actually gave him a fresh and rejuvenating kind of pleasure. His sister's seemingly idle vivacity crackled in his solitude like a small fire in a cold stove. Bright waves of lovely cheerfulness, dark waves of human trust, filled to the brim these rooms he lived in, so that they ceased to be what they had been—merely a space where he moved about at the dictates of his own will. But what amazed him above all about the inexhaustible nature of another presence was the fact that the countless trifling details that went to make up its totality actually produced a quite different answer from what he would have expected: his impatient dread of wasting his time, that unquenchable feeling which had never left him since he could remember, whatever he had taken up in the way of things supposed to be great and important, had astoundingly and utterly vanished. And for the first time quite unthinkingly he loved his day-to-day life.

It went so far that he would even produce a gasp of delight when Agathe—with the seriousness that women have in these matters—offered for his admiration the charming odds and ends

she had been buying. He made a show of being irresistibly
fascinated by the quaint workings of feminine nature, which,
though no less intelligent than masculine nature, is more sensitive
and therefore also more susceptible to inspirations about adorn-
ment—and has a crassness yet further removed from the logic of
the higher human possibilities than is the crassness of the male.
And perhaps indeed he was really fascinated. For the many
little tenderly absurd notions that he came to know—tricking oneself out with beads, curling one's hair with heated tongs, the
foolish importance of how lace or embroidery was draped, the
ruthlessly calculated seductiveness for which colour-schemes were
chosen—these charms so akin to the tinfoil stars one can win at a
fairground rifle-range, charms that every intelligent woman sees
through without in the slightest losing her taste for them—began
to entangle him in the threads of their twinkling craziness. For
the moment one begins to take a serious interest in anything, no
matter how ludicrous or however lacking in aesthetic sense, and
puts it on an equality with other things, it begins to reveal a
harmonious order of its own, to give off the intoxicating scent of
its own self-love, its indwelling urge to play and to be liked.
This was what Ulrich experienced, letting himself be involved in
the nonsense associated with his sister's replanning of her wardrobe. He fetched and carried, admired, approved, was asked for
his advice, helped with ' trying on '. He would stand in front of
the looking-glass with Agathe. Nowadays, when a woman's
appearance is reminiscent of an efficiently plucked fowl ready to
be popped into the pot, it is hard to recall all that charm of other
days, with its intricacies (since obsolete and thus ridiculous) that
were designed to stave off appetite: the long skirt, apparently
firmly tailored to the floor and yet by some miracle in motion,
enclosed yet other mysterious floating skirts, pastel-shaded silken
petals whose light fluttering further concealed a white and still
more exquisite tissue, this last soft foam being the only thing to
touch the body itself. And if these clothes resembled waves in
that they were at once a flowing allurement and yet baffling to the
eye, they were also an ingenious contrivance of intermediate
stations and fortifications surrounding expertly defended wonders
and, for all their perverse artificiality, a consummately curtained
theatre of the erotic, its breath-taking darkness illumined only by

the dim torches of imagination. It was this quintessence of the erotic preliminaries that Ulrich now daily saw in various phases of stage-carpentry and scene-shifting, as it were, himself behind the scenes. And even though a woman's secrets had long been no secret to him, or perhaps rather because all his adult life he had merely run through them as though they were mere ante-chambers or outer gardens, they took on another sort of importance now that there was no gateway or goal for him. The tension that lies in these things now snapped, struck back at him. It would have been hard for him to say what changes it brought about in him. He justifiably regarded himself as a man of emphatically masculine constitution, and it seemed to make sense that such a man might take pleasure in for once seeing the so-often desired from the other side. Yet sometimes this became almost eerie, and he would make laughing protest.

" As though the walls of a girl's boarding-school had shot up all round me in the night and shut me in ! " he protested.

" Is that so frightful ? " Agathe asked.

" I don't know," he admitted.

Then he would call her a carnivorous plant and himself a poor insect that had crawled into the shimmering calyx. " You've closed your petals on me," he said, " and now here I am in the midst of all this colour, scent, and radiance, having lost my own nature and already become part of you, waiting for the males of the species that we are to trap ! "

And indeed it was very odd what he felt, watching the effect his sister had on men—he whose prime concern it was, after all, to ' get her a husband '. He was not jealous—on what basis *could* he have been jealous ?—he subordinated his own welfare to hers, and what he wished for her was that a man worthy of her might soon free her from this phase of transition she had been in since leaving Hagauer. And for all that, whenever he saw her the centre of a group of men paying her their attentions, or in the street whenever some man was attracted by her beauty and, heed-less of her escort, looked her straight in the face, he did not know what to make of his feelings. Here too, since the simple way out— ' male jealousy '—was a closed road to him, he often felt as though he were enclosed in some world that he had never before entered. From his own experience he knew as much of the male's sexual

caracoling as of woman's more wary devices, and when he saw
Agathe exposed to the one and using the other, he suffered. It
was like watching the courtship of horses or mice; the mutual
sniffing and whinneying, the pouting of the lips, the baring of the
teeth, all the symbolic flourishes by which human beings complacently set out to please in making themselves known to others—
all this revolted him, observing it as he did without sympathy; it
was like some immense intoxication welling up from within.
And if he nevertheless put himself in his sister's place, as some deep
urge made him do, sometimes he was afterwards not far from
feeling, not only bewilderment at his own passivity, but the sort
of shame that a normal man feels on being deviously approached
by one who is not. When he confessed as much to Agathe, she
laughed.

" Anyway," she replied, " there are several women among our
acquaintances who take a great interest in you."

What was going on, what did it mean ?

Ulrich said: " Fundamentally it's a protest against the world."
And he also said: " You know Walter. He and I haven't been
able to stand each other for a long time now. But even if he
annoys me and I know that I infuriate him, often at the mere sight
of him I can't help having an affectionate feeling, as though I got
on with him as wonderfully well as in fact I don't get on with him.
Look, there's so much in life that one understands without, so to
speak, having come to an understanding with it. And that's why
having an understanding with a person from the start, even before
one understands him, is as magically beautiful and senseless as the
way in the springtime water comes streaming down all the hills
into the valley . . ."

And what he felt was: ' That's the way it is now . . .' And
what he thought was: ' The moment I manage to have no more
egocentric and selfish feelings towards Agathe, and no single
ugly feeling of indifference either, she draws all the qualities out
of me the way the Magnetic Mountain draws the nails out of the
ship ! Morally I'm atomised into a pure and primal state in
which I'm neither myself nor her. I wonder is that what's meant
by eternal bliss ? '

But all he said was: " It's such fun watching you."

Agathe blushed deeply and asked: " Why is it ' fun ' ? "

" Oh, I don't know.   Sometimes you're embarrassed at having me there," Ulrich said.   " But then you remind yourself that after all I'm ' only your brother '.   And at other times you're not in the least embarrassed if I come on you in circumstances that would be very glamorous for a strange man.   But then suddenly it does strike you that I oughtn't to be looking, and you tell me to look the other way."

" And what's such fun about that ? " Agathe asked.

" Perhaps it makes one happy to follow someone else with one's eyes without knowing why," Ulrich said.   " It's reminiscent of a child's love for its small possessions.   Without the child's intellectual helplessness. . . ."

" Perhaps it's fun for you to play at brother and sister," Agathe said, " only because you're sick of playing at man and woman ? "

" It would be that too," Ulrich said, contemplating her.   " Love is basically a simple urge to get closer, an instinct to grab hold of something.   It has been split into two poles, male and female, with incredible tensions, frustrations, paroxysms and perversions arising in between.   Nowadays we've had enough of that inflated ideology.   It's become nearly as ridiculous as a gastrosophy. Agathe, I'm convinced most people would be glad of it if the connection between a local stimulus and the entire personality could be cancelled out !   And sooner or later there will be an era of simple unassuming sexual comradeship, when boy and girl will stand, reconciled and uncomprehending, gazing at an ancient heap of broken clockwork springs that was once what made Man and Woman tick."

" But if I were to tell you that Hagauer and I were pioneers of that era, you'd take it amiss," Agathe retorted, with a smile as astringent as a good dry wine.

" I'm past taking anything amiss," Ulrich said.   He smiled. " A warrior unbuckled and unhelmed !   For the first time since he cannot remember when," he went on, improving on this, " he feels Nature's own air on his skin instead of hammered iron and sees his body growing so weary and frail that the birds might easily carry it off."

And smiling so—simply forgetting to stop smiling—he contemplated his sister, who was sitting on the edge of a table, swinging one leg in its black silk stocking.   Apart from her chemise she had nothing on but short frilly panties: but these were somehow fragmentary impressions, floating images without intrinsic relation to the total fact of her. ' She's my friend,' Ulrich thought, ' deliciously manifesting himself to me as a woman. What a realistic complication that she really is one ! '

And Agathe asked: " Is there really no such thing as love ? "

" Oh yes, there is ! " Ulrich said. " But it's the exception. One has to distinguish. First of all, there's a physical experience, to be classified under the heading ' cutaneous irritation '. It can be stimulated without any moral associations, even without emotion, purely as a sensory pleasure. In the second case there are usually emotions involved, and though they are intensely associated with the physical experience, only in ways that, with slight variations, are the same for everyone. These culminating moments in love are so inevitably the same that I'm more inclined to place them on the physical, mechanical side than on the emotional. But finally there's also something else, the real psychic experience of love—only it hasn't necessarily anything at all to do with the rest of it. One can love God, one can love the world. Perhaps indeed one can't really love anything but God or the world. Anyway, it isn't necessary to love a human being. If one does, however, the physical side draws the whole world into itself, as it were turning the world inside out——" and here Ulrich suddenly broke off.

Agathe had flushed dark red.

If Ulrich had framed his ideas and chosen his words with the intention of hypocritically suggesting to Agathe's imagination the actions of love-making inevitably associated with them, he would have achieved his purpose.

He looked round for matches, simply to create a diversion and destroy the atmosphere he had unintentionally conjured up.

" Anyway," he said, " love, if that is love, is an exception, and can't provide an example for everyday behaviour."

Agathe had taken the corners of the table-cover and wrapped it round her legs. " Wouldn't strangers," she asked, " if they could see and hear us, think there was something perverse about our feelings ? "

" Nonsense ! " Ulrich maintained. " What each of us feels is the shadowy doubling of his or her self in a complementary nature. Here am I a man, you a woman. It's widely believed that every human being has within him the shadowy or repressed counter-quality to each of his qualities: certainly he feels the yearning for them whenever he isn't damnably satisfied with himself. So my counterpart, coming to light, has slipped into you, and yours into me, and they feel wonderful after this exchange of bodily habitation, simply because they have scant respect for their former habitations and the view to be had from there!"

Agathe thought: ' At other times he's said far more about all these things. Why does he whittle it down?'

What Ulrich said did, of course, fit in quite well with the life they were leading together, as two comrades who occasionally, when other people's company left them free, marvelled that they were a man and a woman and yet also twins. Once such harmony exists between two human beings, their separate relations with the world take on the charm of an invisible hide-and-seek, one hiding inside the other—the charm of exchanging clothes and even bodies, a gay deception, the two distinct masks of exterior appearance concealing their two-in-oneness and so tricking all who have no notion of it. But this playful and over-emphatic merriment— like the way children sometimes make a noise instead of being noisy!—was not in keeping with the gravity that sometimes, from some great height, laid its shadow on the hearts of this brother and sister, involuntarily making them silent.

So it happened once at evening, as they were going to bed and happened to encounter each other once more. Seeing his sister in her long nightdress, Ulrich attempted a little joke.

" A hundred years ago," he said to her, " I might in these circumstances have cried out: My angel! What a pity the expression's gone out of use!" He fell silent, disconcerted by the thought: ' Isn't it the only expression I ought to use for her? Not friend, not woman! Yes, they used to say too: Heavenly creature! I suppose it would be rather absurdly high-flown but still, better than simply not having the courage to believe oneself . . .'

Agathe was thinking: ' A man in pyjamas doesn't look like an angel.'

But he did look fierce and broad-shouldered, and she was suddenly ashamed to feel the desire that this strong face, with the hair tousled, should bring a darkness before her eyes. In some physically innocent way she was sensually stirred; her blood pulsed through her body in wild waves, spreading out through her skin, robbing her inner being of its strength. Since she was not such a fanatic as her brother, she simply felt what she felt. When she was affectionate, she was affectionate—not lit by brilliance of thought, not morally illumined, though that was something she loved in him as much as she was shy of it.

And ever again, day by day. Ulrich summed everything up in the idea: Fundamentally it's a protest against life! Arm in arm they walked about the city. Matched in height, matched in age, matched in their attitude to things . . . Strolling along, side by side, they could not see much of each other. Tall figures, pleasing to each other, it was for sheer enjoyment that they went out into the streets, at every step feeling the breath of their contact with each other in the midst of all the alien life around them. We belong together! That was the feeling, a far from extraordinary one, that made them happy, and half in that feeling, half in resistance to it, Ulrich said: "It's funny we should be so content to be brother and sister. For the world in general it's a commonplace relationship—and surely we put something special into it, don't we?"

Perhaps he had hurt her by saying it. He added: "But it's what I've always wished for. When I was a boy I resolved to marry only a woman I'd have adopted when she was a little girl and brought up myself. As a matter of fact, I think plenty of men have such fantasies—they're quite banal. But once, as a grown man, I positively fell in love with such a child, even though for only two or three hours." And he went on to tell her about it.

"It was in the tram. A little girl—she might have been twelve —got in together with her very young father or elder brother. The way she got in, sat down, casually handed the conductor the money for both their fares—oh, she was entirely the lady, the woman of the world! Yet it was without any slightest trace of childish affectation. It was the same way she talked to her companion, or quietly listened to him. She was marvellously beautiful: brown-skinned, with full lips, strongly marked eyebrows, a slightly tip-tilted nose—perhaps a dark-haired Polish child, or a Southern Slav. I somehow remember her as wearing a dress that

suggested some national costume or other, long jacket, tight waist,
a laced bodice and frills at throat and wrists, all in its way as perfect
as the small person herself. Perhaps she was Albanian? I was
sitting too far away to be able to hear her talk. What struck me
was that the cast of her grave face was developed beyond her
years, so that it seemed completely adult, and yet it was not the
face of a dwarfish little woman, but beyond question that of a
child. On the other hand, this child's face was not at all the
immature preliminary to an adult face. It may be that sometimes
a woman's face is complete at the age of twelve, even spiritually,
as though a masterhand had formed it with the first touches, so
that everything subsequently added in working up the picture only
spoils the original greatness of it. One can fall passionately in
love with such an apparition—mortally, and actually without desire.
I know I glanced round nervously at the other people in the tram,
because I felt every kind of order was slipping away from me.
When that little girl got out, I followed her. But I lost her in
the crowded street," he said, ending his little story.

After they had let it rest at that for a while, Agathe asked,
smiling: " And how does that accord with the age of love being
past and only sex and comradeship being left ? "

" It doesn't accord with it at all ! " Ulrich exclaimed, laughing.

His sister, after some thought, remarked with noticeable
astringency—it seemed to be an intentional reminder of words he
had used on the evening of her arrival: " All men want to play at
little brother and little sister. It really must have some idiotic
meaning. And these little brothers and little sisters say ' father '
and ' mother ' to each other when they're not entirely sober."

Ulrich was taken aback. It was not merely that Agathe was
right: intelligent women are unerring in their observation of the
men they love; but, having no theories, they make no use of their
discoveries except when provoked. He felt somewhat affronted.

" Of course they've got a psychological explanation for that too,"
he said reluctantly. " It's pretty obvious that the two of us are
psychologically suspect. Incestuous tendencies, demonstrable in
early childhood together with anti-social constitution and attitude
of protest against life. Even perhaps inadequately integrated
monosexuality, although I——"

" Nor me either ! " Agathe interrupted, laughing again, though perhaps rather against her will. " I don't at all care for women ! "

" Not that it matters at all," Ulrich commented. " Psychic entrails, that's the gist of it.   You might also say there's a sultanesque urge to be the only one who adores and who is adored, to the exclusion of the rest of the world. In the ancient East it produced the harem, and nowadays we have instead the family, ' love ', and the dog. And I make no bones about saying that the craving to possess another human being so exclusively that nobody else can approach is an expression of personal loneliness in the midst of the human community, one that even socialists will seldom deny.   If you prefer to take it that way, we're nothing but a form of bourgeois debauchery—Oh look, how magnificent ! " he broke off, his grip tightening on her arm.

They were standing at the edge of a small market-place surrounded by old houses. Round about the neo-classical statue of some intellectual giant there were spread out all the bright-coloured vegetables, the big canvas umbrellas of the market-booths, and tumbling fruit, there were baskets being dragged, dogs being chased away from the outspread bravery, and everywhere in the midst of it the red faces of rough men and women. The air pounded and throbbed with raised busy voices and smelt of the sun, which shines impartially on all the earthly hotch-potch.

" Can one help loving the world if one simply sees and smells it ? " Ulrich asked enthusiastically. " And we can't love it," he added, " because we don't agree with what goes on inside the heads of the people living in it. . . ."

This did not happen to be a reservation entirely to Agathe's taste, and she did not answer. But she pressed her brother's arm more tightly, and for both of them it meant as much as if she had gently laid her hand on his mouth.

Laughing, Ulrich said: " Not that I care for myself, anyway ! That's the result of always having some fault to find with people. But even I have to be able to love something, and so a Siamese Sister, who's neither me nor herself, but just as much me as herself, is clearly the only point where everything intersects."

He had cheered up again. And usually his mood drew Agathe with it. Yet they never again talked as they had in the first night of their reunion, and before. That had disappeared like great cloud-castles: when they tower up in the sky, not over the solitary countryside, but over the city streets, all teeming with life, it is hard to believe in them. Perhaps the cause was to be found merely in the fact that Ulrich did not know what degree of solidity might be ascribed to the experiences that moved him; but Agathe often believed he now regarded them as no more than a fantastic freak. And she could not prove to him that it was not so; for one thing, she always talked less than he did, and she could not hit the right note, and did not dare to try. Only she felt that he was shirking the decision, and that he must not do that. So they were both actually hiding in their light-hearted happiness that had neither depth nor weight, and it made Agathe sadder day by day, although she laughed as often as her brother.

29   *Professor Hagauer takes up his pen.*

THIS was changed, however, by action on the part of Agathe's husband, whose existence they had all this time ignored.

One morning, which put an end to these days of delight, she received a heavy letter in a foolscap envelope sealed with a large round yellow seal, imprinted with the white insignia of the Imperial-Royal Rudolfsgymnasium in the town of Y. Instantly, even while she still held the letter unopened in her hand, out of the void there rose a vision of houses: two-storeyed, with the blank mirrors of their well-polished windows and white thermometers outside on the brown frames, one for each storey, so that one could tell what the weather was doing; with neo-classical pediments and scallops over the windows, with heads peering forth out of the walls, and other mythological sentinels that looked as though they had been made in a cabinet-maker's workshop and painted to resemble stone. Brown and wet the streets ran through the town, just as they had entered it as country roads, with well-worn wheel-tracks, and on each side there were the shops with their brand-new window-displays, looking for all of that just like gentlewomen of thirty years earlier, picking up their long skirts and yet not bringing themselves to step off the pavement into the mud of the street. The provinces in Agathe's mind! Ghosts inside Agathe's head! The incomprehensible not-quite-disappearing of it, although she had thought herself free from it once and for all! And still more incomprehensible: having ever been involved in it! She saw the way leading from her front door, past familiar houses, to the school, the way her husband Gottlieb Hagauer went four times a day and which at first she had often gone too, accompanying Hagauer from his home to his work, in the period when she was scrupulous not to spill any drop of the bitter potion meant to cure her. ' I wonder whether he lunches at the hotel these days ? ' she thought. ' Does he tear the leaf off the calendar every morning now instead of me ? ' It had all suddenly become so senselessly acute and actual that it seemed this could never die; and with a very quiet horror she recognised the once familiar sensation of being intimidated, a feeling that was a blend of indifference, loss of courage, satiation with ugliness, and a sense of her own unstable volatility. With a kind of avidity she opened the thick letter her husband had addressed to her.

When Professor Hagauer had returned to his home and his work after attending his father-in-law's funeral and paying a brief visit to the capital, his environment had re-absorbed him exactly as it always did after his short journeys; and with the agreeable consciousness of having neatly dealt with one matter and of now changing his travelling shoes for his house-slippers, in which a man works twice as well, he applied himself to the fact of being home again. He betook himself to his school. He was very respectfully greeted by the porter; he felt himself welcomed whenever he encountered one of the masters subordinate to him. In the headmaster's room he found awaiting his attention the files and forms and the various problems that nobody had presumed to deal with during his absence. When he hastened along the corridors, he was accompanied by the feeling that his steps lent wings to the whole building: Gottlieb Hagauer was a personage, and knew it. Encouragement and good cheer beamed from his brow throughout the establishment under his aegis, and when outside the school he met with enquiries about his wife—how she was and where she was—he answered with the serenity of a man who knows he is

respectably married. It is well known that so long as a male is
capable of procreation he reacts to brief interruptions of his married
life somewhat as if an easy yoke has been lifted, even if he does
not dream of getting into any mischief and, the period of this
relief once ended, takes up his happiness once more refreshed.
Such was the way Hagauer at first unsuspectingly accepted
Agathe's absence, for a while not even noticing how long his wife
remained away.

What actually first drew his attention to it was that very wall-
calendar, with the leaf to be torn off every day, which in Agathe's
memory had become a frightful symbol of life. It hung in the
dining-room, an irrelevant patch on the wall, a New Year's
compliment from a stationery shop that had persisted there from
the day Hagauer had brought it home from school and which, for
its dreariness, Agathe had not only tolerated but tended. It would
have been entirely in Hagauer's nature if after his wife's departure
he had himself taken over the job of tearing the leaves off this
calendar, for it was contrary to his habits to, as it were, let that
part of the wall run wild. On the other hand, he was a man who
always knew on exactly what latitude of the weeks and months he
was situated in the ocean of infinity; further, he anyway had another
calendar in his office at school; and finally, just as he had nevertheless been stretching out his hand to regulate the measurement
of time in his home, he had felt a strange, smiling something that
stopped him, one of those impulses that—as it turned out in this
case—foreshadow things to come, though he himself at this
moment took it for no more than an affectionate, chivalrous sentiment that astonished him and contented him with himself: he
resolved that the leaf marking the day when Agathe had left the
house should remain untouched, as a token of homage and a
souvenir, until her return.

So in the course of time the wall-calendar became a festering
wound, every glance at it reminding Hagauer how long his wife
was staying away. Being thrifty with emotion as with postage-
stamps, he wrote her postcards, giving her news of himself and
asking her, gradually more and more pressingly, when she expected
to return. To all these he got no answer. Before long he ceased
to beam when acquaintances sympathetically asked him if his wife
would have to stay away much longer, attending to her melancholy

duties. But fortunately he always had a great deal to do, since, apart from school and the various clubs he belonged to, the post daily brought him copious invitations, enquiries, letters from people who admired his writings, attacks by people who disagreed with him, proofs to be corrected, journals, and important books, for though Hagauer's bodily person lived in the provinces, as an element in the uncomely impression that the provinces could make on a stranger passing through, his mind was at home in all Europe; and this for a long time helped to prevent his grasping the full significance of Agathe's prolonged absence. Then, however, the mail one day brought him a letter from Ulrich, curtly informing him of the bare fact that Agathe did not intend returning to him and wanted him to agree to a divorce. In spite of its perfectly polite phrasing, this letter was so inconsiderately brief and bald that Hagauer indignantly realised how in writing it Ulrich had been just about as much concerned with his, Hagauer's, feelings on receiving it as with those of an insect he was flicking off a leaf. His first reaction was: Not to be taken seriously—a whim! The letter lay like a mocking spectre in the broad daylight of innumerable other papers and correspondence setting urgent tasks or singing respectful praises. It was only that evening, when Hagauer entered his empty house again, that he sat down at his desk and, with dignified brevity, informed Ulrich that it would be best to regard his letter as never having been written. But shortly after this another letter came from Ulrich rejecting this view of the matter, repeating Agathe's wish (though she did not know of this), and only in somewhat more courteous detail asking Hagauer to do whatever he could to simplify the necessary legal proceedings, as beseemed a man of his high moral principles and as was incidentally desirable if the deplorable concomitants of a public quarrel were to be avoided. Now Hagauer grasped the seriousness of the position. He allowed himself three days' time to compose an answer that would subsequently leave nothing to be desired and nothing to be regretted.

For two of these days he suffered from a sensation as though someone had struck him a blow over the heart. ' A bad dream ! ' he several times said to himself plaintively, and whenever he did not keep himself very firmly in hand, he could not go on believing in the reality of what he was being asked to do. During these days a profound discomfort worked within his breast, very like injured love, and in addition there was an indefinable jealousy directed not so much against a lover—for such he assumed to be the cause of Agathe's behaviour—as against an intangible something that he felt had got the better of him.   It was much the sort of shame that a very tidy man feels when he has broken or mislaid something: something that had had its fixed place in his mind since time immemorial, so that it was no longer noticed, but on which nevertheless much depended, was all at once smashed.   Wan and distraught, in real anguish—a thing that must not be under-esti- mated merely because it lacked beauty—Hagauer went round avoiding people, shrinking from the explanations he would have to give and the humiliations he would have to bear.   Only on the third day did his condition settle into firmness.   Hagauer had just as much of an intense natural dislike for Ulrich as Ulrich had for him, and although this had never properly come to light before, now it suddenly did so when intuitively he put the entire blame for Agathe's behaviour on his brother-in-law, that restless bo- hemian brother of hers who must have quite turned her head. He sat down at his desk and, wasting no words, insisted that his wife should return forthwith, with iron resolution declaring that everything else could be discussed only between her and himself, her husband.

From Ulrich there came a refusal, equally short, in a tone of no less iron resolution.

Thereupon Hagauer resolved to see what he could do with Agathe herself.   He took copies of his correspondence with Ulrich and wrote a long, carefully pondered letter to go with it all.   This then was what Agathe was confronted with when she broke the institutional seal and opened the envelope.

Hagauer himself had had the feeling that all that seemed about to happen simply could not happen.   Coming in after finishing his daily round, that evening he had sat in the ' deserted house ' with a sheet of letter-paper before him, much as Ulrich had done on an earlier occasion, and had equally not known how to begin. But in Hagauer's life the well-known ' buttons method ' had often proved helpful; so he applied it this time too.   This method consists in a systematic approach to one's thoughts, even in connection with agitating tasks, on the principle that a man gets buttons sewn on to his clothes because it would only turn out to be time-wasting if he acted on the observation that one can undress faster without buttons. The English writer Surway, for instance, whose study of this subject Hagauer referred to—because even in his present state of grief he attached importance to comparing Surway's views with his own—distinguishes five such buttons in a successful mental process: (a) conclusions drawn from observations of an event that gives rise to a sensation of difficulty in interpreting its significance; (b) closer attention to and final definition of such difficulties; (c) hypothesis as to possible solution; (d) rational development of conclusions to be drawn from this hypothesis; (e) further observation, resulting in acceptance or rejection of the hypothesis, with successful issue of the thought-process. Hagauer had already found it advantageous to apply a similar method to such a frivolous occupation as lawn tennis, when he was learning to play at the Civil Service Club, and it had lent the game considerable intellectual charm for him. Hitherto however he had never made use of it in purely emotional matters; after all, his everyday mental experiences lay mainly on the professional plane, and where personal affairs were concerned he resorted to that ' proper feeling ' which is a compound of all the feelings that the white race considers possible in a given case and acknowledges as customary, with a certain bias towards whatever is the nearest specific local, professional, or class version of it. The buttons, therefore, could be applied to this extraordinary situation, with his wife demanding a divorce from him, only with the awkwardness that goes with lack of practice. Even ' proper feeling ', in cases of intimate personal difficulty, has a tendency to split into two: on the one hand it told Hagauer that there were many reasons why a man who moved with the times, as he did, was in duty bound not to put obstacles in the way of dissolving a partnership based on mutual trust if one of the two parties wished to dissolve it; on the other hand, if one does not want to do what it says it also says a great deal that acquits one of such obligations, for the lightness with which such things are treated nowadays is something one cannot but deplore. In such a case, as Hagauer indeed realised, a modern person must ' relax ': that is, he must distract his attention, make his muscles go loose and floppy, and listen for whatever then makes itself heard in the deepest depths of his inner being.   With care he brought his meditations to a standstill, stared at the orphaned wall-calendar, and harkened inwardly.   And truly, after a while he was answered by a voice emerging from the deeps that lie beneath conscious thought, which told him exactly what he had already been thinking.   The voice told him there was really no earthly reason why he should put up with such nonsense as Agathe's wildly unjustified proposal.

In this way, however, Professor Hagauer's mind had without warning jumped from button (a) to button (e) in Surway's or some equivalent row of buttons, and this left him once more acutely sensible of the difficulty of interpreting the event he must observe.

' Can it be that I, Gottlieb Hagauer,' Hagauer asked himself, ' am to blame for this distressing development ? ' Scrutinising himself, he found no single point at which he had been at fault. ' Is it because she's in love with another man ? ' he wondered, pursuing the hypotheses for a possible solution.   However, it was difficult to suppose that was the explanation, since when he made himself consider it objectively it failed to appear in what way another man could offer Agathe anything better than he did. Still, since this question was so uniquely prone to be overcast with private vanity, he considered it with the greatest of care, and in so doing he found vistas opening up which he had never previously suspected.   Suddenly, from Surway's point (c) Hagauer found himself on the track of a possible solution via points (d) and (e): for the first time since his marriage he thought of a complex of phenomena that occurred, so far as his information went, only in women whose erotic relationship to the opposite sex was never deep or passionate.   It distressed him that nowhere in his memory could he find any evidence of that open-hearted, guileless, dreamy surrender that he had had some experience of in women during his bachelor period—women whose life was one of sensual pleasure, certainly, but whose acquaintance now gave him the advantage of being able, with due scientific calm, to exclude the possibility that his matrimonial bliss had been destroyed by some third person. Thus Agathe's behaviour was automatically reduced to purely private rebellion against this happiness; and all the more because she had gone without the slightest hint of this future development, and because no rationally founded change of attitude could have taken place within the very short period that had elapsed, Hagauer came to the firm and final conclusion that Agathe's incomprehensible behaviour could be explained only as one of those slowly worked-up-to outbursts against life which are said to occur in personalities that do not know what they want.

But was Agathe's personality really one of those? That still remained to be investigated, and Hagauer thoughtfully combed his moustache with the end of his pen. True, she did usually make the impression of being ' easy to get on with ' and ' companionable ', as he put it; yet even in matters that interested him most she did tend to show very marked indifference, not to say apathy. There was in fact something in her that was not in harmony with himself or other people and their interests; it did not even come into conflict with them; she did laugh or look serious as might be appropriate, but she had—now he came to think it over—in all these years always made a somewhat abstracted impression. It seemed that though she listened attentively to what one told her or explained to her, she never really believed it. On closer investigation it seemed to him that she was downright morbidly indifferent. Sometimes she gave one the impression that she simply did not take in what was going on around her ... And suddenly, before he was himself aware of it, his pen had begun swiftly covering the paper with that handwriting of his which showed so much character. " Heaven alone knows what is going on in your mind," he wrote, " if you think yourself too good to care for the life I am in a position to offer you and which, I may say in all modesty, is a pure and full life. You have always handled it as it were with tongs, so it now appears to me. You have rejected the wealth of human and moral values that even a modest life is able to provide, and even if I were forced to the conclusion that you might conceivably feel yourself in some way justified in so doing, you would still have shown a total lack of the moral will to bring about some change. Instead of that you seem to have chosen an artificial, nay a fantastical way out ! "

He reflected on this for a while. Mentally he mustered the schoolboys who had passed through his guiding hands, to see if he could find a case that might offer a parallel. But before he had really got going with this, there suddenly popped into his mind the missing piece of consideration that he had, with vague discomfort, been looking for. From this moment Agathe ceased to

be a completely individual problem without any clues to its
general nature; for as soon as he reflected on how much she was
ready to forfeit without being blinded by any particular passion,
to his delight he was unerringly led to the supposition, so basic
and so dear to the modern educational outlook, that she lacked
the faculty for supra-subjective thought, as well as any stable
spiritual contact with the world in which she lived. Swiftly he
wrote: " Probably you are far from being clearly aware of what it
is you are setting about, even now. But I warn you against hastily
making any decision that would affect your whole future! You
are perhaps the most complete example of the opposite of the type
of person I myself am, namely one who is life-directed and who
possesses self-knowledge; but for this very reason you should not
lightly deprive yourself of the support that I am for you! "
Actually Hagauer had meant to write something else. For the
human intelligence is not a self-contained faculty without relation
to the rest of the person; its defects are associated with moral
defects—does one not speak of moral imbecility?—just as moral
defects (though this is something more rarely considered) often
misdirect or totally confuse the intelligence in some way that suits
them. Thus Hagauer saw before his mental eye a distinct type
that he was inclined, on the basis of conclusions already arrived
at, to define as ' a special type of moral imbecility associated with
average intelligence and manifesting itself merely in certain
irregular forms of behaviour '. But he could not quite bring himself to use this highly illuminating expression, partly because he
wished to avoid further provoking his run-away wife, partly
because a lay person generally misunderstands such terms when
they are applied to him or herself. Objectively, however, it was
now clearly established that the forms of behaviour to which
Hagauer took exception came under the widely inclusive heading
' sub-normal ', and finally, in this conflict between conscience and
chivalry, Hagauer hit upon a way out: the irregular form of behaviour manifest in his wife could be associated with a fairly
general type of inferiority that was simply feminine, in other
words, it could be termed ' social imbecility '.

Having come to this conclusion, he finished off his letter in a
high moral key. With the prophetic wrath of the scorned lover
and the educationist he depicted Agathe's asocial and morbid

temperament to her as a ' minus variant ' that never at any point grappled vigorously and creatively with the problems of life, in the way that ' the present age ' required of ' the people who live in it '; on the contrary, she was deliberately and obstinately shutting herself up in a solitude of her own, ' with a pane of glass between herself and reality ', constantly on the brink of a danger that could only be called pathological. " If there was anything about me that displeased you," he wrote, " you ought to have tried to combat it. But the fact is that your mental and emotional faculties are no match for the forces of our time and therefore seek to escape from its demands ! Having now warned you about your own character," he concluded, " I repeat that you need reliable support more than most people do. In your own interest I urge you to return forthwith, and explicitly declare that my responsibility as your husband forbids my acceding to your wish."

Before signing this letter Hagauer read it through once more. He decided that the description of the psychological type under discussion was very incomplete, but he refrained from altering anything. He merely made an addition at the end. Exhaling the unaccustomed, proudly accomplished effort of thinking about his wife in a sort of gusty sigh through his moustache, at the same time pondering how much still needed to be said on the problem of ' the modern age ', he interpolated a chivalrously turned sentence about the precious bequest of his venerated late father-in-law, putting this in over the word ' responsibility '.

When Agathe had read all this, a strange thing happened: the gist of these remarks did not entirely fail to make an impression on her. Slowly—after reading the letter standing, without stopping to sit down even before she went through it again word by word —she let it sink, then handed it to Ulrich, who had been observing his sister's agitation with some astonishment.

30 *Ulrich and Agathe in search of grounds for past action.*

AND now while Ulrich was reading, Agathe dejectedly observed the play of expression on his face. He had bent his head over the letter, and his expression seemed to be irresolute, as though he could not decide whether to be mocking, grave, concerned, or contemptuous. Now a heavy weight sank down on Agathe; it came on her from all sides, as though the atmosphere were becoming dense and insupportably sultry, after a phase of unnaturally delicious lightness: what she had done to her father's Last Will and Testament was for the first time oppressing her conscience. But it would be inadequate to say that she was all at once taking the full measure of the guilt she had incurred in real life; rather it was that she vaguely felt a real measure of guilt in relation to everything, including her brother, and it was an indescribably disillusioned feeling. Everything she had done now seemed incomprehensible. She had talked of killing her husband, she had forged a Will, and she had come to live with her brother without wondering whether she was disrupting his life; she had done it all in a state of intoxication whirling with fantasies. And what particularly shamed her at this moment was that she had utterly failed to think of what was most obvious and natural: that any other woman, separating from a husband she did not like, would either look for someone better or work out some other natural way of leading a different life. Often enough, indeed, Ulrich himself had pointed this out; but she had paid no attention. And so here she stood, wondering what he was going to say.

Her behaviour struck her now as so entirely that of someone who was really not quite responsible for her actions that she acknowledged Hagauer's rightness in holding up this picture of herself; and his letter, now in Ulrich's hand, left her aghast in much the way someone might be, charged with a crime and now receiving, into the bargain, a letter from a former teacher expounding his contempt. Naturally she had never allowed Hagauer to have any influence on her; nevertheless the effect of this was rather as if he were entitled to say: ' I have been disappointed in you ' or ' I'm afraid I was never deceived by you, I always felt you would come to a bad end '. Although Ulrich was still attentively reading the letter, without any sign of coming to the end of it, the urge to shake off this ridiculous and distressing feeling made her impatient and she interrupted him, saying:

" Really he's described me quite correctly."

Her tone was artificially calm, but with an undertone of defiance, betraying her desire to be contradicted.

" And even if he doesn't say so," she went on, " it's true all the same: either I must have been not responsible for my actions when I married him without compelling grounds, or I'm being irresponsible now, leaving him on grounds just as inadequate."

Ulrich, who had just been reading for the third time through the passages that made him an involuntary witness to her close relationship to Hagauer, abstractedly muttered something she did not catch.

" But do listen ! " Agathe urged him. " Am I the typical modern woman, with some economic or intellectual involvement in the world ? No. Am I the typical woman in love ? Not that either. Am I the good wife and mother, smoothing things out, simplifying things—the nest-building type ? That least of all. So what's left over ? What am I in the world for at all ? The social round we're caught up in—I may as well tell you candidly —leaves me fundamentally quite cold. And I'm rather inclined to believe that all the music, literature, and art in general that throws these cultured persons into ecstasies is something I could very well get on without, too. Gottlieb Hagauer couldn't: Gottlieb Hagauer needs all that if only to provide him with his allusions and quotations. He at least always has the pleasant and satisfactory sense of being a sort of collector. So isn't he quite right when he reproaches me with not *doing* anything, with rejecting ' the wealth of the beautiful and the moral ', and tells me the most I can hope for is sympathy and tolerance from Professor Hagauer himself ? ! "

Handing back the letter, Ulrich replied with composure: " Let's face it: you are, in fact, socially feeble-minded ! " He smiled, but his tone held a trace of the exasperation set up by having looked into this intimate letter.

But Agathe was not pleased with her brother's answer. It deepened her distress. With diffident mockery she asked: ' If that's the way it is, then why did you insist I should get a divorce and lose a husband's protection—without even telling me ? "

" Oh," Ulrich said evasively, " perhaps just because it's so splendidly easy to adopt a firm manly tone. I bang my fist on the table, he bangs his fist on the table. Then of course I have to bang the table twice as hard. I expect that's why I did it."

Up to now, although her depression prevented her quite realising it, Agathe had really been wildly delighted with her brother for secretly acting in a way completely contrary to the attitude he had displayed all through the period when they had been light-heartedly playing at a brother-and-sister flirtation; for evidently the reason why he was offensive to Hagauer could only be that he meant to raise up obstacles behind her to cut off any possibility of return. Yet now even that hidden joy had gone, leaving only a hollow sense of loss, and Agathe sank into silence.

" We mustn't overlook the fact," Ulrich went on, " that in his own way Hagauer manages to misunderstand you so well that one might call it hitting the nail on the head. Take it from me, in his own fashion, without the aid of private detectives, merely by starting to think seriously about the weakness in your attitude to the rest of mankind, sooner or later he'll discover what you've done to Father's Will. And how are we going to defend you then ? "

So it was that for the first time since they had been together again the subject was brought up once more—the subject of the disastrously delightful trick that Agathe had played on Hagauer. She shrugged her shoulders almost fiercely, with a vague gesture of pushing that away from her.

" Hagauer, of course, has right on his side," Ulrich gently but firmly reminded her.

" He hasn't got right on his side ! " she passionately retorted.

" He's partly right," Ulrich compromised. " In a situation as dangerous as this one must start off by facing facts, including those of one's own character. What you've done may easily land us both in jail."

Agathe looked at him with eyes widened in dismay. In a way she had of course known this, but it had never before been uttered so definitely, in such a matter-of-fact tone.

Ulrich responded with a comforting gesture. " But that's not the worst of it," he went on. " How are we going to keep what you've done—and also the way you did it—free of the reproach that—" he groped for an adequate way of putting it and found none—" well, let's simply say it is really just a little bit what Hagauer means when he says it tends to the shadow side, to the realm of abnormality, of the wrong step that originates in something constitutionally wrong. Hagauer embodies the voice of the world, even if it sounds ridiculous in his mouth."

" Now we're coming to the cigarette-case," Agathe said in a small voice.

" Yes, here it comes," Ulrich said doggedly. " There's something I must tell you that I've had on my mind for a long time."

Agathe tried to stop him. " Isn't it better to wipe it all out ? " she asked. " Perhaps I should have a nice soothing talk with him and offer him some kind of apology ? "

" It's too late for that. Now he could use it against you, to force you to go back to him," Ulrich declared.

Agathe said nothing.

Ulrich began to talk about the cigarette-case that a well-off man steals in a hotel. He had evolved a theory according to which there were only three grounds for such a theft: penury, being a professional thief, or, failing either of those two, some psychological defect. " Once when we talked about this," he added, " you objected that one might do it out of conviction."

" I said one might simply *do* it ! " Agathe emended.

" All right: on principle."

" No, not on principle ! "

" There you are, that's just it ! " Ulrich said. " If one does do such a thing, one must at least have some conviction about it ! There's no getting away from that ! One doesn't ' just do ' things: there are always grounds, either outside oneself or within. It may not be very easy to distinguish one from the other, but don't let's go into that now. The point is: if something is entirely without grounds and one considers it right, or say if a resolve emerges so to speak out of the void, one comes under suspicion of being pathological or mentally defective."

This was, certainly, much more, and worse, than Ulrich had meant to say; it was, however, the main drift of his qualms.

" Is that all you have to say to me about it ? " Agathe asked very quietly.

" No, it isn't," Ulrich answered grimly. " If one has no grounds, one must look for them ! "

Neither of them had any doubt as to where they must look. But Ulrich was after something else, and after a slight pause he went on thoughtfully: " The moment you shift out of harmony with everyone else you commit yourself to everlastingly not knowing what's good or what's bad. So if you mean to be good, you have to be convinced that the world is good. And neither of us is convinced of that. We live in a time when morality is either dissolving or in convulsions. But for the sake of a world that may yet come, one must keep oneself pure ! "

" You mean you believe that can have some influence on whether it comes or not ? " Agathe said sceptically.

" No, I'm afraid I don't believe that. At the most the way I believe it is like this: if even the people who see this don't act rightly, it will certainly not come, nothing will then stop the rot."

" And what can you care whether it's all different in five hundred years from now, or not ? "

Ulrich hesitated. " I do my duty, do you see. Perhaps like a soldier."

Probably because on that unhappy morning Agathe was in need of another and more affectionate sort of comfort than Ulrich gave, she answered: " In the last resort, just like your friend the General ? "

Ulrich was silent.

Agathe could not stop. " But you aren't even sure whether it is your duty," she went on. " You do it simply because that's the way you are and because you enjoy it. And that's all I did too ! "

Suddenly she lost her self-control. Something, somewhere in all this, was very sad. All at once there were tears in her eyes, and a great sob rose in her throat. In order to hide this, to keep it from her brother's eyes, she threw her arms round his neck and hid her face against his shoulder.

Ulrich could feel her weeping and the quivering of her back. A troublesome embarrassment crept upon him: he felt himself turning cold. However many tender and happy feelings he believed himself to have for his sister, in this moment, which ought to have touched him, they were not there; his sensibility was out of gear, it would not work. He stroked Agathe and whispered some words of consolation, but it was hard for him to do it. And because he had no spiritual share in her agitation, the contact of their two bodies affected him like that of two bundles of straw. He put an end to it by leading Agathe to a chair and himself sitting down in another chair some way off. It was then that he gave his answer to what she had said: " That whole thing with the Will is something you don't enjoy at all! And you never will get any joy out of it, either, because it was an untidy thing to do, a disorderly thing!".

" Order? " Agathe exclaimed through her tears. " Duty?! "

She was quite beside herself because Ulrich had behaved so coldly. But she began to smile again. She realised that she must deal with her troubles all on her own. It felt as if the smile she managed to produce were floating somewhere a long way away from her icy lips.

As for Ulrich, he was now rid of his embarrassment. He was even pleased not to have felt the usual bodily tenderness, and it came to him in a flash that this too was something that must be different between the two of them. However, he had no time to think about this, for he could see that Agathe was in great distress, and to help her he began to talk.

" Don't be hurt by the terms I've used," he pleaded, " and don't take them amiss! I dare say I'm wrong to choose words like ' order ' and ' duty '. They do have rather the ring of a sermon. But why," he instantly went off at a tangent, " why the devil should sermons be despised? Surely they ought to give us the highest happiness? "

Agathe had no inclination at all to answer this.

Ulrich let the question drop.

" Don't go and think I'm trying to set myself up over against you as the just man," he begged. " I didn't mean *I* don't do anything wrong. Only what I don't like is doing it secretly! I like morality's highway-robbers, not the sneak-thieves. So I'd like," he said jestingly, " to make a moral robber of you, I don't want you to offend out of weakness."

" So far as I'm concerned, there's no point of honour involved," his sister said from behind her remote smile.

" You know it's frightfully funny that there should be times like ours when all the younger generation's so taken with the Bad ! " he said with a laugh, trying to get away from the personal. " Of course the modern preference for the morally gruesome is a weakness. Probably it comes from bourgeois satiation with the Good—it's sort of sucked dry. I began, myself, by thinking one had to say ' no ' to everything. Everyone who's between twenty-five and forty-five today has had that notion. But of course it was only a sort of fashion. I can quite easily imagine there'll soon be a reaction, with a younger generation that'll nail morality to its masthead again instead of immorality. And then all at once the aged donkeys who never in their lives felt any trace of true moral excitement, who merely uttered moral platitudes on occasion, will suddenly appear in the role of pioneers of a new character ! "

Ulrich had got up and was walking restlessly up and down the room.

" Perhaps we can put it this way," he suggested, "—the Good has by its very nature become almost a platitude, whereas Evil is still criticism. What is immoral gets its divine right from being drastic criticism of what is moral. It shows us that life is also thinkable in other terms. It gives the lie. We prove our gratitude for that by showing some forbearance. The fact that there are people who forge Wills and are themselves beyond question delightful ought to prove that there's something a little awry in the sanctity of private property. Or perhaps it doesn't even need proving. But this is where the task begins: for we must mentally provide, to go with every kind of crime, the potential guiltless criminal, even for infanticide and whatever other worst horrors there may be . . ."

He had been trying to catch his sister's eye, in vain, although he was teasing her about the Will. Now she made an involuntary gesture of protest. She was no theoretician, it was only her own crime that she could think excusable, and his comparisons were merely a renewed affront.

Ulrich laughed. " It looks like an intellectual game, but really," he assured her, " there's a meaning in our being able to juggle like this. It goes to show there's something out of kilter in the way we evaluate our behaviour. And there really is, you know. In a society made up of people who forged Wills you'd certainly be in favour of the inviolability of the law. It's only in a society of righteous people that the thing blurs and turns upside-down. I'll go so far as to say if Hagauer were a rotter, you'd be blazingly righteous. It's a positive disaster that even he's decent! This is the way one gets flung to and fro."

He waited for an answer, but none came. So he shrugged his shoulders and came back to the point.

" We're looking for grounds for you. We have come to the conclusion that respectable people are awfully keen on crime, though of course only in their imagination. It's only fair to add that, to make up for this, criminals—at least to judge by the way they talk—would all like to pass for respectable people. So we can actually arrive at a definition: crimes are that concentration, in the persons of sinners, of all that other people work off in minor irregularities—in imagination and in innumerable little everyday acts and attitudes of spite and beastliness. One might also say: crimes are something in the air, which simply takes the path of least resistance, into certain individuals. One might even say that although they are the acts of individuals incapable of any morality, in their totality they're the collective expression of some universally faulty human attitude to the distinction between Good and Evil. This is what from our earliest youth filled us with the critical spirit that our contemporaries have never got beyond ! "

" But what actually are Good and Evil ? " Agathe interjected. Ulrich did not notice that his free and easy manner was a torment to her.

" Well, as to that I don't know ! " he answered, laughing. " The fact is I've only just noticed for the first time that I loathe Evil. Honestly, until today I didn't know it reached such a pitch with me. Oh, Agathe, you've no idea what it's like," he lamented, in a pensive tone, "—I mean, take science ! For a mathematician—to put it in the simplest terms—minus five is not worse than plus five. A scientist, a research-worker, can't afford to feel loathing for anything, and in certain circumstances he'll be more excited and delighted by a beautiful specimen of a cancer than by a beautiful woman. A man who knows about things knows that nothing's true, that the whole truth will be revealed only at the end of time. Science is amoral. All this glorious thrusting forward into unknown territory gets us out of the habit of being personally concerned with our conscience, in fact it doesn't even give us the satisfaction of taking such a concern quite seriously. And art? Doesn't it amount to a continual creation of images that don't quite correspond to the image of life itself? I'm not talking about bogus idealism or the painting of voluptuous nudes in an age when everyone goes around clothed right up the ears," he said, now lightly again. " But just think of an authentic work of art— have you never felt there was something about it rather like the burning smell from a knife being whetted in a grindstone? It's a cosmic, meteoric, thunderstormy smell—isn't it?—divinely uncanny ! "

This was the only point at which Agathe interrupted him out of real interest. " Didn't you once write poems yourself? " she asked him.

" Oh, you remember about that? When did I make you that confession? " Ulrich asked. " Well yes, we all write poems at some stage. I even went on doing it after I'd gone over to mathematics," he admitted. " But the older I grew, the worse they became. And I can't help thinking, not so much because of my own lack of talent as out of a growing distaste for the untidiness, the bohemian, romantic character of that sort of emotional debauchery . . ."

His sister shook her head almost imperceptibly, but Ulrich noticed it.

" Oh yes ! " he insisted. " A poem should be just as little of an exceptional phenomenon as an act of goodness ! But what then—if I may put the question so—what becomes of the moment of exaltation in the next moment? You have a taste for poetry, I know. But what I mean is it isn't enough to have that fiery smell in one's nostrils and then let it fade away. That's an incomplete attitude, the exact counterpart to the moral attitude that exhausts itself in half-baked criticism." And suddenly coming back to the main subject, he said to his sister: " If I were to take the attitude to this Hagauer business that you were expecting me to take today, I'd have to be sceptical, nonchalant, and ironical. Then the undoubtedly very virtuous children that you or I may yet have would truly be able to say that we were part and parcel of a very bourgeois age of security, when nobody had any worries

except perhaps some idle ones.   And yet we've already gone to
so much trouble about our convictions——!"

Ulrich probably meant to say a good deal more.   He was
actually only leading to a way of coming down on his sister's
side that he had been thinking out, and it was a pity he did not
tell her so.

For suddenly she went and got her outdoor things, with a vague
remark about going out.   "So what it does come to is that I'm a
moral imbecile?" she asked with a forced attempt at lightness.
"I can't make anything of all you say in refutation."

"We're both moral imbeciles!" Ulrich gallantly assured her.
"Both of us!"   And he was somewhat put out by the haste in
which his sister left him without saying when she was coming back.

31   *Meaning to commit suicide, Agathe makes
a new acquaintance.*

IN fact she had hastened away because she did not want to give
her brother another chance to see the tears she could scarcely
restrain.   She was as sad as a person who has lost everything.
Why, she did not know.   It had come over her while Ulrich was
talking.   And again she did not know why.   He ought to have
done something instead of just talking.   What, she did not know.
He was right, of course, in not taking seriously the 'silly coincidence' of her agitation with the arrival of the letter, and right
to go on talking just the way he always did.   But Agathe had to
rush away.

At first she felt only the need to walk and walk.   She rushed
headlong away from the house.   She simply followed the street,
keeping always straight on.   She fled, the way human beings and
animals flee from a catastrophe.   Why, she did not ask herself.
It was only when she began to tire that she realised what she was
intent on: she was not going back, ever!

She meant to walk until evening.   Every step was a step farther away from home. She somehow assumed that by the time she was stopped by the barricade of evening, her resolve would be complete. It was the resolve to kill herself. It was actually not the resolve to kill herself, but the expectation that this resolve would be complete by evening. Behind this expectation there was a desperate seething and whirling inside her head. She had not even anything with her to kill herself with. Her little capsule of poison was somewhere in a drawer or a suit-case. All of her death that was ready was the desire not to have to go back again. She wanted to walk out of life. That was the cause of her walking. With every step she was walking as though straight out of life.

When she grew tired, she began to feel a craving for meadows and woods and to be walking in silence and open air. But to do that one had to have transport. She took a tram. She had been brought up to control herself in front of strangers. So when she bought a ticket and asked for directions there was no sign of agitation in her voice. She sat calm and straight, even her fingers quite still. And as she sat like this, the thoughts came. She would beyond doubt have felt better if she had been able to let herself go; fettered as she was physically, these thoughts were like big packages that she struggled in vain to force through an opening. She bore Ulrich a grudge for what he had said. She did not want to have a grudge against him for it. She told herself she had no right to. What after all did she give him? She took up his time and gave him nothing instead; she disturbed his work and all his habits. At the thought of his habits she felt a pang. So long as she had been in the house, apparently no other woman had entered it. Now Agathe was convinced that her brother must always have some woman. So he was putting himself under constraint for her sake. And since she had no way of compensating him, she was selfish and wicked. At this moment she would have liked to turn back and tenderly beg his forgiveness. But then she instantly remembered how cold he had been. Clearly he was sorry he had taken her on. Oh, all the things he had planned and talked of before he had grown tired of her! Now he no longer mentioned them. Once again Agathe's heart was overwhelmed by the disillusionment that had come with the letter. She was jealous. Senselessly and vulgarly jealous. She felt like hurling herself upon her brother, and felt the passionate, impotent friendship of the person throwing herself or himself straight against a rejection. 'I could steal for him, or go on the streets!' she thought, and though she saw this was ridiculous, she could not help it. Ulrich's talk, with its joking tone and its apparently impartial superiority, was by contrast like mockery. She admired that superiority and all the intellectual urges that went so far beyond her own. But she could not see why all ideas should always apply to all human beings alike! In her shame and humiliation she wanted personal comfort, not general edification! She did not want to be brave! And after a while she reproached herself for being as she was, increasing her grief by imagining that she deserved nothing better than Ulrich's indifference.

This self-mortification, for which neither Ulrich's behaviour nor even Hagauer's distressing letter provided adequate cause, was a temperamental outburst. Everything that Agathe, in the not very long period since she had ceased to be a child, had felt to be her own failure in the face of society's demands had been brought about by the fact that she went through that period with a sense of living without, or perhaps against, real inclinations of her own. She had inclinations towards devotion and trustfulness, for she had never been as at home in solitude as her brother was; and if she had up to now found it impossible to devote herself wholeheartedly to any person or cause, this was simply because she had the potentiality for some greater surrender and devotion, no matter whether it stretched out its arms to the world or to God! For there is, after all, a well-known way of devoting oneself to all humanity through not getting on with one's neighbour, and in the same way a latent, deep-seated yearning for God can spring up in an anti-social type because he or she has a great capacity for love: the religious criminal, in this sense, is no more paradoxical than the elderly person who goes to church because she never got a husband. And Agathe's behaviour to Hagauer, which had taken the completely senseless form of a self-seeking action, was just as much the outburst of an impatient will as was the violence with which she accused herself of having been wakened to life by her brother only to lose it then because of her own weakness.

She was soon out of patience with sitting in the slow-rumbling tram-car; when the buildings along the streets began to be lower and more rural, she got out and continued on foot. The gates of court-yards stood open, and through archways and over low fences her glance fell on artisans and animals, and children at play. The air was filled with a peace that stretched away into the distance, and in it was the sound of voices and the banging of tools: sounds stirring in the bright air with the irregular, soft movements of a butterfly, while Agathe felt herself gliding along past it all, like a shadow, now approaching the rising ground of the vineyards and woodland. But once she paused, outside a yard where coopers were at work, and listened to the good noise of mallets on a wooden barrel. All her life she had liked watching this good sort of work, had always taken pleasure in the modestly significant and well-pondered labour of hands. Even now she could not have enough of the thud of the mallets and the men's moving round and round the barrel. It made her for a while forget her anguish, plunging her into a pleasant unthinking alliance with the world. She always felt admiration for people who could do this sort of thing, skills that arose multifariously and naturally out of universally acknowledged needs. Only she herself had no gift for activity, although she had a number of mental and practical talents. Life was complete even without her. And all at once, before the connection became clear to her, she heard bells ringing and found it hard to stop herself weeping again. The little local church had probably had its bells chiming all this time, but Agathe noticed it only now and in the same moment was overwhelmed by the kinship between these useless chimes, shut out from the good, lavish earth, passionately flying through the air, and her own existence.

At once she began to hurry on, and, accompanied by the chime of bells, which now filled her ears, she passed swiftly between the last houses and came out to where the hillside was—below, dense with vineyards and a few bushes edging the paths and, above, all bright green woods that seemed to beckon her. And now she knew where she was being drawn, and it was a lovely feeling, as though with every step she were sinking deeper into Nature. Her heart pounded with ecstasy and effort whenever she stopped and assured herself that the bells were still going with her, though now hidden high in the air, scarcely audible. It seemed to her she had never before heard bells chiming like this in the middle of an ordinary day, apparently without any particular festive cause, democratically mingling with the natural, self-confident affairs of men. But of all the tongues this thousand-voiced city had this was now the last to speak to her, and there was something about it that took hold of her as though to lift her high and swing her up the hill; yet time and again it let go of her and dissolved into a small metallic sound with no primacy over the chirping, buzzing, and rustling sounds of the countryside. So Agathe climbed and walked onward for perhaps an hour more, until she suddenly found herself in the little shrubby wilderness to which her memory had drawn her.

It enclosed a neglected grave on the edge of the woods, at the place where almost a hundred years ago a writer had killed himself and where, in accordance with his last wish, he had also been laid to rest. Ulrich had said he was not a good writer, even if he was a famous one, and the rather myopic poeticism that was expressed in the wish to be *buried* overlooking a view had got short shrift from him. But Agathe loved the inscription on the big stone slab since the day when they had come for a walk this way and had together deciphered the rain-worn, handsome Biedermeier lettering; and she leaned over the black chains, with their big angular links, that bordered off from life the rectangle of death.

' Here lies one whom the world passed by ' were the words this writer, so discontented with life, had caused to be put on his tombstone, and Agathe thought to herself that the same might be said of her. This thought, here at the edge of wooded hills, above the returning green of the vineyards and the alien, immeasurable city with its trails of smoke slowly stirring in the morning sunlight, moved her deeply. She suddenly knelt down and pressed her forehead against one of the stone posts to which the chains were attached; the unaccustomed pose and the cool touch of the stone gave her a fictitious sense of the stony and passive tranquillity of death, which awaited her. She tried to recollect herself. At first, however, she could not: bird-calls struck upon her ear; there were so many different bird-calls that it astonished her; branches stirred, and since she could not feel any wind, it seemed to her the trees were moving their branches themselves. In a sudden hush there was a faint scuttering sound. The stone that she rested against was so smooth that it felt as if between her forehead and it there were a piece of ice that kept her from quite getting to it. Only after a while did she realise that what distracted her was

the very thing she was trying to call before her mind—that fundamental sense of her own superfluity, a feeling that could be most
simply reduced to saying that life was so complete without her that
she had nothing to do in it, no business to exist. This cruel
feeling was at bottom neither despairing nor affronted, but a kind
of listening and of looking on that Agathe had always known,
being without any stimulus, even any chance, to get into things
herself. There was almost a sort of security in being thus excluded,
just as there is a sort of amazement that forgets to ask any questions.
She might just as well go away. But where? There must be
some place, somewhere. Agathe was not one of those people to
whom a conviction of the emptiness of all illusions affords a kind
of satisfaction equal to a belligerent or spiteful asceticism in accepting one's unsatisfactory lot. She was generous and unthinking
in such matters—not at all like Ulrich, who put every imaginable
difficulty in the way of his own feelings, in order to forbid himself
to have them if they did not pass the test. She was stupid, that
was all! Yes, that was what she told herself. She did not want
to think about things! Defiantly she pressed her lowered brow
against the iron chains, which gave a little and then tightened in
resistance.

In these last weeks she had once more begun somehow believing
in God, but without thinking of Him. There were certain states
of mind in which the world had always seemed different to her
from the way it apparently was, and in such a way that then even
she no longer felt shut out, but lived in a radiance of utter conviction; and now through Ulrich's influence this had almost
become an interior metamorphosis, a total transformation. She
would have been prepared to imagine a God Who opens His world
like a hiding-place. But Ulrich said that was not necessary, it
could only do harm to imagine more than one could experience.
And it was for him to decide such things. But then it was also for
him to lead her, without abandoning her. He was the threshold
between two lives, and all the longing she had felt for one of them
and all her flight from the other led first to him. She loved him,
as shamelessly as one loves life. He reawakened every morning,
in every limb of her body, when she opened her eyes. And he
was looking at her now out of the dark mirror of her anguish.

And only at this point did Agathe remember that she meant to kill herself. She had the feeling that to spite him she had run away from home to God, when she left home with the resolve to kill herself. But now the resolve seemed to be exhausted, to have sunk back to its source, which was that Ulrich had affronted her. She was angry with him—she could still feel that—but the birds were singing, and she had begun to hear them again. She was just as bewildered as before, but now joyfully bewildered. She wanted to do something, she did not know what, but it should strike at Ulrich and not only at her. The infinite cold stupor in which she had been kneeling there now gave way to the warmth of blood vitally streaming back into her limbs as she rose to her feet again.

When she looked up, there was a man standing near her. She was disconcerted, for she did not know how long he had been watching her. As her glance, still dark from her emotion, crossed with his, she realised that he was contemplating her with unconcealed sympathy, apparently with a heart-felt wish to inspire her with confidence. This man—he was apparently of her own social class—was tall and gaunt; his clothes were dark. A short fair beard covered his chin and cheeks, but even so one could see his slightly up-turned, soft lips, which were in remarkably youthful contrast to the grey mingling with the fair hairs of his beard; it was as if under the aging beard the mouth had forgotten to age too. Altogether the face was not an easy one to characterise. Agathe's first impression was that he must be a grammar-school master: the severity in the face was not carved out of hard wood, but rather more resembled something soft that had hardened under the impact of little daily annoyances. But taking this softness as one's point of departure—this softness on which the manly beard had the effect of being deliberately planted in order to comply with some system to which its wearer owed allegiance—one then became aware that in this originally perhaps rather effeminate face there were hard, almost ascetic details, evidently the work of an indefatigable will exerting itself upon the soft material.

Agathe did not know what to make of this face, which left her suspended between attraction and repulsion. But she realised instinctively that this man wanted to help her.

" Life," the stranger said, " offers as much opportunity to strengthen the will as to weaken it. One must never flee from difficulties, but seek to master them!" And in order to see better, he polished his spectacles, which were misted over.

Agathe looked at him, amazed. Obviously he had been watching her for some time; for these words arose out of the midst of an interior conversation.

He in turn seemed rather startled by his own words and he raised his hat—belatedly, but all the more formally for that. But he quickly regained his composure and went straight on. "Forgive my asking if I can help you in any way . . ." he said on a querying note. "It is my belief that a sorrow, nay truly often some profound upheaval within the self, such as I here behold, may more easily be confided to a stranger."

It appeared that the stranger was speaking not without effort; evidently he had been fulfilling a caritative obligation in having anything to do with this beautiful woman, and now that they had begun to walk along side by side, he was positively fighting for words. For, having stood up, Agathe had simply begun slowly walking away from the grave, in his company, out from among the trees into the open space at the edge of the hills, without either of them deciding whether they would now follow one of the paths leading into the valley or, if so, which. Instead, they walked along the hilltop for a fair distance, talking, then turned back, and then came back over the same ground for the third time; neither knew where the other had been going, and each was trying not to interfere with the other's plans.

"Will you not tell me why you were weeping?" the stranger repeated, in the mild voice of a doctor asking where it hurts.

Agathe shook her head. "It wouldn't be easy to explain," she said and suddenly asked him: "But will you answer a question for me? What gives you the certainty of being able to help me without knowing me? I should have thought no one could help anyone!"

Her companion did not instantly answer. He several times opened his mouth to speak, but it appeared that he was forcing himself to wait. At length he said: "Probably one can help only someone whose sufferings are of a kind one has once experienced for oneself."

He fell silent. Agathe laughed at this man's thinking he could have experienced sufferings like hers, which could not fail to fill him with horror if he learnt their cause. But he seemed not to hear her laughter, or to pass it over as a spasm of exhausted nerves.

After a moment's thought, he said calmly: " Naturally I do not mean one is justified in imagining one can show anyone else what to do. But do you see: in a catastrophe panic is infectious and —escape is also infectious ! I mean the sheer fact of escaping, as from a house on fire. All the people inside lose their heads and rush into the flames. What a tremendous help it is then if one single person outside can stand and wave, simply wave his arms —shouting to them, even if they cannot hear his words, that there is a way out. . . . ! "

Agathe was within an ace of laughing at the frightful notions this kindly man harboured in his mind. But precisely because they did not seem to fit him, they moulded the waxen softness of his face almost uncannily.

" Heavens, you talk like a member of the fire brigade ! " she said, deliberately adopting a worldly tone of the flippant and superficial in order to hide her curiosity. " But surely you must have formed some sort of idea of the sort of catastrophe I'm involved in ? " Without her meaning it, some of her real scorn came through; for the plain notion that the man should want to help her made her indignant precisely because of the equally plain gratitude that she felt welling up in her.

The stranger gave her an astonished glance, then recollected himself and replied almost reprovingly: " You are probably still too young to know how very simple our life is. It becomes unmanageably confused only when we think of ourselves. The moment one does not think of oneself, but asks oneself how can one help someone else, it becomes very simple."

Agathe was silent, in thought.

And whether because of her silence or because of the encouragingly open spaces into which his words could go winging out, the stranger continued, though without looking at her: " It is a mere modern superstition to attach so much importance to whatever is personal. Nowadays there is so much talk about the cult of personality, living one's life to the full, accepting life on its own terms. But such vague and ambiguous expressions merely betray that those who hold such ideas have need of some mist to veil the real meaning of their rebellion. For what is it that is supposed to be ' accepted ' ? Everything, in every way, in whatever confusion ? Evolution, an American thinker has said, is always associated with resistance. We cannot develop one aspect of our nature without stunting the growth of another aspect. And what is to be lived to the full ? The mind or the instincts ? One's moods or one's character ? Selfishness or love ? If our higher nature is to be lived to the full, the lower must learn renunciation and obedience."

Agathe was thinking about why it should be simpler to look after others than after oneself. She was one of those far from egotistical people who, though they may always be thinking about themselves, do not look after themselves; and this is much further removed from ordinary selfishness, which is always looking out for its own advantage, than the contented selflessness of those who go round looking after their fellow-men. So what her companion was saying was radically strange to her; yet somehow it did move her, and the separate phrases, the words so emphatically pronounced, sailed perturbingly before her as though their significance were rather to be seen in the air than heard.

They were walking along a ridge that gave her a wonderful view of the deep valley hollowed out below, and it was evident that their present position gave her companion the sense of being on a lecture-platform or in a pulpit. She stopped and with her hat, which she had all this time been carelessly swinging in her hand, drew a line through the stranger's talk, cancelling it out.

" So," she said, " you have formed your own picture of me. I glimpse it through your words, and it isn't flattering ! "

The tall stranger appeared dismayed at the thought that he had offended her. Agathe laughed, with a friendly look at him.

" You seem to confuse what I am with the rights of the free personality," she said. " And, what's more, a somewhat neurotic and rather disagreeable personality."

" I was speaking merely of the fundamental pre-condition of the personal life," he said apologetically. " I confess that the situation in which I found you gave me the feeling that you might find some advice helpful. There is much misunderstanding nowadays about the fundamental pre-condition of life. All this modern neurosis, with all its excesses, comes solely from a slack inner atmosphere without will-power. For without a special exertion of the will no one can gain that integrity and stability which raises him above the sombre *mêlée* of the organism."

Here again were two words, 'integrity' and 'stability', that reminded Agathe of past yearnings and self-reproaches. "Please explain what you understand by this," she asked him. "Surely one can only have a will once one has an aim?"

"It is of no account what *I* understand!" was the answer she received, in a tone at once mild and brusque. "Do not all mankind's great ancient writings tell us, with unsurpassable clarity, what we must do and what we must not do?"

Agathe was nonplussed.

"In order to set up fundamental ideals of life," her companion expounded, "one requires a penetrating knowledge of life and of human beings, as well as heroic mastery of the passions and of egotism, in such degree as has been granted to only a very few personalities in the course of many thousands of years. And in all epochs these teachers of humanity have acknowledged one and the same truth."

Agathe involuntarily resisted, as anyone does who thinks better of his youthful flesh and blood than of dead sages' bones. "But," she exclaimed, "precepts that were originated thousands of years ago can't possibly apply to modern conditions!"

"They are not nearly so remote as sceptics would have us believe, sceptics who have lost touch with living experience and self-knowledge!" her companion answered with bitter satisfaction. "The profound verities are not arrived at in debate, as Plato well said. Man hears them as·a living interpretation and fulfilment of his self! Believe me, what makes man truly free, and what deprives him of his freedom, what gives him true bliss and what destroys it—that is something not subject to 'progress', it is something that every honest human being knows in his heart of hearts, if only he will listen to it!"

Agathe liked the expression 'living interpretation', but a sudden idea had come to her. "I suppose you must be religious?" she asked. She gave her companion a look full of curiosity.

He did not answer.

"You don't happen to be a priest, do you?" she went on, but her mind was put at rest by his beard; the rest of his appearance she had been ready to fit in with this surprising notion. It must be said to her credit that she could not have been more astounded if the stranger had casually referred to 'our sublime ruler, the divine Augustus '. Though she knew that religion played a great part in politics, the ideas that are made so much of in public life are something one is so used to not taking seriously that the suggestion that the various 'Christian' parties might be made up of Christian members tends to seem as wild as expecting every village postmaster to be a philatelist.

After a lengthy, somehow indecisive pause the stranger replied:

" I should prefer to leave your question unanswered. You are too remote from all these things."

But Agathe was in the grip of intense curiosity. " I should be glad if you would tell me who you are," she demanded.

This was admittedly a feminine privilege that could not very well be denied. Once again the stranger showed the same rather ludicrous uncertainty as when he had belatedly raised his hat. His arm seemed to twitch as though he were thinking of once more formally uncovering. But then something stiffened in him, one army of thoughts seemed to engage another in battle and finally to come out victorious: it was thus rather than that a little easy thing was easily done. " My name is Lindner. I teach at the Franz-Ferdinand-Gymnasium," he said, after a moment's reflection adding: " I am also on the University teaching-staff."

" Then perhaps you know my brother ? " Agathe asked eagerly, giving him Ulrich's name. " He read a paper recently, I think to the Pedagogic Society, on Mathematics and the Humanities, or something of the sort."

" I know his name. As a matter of fact I was at that lecture," Lindner admitted.

It seemed to Agathe that there was some negative implication in this, but she forgot it at Lindner's subsequent question.

" Was your father the distinguished jurist ? "

" Yes, he died a short time ago and now I live with my brother," Agathe said chattily. " Won't you come and see us ? "

" I'm afraid I have no time for social calls," Lindner answered brusquely, his eyes downcast in uncertainty.

" But then you mustn't mind my coming to see you," Agathe continued, without paying any attention to his reluctance. " I need advice!" And, since he had gone on addressing her as 'Fräulein', she added: " I'm married, my name is Hagauer."

" Can it be," Lindner exclaimed, " that you are the wife of that estimable educationist, Professor Gottlieb Hagauer?" He had begun the question on a note of high enthusiasm, which towards the end became rather hesitantly muted. For Hagauer was two things: he was an educationist, and he was a progressive educationist. Lindner was actually opposed to his ideas. What a relief it is, when a lady has just made the impossible suggestion of visiting a man at his house, if the shifting mists of the feminine psyche part to reveal a familiar enemy; it was the decline from the first to the second of these feelings that was reflected in his change of tone.

Agathe noticed this. She did not know if she ought to tell Lindner what her relations with her husband now were. It might make an immediate end of everything between herself and this new friend if she were to tell him; she felt that clearly. And she would have been sorry; for precisely because many things about Lindner made her inclined to laugh at him, he also gave her the feeling she could trust him. The impression, borne out by the man's appearance, that he wanted nothing for himself drove her, in some odd way, to honesty: he quieted all cravings, and then honesty sprang up of its own accord.

" I'm on the point of getting a divorce," she finally announced.

What followed was a silence. Lindner seemed to be dejected, and Agathe thought he was really quite pitiful.

At length he said, with an offended smile: " I thought it must be something of that kind, when I first caught sight of you."

" You don't mean to tell me you're also opposed to divorce!" Agathe exclaimed, giving free rein to her annoyance. " But of course you must be! Still, you know, it is really rather behind the times!"

" At least I cannot take it so much as a matter of course as you do," Lindner said thoughtfully, defending his own position. He removed his spectacles; polished them, put them on again, and surveyed Agathe. " I think you have too little will-power," he observed.

" Will-power? My will, for what it's worth, is to get a divorce!" Agathe cried, knowing it was not a very rational answer.

" That is not the sense in which I mean it," Lindner gently

corrected her. " I am of course prepared to believe you must have adequate grounds. But the fact of the matter is that I see these things in a different light. The free and easy morals that prevail nowadays amount, in practice, merely to a sign that an individual is inexorably chained to his own ego, incapable of living and acting in wider perspectives. Our worthy literary men," he added jealously, with an attempt, which only turned sour on his lips, to joke about Agathe's impassioned pilgrimage, " who play upon and flatter young ladies' feelings and are rewarded by being accorded excessive admiration, are naturally in an easier position than I am when I tell you that marriage is an institution involving responsibility and the person's mastery of his or her passions ! Before any individual absolves himself or herself from the obliga- tion to comply with the external safeguards that humanity has, with wise self-knowledge, set up against its own unreliability, he or she would do well to tell himself or herself that isolation from and violation of obedience to the higher totality are worse dis- asters than the body's disappointments, which we so sorely fear ! "

" That sounds like a code of law for archangels," Agathe said. " But I can't see that you're right. I'll walk a bit farther with you, and you must explain how anyone can think that way. Where are you going now ? "

" I must go home," Lindner said.

" Would your wife be inconvenienced if I came home with you ? In town we can take a taxi. I have plenty of time ! "

" My son will be coming home from school," Lindner said with dignified evasiveness. " We always lunch punctually. That is why I must go home. My wife, alas, died suddenly some years ago," he added in correction of Agathe's assumption. And with a glance at his watch he said nervously and crossly: " I must hurry ! "

" Then you must explain it to me another time. It matters to me ! " Agathe insisted with animation. " If you won't come to see us, I can come to you, can't I ? "

Lindner gasped for air, but it was no good. Finally he said: " But a lady cannot call on a man ! "

" Oh yes, I can ! " Agathe assured him. " You'll see, some day I shall just appear. I haven't decided when. There's no harm in it, you know ! "

And with this she took her leave of him, starting down a path leading in another direction.

'You have no will-power!' she said under her breath, trying to imitate Lindner. But the word 'will-power' was fresh and cool in her mouth. It had overtones of pride, toughness, and confidence, a strong beat of the heart. The man had done her good.

32 *The General meanwhile takes Ulrich and Clarisse to the lunatic asylum.*

WHILE Ulrich was alone at home, the War Ministry telephoned to ask whether His Excellency the chief of the Department for Educational and Cultural Affairs could speak to him privately if he called in half-an-hour, and thirty-five minutes later General von Stumm's official carriage came dashing up the gravel sweep.

"A nice thing!" was the General's way of greeting his friend, who was immediately struck by the absence of the orderly customarily there to carry the spiritual bread. The General was in full dress and was even wearing his decorations. "A nice mess you've got me into!" he asseverated. "There's this big do at your cousin's tonight, I haven't even had time to consult with my chief about it, and you spring a mine under my feet—I've just heard we're bound for the mad-house, we've got to be there in an hour or less!"

"But why on earth?" Ulrich not unnaturally asked. "Surely these things are usually arranged with plenty of notice to suit everyone's convenience?"

"Don't ask so many questions!" the General implored him. "Just go and ring up your lady-friend or cousin or whatever she may be, and tell her we're calling for her!"

Ulrich rang up to the grocer's shop where Clarisse was in the habit of doing her local shopping, and while he was waiting for her to be fetched to the telephone, he inclined one ear to the General's

tale of woe.   In order to comply with the wish that Ulrich had
expressed on Clarisse's behalf, Stumm had had a word with the
chief of the Medical Corps, who had then got in touch with a
celebrated colleague, the head of the University Hospital, where
Moosbrugger's case was awaiting a top-level opinion.   As a result
of a misunderstanding on both these gentlemen's part, the appointment had been made forthwith, and Stumm had been (very apologetically) informed of this only at the last moment, as also of the
fact that the distinguished alienist was likewise expecting him, in
person, and looking forward to his visit with much pleasure.

" I feel sick ! " he declared.   It was a time-honoured formula
that meant he wanted a drink.

When he had tossed off his schnaps, his nerves relaxed.

" What business have I got going to a mad-house ?   It's all for
your sake ! " he lamented.   " What on earth am I going to say to
this blanketty-blank professor if he asks me what I've come
for ? "

At this moment Ulrich heard Clarisse's voice at the other end
and when he gave her the news the telephone resounded with a
jubilant war-cry.

" It's all very well ! " the General said fretfully.   " But apart
from that I've simply got to talk to you about this evening's do.
And I've got to see His Excellency about it too.   And he leaves
the office at four ! "   He looked at his watch, and despair pinned
him to his chair.

" All right.   I'm ready," Ulrich declared.

" Your delightful sister isn't coming with us ? " Stumm asked
in surprise.

" My sister's not at home."

" Pity ! " the General affirmed.   " She's the most admirable
woman I've ever seen."

" I thought Diotima was ? " Ulrich remarked.

" So she is," Stumm replied.   " She's admirable too.   But
since she's been going in for sexual enlightenment, she makes me
feel like a kid at school.   Mind you, I like looking up to her.
God knows, war's a plain and tough job, as I'm always saying.
But sex just happens to be the very territory where, as you might
say, it goes against one's honour as an officer to let oneself be
treated as a layman."

Meanwhile, however, they had got into the carriage and been driven off at a very brisk trot.

" This lady-friend of yours—I hope she's good-looking ? " Stumm enquired sceptically.

" She's original, anyway," Ulrich told him. " But you'll see for yourself."

" And so tonight," the General said with a sigh, " something gets going. I expect something to happen."

" That's what you always say when you come to see me," Ulrich retorted, smiling.

" Maybe I do, but it's true all the same. And this evening you'll be present at the encounter between your cousin and the Widow Drangsal. I trust you haven't gone and forgotten all I told you about that ? Well now, the Widow Drangsal—you know that's what your cousin and I call her between ourselves—she's been pestering your cousin for so long and now it's come to a head. She's been working on everyone, and tonight the two of them have it out. We've only been waiting for Arnheim, so that he can form his opinion too."

" Oh, he's back, is he ? " Ulrich, who had not seen Arnheim for a long time, had not heard this.

" He's back," Stumm said. " For a few days. So we had to get things moving, you see." He broke off, bounding up from the upholstery, on which they were rocking along, with a speed nobody would have expected of him. " Idiot ! " he barked into the ear of the orderly, who was seated on the box in civilian livery, driving the departmental horses. Helplessly shaken to and fro, Stumm clung to his orderly's back as he anathematised him. " This isn't the way ! "

The mufti-clad soldier kept his back as stiff as a board, showing no reaction to the General's intervention in his prescribed duties other than turning his head exactly ninety degrees, so that he could see neither the General nor his horses, and smartly reported to the empty air that the direct route was for some distance out of service owing to repairs in progress but that they would rejoin the road after making the necessary détour.

" There you are, so you see I was right ! " Stumm exclaimed as he plumped back on to the seat, glossing over his futile outburst of impatience partly for the orderly's benefit and partly for Ulrich's.

" Now the chap's got to drive a longer way round, and here am I still having to see the chief, who wants to get away from the office by four and has to brief the Minister before he goes. The fact is," he added in a lower voice, exclusively for Ulrich's ear, " His Excellency the Minister's announced he'll make a personal appearance at Tuzzis' this evening ! "

" Whatever next ? ! " Ulrich exclaimed in proper surprise at this announcement.

" Ah, I've kept on telling you there's something in the air."

Now Ulrich pressed him to reveal what actually was in the air. " Come on, out with it," he demanded. " What's the Minister after ? "

" Oh, he doesn't know himself," Stumm answered cosily. " H.E. has a sort of feeling that ' the time has come '. Old Leinsdorf's also got a feeling that the time has come. Furthermore, the Chief of the General Staff has the feeling the time has come. If enough people have it, there's bound to be something in it."

" But the time come for what ? " Ulrich insisted.

" Well, there's no need to know that yet ! " the General set him right. " These are just what you might call absolute impressions. By the way," he asked, abstractedly or perhaps pensively, " how many of us are there going to be ? "

" How do you expect me to know ? " Ulrich retorted in astonishment.

" No, I meant," Stumm explained, " how many of us are going to the looney-hatch ? Sorry, old boy ! Funny, isn't it, a misunderstanding like that ? Fact is there are days when a chap has such a lot on his mind. Anyway, how many of us are there going to be ? "

" I don't know who else may come along. Anything from three to six people."

" What I was getting at," the General said, pondering, " if there are more than three of us, we'll need another cab. Appearances, you know—I'm in uniform."

" Oh of course," Ulrich said reassuringly.

" I can't very well drive about squashed up with a lot of people like a sardine."

" Of course not. But tell me, what's all this about absolute impressions ? "

" Only the trouble is will we find a cab away out there ? " Stumm went on worrying. " It's at the back of beyond, isn't it ? "

" We'll pick one up on the way," Ulrich decided firmly. " And now kindly explain how you've all got this absolute impression of yours that the time has come for whatever it may be."

" There's no explaining it," Stumm retorted. " Look, if I say something's absolutely like this or that and not otherwise, it means just that: that I can't explain it. The most you could add is that the Drangsal woman's a pacifist, sort of, probably because she's launching Feuermaul on the world and he writes poems about ' man is good '. There are a lot of people believe that now."

Ulrich refused to take this seriously. " It's only a short time ago you were telling me the opposite. You told me everyone in the Campaign's in favour of action, and taking a strong line, and all that ! "

" So they are too," the General granted him. " And then, you see, there are influential circles backing the Widow—she's got a great knack for that. There's this demand that the National Campaign should produce an act of human goodness."

" Oh, indeed ? " Ulrich said.

" Yes. It all just goes to show how you don't bother about anything any more ! Other people are worried about it. Just let me remind you that the fratricidal war of 'sixty-six only happened because those fellows in the Frankfurt Parliament went and declared all the Germans in the world were brothers. Of course I'm not going the lengths of saying the War Minister or the Chief of General Staff might be worried. That'd be nonsense. But you know how one thing leads to another. That's the gist of it. See what I mean ? "

It was not very clear, but it made sense. And the General added a very wise remark.

" Look here, you're always wanting to get things clear," he said to his companion reproachfully. " And I admire you for it. But you ought to try thinking in historical terms for once. The question is : How on earth can all the people directly concerned in an event know in advance if it'll turn out to be a great one ? Purely and simply because they tell themselves it's great ! So if

I may indulge in paradox, I'd put it this way: the history of the world is written before it happens. It starts off by being just a lot of bally-hoo. And the next thing is the people with the energy to get things done have a very difficult job facing them."

"You're right about that," Ulrich said appreciatively. "And now tell me the whole story!"

But although the General himself wanted to talk about it, there was so much he had on his mind, during these minutes when the horses' hooves were beginning to beat along softer ground, that he suddenly gave way to other anxieties.

"Here I am got up like a Christmas-tree in case the Minister wants to see me too," he exclaimed, stressing the fact by patting his pale-blue tunic and the rows of medals dangling on his breast. "Doesn't it strike you it might lead to some awkward moments if I appear in full-dress before the loonies? For instance, what am I going to do if one of them insults the Emperor's coat? I can't very well draw my sword. On the other hand, I can't risk letting it pass, either."

Ulrich reassured his friend by pointing out that he would doubtless be wearing a doctor's white coat over his uniform. Yet before Stumm had time to declare himself fully satisfied with this solution, they were met by Clarisse in a smart summer dress, impatiently coming along the road to meet them, escorted by Siegmund.

She told Ulrich that Walter and Meingast had refused to come. And after a cab had been found for the other two, the General said in a gratified manner to Clarisse:

"Coming down the road like that—my dear young lady, you were positively an angelic vision."

But by the time he descended from his carriage at the gate of the hospital, Stumm von Bordwehr was red in the face and looking rather uncomfortable.

33 *The lunatics hail Clarisse.*

CLARISSE was twisting her gloves in her hands, looking up at the windows and fidgeting all the time while Ulrich paid off the cab. Stumm von Bordwehr protested against Ulrich's doing it, and the cabby meanwhile sat on his box, smiling complacently, while the two gentlemen politely wrangled. Siegmund, as usual, found a grain of dust to brush off his coat with his fingertips and then gazed about him with a vacant expression.

In a low voice the General said to Ulrich: " Strange woman your friend is. On the way here she was telling me about *will-power*. I didn't understand a word of it ! "

" That's just like her," Ulrich said.

" Pretty, though," the General whispered. " Like a fourteen-year-old lass in the ballet. But what did she mean by saying we were coming here to make ourselves over to our ' illusion ' ? The world's ' too free of illusion ', she says. D'you know anything about that ? Jolly awkward it was, there simply wasn't anything I could think of saying."

The General was obviously delaying the paying off of the cab only to have a chance of asking these questions. But before Ulrich could answer, he was saved the trouble by the appearance of an emissary from the Superintendent, who conveyed to the General his chief's apologies for some delay owing to the unavoidable pressure of his duties, and conducted the whole company upstairs and into a waiting-room.

With her eyes Clarisse took in every stone of the staircase and the corridors, and even in the little waiting-room, which, with its chairs upholstered in threadbare green velvet, was reminiscent of an old-fashioned first-class waiting-room at a railway-station, her gaze was all the time slowly moving about. There the four of them sat, when they had been left to wait, and at first found nothing to say.

After a while, to break the silence Ulrich asked Clarisse teasingly if the thought of meeting Moosbrugger face to face did not make her blood run cold.

" Oh ! " Clarisse said disparagingly, " he's never known any but surrogate women, so it had to come to this."

The General tried to restore his credit, something having meanwhile occurred to him. " Will-power's the very latest thing nowadays," he said. " It's a problem we're much concerned with in the Patriotic Campaign too."

Clarisse smiled at him and stretched her arms to ease the tension in them. " Waiting like this, one feels what's to come in one's limbs, as if one were looking through a telescope," she replied.

Stumm von Bordwehr reflected. He did not want to appear at a loss again.

" True ! " he said. " It may be connected with the modern interest in physical culture. That's another thing we're concerned with in the Campaign."

At this point the Superintendent swept in, with a whole entourage of assistants and nurses, was very gracious, especially to Stumm, mumbled something apologetic about urgent business, and regretted that this was all he would see of them, instead of being able to show them round himself. He introduced Dr. Friedenthal, who was to act for him.

Dr. Friedenthal was a slim, tall man with a thick mop of hair and a tendency to flabbiness. As he was introduced he smiled like an acrobat just about to climb his ladder in order to perform a *salto mortale*.

When the Superintendent had gone, overalls were brought.

" To avoid upsetting the patients," Dr. Friedenthal explained.

As Clarisse slipped into hers, she felt a peculiar increase in strength. A little doctor—that was what she was like. She felt very masculine and very white.

The General looked round for a looking-glass. It was difficult to find an overall that fitted him, with his odd proportions of girth to height. When they finally managed to get him entirely enveloped, he looked like a child in an over-long nightshirt.

" You don't think I ought to take my spurs off ? " he asked Dr. Friedenthal.

" Army medical officers wear spurs," Ulrich pointed out.

Stumm made one last helpless, complicated effort to see what he looked like from behind, with the physicianly robe draped in wide folds all round him and the hem catching on his spurs. Then they set out.

Dr. Friedenthal begged them not to show any sign of perturbation, whatever they encountered.

"Well, it's all gone smoothly so far," Stumm whispered to his friend. "Trouble is it doesn't really interest me, I could be making far better use of the time talking over this evening's do with you. Now look, you said you wanted me to be quite frank about the whole thing. It's perfectly simple: everyone's arming to the teeth. The Russians have got entirely new field-artillery. Are you listening? The French turned their two-year conscription period to account to enlarge their army terrifically. The Italians——"

They had once more descended the princely, ancient staircase that they had just come up and, turning off the main hall, found themselves in a network of small rooms and twisting passages with white-washed beams in the ceiling. These were for the most part administrative and domestic offices; they were rather poky and sombre, but there was a shortage of space in this old building. Here they encountered sinister persons going about their unknown business, some in hospital uniform, some in mufti. One door bore a notice saying 'Reception', another 'Men'.

The General's flow of talk dried up. He had premonitions of unaccountable things that would start happening at any moment, things so extraordinary that they would require great presence of mind to deal with them. Against his will he found himself occupied with the question how to cope with the situation if an irresistible need should compel him to separate from the party and he, being thus alone, without a specialist at his side, in a place where all men are equal, should encounter a lunatic.

Clarisse, on the other hand, kept walking half a pace ahead of Dr. Friedenthal. The fact that he had said they must wear doctors' white coats in order not to alarm the patients buoyed her up, like a lifebelt, on the swell of her impressions. All sorts of pet ideas of hers were going through her mind, questions of Nietzsche's: ' Is there a pessimism of strength? An intellectual predisposition to all that is hard, frightful, evil, and problematic in life? A desire for the terrible as the one worthy enemy? Is

madness perhaps not necessarily a symptom of degeneration?'
She was not thinking these questions in so many words, but remembering them as a whole. Her thoughts had pressed all this
together into one very small package, marvellously reducing it to
the smallest possible bulk, like a burglar's tools. For her this
journey was half philosophy and half adultery.

Stopping at an iron door, Dr. Friedenthal took a flat key out
of his pocket. As he opened the door, dazzling brightness fell
upon the explorers, and they stepped out of the building. At the
same moment Clarisse was transfixed by a fearful piercing cry
such as she had never heard in all her life. For all her courage,
she shrank.

" Just a horse ! " Dr. Friedenthal said, smiling.

And in fact they were on a road that led from the front gate,
along the side of the main building, round to the kitchen yard at the
back. It was in no way different from other such pieces of road,
with old wheel-tracks and homely weeds on it, and the sun blazing
down. And yet not only Clarisse, but all the others with the
exception of Friedenthal, felt an odd surprise, even something
rather like a startled, confused resentment, at finding themselves
on an ordinary, normal road after the ordeal of their long adventure
through dark passages. In the first instant this freedom was
disconcerting even if also extremely pleasant; it took some getting
used to. With Clarisse, in whom all clashes were most direct,
the tension broke in a loud giggle.

Dr. Friedenthal strode, smiling, ahead along the road, and then
opened a small but heavy iron door in a high wall on the other
side, leading into a park.

" This is where it starts," he said gently.

And now they found themselves really in that world which had
been inexplicably drawing Clarisse towards it for weeks past, and
not merely with the gruesome attraction of something incommensurable and impenetrable, but as though she were destined
there to experience something she could not imagine beforehand.
At first, however, there was no way in which this world seemed
differently from any old park: in one direction the greensward
rose slightly towards some groups of tall trees, among which there
were small, white buildings rather like villas. The sweep of sky
behind them suggested the presence of a view from there, and on

one such view-point Clarisse saw patients with warders, standing or sitting about in groups, looking like white-clad angels.

General von Stumm thought this a suitable place to resume his talk with Ulrich.

"You see, I'd just like to prime you a bit for this evening," he began. "The Italians, the Russians, the French, and the English as well, you know, they're all arming, and we——"

"You chaps want your artillery, I know that," Ulrich interrupted.

"Among other things," the General went on. "But if you won't let me finish what I'm trying to say, we'll have got among the crackpots and won't have any more chance to talk. What I was going to say is, here we are, bang in the middle of it all, militarily speaking in a very dangerous position. And with things being like this, there are people among us—and now I'm talking about the Patriotic Campaign—crying out for nothing but human goodness!"

"And that's what you chaps are against. Yes, yes, I realise that."

"Quite on the contrary!" Stumm asserted. "We're not against it! We take pacifism very seriously! Only we want to get our artillery budget through. And if we could do that what you might call hand in hand with pacifism, that'd be the best way of safeguarding ourselves against all those misunderstandings—flying off the handle about 'imperialism' and how one's endangering peace! I don't mind admitting to you, old boy, that's why we actually are a bit in league with the Widow Drangsal. On the other hand, that's something one has to be careful about. Because on the other hand, of course, the party in opposition to her, the nationalist group, which we have in the Campaign too now, is against pacifism but in favour of getting the army up to scratch."

The General had to swallow down, however bitterly, the rest of what he meant to say, for they had almost reached the top of the incline and Dr. Friedenthal was waiting to gather his little company about him. The angelic site turned out to have a slight fence round it. Their guide strode through this compound without paying it much attention, as though this were a mere prelude.

"A 'quiet' section," he explained.

There were only women here. They wore their hair loose on

their shoulders, and their faces were repulsive, the features thickened, fat and soft. One of them at once came running up to the doctor, thrusting a letter upon him.

" It's always the same thing," Dr. Friedenthal said and read the letter aloud: " ' Adolf, dearest ! When are you coming ? Have you forgotten me ? ' "

The woman, who was perhaps sixty, stood there, blank-faced, listening. " You'll send it straight off, eh ? " she asked.

" Of course," Dr. Friedenthal said, tearing the letter up under her eyes and smiling meanwhile at the attendant nurse.

Clarisse instantly challenged him. " How can you do such a thing ? " she exclaimed. " Mad people must be taken seriously ! "

" Come along," Dr. Friedenthal said. " There's no point wasting our time here. If you like, afterwards I can show you hundreds of such letters. I dare say you noticed the old woman was quite unmoved when I tore it up."

Clarisse was taken aback. What Dr. Friedenthal said was quite true, but it disturbed her thoughts. And before she could re-arrange them, they were disturbed again.

The moment they moved off another old woman, who had obviously been waiting for this, lifted her skirt and revealed to the men passing her an expanse of hideous aged thigh, and pelvis as well, above the coarse woollen stockings she wore.

" The beastly old trollop ! " Stumm von Bordwehr muttered, so outraged and disgusted that for a while he forgot all about politics.

But Clarisse had found that the thigh resembled the face. In fact both probably showed the same signs of fatty degeneration. For Clarisse, however, this gave rise to the first sense of strange interrelatedness she had here, the sense of a world in which everything worked differently from what one would grasp by means of ordinary concepts. It suddenly occurred to her, too, that she had not noticed just when the white-clad angels became transformed into these women, and indeed that even while she had been walking through the midst of them she had not noticed which of them were patients and which were nurses. She turned round and looked back, but the path had followed a curve round a house, so that she could no longer see them. Still with her head half-turned over her shoulder, she stumbled on, like a child, after the others. And the series of impressions that began here and now no longer formed the transparent, flowing stream of events that one accepts as life, but a frothy torrent, with only here and there a smooth patch that would afterwards remain in her memory.

" Another ' quiet ' section. Men this time," Dr. Friedenthal announced, collecting his party at the door of the house.

When they paused at the first bed, in a considerately lower voice he told them that its inmate was a case of ' depressive dementia paralytica '.

" Longstanding syphilis. Delusions of sin, nihilistic obsessions," Siegmund whispered to his sister in further explanation.

Clarisse found herself face to face with an old gentleman who had the appearance of once having belonged to the upper reaches of society. He was sitting bolt upright in bed. He was perhaps in his late fifties; his complexion was very white. His apparently well-cared-for face—that of a highly cultivated man—was framed in thick white hair and was as insufferably noble-looking as are only faces described in fifth-rate novels.

" Couldn't someone do a portrait of him ? " Stumm von Bordwehr asked. " He's the perfect model of intellectual beauty. I'd like," he said, turning to Ulrich, " to give the portrait to your cousin."

Dr. Friedenthal smiled a melancholy smile and explained: " The noble expression is caused by the slackening of the facial muscles." With a swift gesture he demonstrated that the pupils of the eyes did not contract in bright light, and then conducted the party further. There was little time for all there was to be seen. The old gentleman, who had nodded mournfully to all that was said at his bedside, was still muttering in a low, worried voice when they paused, some beds farther on, to consider the next case Dr. Friedenthal drew to their attention.

This time it was someone who was himself engaged in artistic activity: a cheerful, fat painter, whose bed was beside the sunny window. He had paper and a great many pencils strewn on his bed, and was said to use them all day long. What instantly struck Clarisse was his blithe, unwearying activity. ' That's the way Walter ought to paint ! ' she thought to herself.

Observing her interest, Dr. Friedenthal grabbed a sheet from the fat man and handed it to Clarisse. The painter snickered, with a coquettish air, like a maidservant whose bottom has been pinched.

What Clarisse saw, to her astonishment, was a sketch for a large composition, the drawing sure and accomplished, entirely sensible, in spirit even commonplace, with many figures perspectively involved with each other in a large room the details of which were executed with the painful correctness, the schoolmasterly sanity, of something straight from the National Academy.

" Surprisingly accomplished ! " she involuntarily exclaimed.

Dr. Friedenthal smiled as if flattered.

" Sucks to you ! " the painter exclaimed. " There you are, you see, the gentleman likes it ! Show him some more, go on ! Surprisingly good, he said ! Go on, show him ! I know you just laugh at me, but he likes it ! " He spoke good-humouredly, holding out the rest of his pictures to the doctor, with whom he was apparently on excellent terms, even if his art was not appreciated.

" We've no time for you today," Dr. Friedenthal told him. Turning to Clarisse, he summed up his criticism in the words: " He's not schizophrenic, but I'm afraid he's the only artist we have at the moment. Schizophrenics are often splendid artists, absolutely modern."

" And insane ? " Clarisse queried.

" Why not ? " Dr. Friedenthal mournfully retorted.

Clarisse bit her lip.

Meanwhile Stumm and Ulrich were already waiting on the threshold of the next ward and the General was saying: " Looking at this makes me really sorry I called my orderly an idiot this morning. I'll never do it again." For the ward they were gazing into was apparently for extreme cases of congenital idiocy.

Clarisse, who had not yet seen this, was thinking: ' So even such a respectable, generally recognised art as the academic sort has its sister-art in the lunatic asylum—a sister denied, deprived, and yet so like that one couldn't tell the difference . . .' This almost struck her more than Dr. Friedenthal's remark that some other time he would be able to show her Expressionist artists. However, she resolved to take that up. She had bent her head and was still biting her lip. Something wasn't quite right about all this. It seemed glaringly wrong to lock up such gifted people.

Doctors did no doubt understand about disease, she thought, but they probably did not yet understand all the implications of art. She had the feeling that something must be done about this. Still, she did not lose heart, for the fat painter had from the first moment referred to her as ' the gentleman '; that struck her as a good sign.

Dr. Friedenthal was scrutinising her with curiosity.

When she felt his gaze, she looked up, with that thin-lipped smile of hers, and went towards him. But before she could say anything, her thoughts were blotted out by an appalling sight.

In the next ward, all crouching or drooping in their beds, were a row of ghastly creatures. Everything about their bodies was crooked, twisted, paralysed, squalid. Their teeth protruded in all directions. Heads waggled. Some heads were too big, some too small, some misshapen. Jaws hung slack, slobbering, or brutish ruminating movements were made by mouths empty of food, empty of words. It seemed as though leaden bars many yards thick must lie between these souls and the living world; and after the quiet chuckling and buzzing in the other room the silence was oppressive, broken only by obscure gruntings or groanings. Such wards for advanced dementia cases or low-grade idiots are one of the most horrifying things one can encounter in all the hideousness of a mental hospital. Clarisse felt herself plunged headlong into a ghastly darkness where nothing could be distinguished from anything else.

But their guide Friedenthal could see even in the dark. Pointing to several beds, he explained: " This is idiocy, and that over there is cretinism——"

Stumm von Bordwehr pricked up his ears. " You mean a cretin isn't the same as an idiot ? " he asked.

" No," the doctor said. " There's a medical distinction."

" Interesting," Stumm said. " In ordinary life you'd never think of a thing like that."

Clarisse walked from bed to bed. She tried to pierce the patients with her gaze, exerting herself to the utmost without managing to understand the slightest thing about these faces, which appeared to have no cognisance of her. All thought was extinguished in this confrontation.

Dr. Friedenthal followed her, quietly commenting: " Congenital amaurotic idiocy", "Tubercular hypertrophic sclerosis", "Idiotia thymica". . .

The General, who had by now come to feel he had had enough of 'these idiots' and assumed the same applied to Ulrich, glanced at his watch and said:

"Now let's see, where did we leave off? We must make use of the time." And somewhat startlingly he began: "So please bear this in mind: the War Ministry finds itself backed by the pacifists on one side and the nationalists on the other——"

Ulrich, who was not so nimble at detaching himself from his environment, gazed at him blankly.

"No, no, I'm not joking!" Stumm protested. "This is politics I'm talking! Something must be done. But that, you know, is where we came in. If we don't get a move on, we shall have H.M.'s jubilee on top of us—and a nice lot of fools we'll look. But what *is* to be done? It's a logical question, isn't it? And roughly what it all comes to, what I've been telling you, is some of our crowd expect us to help them to love all humanity and the rest of them expect us to let them play Old Harry with the other chaps so that the nobler blood may be victorious, or however one puts it. Either way, there's something in it. And what you've got to do, to make no bones about it, old boy, is somehow combine the two so that no harm's done."

"Me?" Ulrich asked incredulously, when his friend had thus exploded his bomb. He would have burst out laughing if they had been anywhere else.

"Yes, of course you," the General maintained firmly. "I'll do my damndest to support you, but after all it's you that's Secretary to the Campaign and Leinsdorf's right-hand man."

"I'll apply to get you admitted to this institution," Ulrich countered with determination.

"Oh, all right," the General said. From his training in strategy and tactics he knew that when faced with unexpected resistance one did best to retire at once, in good order. "You get me in here and perhaps I'll get to know someone who's found the greatest idea in the world. The people outside seem to have lost their taste for the search anyway." He glanced at his watch again. "I gather there are some of them that are the Pope or the universe. That's what I've heard. We haven't seen any of *them* yet, and they're just the ones I was looking forward to. Your friend's terribly thorough," he lamented.

Dr. Friedenthal gently detached Clarisse from contemplation of the defectives.

Hell is not interesting; it is merely terrible. Whenever it has not been humanised—as by Dante, who populated it with men of letters and other public figures, thus distracting attention from the penal technicalities—whenever anyone has simply tried to give an original idea of it, even the most imaginative people have not got beyond oafish torments and puerile distortions of earthly peculiarities. But it is precisely the emptiness of the thought of inconceivable, inexorable, everlasting punishment and torment, the premise of a change for the worst impervious to any attempt to reverse it, that has the attraction of an abyss. The same is true of lunatic asylums, which on earth are the ultimate habitation of the lost. They are as lacking in imagination as Hell itself. Many people who are ignorant of the causes of mental disease are afraid of nothing so much—apart from the possibility of losing their money—as that one day they might lose their reason. It is remarkable how many people are plagued by the thought of suddenly losing themselves. It is probably overestimation of what we find in ourselves that makes us overestimate the horror that—as it seems to sane people—surrounds the institutions where the insane are confined. Clarisse too was suffering a faint disappointment, arising from some vague expectation she had acquired with the rest of her education. With Dr. Friedenthal it was the contrary. He was accustomed to making this journey. The elements of his daily routine were keeping order as in a barracks or in any other collective institution, alleviating such pains as became marked, dealing with complaints, preventing deterioration wherever possible, occasionally achieving some slight improvement, sometimes even a cure. Observing much, knowing much, but never possessing an adequate explanation of all the patterns: that was his intellectual lot. Going his round through the various buildings, prescribing medication for coughs, colds, constipation, sores and wounds, with sedatives here and there: that was his daily work as a physician. The spectral horror of the world in which he lived was something he felt only when his sense of contrast was stimulated by contact with the

ordinary world.   This was something that could not be done every
day, but visits such as this of Clarisse and her friends were such an
occasion, and that was why what they were shown had been
thought out with some of a theatrical producer's sense of effect.
So the moment Dr. Friedenthal had roused Clarisse from her
absorption, he went on to something new and more dramatic.

Scarcely had they left that ward when they were joined by
several large men in crisp overalls, with bulky shoulders and
jovial sergeant-majorly faces.   It happened so mutely that it was
like a roll of drums.

" Here we come to an ' acute ' section," Dr. Friedenthal
announced.

Indeed, they could already hear a screaming and squawking,
which they were steadily approaching; it was like the uproar from
an enormous aviary.   When they reached the door, they saw that
it had no handle.   One of the warders opened it with a special
key.

Clarisse moved to go in first, as she had done everywhere so
far, but she was grabbed by Dr. Friedenthal.

" Not here! " he said in a significant and weary tone, without
apology.

The warder who had opened the door pushed it only slightly
ajar, filling the space with his huge body, and after he had first
listened, then peered inside, he made a quick dash in, followed by
a second warder, who took up his position on the opposite side of
the door.

Clarisse's heart began to thud.

" Advance-guard, rear-guard, flank cover," the General said
appreciatively.

Thus covered, they went in, and the huge warders accompanied
them from bed to bed.

Those in the beds produced a continuous agitated flutter,
screaming, rolling their eyes, waving their arms.   It was as if each
of them were shouting out into some space that existed only for
him; and yet too they all seemed to be engaged in one vast
tumultuous discussion, like exotic birds all shut up in one cage
and each of them chattering in the language of some other island.
Some of them were free, others were tied to the bed with bandages
which prevented them from moving their hands much.

" Safeguard against attempted suicide," the doctor explained, and went on to name the forms of insanity: paralysis, paranoia, dementia praecox—names that might indeed have been those of species of exotic birds.

At first Clarisse was again intimidated by confused impressions, and could not get her bearings. And so it was something like a token of things going well when somebody waved to her excitedly from a distance, calling out something to her while she was still separated from him by a number of beds. He was shuffling about in his bed as though making desperate efforts to free himself in order to dash towards her, and his shouts of lamentation and rage made themselves heard even above the general chorus, drawing Clarisse's attention to him ever more. The nearer she came to him, the more she was perturbed by the impression that it was only to her he wanted to talk, whereas she was completely unable to understand what he was trying to say. When the party at length reached this bed, the senior warder said something to the doctor in such a low voice that Clarisse could not catch the words, and Dr. Friedenthal gave some instructions, looking very grave. Then, however, he made a light remark and spoke to the patient. The madman did not immediately answer, but then suddenly asked: " Who's he ? " indicating Clarisse.

As though Siegmund had been meant, Dr. Friedenthal said, with a glance at him, that he was a medical man from Stockholm.

" No, that one ! " the patient insisted, pointing to Clarisse again.

Dr. Friedenthal smiled and said she was a woman doctor from Vienna.

" No, it's a man," the patient further insisted and then fell silent.

Clarisse felt the beating of her heart. So here was another who took her for a man !

Then the patient said slowly: " He's the seventh son of the Emperor."

Stumm von Bordwehr nudged Ulrich.

" That's not true," Dr. Friedenthal answered and kept the game going by turning to Clarisse with the appeal: " Please, you tell him he's mistaken."

"It's not true, my friend," Clarisse said in a low voice, so agitated that she could scarcely speak.

"Oh, you're the seventh son all right," the patient said obstinately.

"No, no," Clarisse assured him, in her excitement smiling at him with lips as petrified as if she were enacting a love-scene and overcome with stage-fright.

"Yes, you are," the patient repeated, looking at her, in a way she could not find words for.

She was quite incapable of thinking of anything to say. She gazed, with a helplessly friendly expression, into the eyes of the madman who took her for a prince, and simply went on smiling. And something remarkable took place within her: it began to seem possible to grant that he was right. Under the pressure of his repeated assertion something dissolved in her, on some plane she lost control of her thoughts, and new patterns formed, their outlines looming out of mist: he was not the first to ask who she was and to take her for a man. But while she was still held in this strange bondage, still gazing into this face, as unable to determine its age as to place any of the other vestiges of normal life that were left in it, something incomprehensible began to happen in the face, indeed in the whole man. It seemed as though her gaze suddenly became too heavy for the eyes on which it rested, and something in the eyes began to slide and fall. The lips also began to tremble, producing a vague jabbering in which clearly articulated obscenities came thicker and faster, like big drops flowing ever closer together. Clarisse was so overwhelmed by this slithering alteration that she felt as if something were slipping away from herself, and involuntarily she made a movement towards the unhappy creature, holding out both arms to him. And before anyone could interfere, the madman leapt to meet her: he flung aside the bed-clothes, knelt up at the end of the bed, and began masturbating like a caged monkey.

"Stop your filthy tricks!" the doctor said swiftly and sternly, and at the same moment the warders seized the man and the bed-clothes and in a flash had reduced both to an immobile flat bundle. Clarisse had turned dark red. She had the sensation one gets in a lift, when the ground drops away from under one's feet. Suddenly it seemed as though all the patients they had already passed were shouting after her and those they had not yet come to were shouting to her. And as luck would have it—or the infectious power of excitement—the harmless-looking old man in the next bed, who had been making friendly little jokes at the visitors while they stood near him, the moment Clarisse hurried past him leapt up and began vituperating, using vile words, and with a horrible foam gathering on his lips. He too was instantly seized by the warders, who were like a ponderous press crushing all resistance.

But the conjurer Friedenthal had still more in store. With the warders covering their retreat just as they had covered their entry, they left the ward at the far end, and suddenly were plunged into a benign silence. They were in a clean, cheerful corridor with lino-leum on the floor, where they soon encountered a number of people, with pretty children, all dressed in their Sunday best and all confidently and politely saying: " Good-morning, doctor." These were visitors waiting to see their relatives. Once again there was the disconcerting encounter with the sane world: for a moment these discreet and well-behaved people in their best clothes seemed like dolls, almost like very well-made artificial flowers.

Dr. Friedenthal walked swiftly through this crowd and now told his visitors that he was taking them to a section containing murderers and other criminal lunatics.

They came to another iron door, and here the warders' ex-pression and cautious behaviour suggested the worst. What they came into then was a cloistered court-yard, which resembled one of those gardens of modern design that contain many stones and few plants. The empty air was like a great cube of silence. It was a moment or two before anyone noticed people sitting dumbly along the walls in the cloisters. Not far from the entrance some idiot boys sat hunched up, dirty-nosed, unsavoury, as motionless as though some sculptor had had the grotesque fancy to carve them on the columns of the doorway. Near them, the first figure by the wall, some distance away from the rest, was a working-class man still in his dark Sunday suit, though without collar and tie, as if he had only just been admitted there; he had an infinitely pathetic look of not belonging anywhere. Clarisse suddenly imagined the grief she would cause Walter if she left him, and it almost made her weep. It was the first time this had ever happened. But she got over it quickly, for the other men she was now conducted past merely had that air of taciturnity and being used to it all which old convicts have. They greeted the doctor timidly and civilly, and produced trivial requests. One of them, however, a young man, became obstreperous in his complaints: heaven alone knew what oblivion he was emerging from. He demanded that the doctor should order his release, with an explanation of why he was there at all. And when Friedenthal avoided the issue by answering that it was not he but the Superintendent who decided these things, the young man became more pressing. His pleas became repetitive, a chain of repetitions that ran faster and faster, and gradually the note of urgency in them became threatening, until finally it turned into a brutish, senseless raging. When he reached that point, the huge warders pushed him down on to the bench again, whereupon he relapsed into his silence, creeping back into it like a beaten dog, without having received any answer. Clarisse was by now familiar with this, and it was simply assimilated into the general excitement she felt.

There was in any case no more time. The warders were banging on another iron door at the far end of the cloisters. This was something new: hitherto they had opened the doors with precautions, but without announcing their arrival. Here they banged their fists four times on the door and listened to the sounds coming from inside.

" This," Dr. Friedenthal expounded, " is the sign for everyone inside to stand by the wall, or sit on the benches that go along the walls."

And indeed, as the door opened slowly, inch by inch, they saw that all the men who had been wandering about, quietly or noisily, were reacting as obediently as well-drilled prisoners. For all this, as they entered the warders took such precautions that Clarisse suddenly clutched Dr. Friedenthal's sleeve and asked him, excitedly, if Moosbrugger was here. Dr. Friedenthal merely shook his head. He had no time to answer, for he was in a hurry to tell the party that they must keep at least two paces distance from the patients. The responsibility for this particular visit did seem to cause him some anxiety. They were seven against thirty, in a remote, walled building inhabited only by insane men, almost each one of whom had committed at least one murder.

People who are accustomed to carrying arms feel more exposed

when without them than others do. It therefore casts no slur on
the General that, having left his sword in the waiting-room, he
asked the doctor:

" By the way, you're armed, of course ? "

" With alertness and experience," Dr. Friedenthal replied,
evidently pleased at being able to show off. " It's all a matter of
nipping any disturbance in the bud."

In fact, the moment anyone made the slightest move to break
ranks, the warders rushed at him and thrust him back into his
place. These were the only acts of violence. Clarisse did not
approve of them. ' The doctors don't seem to take account of it,'
she said to herself, ' that these people are shut up together all day
long and don't do each other any harm. It's only for us, coming
in out of the alien world, that they're dangerous.' And she wanted
to speak to one of them. All at once it seemed to her that she
must surely be able to find the right way of communicating
with them. Close to the door, in a corner, there was a sturdy
man of middle height, with a brown beard and piercing eyes, who
was leaning against the wall with his arms folded, surveying the
visitors sullenly. Clarisse took a step towards him. But Dr.
Friedenthal instantly laid a hand on her arm and stopped her.

" Not that one," he said in a low voice.

He picked out another murderer for Clarisse's benefit and spoke
to him. This was a small, squat man with a pointed head shaved
like a convict's. The doctor apparently knew him for tractable.
The man instantly stood to attention, as he answered smartly,
showing two rows of teeth that somehow looked disturbingly like
two rows of gravestones.

" Try asking him why he's here," Dr. Friedenthal whispered to
Clarisse's brother.

Siegmund asked the man with the pointed head: " Why are you
here ? "

" You know very well why," was the short answer.

" I don't know actually," Siegmund said rather foolishly; he
did not want to give up at once. " Come on, tell me why you're
here."

" You know very well ! " the man answered more emphatically.

" Why are you rude to me ? " Siegmund asked. " I really don't
know."

'What a fake it all is!' Clarisse thought, rejoicing when the man simply answered:

"Because I choose!   I can do what I like!!"   And he repeated: "I can do what I like!" baring his teeth at them.

"Well, there's no need to be uncivil about it," the wretched Siegmund said, not being able to think of anything new to say either.

Clarisse was furious with him for behaving as stupidly as someone teasing a caged animal in the zoo.

"It's no business of yours!   I do what I like, see!   What I like!" the insane man barked like an N.C.O., and he laughed— something in his face laughed, but it was neither the eyes nor the mouth, both of which expressed only a wild anger.

Even Ulrich thought: 'I shouldn't care to be alone with that chap now.' Siegmund clearly found it difficult to stand his ground, since the madman had stepped towards him, and Clarisse was wishing he would seize her brother by the throat and bite him in the face.   Dr. Friedenthal seemed to be complacently letting the scene take its course on the principle that Siegmund was, after all, a medical man too and should be able to cope with the situation; he seemed to be enjoying Siegmund's embarrassment. With his sense of the theatrical, he let it work up to a high pitch and only then, seeing that Siegmund was beyond uttering another word, broke it off.   But Clarisse once again felt the urge to meddle. This urge had been growing stronger as the man's answers came drumming out ever more violently, and now suddenly she could not contain herself.   She walked up to the man and said:

"I'm from Vienna."

It was as meaningless as some random note blown on a bugle. She did not know what she meant or why she had said it; she had not stopped to wonder if the man knew what city he was in, and indeed if he did, that made her remark all the more pointless. But somehow she felt tremendously confident about it.

And in fact miracles do sometimes happen even now, though by preference in lunatic asylums.   For when she had said that and was standing, flaming with excitement, face to face with the murderer, a sort of radiance suddenly came over him.   His tombstones of teeth disappeared behind his lips and the glare in his eyes gave way to benevolence.

" Ah, Vienna, city of dreams ! There's no place like Vienna ! "
he said with the lower-middle-class smugness that always has its
clichés ready.

" I congratulate you ! " Dr. Friedenthal said, laughing.

But for Clarisse this episode was serious and important.

" And now we'll go and see Moosbrugger," Dr. Friedenthal
said.

However, this was not to be.

They had departed, again with all due precautions, from the
high-walled courtyards and were outside, walking up the incline
towards a pavilion some distance away when a warder came
running towards them; he had evidently been in search of them
for some time. Going up to Friedenthal, he whispered to him at
some length. To judge by the doctor's expression, as he listened
and occasionally interrupted to ask questions, it seemed to be
something important and disagreeable. Finally Dr. Friedenthal
turned back to the others with a grave, apologetic air and told them
that he was called away to deal with an incident in one of the wards;
there was no telling how long he would be needed, so he was
afraid he must cut short their tour of inspection. He addressed
his apologies primarily to the distinguished official personage whose
general officer's uniform was concealed by the hospital overall.
Stumm von Bordwehr expressed his gratitude by saying he had
seen enough to be thoroughly impressed by the outstanding
organisation and discipline prevailing in the institution and that one
murderer more or less was really immaterial. Clarisse, however,
looked so disappointed, even distressed, that Dr. Friedenthal
proposed to make up the visit to Moosbrugger, with some other
interesting cases, some other time. ' He would ring up Siegmund,
he said, as soon as there was a chance of making an appointment.

" That's awfully good of you," the General said on behalf of
them all. " For my own part, as a matter of fact, I can't be sure
that the other calls on my time will allow me to be present."

With this reservation it was agreed that another visit would be
arranged. Dr. Friedenthal then set off along a path that soon took
him out of sight on the other sight of the hill, and the visitors were
conducted back to the gate by the warder into whose charge Dr.
Friedenthal had given them. Leaving the path, they took a short
cut across the grass slope, between fine beeches and plane-trees.

The General had removed his overall and was jauntily carrying it over his arm as one might carry a motorist's dust-coat on an outing in the country. But nobody seemed to feel like talking. Ulrich showed no interest in being further primed for the evening's reception. Stumm was in any case already intent on the problems awaiting him in his office, and the utmost he could do was carry out what he felt was the obligation to make some sociable remarks to Clarisse, whom he was gallantly escorting. Clarisse however was absent-minded and rather silent. 'Perhaps', Stumm thought to himself, 'she hasn't got over that embarrassing filthy fellow?' He felt an urge somehow to explain why in the special circumstances it had been impossible for him to offer her any chivalrous protection; on the other hand, it was plainly better to say nothing more about it at all. So the walk back passed in silence and some constraint.

Only when Stumm von Bordwehr had got into his carriage—Ulrich having undertaken to see Clarisse and her brother home—did his spirits revive, and he thereupon got an idea that made these recent oppressive experiences take on an intelligible shape. He had extracted a cigar from the big leather case he always had with him and, leaning back in the cushions, blowing the first little blue clouds into the sunny air, he said comfortably:

" Must be awful being out of your mind like that ! Just fancy, all that time we were in there I didn't see a single one of them smoking. People don't realise how well off they are so long as they're in their right minds."

34   *A great event is on the way. Count Leinsdorf and the river Inn.*

IT was on the evening of this eventful day that the great reception was held at Tuzzis'.

The Collateral Campaign paraded in all its glory and brilliance: eyes beamed, jewels glittered, wit flashed, and there was a blaze of names and titles. From this a poor lunatic might draw the conclusion that at such a reception eyes, jewels, names, and wit all amounted to much the same thing; and he would not be so very mistaken. Everyone who was not idling on the Riviera or by the North Italian lakes had put in an appearance, with the exception of a few people who, regarding ' the season ' as already over, on principle refused to admit the existence of any more ' occasions '.

To make up for their absence, there were a fair number of people who had never been there before. The long delay since the last gathering, which caused these gaps to appear in the list of *habitués*, and the unaccustomed haste with which Diotima had finally sent out invitations, explained the presence of people whom she would otherwise never have asked. Count Leinsdorf had himself given his friend a list of people whom he suggested asking for political reasons, and once the principle of her *salon's* exclusiveness had been sacrificed to higher considerations, she had no longer attached so much importance to the rest. It was in fact Count Leinsdorf who was the sole mover of this festive assembly. Diotima's own view was that humanity could be helped only if dealt with couple by couple. But Count Leinsdorf maintained firmly: " Capital and Culture have not done their duty by the historical development. We must make one last attempt with them."

And Count Leinsdorf constantly returned to this point.

" My dear, have you not made your resolve yet ? " he kept on asking. " It's high time. All sorts of people are coming out with destructive opinions. We must give Culture one last chance to hold the balance with them."

But Diotima, being distracted by the fascination of the multiple forms of human coupling, was deaf to all else.

Finally Count Leinsdorf admonished her: " But really, my dear, I scarcely know you these days ! Now we've given everyone the slogan ' Action !', and I myself have had something to do with —well, yes, to you I can say what I could not say to everyone— it was I who got the Minister of the Interior to resign. It was managed on a very high level, don't you know—a very high level indeed. But of course it had become really quite a scandal, and no one had the courage to put a stop to it. There, that's just for your own ears. And now," he went on, " the Premier has asked that we should bestir ourselves more intensively, in the Enquiry as to the Wishes of the Relevant Sections of the Population, with regard to the reform of home affairs, because of course the new Minister cannot be expected to have it all at his fingertips. And just at this point you are leaving me in the lurch, you who have always been the last to give up? We *must* give Capital and Culture a last chance! That's the way it is, don't you know: either— or somehow else!"

This somewhat obscure conclusion he produced so menacingly that there was no mistaking it: he knew what he wanted. And Diotima obligingly promised to hurry. However, she then forgot about it and did nothing.

And so one day Count Leinsdorf had one of his well-known fits of energy, which drove him straight to her, transported by his forty-horsepower motor.

" Has anything happened yet? " he asked.

Diotima could not but admit that nothing had.

" Do you know the river Inn, my dear? " he asked.

Naturally Diotima did know the Inn, which was the most famous of all Kakania's rivers with the exception of the Danube, and richly interwoven with the country's geography and history. She gazed on her visitor somewhat dubiously, doing her best to smile.

But Count Leinsdorf remained grave. " Leaving aside Innsbruck," he declared, " just think what ludicrous backward little rustic places all those towns in the Inn valley are! And, do you know, it never struck me before, never! " He shook his head. " You see, I happened to be looking at a motoring-map today," he said, finally beginning to explain himself, " and I noticed that the Inn rises in Switzerland. Well, as a matter of fact I knew that before, we all know that, but we never give it a thought, do we? Maloja's where it rises, and a ludicrous little stream it is, no wider than the Kamp or the Morava in our own territory. But what have the Swiss made of it? The Engadine! The world-famous Engadine! The *Engad-Inn*, my dear! Did it ever occur to you that the whole Engadine comes from the name ' Inn '? That's what I hit on today. Whereas we, of course, with our insufferable Austrian modesty, never make anything out of what belongs to us."

After this conversation Diotima hastened to propose a date for the reception Count Leinsdorf wanted, partly because she saw that she must fall in with His Highness's wishes, partly because she was afraid of driving her exalted friend to desperation if she continued to refuse.

But when she promised it to him, Leinsdorf said: "And I do beg you, dearest lady, this time don't fail to invite—er—yes, the widowed lady, don't you know, whom you've nicknamed Drangsal. Her close friend, the good Wayden lady, has been after me about it for weeks—simply won't leave me in peace."

This too Diotima promised, although at any other period she would have regarded toleration of her rival hostess as a dereliction of duty towards her country.

35

A great event is on the way.   Meseritscher of the press.

WHEN the reception-rooms were overbrimming with the brilliance of festive lights and of the assembled company, not only was His Highness notably ' among those present ', as the gossip-columnists say, but besides other exalted aristocratic personages, who he had taken care should appear, there was also His Excellency the Minister for War and, in his entourage, the now intensely intellectual, culturally preoccupied, and somewhat fatigued person of General Stumm von Bordwehr. 'Another distinguished guest' was Paul Arnheim (most effectively reported with untitled simplicity, public relations having thoughtfully decided in favour of litotes, namely that ingenious form of understatement which consists in, so to speak, removing some trifle from one's own person, as a king may draw off a ring, and placing it upon the person of another). 'Also present' was everyone worth mentioning from the various Ministries (the Minister of Education and Public Worship had apologised to His Highness, whom he had seen at the Upper House, for not putting in a personal appearance, since he had had to go to Linz that day for the consecration of a large roodscreen). Numerous embassies and legations were represented by 'leading diplomats'. There were 'distinguished figures from the industrial world, as from the worlds of the arts and sciences '—a sturdy old cliché that took command of Gossip's pen when it came to listing, in the inevitable order, these three branches of activity in bourgeois society. Then the adept pen conjured up its paragraph on the ladies' dresses: *beige*, blush-pink, *cérise*, cream . . . embroidered . . . draped . . . caught in at . . . falling from the waist in . . . And, named between the Countess Adlitz and Frau Generaldirektor Weghuber, there was 'that well-known figure' Frau Melanie Drangsal, widow of the internationally celebrated surgeon 'and herself a hostess whose drawing-room is a favourite haunt of leading lights in the cultural life of our day '. Right at the end of this part of the report there was mention too of Ulrich von So-and-So, 'escorting his sister '. Gossip had considered writing ' whose name is, of course, associated with that selfless activity in the service of the Campaign's spiritually lofty and patriotically admirable aims which . . .' or even ' a coming man ': for word had long ago gone round that many people were expecting this *protégé* of Count Leinsdorf's to involve his patron in some second imprudent measure, and it was extremely tempting to get it on record early that one had one's finger on the pulse of events. However, those who are in the know always find their greatest satisfaction in silence, and all the more so if they are wary in their ways. It was to this, then, that Ulrich and Agathe owed the uncommented mention they received at the bottom of the list, immediately before all those representatives of society and culture who were tipped into the mass grave of ' many other eminent and distinguished persons '. Of these, indeed, there were a great many, among them the well-known jurist, Hofrat Professor Schwung, who was in town while sitting on a government commission, and this time, too, the young poet Friedel Feuermaul: for although it was known that he had been among the moving spirits behind this evening's gathering, that was by no means the same thing as having the solid importance attached to glittering titles and the triumphs of *haute couture*. Such people as Acting Bank-Director Leo Fischel, with his wife and daughter—who had got themselves invited as a result of immense efforts on Gerda's part, without calling in Ulrich's aid, which meant that it was only thanks to the carelessness temporarily prevailing—simply disappeared into an obscure corner. Only the wife of a well-known jurist—well-known, but for purposes of such an occasion still below the level of the hostess's notice—a lady who rejoiced, though Gossip was unaware of it, in the secret name of Bonadea, was subsequently exhumed from the anonymous mass and set among those reported as 'wearing' or 'in' whatever it was; for her sensational looks aroused general admiration.

Gossip, the ubiquitously vigilant curiosity of the Public, was a man. As a rule, of course, a large number of individuals go to make up the personification. But in Kakania at this period there was one who overtopped all the rest, and this was Regierungsrat Meseritscher. This newspaper correspondent and editor of *The Parliamentary and Social Gazette*, founded by himself, had been born in Meseritsch in Wallachia—which helped to explain his name—and had come to the capital in the 'sixties of the previous century as a young man who had abandoned the prospect of taking over the parental tavern in his native township in favour of journalism, to which he was attracted by the brilliant rays of liberalism, then at its zenith. Before long he had made his contribution to that era by founding a news agency, which began by supplying newspapers with small items of local news deriving from police sources. Thanks to the industry, reliability, and thoroughness of its owner this agency, in its original form, not only earned the gratitude of the newspapers and the police, but was before long noticed by other authorities, which found this a convenient means of publishing news that they wished to disseminate without themselves being associated with it; the agency was soon in a privileged position, with a monopoly of sources not merely of semi-official but also of official information. Being a man of enterprise and an untiring worker, when he saw how successful this line was becoming Meseritscher extended his activities to include Court and social news; indeed he would probably never have left Meseritsch for the capital if he had not always had a vision of this, however vaguely. Unerring lists of 'those present' were his speciality. His memory for faces, names, and whatever was said about people was extraordinary, and this assured him of a strong position in relation to drawing-rooms as to law-courts. He knew 'the great world' better than it knew itself, and his unflagging attentiveness enabled him to make people who had met in public the night before really acquainted with each other only the next morning in his columns—like an aged cavalier in whom everyone has been confiding for decades about everything from prospective betrothals to what they have ordered from their dressmakers. And so on every sort of public and private occasion this zealous, nimble, over-obliging, affable little man was to be seen, himself an institution, and in the later years of his life it was only his presence and subsequent commentary that conferred indisputable prestige on a social gathering.

Meseritscher's career had reached its peak when the rank of Regierungsrat was bestowed on him. Now, there was a peculiarity associated with this title of ' Government Councillor '. Kakania was of course the most peace-loving country in the world, but at some stage it had had the inspiration, in the profound innocence of its conviction that there was certainly no longer any such thing as war, of arranging officialdom in a hierarchy corresponding to that of military rank; it had even bestowed appropriate uniforms and badges on these officials. The rank of Government Councillor was equivalent to that of lieutenant-colonel in His Imperial and Royal Majesty's army; but even though this was in itself no very high rank, it had the interesting peculiarity, in so far as it came to be bestowed on Meseritscher, that it should not have been bestowed on him at all. For according to an immutable tradition, which, like everything immutable in Kakania, was modified only in exceptional cases, Meseritscher actually should have been made an Imperial Councillor. Anyone would naturally suppose that an Imperial Councillor was something loftier than a Government Councillor; but that was not so. An Imperial Councillor was the equivalent only of a captain. Now Meseritscher should have become an Imperial Councillor because this was an honour bestowed, apart from civil servants, on those engaged in certain ' arts and crafts ', namely such as Court hairdressers and coach-builders, which therefore meant that it was also extended to writers and artists; whereas Government Councillor was at that time an honour bestowed exclusively on civil servants of a certain rank. The fact that Meseritscher was the first and only one to receive it thus signified more than the mere loftiness of the distinction itself, more indeed even than the daily challenge implicit in it to not take over-seriously whatever happened in this country of one's birth. The unjustifiable handle to his name did in a subtle and discreet way confirm the indefatigable chronicler's close association with Court, State, and Society.

Meseritscher had been a model for many journalists in his time, and he was on the committees of many representative literary bodies. It was also rumoured that he had had a uniform with a gold collar made for himself, which however he only wore sometimes at home. But this was probably not true, for in the innermost recesses of his being Meseritscher had always preserved certain memories of the family tavern in Meseritsch, and a good taverner does not himself drink. A good taverner knows the secrets of all his ' regulars ', but he does not make use of everything he knows. He never joins in discussions to put forward his own view, but he does take pleasure in noting and recounting everything in the way of fact, anecdote, or funny story. And so Meseritscher, who was to be met with on every festive occasion as the acknowledged reporter of the presence of beautiful women and distinguished men, himself had never even thought of going to a good tailor; he knew all the backstairs intricacies of politics and himself never dabbled in politics even to the extent of a single line of print; he was informed about all the inventions and discoveries of his time and understood no single one of them. For him it was enough to know that all this existed, that it was all ' also present '. He honestly loved his time, and in return his time accorded him a certain degree of affection because he daily reported that it was there.

When, on his entry, Diotima caught sight of him, she instantly beckoned him to her side.

" Dear Meseritscher," she said, as sweetly as she knew how, " I'm sure you didn't take His Highness's speech in the Upper House as representing our position—and of course you won't have taken it *literally* ! "

The fact was that His Highness, having brought about the Minister's downfall and being exasperated by his many worries, had made a widely noticed speech in the Upper House, charging his victim with having shown a total lack of the true constructive spirit of collaboration and severity, and not only this: he had also let his enthusiasm carry him to the lengths of making general observations that in some inexplicable way culminated in a survey of the importance of the press, in which he charged this ' institution now risen to the position of a great power ' with pretty well everything that an independent, non-party, Christian gentleman could charge an institution with that was in his view just about the dead opposite of what he was himself.   This was what Diotima diplomatically wished to smooth over, and as she went on speaking of Count Leinsdorf's true attitude in language that became steadily more beautiful and more unintelligible, Meseritscher listened pensively.

Then suddenly he laid a hand on her arm and generously cut her short.

" Lady, don't you worry about that," he said comprehensively. " His Highness is a good friend to us, isn't he ?   Well then.   He was drawing the long bow all right.   But a gentleman like him, why shouldn't he ? "

And in order to prove that he had not taken anything in bad part, he added:

" I'm just going over to wish him a good evening."

That was Meseritscher all over !

Yet before he moved off, he turned back to Diotima once more and asked confidentially:

" And what's the odds on Feuermaul, dear ? "

Smiling, Diotima shrugged her beautiful shoulders.   " Really nothing so very overwhelming, my dear Councillor.   But we don't care to have it said that we rebuffed anyone who came to us with good will."

' Good will—that's rich, at that,' Meseritscher thought to himself on his way to Count Leinsdorf.   But before he got so far, before he had even reached the end of his thoughts, which he would gladly have known the end of himself, he was cordially stopped by his host.

" My dear Meseritscher," Permanent Secretary Tuzzi said, smiling, " official sources of information having once again dried up, I apply to the semi-official fount of news.   Can *you* tell me anything about this Feuermaul we have among us tonight ? "

" And what should I be able to tell, Mr. Permanent Secretary ? " Meseritscher said mournfully.

" They say he's supposed to be a genius."

" That's rich! " Meseritscher answered. If one wishes to be able to report, with speed and accuracy, whatever there is in the way of news, what is new must not be too different from what is old, from what one knows already. Nor is genius any exception to this rule—that is to say, real acknowledged genius, whose significance can be quickly assessed by its own time. How different, of course, with the sort of genius that is not instantly acknowledged as such! About this there is something utterly of the non-genius, and the trouble is that even this is not its own monopoly, so it is easy to go wrong about it in every respect. Thus there was for Regierungsrat Meseritscher a solid stock of geniuses, which he tended with love and care; but he was not keen on adding to current stock. The older and more experienced he grew, the more, indeed, he had developed the habit of regarding rising artistic genius—and this applied especially to genius in the, to him, neighbouring field of literature—merely as a frivolous attempt to disturb him in his serious work of reporting, and he hated it in the goodness of his heart until it reached the stage where it was fit to be included in his accounts of ' who ' was ' there '. But Feuermaul was still a long way from that point; he was only on the way to being put there, and Regierungsrat Meseritscher was not at all sure that he approved of this.

" They say he's supposed to be a great poet," Permanent Secretary Tuzzi said, a little vaguely and hesitantly.

Meseritscher retorted firmly: " And who says so? The critics on the book-page! And I ask you, Permanent Secretary, what does that amount to? It's the experts say it," he went on. " And what are the experts, anyway? There are some say the opposite. And there've been cases of experts saying one thing one day and something different the next. Who cares for them? Real fame is having arrived among the ordinary public, *that's* when fame is reliable. You want to know what I think? All anyone ought to know about a great man is when he arrives in town and when he leaves again."

In a melancholy way he had talked himself into a state of fervour, and his gaze was fixed on Tuzzi.

But Tuzzi maintained a resigned silence. " What's going on here this evening, Mr. Permanent Secretary? " Meseritscher asked.

Smiling absent-mindedly, Tuzzi shrugged his shoulders. "Nothing. Not really. A little spurt of ambition. Have you ever read a book of this Feuermaul fellow's?"

"I know what he writes about: peace, friendship, goodness, and what-have-you."

"So you don't think much of him?" Tuzzi queried.

"Lord love you!" Meseritscher began, wriggling. "Am I an expert?"

Before he could go on, Frau Drangsal came bearing down upon the two of them, and Tuzzi had to take a courteous step in her direction. Meseritscher saw his chance to make a resolute dash into a breach he had just glimpsed in the circle round Count Leinsdorf and, without letting anyone else stop him, he manoeuvred into position next to His Highness.

Count Leinsdorf, who was standing talking to the Minister and several other gentlemen, retired slightly as soon as Regierungsrat Meseritscher had expressed his deep respects to them all, and drew Meseritscher to one side.

"Meseritscher," His Highness said earnestly, "promise me that there will be no misunderstandings. The gentlemen of the press never seem to know what to write. The position is this: since last time there has been no change whatever in the position. Perhaps there will be some change. That we don't know. For the time being we must not be disturbed. So I beg you, even if any of your colleagues ask you—this whole evening here is purely and simply a private party given by Frau Tuzzi."

Meseritscher's eyelids slowly conveyed that he had understood the top-level instructions just received and felt the weight of responsibility. And since one confidence deserves another, he moistened his lips—which then gleamed as only his eyes should have done—and asked:

"And how about Feuermaul, Your Highness, if it's a fair question?"

"Why on earth shouldn't it be?" Count Leinsdorf asked in astonishment. "There's absolutely nothing to be said about Feuermaul! The young man was invited because Baroness Wayden wouldn't take no for an answer. What else should there be? Do you happen to know anything?"

Up to this point Regierungsrat Meseritscher had attached no

importance to the matter of Feuermaul, assuming it to be merely one of the social rivalries he ran into every day. But now that even Count Leinsdorf denied, and so emphatically denied, that there was anything in it, he necessarily had to revise his view of it. He was now convinced that something important was in the wind. 'What are they up to now?' he brooded as he strolled farther through the throng. He passed in review the most audacious possibilities in home and foreign policy. But after a while he decided abruptly: 'Ten to one it's a dud', and refused to let himself be diverted any longer from his reporting activities.

For however much it seemed to be in conflict with the meaning of his life, Meseritscher did not believe in great events. What was more, he did not hold with them. If one is convinced that one lives in a very important, very splendid, very great time, one cannot endure the notion that anything additionally important, splendid, and great can happen in it. Meseritscher was no Alpinist, but if he had been, he would have said that this attitude of his was as correct as putting up look-out towers in the middling high mountains and never on the great peaks. Lacking such a comparison, he made do with a sense of perturbation and the resolve to settle the matter by on no account mentioning Feuermaul's name in his account of this evening's party.

36 *A great event is on the way. Bringing a meeting with some old acquaintances.*

ULRICH, who had been standing near his cousin while she was speaking to Meseritscher, asked her as soon as they were alone for an instant:

" How did your meeting with the Widow go off? I'm afraid I came in too late for it."

Diotima raised her thick eyelashes to give him a world-weary glance, then let them sink again.

" Charming, naturally," she said. " She'd been to see me. We shall arrange something or other this evening. Not that it matters in the least."

" You see ! " Ulrich said. It was the tone in which they had been used to talk and sounded as if it were meant to draw a final line under that relationship.

Diotima turned her head and looked at her cousin questioningly.

" I mean I told you so," Ulrich said. " It's all practically over, without having ever existed."

He felt a need to talk. When he had got home in the afternoon, Agathe, who had meanwhile returned, had been on the point of going out again, and before coming here they had only exchanged a few very brief remarks (Agathe had called the gardener's wife in to help her to dress).

" I warned you," he said.

" Of what ? " Diotima drawled.

" Oh, I don't know. Everything ! "

It was true: he no longer knew himself what he had warned her against. Against her ideas, her ambition, the Collateral Campaign, love, the mind, the Universal Year, intrigues, her *salon*, her passions. . . . Against sensibility and the heedlessness of taking things just as they came. Against immoderation and against correctitude. Against adultery and against marriage. There was nothing he had not warned her against. ' Well, that's what she's like ! ' he thought to himself. To him everything she did was absurd, and yet she was so beautiful that it was sad.

" I warned you," Ulrich repeated. " And one gathers that all you're interested in now is the theory of sex life."

Diotima let this pass. " Do you think the Widow's *protégé* is gifted ? " she asked.

" Certainly," Ulrich answered. " Gifted, young, immature. His success and this woman between them will be the ruin of him. In this country of ours the very babes in arms are ruined by being told what marvellous instincts they have and that any intellectual development would only be to their disadvantage. He comes out with good things from time to time, but he can't let ten minutes pass without uttering some nonsense." He came closer to Diotima's ear. " Do you really know anything about the woman ? "

Diotima shook her head almost imperceptibly.

" She's dangerously ambitious," Ulrich said. " But she ought
to be of interest to you in your new studies—where lovely women
once wore a fig-leaf what she wears is a laurel-leaf! The sort
of woman I can't stand ! "

Diotima did not laugh. She did not even smile, but merely
inclined her ear to her cousin.

" And what do you think of him as a man ? " he asked.

" Pathetic," Diotima murmured. " A little lambkin running to
fat before its time."

" Why not ? Masculine beauty is only a secondary sexual
characteristic," Ulrich said. " What's primarily exciting about a
man is his expectation of success. In ten years Feuermaul'll be an
international celebrity. The lady's connections will take care of
that. After which she'll marry him. If he remains a celebrity,
it'll be a happy marriage."

Recollecting herself, Diotima gravely put him right: " Happiness
in marriage depends on factors that one can learn to judge only by
disciplining oneself."

She then left him behind, as a proud ship leaves the quay at
which it has been moored. Her duties as hostess bore her away,
with a scarcely perceptible nod to him; she gave him no glance as
she cast off. But she did not mean it in an unfriendly way; on the
contrary, Ulrich's voice had affected her like music remembered
from her youth. She even wondered what conclusions one might
arrive at from a sexual-scientific consideration of him. Oddly
enough, in all her detailed research into these problems she had
never yet considered his case.

Looking around, Ulrich found a gap in the festive hugger-
mugger, a sort of optical channel—which was perhaps what
Diotima's gaze had gone down when she moved away from him—
at the end of which, in the room beyond the next, he saw Paul
Arnheim in conversation with Feuermaul, with Frau Drangsal
benignly listening. So she had brought the two men together.
Arnheim's one hand, holding a cigar, was raised as though in an
unconscious gesture of self-defence, but he was smiling very
charmingly. Feuermaul was talking vivaciously, holding his own
cigar with two fingers and sucking at it, between sentences, with
the greed of a calf pulling at the maternal udder. Ulrich could
imagine the sort of thing they were saying, but he did not feel

like dwelling on it.   He remained standing where he was in happy
isolation, looking round in search of his sister.   He discovered
her in a group of men more or less strangers to him, and for all
his abstraction a little chilly shudder ran through him.   But at the
same moment he was mildly poked in the ribs by Stumm von
Bordwehr, while on the other side Hofrat Professor Schwung
approached—only to be stopped a few paces away by one of his
Viennese colleagues.

"Found you at last!" the General murmured with relief.
"The Minister wants to know what an ethos is."

"What on earth for?"

"I don't know what for.   But come on, what is it?"

"An eternal verity," Ulrich offered in definition, "that is
neither eternal nor true, but valid only for a time so that the
time has a standard to diverge from.   It's a philosophical and
sociological term, not much used."

"Aha, that'll be it," the General said.   "Fact is, Arnheim's
been saying the view that man is good is only an ethos.   And
Feuermaul said he didn't know what an ethos was, but man was
good—that was an eternal verity, he said.   So then Leinsdorf
said: 'That's right enough.   There aren't really any wicked
people, for nobody can really want what's bad.   There are only
people led astray.   People are neurotic these days simply because
in times like these there are so many sceptics who don't believe
in anything solid.'   I couldn't help thinking: pity he wasn't with
us this afternoon!   But anyway, he himself is of the opinion that
people must be forced to see what's good for them.   And so the
Minister wants to know what 'ethos' means.   I must just pop
over and tell him.   I'll come straight back.   You just stay here
so that I can find you again.   Fact is, there's something else I've
got to talk to you about, urgently.   Then I'll take you to the
Minister."

Before Ulrich could demand enlightenment, he found Tuzzi's
hand slipped round his arm.

"It's a long time since we've seen you," Tuzzi said, and went
on: "Do you remember, I said we'd have to deal with a pacifist
invasion sooner or later?"   He looked cordially at the General as
he said it.

But the General was in a hurry and merely answered that

though as an officer he had another ethos, any sincerely held conviction . . . The rest of it vanished with him. Actually he was always irritated by Tuzzi, and irritation is not conducive to clear thought.

The Permanent Secretary blinked gaily at the General's retreating form, then turned back to his ' cousin '.

" The oil-fields, of course, are only a blind," he said.

Ulrich looked at him in astonishment.

" You don't meant to say you don't know about the oil-fields ? " Tuzzi asked.

" Oh yes," Ulrich answered. " I was just startled by your speaking of it." And to cover up his gaffe he added: " You're so very good at keeping things dark."

" I've known about it for a long time," Tuzzi said complacently. " It was Arnheim, naturally, who got Leinsdorf to get this young man Feuermaul here this evening. Do you happen to have read any of his books ? "

Ulrich admitted that he had.

" An arch-pacifist ! " Tuzzi said. " And the Widow Drangsal, as my wife calls her, is so ambitious about mothering him that if need be she'll wade through rivers of blood for the sake of pacifism, though it's not her own line at all—artists are her line." Tuzzi reflected for a moment and then declared: " Pacifism's the main thing, naturally. The oil-fields are only a piece of diversionary tactics. That's why Feuermaul's being pushed into the forefront with his pacifism, because that'll make everyone think: ' Aha, this is diversionary tactics ! ' and be convinced that behind it it's the oil-fields that matter. Very neatly contrived, but much too clever not to be noticed. You see, if Arnheim has the Galician oil-fields and a contract to supply the War Ministry, of course we have to defend the frontier. It means we also have to provide oil-bases on the Adriatic for the Navy, which means upsetting the Italians. But if we start provoking our neighbours in this way, everyone becomes all the more conscious of the need for peace, there's more and more peace-propaganda, and finally, if the Czar comes out with some idea or other about Perpetual Peace, he'll find the ground psychologically prepared for it. That's what Arnheim's after ! "

" And you've something against it ? "

" That's not what we have anything against," Tuzzi said.
" But you may recall my once explaining there's nothing so
dangerous as peace at any price. We must defend ourselves
against the amateurs."

" But Arnheim's an armaments manufacturer!" Ulrich objected,
smiling.

" Of course he is!" Tuzzi murmured with some exasperation.
" For heaven's sake, you mustn't be so naïve about these things!
He'll have his contract in his pocket. And at the worst our
neighbours will go on arming too. Mark my words: at the decisive
moment he'll come out hot and strong as a pacifist. Pacifism's a
safe, permanent line for the armaments business. War's a risk."

" My own impression is the military party don't really mean any
harm," Ulrich said. " They only want to use the business with
Arnheim in order to make it easier to bring their artillery up to
date, that's all. And after all, everyone in the world today is
arming only for the sake of peace. So they probably think it's
quite in order to do it for once with the aid of the pacifists."

" And how," Tuzzi asked, ignoring this flippancy, " do these
gentry imagine this is to be done? "

" I don't think they've reached that point yet. For the present
they seem to be just taking soundings."

" Of course!" Tuzzi agreed crossly, as though he had expected
nothing else. " The military ought to confine themselves to
thinking about war and leave other matters to those qualified to
deal with them. But rather than do that, they dabble in what
doesn't concern them and get everybody into danger! I repeat:
there's nothing so dangerous in diplomacy as amateurish talk about
peace. Every time the craving for peace has risen to a given pitch
and there was no more holding it, it's led straight into war. I
can give you chapter and verse for that."

By now Hofrat Professor Schwung had detached himself from
his colleague. He greeted Ulrich with the utmost cordiality, in
order to get introduced to his host. Ulrich obliged, with the
remark that this distinguished jurist was as opposed to pacifism
in the sphere of the penal code as the Permanent Secretary to the
Ministry for Foreign Affairs was in the sphere of politics.

" But good gracious," Tuzzi protested, laughing, " you've
misunderstood me entirely! "

After pausing a moment in doubt as to the next move, Schwung associated himself with this protest, saying that he would not like his view of diminished responsibility to be regarded as blood-thirsty and inhuman.

" On the contrary ! " he exclaimed, spreading his voice, since he could not very well spread out his arms in one of the usual theatrical tricks that some lecturers go in for.   " It is precisely the pacification of the human animal that makes us adopt a certain severity. I don't know whether I can assume that Permanent Secretary Tuzzi has heard of the endeavours in this respect that I am at present engaged in ? "   And he turned to his host.

Not having heard anything about this controversy as to whether an insane criminal's diminished responsibility must be attributed solely to his ideas or solely to his will, Tuzzi hastened to agree all the more politely with everything Schwung said.

And Schwung, being well content with the effect he had pro-duced, then began to sing the praises of the serious view of life he found represented by this evening's gathering. He mentioned that, listening to conversations here and there, he had again and again heard the expressions ' masculine severity ' and ' moral soundness '.   " Our culture," he said, contributing his own mite, " is all too sadly corrupted by inferior types, moral imbeciles." And he asked: " But what is actually the aim of this evening's gathering ?   I have been struck by how often, as I strolled about, I have heard positively Rousseau-ian opinions as to the inborn goodness of man."

Tuzzi, to whom this was principally directed, maintained smiling silence. Since the General had now got back to Ulrich's side, Ulrich, who wished to escape from his clutches, introduced him to Schwung on the pretext that he was better qualified than anyone else present to answer the question. Stumm vehemently disclaimed this, but neither Schwung nor Tuzzi would give quarter. Ulrich was already beating a jubilant retreat when he was caught by an old friend, who said:

" My wife and daughter are here too."

It was the Bank-Director Leo Fischel.

" Hans Sepp has passed his State examination," he recounted. " What do you say to that ? All he has to do now is to get a university degree ! We're all in that corner over there "—he

pointed towards the farthest room. "We don't really know any-
body here. Not that we've seen anything of you for a long time,
if it comes to that. Your father, wasn't it—ah yes, yes. Hans
Sepp got us the invitation for this evening, my wife was dead set
on it. So you see the lad isn't quite without parts. They're
sort of semi-officially engaged now, Gerda and he. You didn't
know that, I suppose? But you know, Gerda—I don't really
know whether the girl loves him or if it's only an idea she's got
into her head. Why won't you come over and join us for a
bit?"

"I'll be along a little later," Ulrich promised.

"Yes, do that," Fischel urged, and fell silent. Then he
whispered: "That's our host, isn't it? Won't you introduce me. . . .
We haven't met either of them."

But when Ulrich showed signs of remedying this, Fischel
stopped him.

"And the great philosopher?" he asked. "What's he up to?
My wife and Gerda are crazy about him, of course. But what
about the oil-fields? What they're saying now is that it was a
canard, but I don't believe it. Denials are just the order of the
day. You know, it's just like when my wife's annoyed with a
servant-girl—suddenly it comes out she tells lies, she's immoral,
she's impertinent—all purely spiritual defects, as you might say.
But if I have a quiet word with the girl and promise to raise her
wages, that's the last you hear about the spirit. No more spiritual
trouble at all, everything's as right as rain, and my wife doesn't
know why. You follow me? You agree that's how it goes?
There's too much solid commercial probability in those oil-fields
for anyone to believe a *démenti*."

And because Ulrich showed no sign of talking, and Fischel
wanted to return to his wife in the glory of one who had inside
information, he started off again.

"It must be admitted it's all very nice here. But my wife is
wondering what all this queer talk is about. And what's this
Feuermaul chap?" he added. "Gerda says he's a great poet.
Hans Sepp says he's only a careerist who's taken everyone in."

Ulrich suggested that the truth probably lay midway between.

"Now that's very well put," Fischel said gratefully. "Truth
always does lie in the middle, doesn't it? That's what everyone

forgets nowadays, everyone's so extreme. What I always say to
Hans Sepp is: everyone's entitled to his opinions, but the only
solid opinions are those that enable one to earn a living, because
that shows that other people can appreciate them too."

There had been some impalpable but important change in Leo
Fischel. But Ulrich unfortunately neglected to investigate this.
He merely passed on Gerda's father to the group talking with
Permanent Secretary Tuzzi.

In that group Stumm von Bordwehr had meanwhile grown
eloquent. Not being able to pin Ulrich down but being charged
with a tremendous urge to get some ideas off his mind, he worked
it off on the first listeners he found.

" How does one explain this gathering tonight ? " he exclaimed,
repeating Hofrat Schwung's question. " I should like to put it
this way, as it were on sober reflection: by not explaining it at all !
I'm not joking, gentlemen," he went on, not without modest pride.
" This afternoon I happened to ask a young lady who had asked
me to show her round the University Psychiatric Hospital, I just
happened to ask her what she was actually interested in there, so
as to be able to explain it to her the right way. She gave me a
very interesting answer, outstandingly thought-provoking. What
she said was: ' If one is to explain everything, man will never
change anything in the world '."

Schwung shook his head in disapproval of this assertion.

" Well, I don't know exactly what she meant," Stumm disclaimed, " and I'm not identifying myself with it, but you can't
help feeling there's a core of truth in it. You know, I have to
thank for instance my friend who has so often given His Highness,
which means the Campaign too, the benefit of his ideas "—and he
bobbed his head in acknowledgment towards Ulrich—" for much
instruction. But what is taking on form here this evening is a
certain distaste for instruction. Which brings me back to what I
began by saying."

" But still, you do want," Tuzzi began and then altered it to:
" It's said that the War Ministry is trying to jump everyone here
into a patriotic resolution, collecting public money, or something
of that sort, for re-arming the Artillery. Naturally for purposes
merely of demonstration, so bringing Parliament under the pressure of public opinion."

" That, certainly, is the way I should understand a good deal
I have heard this evening," Hofrat Schwung concurred.

" It's much more complicated than that, Permanent Secretary ! "
the General said.

" And Herr Dr. Arnheim ? " Tuzzi asked bluntly. " Not to beat
around the bush, are you sure that all Arnheim wants is the Galician oil-fields, which hang together with the artillery problem ? "

" I can only speak for myself and of what I have to do with it,
Permanent Secretary," Stumm protested, and said again: " And
it's all much more complicated than that ! "

" Of course it's more complicated," Tuzzi agreed with a smile.

" Naturally we need the guns," the General said, warming to the
subject, " and it may turn out to be advantageous in that respect to
collaborate with Arnheim on the lines you indicate. But I repeat,
I can speak only from my own point of view as a public-relations
officer concerned with cultural questions, and so I put it to you:
What is the use of cannon without the spirit ? "

" And why then was such importance attached to involving
Herr Feuermaul ? " Tuzzi asked mockingly. " That, after all, is
defeatism pure and simple."

" Allow me to disagree," the General said firmly. " On the
contrary, it's the spirit of the times ! The spirit of the times has
two currents today. His Highness—he's over there with the
Minister, I've just been speaking to them both—His Highness, for
instance, says the slogan ' Action! ' must go forth, the trend of the
times demands it. And it's a fact that nowadays people take
much less delight in the great idea of humanity than they did, say,
a hundred years ago. On the other hand, of course, there is something in the humanitarian attitude, only His Highness says: if
anyone does not want what would make him happy, in certain
circumstances one must force it on him. So His Highness is for
the one current, but that doesn't mean that he dissociates himself
from the other."

" I don't quite follow that," Professor Schwung demurred.

" Not that it's easy to follow," Stumm readily admitted.
" Well, supposing we start from the point that I see two currents
in the spirit of the time. The one current says that man is good
by nature, so long as he's left to himself, as one might say——"

" Good ? " Schwung interrupted. " Surely nobody thinks in

such naïve terms nowadays ? We are no longer living in the world of eighteenth-century idealism ! "

" Well, I don't know about that," the General said, rather nettled. " You only have to think of the pacifists, the vegetarians, the anti-capital-punishment people, the nature-cure reformers, the anti-intellectuals, the conscientious objectors—I can't call them all to mind off-hand—and all the people who as it were put their trust in humanity, they all form one big current. But if you prefer," he went on, in that obliging way of his which was so attractive, " we can just as easily start from the opposite point of view. So let's start from the fact that man must be subdued because left to his own resources, on his own, he never does the right thing. I dare say we'll find it easier to agree about that. The masses need a strong hand, they need leaders to be tough with them instead of merely talking, in short what they need to be ruled by is the spirit of action. The fact is, human society con-sists, as you might say, of only a small number of volunteers, who have the necessary training, and of millions, lacking all higher ambition, who serve only because they must. Isn't that roughly the situation ? And because this has gradually come to be recognised here too in our Campaign, as a result of experience, the first current (you follow me, what I've just been talking about was the *second* current in the spirit of the times), well, the first current is, as you might say, alarmed by the possibility that the great idea of love and faith in man might get entirely lost. And so then there were forces at work that—there you have it—sent forth Feuermaul into our midst, to save, at the eleventh hour, whatever can still be saved. So it's all much easier to understand than it looks at first glance, isn't it ? " Stumm remarked.

" And what's going to be done ? " Tuzzi asked.

" I suppose," Stumm answered, " nothing. By now we've had a lot of currents in the Campaign."

" But there's an intolerable contradiction between these two ! " Professor Schwung expostulated. To him, as a jurist, such ambiguity was intolerable.

" Not if you really go into it," Stumm disagreed. " You see, the other current also sets out to love humanity. Only its view is that to be loved humanity must first of all be forcibly changed. It's what you might call a purely technical distinction."

Now Director Fischel spoke up. "Having missed the beginning, I'm afraid I don't have a complete picture. But if I may say so, it seems to me that in principle respect for humanity is on a higher level than its opposite. This evening I've heard some incredible views—undoubtedly exceptional, but still—incredible views about people of other convictions and particularly of other nations!" With his mutton-chop whiskers and his *pince-nez*, always slightly askew, he looked like an English *milord* sworn to belief in the great ideals of Magna Carta and Free Trade. He refrained from mentioning that the horrifying views had been voiced by Hans Sepp, his future son-in-law, who was thoroughly at home in 'the second current of the spirit of the time'.

"Bloody-minded views?" the General asked, always eager for information.

"Extraordinarily bloody-minded," Fischel confirmed.

"Perhaps," Stumm suggested, "they were talking about 'stiffening up'. It's easy to confuse the two."

"No, no!" Fischel exclaimed. "Utterly nihilistic, positively revolutionary views! I don't know, General, whether you're in touch with our misguided younger generation. I couldn't help being surprised to find such people admitted to this evening's gathering."

"Revolutionary views?" Stumm asked, taking this in rather bad part. He smiled in as chilly a manner as his plump face allowed him to. "I'm afraid I must confess, Herr Director, that I'm by no means an out-and-out opponent of revolutionary views. Oh of course only so long as it doesn't actually come to any sort of revolution. But there's often an uncommonly large amount of idealism in that sort of thing. And as for 'admitting to this gathering', the Campaign, which aims to cover the whole of the country, has no right, you know, to reject constructive forces in whatever mode they may express themselves."

Leo Fischel was silent. Professor Schwung attached little value to the opinions of a dignitary who did not belong to the civil hierarchy. And Tuzzi had been dreaming: 'First current . . . second current. . . .'

It reminded him of two similar expressions, 'first reservoir . . . second reservoir . . .', but without his consciously remembering the actual words or the talk with Ulrich in which they had occurred. But an incomprehensible jealousy of his wife stirred in him, associated, through intangible links that he could not get hold of, with this innocuous General. When the pause that now arose recalled him to reality, he resolved to show Stumm that he was not the man to be diverted from the main point by devious talk.

" Summing it up, General," he began, " the military party———"

" But my dear Permanent Secretary, there *is* no military party ! " Stumm instantly interrupted. " People are always talking about ' the military party ', whereas by their very nature the military are above party ! "

" Well then, the military authorities," Tuzzi emended, chafing at the interruption. " You were saying that what the Army needs is not merely guns, but the spirit to go with them. What may the spirit be that you intend loading your cannon with ? "

" Ah, you're going much too far, Permanent Secretary ! " Stumm deprecated. " It all started with my being asked to explain tonight's gathering to these gentlemen, and I said one couldn't explain anything really. That's all I'll take my stand on. If the spirit of the times really has the two currents I was describing, at least they're both not in favour of *explaining* anything. What people are for nowadays is driving-forces, the forces of the blood, and all that sort of thing. I don't subscribe to it, certainly, but there's something in it."

At these words Director Fischel began to fume again, saying it was immoral for the military even to think of coming to terms with the antisemites in order to get their guns.

" My dear Herr Director ! " Stumm said soothingly. " First of all, a bit of antisemitism more or less is neither here nor there, when people are as anti-minded as they are anyway, the Germans anti the Czechs and the Magyars, the Czechs anti the Magyars and the Germans, and so forth, everyone against everyone else Secondly, if anyone was ever international it was always the Austrian Army Officers' corps. You only have to look at all the Italian, French, Irish, and heaven knows other names you come across in the Army list. We even have an Infantry General von Kohn, he's corps commandant in Olmütz ! "

" All the same, I'm afraid you take too much on yourselves," Tuzzi broke in on this renewed diversion. " The War Ministry's internationally-minded and bellicose, but at the same time tries to come to terms with the nationalist movements and the pacifist ones. That's almost more than a professional diplomat could do. Working out military policy in terms of pacifism is what's now engaging the energies of the oldest hands in diplomacy all over Europe."

" Oh, but it's not us at all that's engaged in politics ! " Stumm protested, once more, in a tone of weary lament over so much misunderstanding. " His Highness wanted to give Capital and Culture a last chance to be of one mind: that's how this gathering came about. Naturally, if the civilian mind turned out quite incapable of coming to accord, that would put us in a position——"

" In a position to what ? That would be interesting to know ! " Tuzzi exclaimed, trying to extract the dilatory statement.

"Well, in a very difficult one of course," Stumm said discreetly and circumspectly.

While these four gentlemen were engaged in this discussion, Ulrich had unobtrusively slipped away in search of Gerda. He steered very clear of the group round His Highness and the War Minister, lest he should be beckoned over to join them.

From some way off he saw Gerda, sitting by the wall beside her mother, who was gazing rigidly into the room, and with Hans Sepp standing on the other side of her with a restless, defiant expression. Since that last disastrous encounter with Ulrich she had grown even thinner and, as he saw more distinctly the nearer he came, in the same measure more barrenly lacking in prettiness; and yet too in some fateful way this lent her charm as she sat there, slack-shouldered, out of harmony with her surroundings. When she caught sight of Ulrich, her face suddenly flushed scarlet and then grew paler than ever, and she made an involuntary movement, bending forward from the waist like someone who feels a twinge at the heart and is unable to lift a hand to press against the pain. He had a fleeting vision of the scene when, savagely abandoned to the animal advantage he had in exciting her body, he had misused her will. Here now that body sat, its forms known to him under the dress—sat on a chair, receiving orders from the will to hold itself proudly, and yet trembling. Gerda did not bear him a grudge, he could tell, but she wanted to be ' finished ' with him at any price. He slowed down a little in order to savour this to the full, and this luxurious tarrying was perhaps in keeping with the relationship between these two people, who could never quite come together.

Ulrich was already quite close to her, aware of nothing now but the quivering of her face, expectantly raised to him, when he was assailed by something imponderable, some mere shadow or wafted warmth, and realised that Bonadea was passing him—without speaking, but doubtless quite deliberately, probably having trailed him through the room. He bowed to her.

The world is very pleasant if one takes it as it is. For one instant the naïve contrast between the voluptuous and the skimpy, embodied in these two women, seemed as great as that in the mountains between pasture and rock. He felt as if he were slipping right out of the Collateral Campaign, even though with a smile of compunction.

When Gerda saw this smile slowly coming to meet her outstretched hand, her eyelids quivered.

At this moment Diotima noticed that Arnheim was leading young Feuermaul in the direction of Count Leinsdorf and the War Minister, and skilled tactician as she was, thwarted this move by having the servants come in with trays of refreshments.

37   *A comparison.*

SUCH conversations as those just reported went on by the dozen, and all had something in common that is not very easy to describe, but which cannot be passed over if one does not share Regierungsrat Meseritscher's belief that a dazzling description of a party consists of listing: X and Y were there, wearing this and that, and made this remark and the other, which is of course what many people take to be genuine narrative art. And so Friedel Feuermaul was not being a wretched sycophant (he was never that), but only having timely inspiration in the right quarter when he said of Meseritscher, in Meseritscher's hearing: " He's the Homer

of our time, you know! No, quite seriously," he went on to
Meseritscher, " in my eyes there is something really great in the
epically immutable ' and ' with which you link all persons and
events." He had got hold of Meseritscher when the editor of
The Parliamentary and Social Gazette approached, being reluctant
to leave without having paid his respects to Arnheim. But it
still did not get Feuermaul's name into the list of those present.

Without going into the subtler distinction between idiots and
cretins, let it suffice to recall that an idiot of a certain degree of
idiocy cannot grasp the concept ' parents ', whereas the notion
' father and mother ' is quite familiar to him. Now it was this
simple, unadorned conjunction ' and ' by means of which Meseritscher related social manifestations to each other. It may further
be recalled that idiots possess something, in the simple concreteness of their mode of thought, which is generally observed
to make a mysterious appeal to the sentiments; and that poets also
appeal primarily to the sentiments, and in much the same way,
in so far as their thought is also as obvious as possible. And so
if Friedel Feuermaul hailed Meseritscher as a poet, he might just
as well—that is to say, with the same feelings floating in him
darkly, which in his case meant the same as in a sudden illumination—have hailed him as an idiot. The element common to
both cases is a mental condition that cannot be spanned by comprehensive concepts or refined by distinctions and abstractions, a
mental condition of the crudest pattern, most clearly characterised
by its way of limiting itself to the use of that simplest of co-ordin-
ating conjunctions, the helplessly additive ' and ', which for those
of little mental capacity replaces all more intricate relationships.
It seems that the world itself, despite all the mind it contains,
is in a mental condition not far removed from that of idiocy. The
conclusion is hard to avoid if one tries to understand all that goes
on in this world, in its totality.

Not that those who first propound, or those who come to share,
such a view are the only intelligent ones! It is not in the least
the individual that counts, any more than it is the plots he con-
trives—such as were being engineered, with more or less ingenuity,
by everyone who had come to Diotima's reception this evening.
For when General von Stumm, for instance, during the diversion
caused by the arrival of refreshments, got into a conversation with

His Highness in the course of which he argued in a genially obstinate and respectfully audacious tone, insisting: " Forgive a simple soldier-man, Your Highness, for profoundly disagreeing, but people's pride in their race is not only arrogance, there's something nice and noble in it as well," he knew exactly what he meant by these words, though he did not know exactly what they conveyed. This sort of bland talk has an enveloping aura round it; it is like trying to get a single match out of a full box while wearing thick gloves.

And Leo Fischel, who had clung firmly to Stumm when he realised that the General was impatiently making off in His Highness's direction, added:

" People must be differentiated not according to race, but according to merit."

What His Highness said in reply was logical. Disregarding Director Fischel, who had just been introduced to him, he said to Stumm:

" What do the middle-classes need *race* for ? They've always been up in arms about a little thing like a Court Chamberlain needing to have sixteen quarterings, and now what are they doing themselves ? Imitating, that's it, and exaggerating too. More than sixteen ancestors is downright sheer snobbery." For His Highness was fretful, and so it was only natural that he should speak thus. Nobody denies that man is rational; it is only questionable how he uses his rational powers for social purposes.

His Highness was vexed by the invasion of ' national ' elements into the Collateral Campaign—which he himself had brought about. Various political and social considerations had forced it upon him. He himself, however, recognised only ' the Austrian people '. His political friends had advised him in terms such as: ' What harm does it do anyway if you listen to what they have to say about race and purity and blood—as if anyone took it seriously when people *talk* ! ' ' But they talk about human beings just as if they were brute beasts ! ' Count Leinsdorf had objected: he himself, after all, had a Catholic view of human dignity, which prevented him from seeing how the ideals of the chicken-farm and horse-breeding could be applied to the children of God, although as a large land-owner he knew all about such things. To this his friends had replied: ' Needn't take such a dim view of it, you know. Perhaps it isn't all that bad. Probably better, anyway, than talking about human rights and all that sort of foreign revolutionary stuff, the way they've always done.' At length His Highness had seen that there was something in this. But His Highness was also vexed because this fellow Feuermaul, whom he had forced upon Diotima, merely created fresh confusion in the Collateral Campaign and disappointed him. Baroness Wayden had praised him to the skies, and he had ended up by yielding to her importunities. ' Yes, you're quite right,' he had admitted, ' the way things are going at the moment it's easy for us to get a reputation for Germanising. And you're right too about its being no harm to invite a poet who says one *must* love all mankind. But don't you see, I really can't spring that on Frau Tuzzi ! ' Still, Baroness Wayden had persisted, and she must have found new and effective arguments, for by the end of their next conversation Leinsdorf had promised to get Diotima to produce an invitation for Feuermaul. ' Not that I like doing it,' he had said. ' But the strong hand in the velvet glove needs fine words if people are to understand it, you're right about that. And I quite agree everything's been going too slowly, there hasn't been the right enthusiasm recently.'

But now he was dissatisfied. His Highness was far from thinking other people stupid, even though he did think himself more intelligent than they were, and he could not understand why all these intelligent people assembled here made such a poor impression on him. Indeed, life as a whole made this impression on him, as though alongside a state of intelligence manifested in individuals, as also in official institutions—among which, it will be remembered, he reckoned faith and science as well—there were a state of utter irresponsibility in the sum total. There were always new ideas popping up, which enflamed passions and then, after being a nine days' wonder, disappeared again. There was the way people were always running after someone or something and stumbling from one superstition into another. One day they would be cheering His Majesty, and another time they would be delivering the most shocking inflammatory speeches in Parliament: and none of it ever amounted to anything, anyway ! If this were reduced to a millionth of its social dimensions, as it were to the measure of one individual brain, what one would get was

precisely the picture of the incalculable, forgetful, ignorant behaviour and the demented hopping around that had always been
Count Leinsdorf's picture of a lunatic, though actually he had
hitherto had little occasion to think about it. Somewhat disgruntled, here now he stood surrounded by people, reflecting that
it had been precisely the Collateral Campaign that was to bring 'the
True' to the light of day. He found himself unable to formulate
some idea about faith that was vaguely there in his mind; he simply
felt something as pleasantly soothing as the shade of a high wall—
a church wall, probably.

" Funny ! " he said after a while to Ulrich, having abandoned
this thought. " If you look at it all with a bit of detachment, you
can't help being reminded, in a way, of starlings—you know the
way they flock together in the fruit-trees, in the autumn."

Ulrich had come back after talking to Gerda. That encounter
had not fulfilled the promise of its beginning. Gerda had not
managed to utter more than brief replies to whatever he said,
replies that were as though laboriously hacked off something that
stuck like a wedge in her breast. Hans Sepp had made up for this
by talking a great deal, assuming considerable airs as her watchdog
and letting there be no doubt that he was not to be intimidated
by this decadent environment.

" You don't know the great racial theorist Bremshuber ? " he had
asked Ulrich.

" Where is he to be found ? " Ulrich had asked in his turn.

" In Schärding on the Laa," Hans had told him.

" What does he do there ? " Ulrich had asked.

" Oh, what does that matter ! " Hans had said. " There are
new people on the way to the top ! He's a pharmacist."

Ulrich had said to Gerda: " I hear you're formally engaged
now."

And Gerda had said: " Bremshuber demands the ruthless
suppression of all who don't belong to the German race, and that's
certainly not so cruel as toleration and contempt ! " Her lips had
begun trembling again as she struggled to get this out; the words
seemed somehow askew, as though they were pieces of something
smashed.

Ulrich had merely gazed at her, shaking his head. " That sort
of thing is not in my line," he had said and had held out his hand to

say goodbye to her.   Now, having returned to Leinsdorf's side, he felt as innocent as a star in the infinity of space.

" But if you don't look at it with detachment," Count Leinsdorf continued slowly, after a pause, " it all goes round in your head like a dog trying to catch its own tail.   You know," he added, " now I've done what my friends said and I've done what Baroness Wayden said, but if you go round listening to what we're saying here, each bit of it sounds very sensible, but precisely in the refined spiritual context that we're in search of it sounds completely haphazard and incoherent."

Round the War Minister and Feuermaul, whom Arnheim had after all managed to introduce, a group had gathered to which Feuermaul was holding forth, loving all mankind.   Arnheim had moved away again, and round him now a second group was forming, in which Ulrich after a while saw Hans Sepp and Gerda. Feuermaul could be heard exclaiming:

" One understands life not by learning, but by goodness.   One must believe in life ! "

His patroness, standing very straight behind him, pressed the point home by adding:

" After all, Goethe was not a doctor of letters ! "

In her eyes, indeed, Feuermaul much resembled Goethe.

The War Minister also held himself very straight, smiling with the same endurance he was wont to show when taking the salute at a parade.

Count Leinsdorf asked: " Tell me, where does this Feuermaul chap come from, actually ? "

" His father owns some factories in Hungary," Ulrich replied. " I believe it's something to do with phosphorus, which kills the workers off by the age of forty.   Occupational disease.   Necrosis of the bone."

" H'm, yes.   But the son ? " Leinsdorf was unmoved by the factory-workers' fate.

" He was supposed to go to the University.   Law, I believe. The father's a self-made man, and he's said to have been very put out because his son didn't take to learning."

" Why didn't he take to learning ? " Count Leinsdorf asked. He was very thorough this evening.

" Goodness knows—probably a case of Fathers and Sons,"

Ulrich said, shrugging his shoulders. " If the father's poor, the sons love money. If the father has money, the sons love mankind. But I expect, sir, you've heard about the father-and-son problem in our time ? "

" Oh yes, I know. But why is Arnheim taking this young Feuermaul under his wing? Has it got something to do with the oil-fields ? " Count Leinsdorf asked.

" You think there's something in that, sir ? " Ulrich exclaimed.

" Of course there's something in it," Leinsdorf replied patiently. " But what I still don't understand is this—we always knew people should love each other and that the government needs a strong hand to make them do it, so why should there suddenly be any either-or about it ? "

Ulrich answered: " Well, sir, you always wanted a general manifestation arising out of the midst of the people, and this is what it's bound to look like."

" Ah, that's not true ! " Leinsdorf earnestly disagreed. But before he could go on, they were interrupted by Stumm von Bordwehr, who had come hurrying over from the Arnheim group, excitedly wanting some information from Ulrich.

" Forgive my butting in, Your Highness," he begged. " I need to know," he said, turning to Ulrich, " can it really be maintained that man acts only according to his impulses and emotions, and never according to reason ? "

Ulrich looked at him rather blankly.

" There's one of these Marxist chaps over there," Stumm explained, " so to speak asserting that a person's economic foundations entirely determine his ideological superstructure. And there's a psychoanalyst arguing with him. *He* says the ideological superstructure is entirely a product of the instinctual foundations."

" It's not as simple as all that," Ulrich said, wishing he could escape.

" That's just what I say ! But it didn't do any good," the General immediately went on, not taking his eyes off Ulrich.

But Leinsdorf now entered the discussion. " Now there, you see," he said to Ulrich, " is something rather like the question I was just going to raise myself. Apart from whether the foundations are economic or sexual or whatever these fellows may think

—what I was going to say just now is this: why are people so
unreliable in their superstructure? That's it, you know. As the
poet has it, 'it's a mad world, my masters!' Sometimes one
comes near to thinking it's literally true."

"That's the psychology of the masses, Your Highness!" the
erudite General pointed out. "So far as it applies to the masses,
it makes very good sense to me. The masses are moved only by
impulses, and of course that means by the impulses that most
individuals have in common, that's only logical. That's to say,
of course, it's illogical. The masses are illogical, they make use of
logical ideas only as trappings. What they're really guided by is
simply and solely *suggestion*. If you give me the newspapers, the
wireless, the cinema industry, and perhaps a few other means of
influencing public opinion, I undertake inside a few years—as
our friend Ulrich once said—to turn everyone into cannibals!
That's precisely why mankind needs strong leadership! But of
course Your Highness knows that much better than I do. Still,
I can't make myself believe that *individuals*, who are in many cases
so highly developed, aren't logical, even if Arnheim says so."

Ulrich wondered what on earth he could offer his friend by
way of contribution to the very random controversy. As an
angler's hook may catch not a fish but a bunch of weeds, so the
General's question had a tangled hunch of theories dangling from
it. Does man act only according to his emotional impulses, does
he only do, feel, and indeed think, that to which he is impelled
by unconscious streams of longing or the milder current of
pleasure, as is nowadays widely assumed to be the case? Or does
he perhaps, after all, act according to reason and will—as is also
widely assumed today? Is he particularly at the mercy of certain
impulses, such as the sexual, as is nowadays assumed? Or at the
mercy not of sexual preconditions, but of the psychological effect
of economic conditions, as is also assumed? An organism as
complex as man can be regarded from many sides, and one can
choose one or the other axis in the theoretical picture: what one
gets is partial truths, out of the interpenetration of which truth
slowly rises higher. Or does it really rise higher? Every time
a partial truth has been taken for the sole explanation of things,
there has been a heavy price to pay. On the other hand, nobody
would have arrived even at the partial truth if it had not been over-

estimated.   So the history of truth and the history of feeling are
in many ways interlinked; but that of feeling remains obscure.
Indeed to Ulrich's way of thinking it was not a history at all, but a
wild tangle.   It was amusing to reflect, for instance, that the
religious ideas, and therefore probably the emotional ideas as
well, that the Middle Ages had about man were full of belief in
man's reason and will, whereas nowadays many highly educated
men, whose only passion—if they have one at all—is smoking too
much, regard feeling as the basis of all human activity.   Such
were the thoughts going through Ulrich's mind, and it is not surprising that he felt no desire to give any answer to Stumm's
oratory.   In any case, Stumm was not really looking for an answer,
but simply letting off steam before going back where he had come
from.

" Count Leinsdorf ! " Ulrich said mildly.   " Do you remember
I once proposed that you should found a world secretariat for all
those problems that make equal demands on the spirit and on
precision ? "

" Indeed I do remember," Leinsdorf replied.   " I told His
Eminence about it, and he was heartily amused.   What he said
was, you'd come on the scene too late."

" And yet this is the very thing you've been sensing the lack
of, Your Highness ! " Ulrich went on.   " You have observed that
the world has forgotten today what it was wanting only yesterday,
that it has moods that have no sufficient grounds, that it is in a
perpetual state of excitement, that it never reaches a conclusion,
and that if one could picture brought together in one single head all
that goes on in all the heads that make up mankind, one would be
confronted with a whole series of well-known degenerate phenomena that we all recognise as constituting mental defectiveness,
and——"

" Outstandingly correct ! " Stumm von Bordwehr exclaimed,
once more with a welling up of his pride in the information he had
acquired that afternoon.   " That's the very spit and image of—
tch, tch !   I've gone and forgotten what the particular kind of
insanity's called, but that's exactly it ! "

" No," Ulrich said with a smile, " I don't think it's exactly
any particular kind of insanity, really.   After all, what distinguishes a sane person from an insane one is that the sane person

is full of countless insanities, and the insane person is possessed by only one."

" Oh, very good ! " Stumm and Leinsdorf both applauded. " Quite brilliant ! "   And then they both asked: " But what does it mean, actually ? "

" It means this," Ulrich began: " If I may take ' morality ' to mean the regulation of all those faculties that include feeling, imagination, and the rest of it, I should say that in the moral scheme each of these faculties adjusts itself to the others and thus appears to have some stability, but that all of them together, in the moral picture they represent, don't get beyond the state of delusion."

" Come, that's going too far," Count Leinsdorf said good-humouredly.

" But I say," the General said, also protesting, " everyone must have his own morality, mustn't he ?   I mean, you can't dictate to people whether they're to prefer cats or dogs ! "

" Can one dictate that, sir ? " Ulrich asked His Highness, very intently.

" Well, in the old days," Count Leinsdorf said diplomatically, though he felt himself touched in his religious conviction that there was such things as ' the True ' in every sphere, " things were better in the old days.   But nowadays ? "

" Then we're left with what we may call the permanent war of religion," Ulrich pointed out.

" You call that a war of religion ? " Leinsdorf asked with interest.

" Well yes—what else ? "

" H'm—not at all bad.   Yes . . .   Quite a good description of modern life.   Ah, I always knew there was not at all a bad Catholic tucked away in you somewhere."

" I'm a very bad one," Ulrich answered.   " I don't believe God has been among us yet.   I believe He is still to come.   But only if we shorten the way for Him, as we haven't shortened it yet."

His Highness put this aside with the dignified words: " That's above my head."

38

A great event is on the way.   But nobody has noticed it.

THE General for his part exclaimed:

" I'm afraid I must rush back to His Excellency, but you must explain all this to me another time, I won't let you off!   I'll join you again a little later, if I may."

Leinsdorf created the impression of wanting to say something. His thoughts seemed to be working strongly within him.   But Ulrich and he had scarcely been alone for a moment when they were surrounded by people borne towards them by the perpetual drifting of the company and the attraction exercised by His Highness.   There was no more talk about what Ulrich had just said, and he was the only person thinking about it a moment later when an arm was slipped through his and he looked round to see Agathe.

" Have you discovered grounds for my defence yet ? " she asked with caressing malice.

Holding her arm firmly, Ulrich drew her away from the people who had gathered around.

" Can't we go home ? " Agathe asked.

" No," Ulrich said.   " I can't leave yet."

" I suppose," Agathe said, teasing him, " you can't leave the times to come, for the sake of which you're keeping yourself pure here ? "

Ulrich pressed her arm.

" I think it's very much in my favour," she whispered in his ear, " that I oughtn't to be here at all, but in jail."

They looked for somewhere where they could be alone.   The party had by now worked up to boiling-point and was all a whirl. All the same, it was still possible to distinguish the two main groups of thought: round about the War Minister the talk was of peace and love, and round Arnheim, at the moment, about how German love of peace flourished best in the shelter of German might.

Arnheim inclined a benevolent ear to this, because he never

refused to listen to an opinion sincerely held, and had a particular liking for new opinions. His only worry was lest the oil-fields affair might meet with opposition in Parliament. He was resigned to the probability that there would be opposition from the Slav politicians, and hoped he could count on support from the German-ophiles. At government level all seemed to be going well, except for a certain antagonism in the Ministry of Foreign Affairs; this he did not think very important. Tomorrow he was going to Budapest.

There were plenty of hostile 'observers' round about him and the other leading personages here. They were quickly identifiable by the fact that they said 'yes' to everything and were the most charming people, whereas the others mostly put forward contrary opinions.

Tuzzi tried to convince one of them of the following:

"What people say doesn't mean a thing. It never means anything."

The other man quite believed it; he was a member of Parliament. But it did not make him alter the opinion he had come with, namely that there was some mischief going on here.

His Highness, on the other hand, spoke up for the significance of the evening's assembly by saying to someone else:

"My dear sir, since eighteen-forty-eight even revolutions have been carried out simply by doing a lot of talking."

It would be a mistake to regard such differences as embodying nothing but a permissible divergence from the usual monotony of life. Yet this mistake, with all its grave consequences, is made as often as the expression 'That's a mere matter of feeling!' is used—one without which our intellectual apparatus is quite unthinkable. This indispensable expression separates that in life which *must* be from that which *can* be.

"It separates the given order," Ulrich said to Agathe, "from the field in which the individual personality is free to follow its own bent. It separates what is rationalised from what passes for irrational. In the way it is generally used it amounts to the admission that to be humane on the main counts is something we're compelled to, but to be humane in minor details is suspect, mere frivolity. People are persuaded that life would be a peniten-tiary if we hadn't free choice in our preference for wine or water, for being atheists or *bien-pensants*. But nobody dreams of believing that what's a matter of feeling is really left to one's own choice. In fact, though there's no clear dividing-line, there are matters of legitimate and of illegitimate feeling."

The feeling between Ulrich and Agathe was not what would be called a legitimate one, although at the present moment, as they looked round, still arm in arm, for some corner to retreat to, they were merely talking about the party and secretly, wildly rejoicing at being united again after their estrangement. On the other hand, the alternative of either loving all one's fellow-men or first of all exterminating some of them obviously covered two aspects of one legitimate feeling: otherwise there would not have been such fierce discussion about it in Diotima's drawing-room and in His Highness's presence, splitting the company into two profoundly antagonistic groups.

Ulrich maintained that the concept 'matter of feeling' had rendered the cause of feeling itself the worst possible service. And when he undertook to give his sister an account of the peculiar impressions he had got from the present gathering, he soon found himself saying things that against his own will turned into a continuation of the talk broken off that morning—and doubtless also an attempt to justify what he had said then.

" Well, I really don't know where to start," he said, " if I'm not to bore you. May I tell you what I understand by ' morality ' ? "

" Do," Agathe said.

" Morality is the regulation of behaviour in any given society, and more especially the regulation of its inner impulses, that is, of its feelings and thoughts."

" That's a lot of progress inside a few hours ! " Agathe commented, laughing. " This morning you said you didn't know what morality was."

" Of course I don't know ! But that doesn't stop me from giving you a dozen definitions. The oldest one is that God revealed the whole of life's order to us, down to its last details——"

" That would be the nicest one," Agathe said.

" But the most probable one," Ulrich said emphatically, " is that morality, like every other form of human order, is a result of pressure and compulsion. One lot of people get to the top and simply impose on the others the principles and prescriptions that will ensure that they remain on top. At the same time, however, this morality becomes the code of those who have caused it to prevail. So it is at the same time an example. And, again at the same time, it undergoes change as a result of repercussions. This is naturally much more complicated than one can explain briefly, and because it doesn't happen without the intellect's taking some part, though again not by means of the intellect at all, but merely empirically, what you finally get is a network too fine to analyse, which extends over everything apparently as independently as the God-created heavens. Now everything refers to this complex, but the complex itself refers to nothing. In other words, everything is moral, but morality itself is not ! "

" That's delightful of it," Agathe said. " But that reminds me: today I got to know a good man."

Ulrich was somewhat taken back by being sidetracked like this, and when Agathe began telling him about her meeting with Lindner, he first of all tried to find a place for it in his present train of thought.

" Good men are two a penny here this evening, if that's what you want," he said. " But if you let me go on, I'll tell you why the bad men are also here."

As they talked they had gradually edged their way out of the throng until they reached the hall. Ulrich wondered where they could hide themselves away for a while. Diotima's room occurred to him, and also Rachel's little bedroom, but he did not want to enter either of them again. So for a while Agathe and he remained standing among the empty coats with which the hall was populated. And suddenly he did not know how to go on.

" I really ought to start all over again," he said, with an impatient, helpless gesture.

And suddenly he said:

" You don't want to know if what you've done is good or evil. You're just uneasy because you do both without any solid grounds ! "

Agathe nodded.

He had taken both her hands in his.

The opaque glimmer of his sister's skin, with its fragrance of plants unknown to him, a fragrance rising from the low-cut bodice of her dress, for a moment lost all earthly meaning. The pulsing of the blood was like an echo between one hand and the other. A deep moat seemed to shut them both off from this world, enclosing them in a land of nowhere.

Now he could not find words in which to hold this fast. He could not use the phrases he had so often used for it before. ' Don't let's act on the inspiration of the moment, but always out of a condition that goes to the last horizon.' ' So that it takes us to the very centre, from where one never comes back again to take it all back.' ' Not from the edge, and the varying conditions at the edge, but out of the one, single, immutable happiness.' Such phrases came to his mind indeed, and he might well have spoken them aloud if it had been that the two of them here were simply talking. But because such words applied to the present moment with such intense immediacy, it was impossible. And that it was so left him helplessly agitated.

Agathe understood him perfectly. And it ought to have made her happy that now, for the first time, the shell encasing her ' hard brother ' had broken, like an egg falling on to the floor, revealing the soft fluid part within. But to her own surprise it was this time her feelings that were not quite ready to join with his. Between this morning and this evening there lay the strange encounter with Lindner, and although the man had merely aroused her astonishment and curiosity, even this tiny grain was enough to prevent the unending mirror-reflection of eremitic love from coming into being.

Ulrich felt this from the touch of her hands, even before she made any answer.

And Agathe made no answer.

He guessed that this unexpected silence was connected with the experience he had just had to listen to her describing. Abashed, and confused by the recoil of his own unanswered feelings, he said, shaking his head:

" It's really rather annoying how much you seem to expect from such a person's goodness ! "

" I dare say it is," Agathe admitted.

He gazed at her. He realised that this experience meant more to his sister than the various attentions paid to her by other men since she had been in his care. He knew a little of the man Lindner. For Lindner took some part in public life; he was in fact the man who, at that very first session of the patriotic Campaign, had made the short speech (received with such painful silence) about 'the historic moment' or whatever it was—awkward, sincere and insignificant. Ulrich involuntarily turned his head to look round for him; but of course he had not seen the man in this gathering, for he remembered now that he had not been asked again. He must have come across him somewhere else, probably at the meetings of some learned society, and he must also have glanced at some publication or other of his, for as he concentrated his memory, microscopically tiny scraps of images from the past congealed, like a viscous drop of something disagreeable, crystallising into the judgment:

"A dreary ass! Anyone with standards of a certain level can't take such a man any more seriously than one takes your exhusband Hagauer."

This was what he said to Agathe.

Agathe met it with silence. She even pressed his hand.

And he felt: 'It simply doesn't make sense, whatever it is, but there's no stopping it!'

At this moment other people came into the hall, and brother and sister drew slightly apart.

"Shall we go in again?" Ulrich asked.

Agathe said 'no' and looked round for some escape.

It suddenly struck Ulrich that there was one place they could escape to, and that was the kitchen.

In the kitchen batteries of glasses were being filled and trays were being loaded with cakes. The cook was bustling about with tremendous zeal, and Rachel and Soliman were standing by for fresh supplies, but not whispering to each other, as they had previously done on such occasions; they kept some distance apart and remained impassive. Little Rachel dropped a curtsey as Agathe and Ulrich came in. Soliman merely rolled up his eyes respectfully.

"It's stuffy over there," Ulrich said. "Can we come and have a drink here?"

He sat down, with Agathe beside him, on the window-seat and put a glass and a plate within reach, so that if anyone should discover them, it would just look as if two old friends of the family were having a little fun on their own.

Then he said with a small sigh: " So it's merely a matter of feeling whether one finds such a Professor Lindner ' good ' or insufferable."

Agathe was concentrating on unwrapping a sweet.

" Which is to say," Ulrich went on, " feeling is not true or false ! Feeling always remains a private affair ! It remains the prey of suggestion, fantasy, persuasion ! You and I are no different from all of them in there. You know what those people in there want ? "

" No. But surely it doesn't matter ? "

" Perhaps it does matter. For they form two parties, each of which is as right—or as wrong—as the other."

Agathe said she could not help thinking it better to believe in human goodness than only in guns and politics, even if the manner of the belief was absurd.

" What's this fellow Lindner like ? " Ulrich asked.

" Oh, that's impossible to say. He's good ! " Agathe replied, laughing.

" You can't make any more of what strikes you as good than of what strikes Leinsdorf as good," Ulrich retorted in annoyance.

Both their faces were tense with excitement and laughter: the superficial current of the cheerfully civilised expression was impeded by deeper currents flowing the other way. Rachel could feel this under her little cap, at the very roots of her hair; but she felt so wretched herself that this sensation was dim compared with what her sensations had been once, indeed it was like a memory of better days. The pretty curve of her cheeks had grown rather hollow, and the dark glow of her eyes was dimmed by discouragement. Had Ulrich been in the mood to compare her beauty with his sister's, he would infallibly have been struck by how Rachel's former dark brilliance had crumbled, like a piece of shining coal crushed to dust by a waggon-wheel. But he was not paying any attention to her. The fact was that Rachel was pregnant, and nobody knew it but Soliman, who failed to understand the reality of the disaster and had nothing to offer but silly romantic schemes.

" For centuries," Ulrich went on, " the world has known truth of thought and hence, at least to a certain degree, rational freedom of thought. And in all this same time the feelings have had

neither the austere school of truth nor freedom of movement.
For every morality, in the period during which it was valid,
regulated feeling only quite rigidly and only in so far as certain
principles and basic feelings were needed for whatever sort of
action that morality required. The rest was always left to the
individual to decide—to the private play of emotion, to the vague
endeavours of art, and to academic debate. So morality has
adapted our feelings to the needs of morality. It has neglected
to develop them, even though it itself depends on them. For
morality is, after all, order and integrity of feeling." He broke
off. He felt Rachel's fascinated gaze; for even if she could no
longer summon up her former enthusiasm for ' the gentry's '
affairs, she was drawn to the eagerness in his face. " Oh, I don't
know, perhaps it's comical to be always talking about morality,
even in the kitchen," he said, suddenly overtaken by shyness.

Agathe was gazing at him intently and thoughtfully.

Leaning closer to her, he added softly, with a rather wry little
flickering smile:

" But it's only another form of the passionate condition that
takes up arms against the whole world."

Without meaning to do so, he had brought about a repetition
of that morning's conflict by again seeming to put himself in the
not very attractive light of one who is always lecturing. He could
not help it. For him morality was neither conformism nor the sum
of acquired knowledge: it was the infinite fullness of life's
potentialities. He believed that morality held the capacity for
constant intensification. He believed in stages of moral experience,
not merely, as most people do, in stages of moral apprehension—as
though morality were something cut-and-dried and only man were
not yet pure enough for it. He believed in morality without believing in any particular code of morals. What is generally
understood by morality is something like a system of police
regulations for keeping life in order; and because life does not
answer to even these, they come to look as if they were by nature
something that could never quite be lived up to and hence, in a
rather sordid way, like an ideal. But morality must not be reduced to this level. Morality is imagination. That was what he
wanted to make Agathe see. And the second thing was that there
is nothing arbitrary about the imagination. Once the imagin-

ation has been surrendered to arbitrary whim, there is a price to pay.

The words twitched on the tip of Ulrich's tongue. He was on the verge of talking about the all too little regarded distinction between the way in which the various epochs have developed the rational mind, and the way in which they have kept the moral imagination closed and static. He was on the verge of talking about this because the consequence is a line that runs, despite all scepticism, more or less straight all through history, a rising line of rational intellect and intellectual patterns, and, contrasting with it, a mound of broken shards, which are feelings, ideas, and life's potentialities, heaped up in strata just as they came into existence— always no more than side-issues—and subsequently were discarded. And another consequence is that there are, after all, innumerable possibilities for forming an opinion this way or that as soon as anything extends into the realm of principles, but that there is no single possibility of harmonising these opinions. And yet another consequence is that these opinions lash out at each other because there is no chance for them to agree. And all in all the consequence is that the emotions are something that slop to and fro in mankind like water slopping about in a rickety tub.

Ulrich had an idea that had been haunting him all this evening. It was actually an old idea of his, and this evening's doings had merely kept on offering evidence of its truth. He had wanted to show Agathe where the mistake was and how it could be repaired if all men were so minded. And behind this there was really only the sorrowful intention to prove that until that was done, it was not safe to trust even the discoveries of one's own imagination.

And with a little sigh, as a hard-pressed woman offers one last struggle before she surrenders, Agathe said:

" So one must always do things ' on principle ', is that it ? "

And she looked him in the eyes, answering his smile.

" Yes," he said. " But only on *one* principle ! "

Now this was something quite different from what he had thought he was going to say. This again emanated from the realm of the Siamese Twins and of the Millennium, where life grows in magical stillness, like a flower; and even if it was not a mere flight of fancy, yet the frontiers of thought it pointed to are solitary and treacherous.

Agathe's eyes were shiny as split agate. If at this instant he had said just a little more, or had touched her with his hand, something would have happened—something that evaporated before she even knew what it was. For Ulrich did not want to say more.

He took a fruit and a knife, and began to peel the fruit. He was happy because the distance that had a little while ago separated him from his sister had melted into some incommensurable nearness. But he was also glad that there was now an interruption.

It was the General who came peering into the kitchen with the knowing glance of a patrol-leader surprising an enemy bivouac.

" Here I come butting in," he exclaimed as he entered. " But it's not as if I were bearing off anyone that matters, he's only your brother ! " he said to Agathe, and to Ulrich: " They're looking for you like a needle in a haystack."

And so it came about that Ulrich said to the General what he had meant to say to Agathe. But first of all he asked: " Who are ' they ' ? "

" I was supposed to bring you to the Minister ! " Stumm said reproachfully.

Ulrich waved that aside.

" Not that it matters now," the General said in his easy-going way. " The old boy's just gone, anyway. But on my own count, as soon as *madame* has chosen some better company than yours I must interrogate you on what you meant by ' religious war '— always supposing you have the decency to recall your own words."

" We're just talking about that," Ulrich replied.

" Now, that's jolly interesting ! " the General exclaimed. " And so *madame* is also studying the subject of morality ? "

" It's my brother," Agathe corrected him, smiling. " He never talks about anything but morality."

" And it's been all over the agenda this evening," Stumm sighed. " Leinsdorf, for instance—only a few minutes ago he was saying morality's every bit as important as eating. Not that I can agree with that ! " Having made this pronouncement, Stumm bent forward, with relish, over the sweets that Agathe held out to him. It was a sort of joke.

" I can't agree either," Agathe said consolingly.

" An officer and a woman must both have a morality, but they
don't care to talk of it," he improvised. " Isn't that right ? "

Rachel had brought him a kitchen chair and was zealously
dusting it with her apron when these words of his stabbed her to
the heart. She nearly began to cry.

But Stumm was already prompting Ulrich: " Come on, now,
what's all this about the war of religion ? " Yet before Ulrich
could say anything, he himself went on: " Fact is, I suspect your
cousin's prowling about looking for you everywhere, and I only
beat her to it thanks to my military training. So I must make good
use of my time. Honestly, I don't like it the way things are going
on in there. It's letting the side down. And Diotima—I don't
quite know how to put it—she's let them get the bit between their
teeth. D'you know what they've resolved ? "

" Who has resolved ? "

" A lot of people have left. Some people have stayed behind,
making careful mental notes about it all," the General elaborated
obscurely. " Fact is, one can't tell who's resolving."

" Then perhaps it would be better," Ulrich suggested, " if you
started by saying what they've resolved."

Stumm von Bordwehr shrugged his shoulders. " Oh well,
fortunately it isn't a resolution in a proper committee-meeting
sense of the word," he said. " All the responsible people had
left by then, thank heaven. So it's only what you might call a
private resolution, a suggestion, a minority vote. I shall take the
line that we have no official knowledge of it. But then you must
tell your secretary, because of the minutes, to make quite sure
that nothing of the sort gets in. Your forgiveness," he said to
Agathe, " for talking shop like this."

" But do tell us what happened," she too urged.

Stumm made a sweeping gesture. " Feuermaul—if you remember about this young man we only invited, really, because—
well, I don't know quite how to put it—because he's an exponent
of the spirit of the times and because we had to invite the opposite
exponents this evening anyway. We'd hoped that for all that,
perhaps even with some intellectual stimulation, we'd be able to
get down to talking about the things that unfortunately matter.
Well, your brother knows all about that. The Minister was to
have been got together with Leinsdorf and Arnheim, to see if

Leinsdorf had no objection to certain—certain patriotic views.
And all in all I'm fairly pleased with the way things have gone,"
he said, turning back confidentially to Ulrich. " So far, so good.
But while this was going on, this Feuermaul and the others—"
here Stumm felt obliged to interpolate for Agathe's benefit:
" that's to say, the exponent of the view that man is as it were a
peaceful and lovable creature that must be nicely treated and the
exponents of what you might roughly call the opposite view, who
maintain the way to keep order is the iron hand and whatever goes
with it—well, Feuermaul got into an argument with them, and
before anyone could stop it they'd put their heads together and
drawn up this resolution."

" Together ? " Ulrich queried.

" Yes. Oh, I may sound as if I was making light of it," Stumm
declared, retrospectively quite well pleased with the absurdity of
what he had told them. " But nobody could have expected that.
And if I tell you what the resolution was, you won't believe your
ears ! Seeing that this afternoon I was supposed to be visiting
Moosbrugger, semi-officially, the whole Ministry'll go and believe
I put them up to it."

Here Ulrich burst out laughing, and did so again and again as
Stumm went on with his story; only Agathe could really understand this. Stumm rather huffily observed that he seemed to be a
bit wrought-up. But what had happened was so exactly on the
pattern that Ulrich had been explaining to his sister that he could
not help finding it hilariously funny.

At the last moment the Feuermaul group had decided they must
save whatever could still be saved. In such cases the object is
generally less clear than the intention. The young poet Friedel
Feuermaul—who went round trying to look like the youthful
Schubert, for he adored everything to do with Old Vienna, he
himself having been born in a small provincial town in Hungary—
firmly believed in Austria's mission, and above and beyond this he
believed in mankind as a whole. It was obvious that a project like
the Collateral Campaign, if it did not include himself, must make
him uneasy. How could a broadly humanitarian project in an
Austrian key, or an Austrian project in a broadly humanitarian
key, prosper without him ? ! Admittedly he had said this only to
his friend Frau Drangsal; but she, as a widow in the reflected

glory of a reputation that had been a credit to the nation and as, furthermore, a hostess whose intellectually brilliant drawing-room had only in this last year been outshone by Diotima's, had repeated it to every influential person with whom she came into contact. So a rumour had got about that the Collateral Campaign was in peril, unless—an ' unless ' and a peril that, naturally enough remained undefined, for first of all Diotima had to be brought to the point of inviting Feuermaul to her house, and then one would perhaps see more clearly. But the rumour of some peril, apparently emanating from the patriotic Campaign, was noted by those alert politicians who acknowledged no *patria*, or Fatherland, but only that little old body, Mother ' people ', who lived in a forced marriage together with the State, by which she was always being knocked about. These politicians had long suspected that all the Collateral Campaign would produce was some new form of oppression. And even though they were civil enough to conceal this suspicion, they attached less importance to averting that—for there had always been despairing humanists among the Germans, but as a whole what were they but oppressors and parasites on the State?—than to the useful hint that Germans themselves were admitting how dangerous their ' popular ' nationalism was. Thus Frau Drangsal and the poet Feuermaul were buoyed up, in their endeavours, by a sense of sympathetic support that they did not bother to investigate, and Feuermaul, who was acknowledged to be a man of ' feeling ', was obsessed by the idea that someone must say something, counselling love and peace, to the War Minister in person. Why it should be the War Minister, of all people, and what part he was supposed to play thereafter also remained obscure; but the inspiration itself was so dazzling and dramatic that it did not need any arguments to support it. In this Stumm von Bordwehr concurred—for the fickle General also occasionally let his zeal for culture bear him into the Drangsal drawing-room, though Diotima knew nothing of this. It was also he who brought it about that the original view—that Arnheim the armaments magnate was an element in the peril—gave way to the view that Arnheim the thinker was an important element in all that was good.

So far all had been going as might have been expected. And the fact that the Minister's chat with Feuermaul despite all Frau

Drangsal's aid produced nothing but some flashes of Feuermaulian brilliance, to which His Excellency inclined a tolerant ear, was also merely the sort of thing to be expected in life. But Feuermaul still had reserves to call upon; and because his forces were made up of men of letters both young and elderly, of Hofräte, librarians, and some pacifists, in short of all sorts of people in all sorts of positions who were united by their sentiment towards 'the old country' and its mission to mankind—a sentiment that would as easily have turned to bringing back the obsolete omnibus with its three-horse team as to propaganda for Viennese porcelain —and because these faithful had in the course of the evening made diverse contacts with their opponents, who likewise did not go round with knives unsheathed, many discussions had sprung up in which opinions whirled blindly in all directions. This was the tempting prospect before Feuermaul when his talk with the War Minister was over and Frau Drangsal's attention was somehow diverted for a while. All Stumm von Bordwehr was in a position to report was that Feuermaul had got into an extremely lively discussion with a young man who, from Stumm's description, might very well have been Hans Sepp. He was in any case one of those who must have a scapegoat, which they blame for all the evils they cannot cope with: nationalist arrogance is only one special case of this, the case in which honest conviction makes one choose a scapegoat not of one's own breed and indeed with as little resemblance to oneself as possible. Now everyone knows what a great relief it is, when annoyed, to have someone on whom to work off one's anger, even if it all has nothing to do with him. What is less well known is how this applies to love. Nevertheless, it is so: love must often be worked off on someone with whom it has nothing at all to do, simply because otherwise it would find no outlet. Feuermaul, for instance, was a bustling young man who could be quite unpleasant in the struggle for his own advantage, but his love's scapegoat was 'mankind', and once he had thought of 'man' in this general form there was no holding his unspent goodness. Hans Sepp, on the other hand, was a decent chap who could not even bring himself to deceive Director Fischel, and his scapegoat was 'man' in all his non-German varieties, on whom he resentfully blamed everything he could not alter. Whatever they had started by talking to each other about, no doubt they had both mounted their hobby-goats and charged each other. For as Stumm recounted:

"Honestly I don't know how it happened. In a twinkling there were a lot of other people listening to them, and the next minute there was a crowd, and in the end everyone who was still there was standing round them."

"And do you know what they were arguing about?" Ulrich asked.

Stumm shrugged his shoulders. "Feuermaul shouted at the other chap: 'You think you hate, but you can't do it! Love is innate in everyone!' Or words to that effect. And the other one yelled at him: 'And you think you love, do you? But you're incapable of it, you—you——' well, I can't repeat it exactly, because, being in uniform, I had to hold a little aloof."

"Oh," Ulrich said, "I see the point." And he turned to Agathe, his eyes seeking hers.

"No, the point is the resolution!" Stumm reminded him. "First of all they nearly had each other's blood, and in two ticks they were drawing up their rotten resolution together!" In all his rotundity Stumm made the impression of deadly seriousness. "The Minister made off at once," he added.

"And what *did* they resolve?" both brother and sister asked.

"Well, I can't tell you that exactly," Stumm answered. "Naturally I took myself off as well, before they'd finished. Anyway it's always difficult to get that sort of thing clear. It was something on behalf of Moosbrugger and against the Army."

"Moosbrugger? But how on earth?" Ulrich laughed.

"How on earth?" the General repeated, very ruffled. "It's all very well for you to laugh, old boy, but it's likely to get me into very bad odour, very bad odour indeed. At best it'll take me days to do all the paper-work it'll bring down on me. How does anyone know 'how on earth' with people like that? Perhaps it was that old Professor who's to blame, the one who goes round talking in favour of hanging and against being soft. Or it may be because there's been a lot in the newspapers about that monster again in the last few days. Anyway, he suddenly cropped up. All this has got to be undone again!" he declared with unusual firmness.

At this point some more people came into the kitchen, following each other at brief intervals: Arnheim, Diotima, and then Tuzzi, and even Count Leinsdorf.

Arnheim had heard the voices from outside in the hall. He had been on the point of slipping quietly away, hoping that the disturbance that was going on would enable him to escape another heart-to-heart talk with Diotima; for tomorrow he was leaving town again for some time. But curiosity lured him to glance into the kitchen, and once again Agathe had seen him he felt it impossible to withdraw. Stumm instantly besieged him with questions as to how things now stood.

" I can even give it to you verbatim," Arnheim replied with a smile. " It was so quaint that I couldn't resist making a quiet note of it."

He extracted a small card from his wallet and slowly read, from his own shorthand, the substance of the proposed manifesto:

" ' The patriotic Campaign has passed the following resolution, proposed by Herr Feuermaul and Herr '—I didn't catch the other name. ' It is right and fitting that each individual should be prepared to die for his own ideas, but anyone who causes men to die for ideas not their own is a murderer.' That was the proposed wording," he added, " and I didn't get the impression that there were going to be changes."

" That's it ! " the General exclaimed. " Now I remember the words myself. Disgusting, absolutely disgusting, these intellectual debates ! "

Arnheim said mildly: " It is a symptom of modern youth's craving for stability and leadership."

" But it wasn't only the younger generation that was in it," Stumm answered, looking quite shocked. " There were old men standing around, nodding their bald heads ! "

" Then it's symptomatic of the general craving for leadership," Arnheim emended, amiably admitting this. " It's very widespread nowadays. Incidentally, this resolution is borrowed from a recent book, if I'm not mistaken."

" Indeed ? " Stumm said.

" Yes," Arnheim said. " And of course it must be treated as never having happened. But I think it would be rewarding, supposing one could only find the way, if the spiritual craving that found expression in this resolution could be directed to a useful end."

The General appeared somewhat relieved. Turning to Ulrich, he asked:

" Have you any notion what could be done? "

" Naturally! " Ulrich replied.

Arnheim's attention was diverted by Diotima.

" Right then," the General said in a low voice. " Fire away! I must say I'd be glad if the leadership remained among ourselves."

" You must get a clear picture of what actually happened," Ulrich said, taking his time. " These people aren't so far out, you know, when one of them accuses the other of wanting to love if only he could, and the other retorts that exactly the same applies to hatred. You see, it's true of all the feelings. Nowadays there's a conciliatory element in hatred. On the other hand, in order to feel what would really be love for another human being—" Ulrich stopped short and said abruptly: " I maintain, two such people have never yet existed."

" I'm sure that's very interesting," the General said quickly, " though I don't in the least understand how you can say such a thing. But tomorrow I have to write a report on what's been going on here this evening, and I implore you to bear that in mind! In Army circles what counts is always being able to report progress. A certain optimism is indispensable, even in defeat—it's the Army tradition. And so how can I report what's happened so that it looks like progress? "

" Say," Ulrich said with a twinkle in his eye, " it was the vengeance of the moral imagination! "

" But you can't say that sort of thing in a War-Ministry report! " Stumm said irritably.

" All right then, put it differently," Ulrich resumed seriously. " Say: all creative epochs have been serious. There is no profound happiness without profound morality. There is no morality if there is no solid basis for it. There is no happiness that is not founded in a conviction. Not even animals live without morality. But mankind no longer knows what moral——"

Stumm broke in on this, as it seemed, calmly fluent dictation: " My dear old boy, I can talk about troops' morale or battle morale or a woman's morals, but only in concrete cases. Morals

or morality as a thing in itself is something you can't put in a
military report any more than you can put in imagination or God
Almighty. You know that as well as I do ! "

Diotima looked at Arnheim standing at her kitchen window,
and it was a strangely intimate sight at the end of a long evening
when they had only exchanged a few circumspect words.
Paradoxically, she suddenly felt a wish to continue her incon-
clusive chat with Ulrich. Her head had been flooded with a
soothing despair, pouring in from several directions at once, which
had then diminished and levelled out into a rather pleasant,
reposeful state of expectation. The long-foreseen collapse of the
Council left her unmoved. Arnheim's faithlessness also left her,
as she thought, almost unmoved. He had looked across at her as
she came in, and for a moment the old feeling had come back:
living space united them. But then she recalled that he had been
avoiding her for weeks, and the thought: ' Sexual coward ! ' gave
her back enough strength in her knees to pace regally towards
him.

Arnheim saw it all: her catching sight of him, her faltering, the
melting of distances. Hovering over frozen roads, innumerable
roads leading to and fro between them, lay the premonition that
this ice might thaw again. He had moved aside from the others,
but at the last moment both he and Diotima made a turn bringing
them together with Ulrich, General Stumm, and the others, who
were on the other side.

In all its manifestations, from the great ideas of extraordinary
men down to the sentimental trash that is such a bond between the
nations, what Ulrich called moral imagination, or, more simply,
feeling, has for hundreds of years been in a perpetual state of
fermentation without ever, as it were, maturing into wine. Man is
a being who cannot live without enthusiasm. And enthusiasm is
the state in which all his feelings and ideas are of the same spirit.
You would suppose almost the contrary: that it is the state in which
one feeling is overwhelmingly strong, a single feeling carrying all
others before it—in short, the state of being carried away. Or
were you not going to say anything about it at all ? Anyway, that
is the way it is. That is one way it is. But there is no fixed point
in the strength of such an enthusiasm. It is only by contact with
each other that feelings and ideas gain permanence, only as a sum

total; they have to be somehow aligned with each other and sweep each other along. And by every means known to him, by means of intoxicants, fantasies, suggestions, faith, conviction, often solely by the aid of stupidity, with its simplifying effect on things, man is always trying to achieve a condition approximating to this. He believes in ideas not because they are sometimes true, but because he must believe. Because he must keep his emotional impulses in order. Because he must have some illusion to stop up the gap between the walls of his life, through which his feelings would otherwise go streaming out to all four quarters of the sky. Probably it would be best, instead of surrendering to transient and delusive conditions, at least to search for the terms on which one can feel authentic enthusiasm. But although the number of decisions dependent on feeling is infinitely greater than the number of those that can be made by means of pure reason, and all the events by which mankind is moved have their origin in the imagination, it appears that only the purely rational problems have ever been got into any suprapersonal order; and for the rest of man's problems nothing has been done that could deserve the name of a common endeavour, or which even indicates any insight into the desperate necessity for such an endeavour.

This was the gist of what Ulrich said, under very understandable protest from the General.

All he saw in this evening's happenings, even if they were somewhat tumultuous in character and were, as a result of prejudiced misinterpretation, to have various grave consequences, was a demonstration of infinite chaos. Feuermaul at this moment struck him as of as little importance as love of mankind, nationalism as of as little importance as Feuermaul; and it was in vain that Stumm urged him to say how in the world one could distil the ideas of some tangible progress out of this highly personal attitude.

" Well," Ulrich said, " report that it's the Millennial War of Religion. And say that never before have people been so inadequately armed for it as in this time, when the rubble of futile feelings, the rubble one age bequeaths to another, has piled up as high as a mountain, without anything being done about it. So the War Ministry can sit back, with its mind at rest, and wait for the next collective disaster."

Ulrich was prophesying the fate of Europe, though he did not realise it. Indeed, he was not concerned with real events at all; he was fighting for his own salvation. And he was trying to obstruct and delay that by every possible means. And that too was why he laughed and tried to throw the others off the scent by mocking and exaggerating. He was now exaggerating for Agathe's benefit; he was continuing his talk with her, and not only the last one. Actually he was erecting a bulwark of ideas against her, knowing that at a certain point there was a little bolt and if it were slid back, everything would be flooded and buried under feeling. And in his heart he never stopped thinking of this bolt.

Diotima was standing near him, smiling. She had some aware-ness of the effort Ulrich was making for his sister's sake. She was mournfully touched and forgot all about sexual enlightenment, and something opened wide: doubtless it was the future. But her lips also opened a little.

Arnheim asked Ulrich: " And so you think something might be done about it ? " The way he put it conveyed that he recognised the seriousness under the exaggeration but also regarded the seriousness as exaggerated.

Tuzzi said to Diotima: " Something must in any case be done to prevent this affair from becoming public."

" Isn't it obvious ? " Ulrich said in answer to Arnheim. " We find ourselves faced with too many possibilities of feeling and too many possible forms of life. But isn't this difficulty very like the difficulty that the intellect overcomes when confronted with a tremendous number of facts and a history of the relevant theories ? We've managed to provide the intellect with a strict, even though incomplete, attitude. I don't need to describe it to you. So isn't it likely that something similar might be done for the feelings ? We all want to discover what we're alive for, there's no doubt about that: it's one of the main sources of all the violence in the world. Other times set about it with their own inadequate means. But the great age of empiricism has not yet given its mind to this at all."

Arnheim, who was quick to apprehend and who had a taste for interrupting, laid his hand on Ulrich's shoulder in a beseeching gesture. " But that would mean an expanding relationship to God ! " he exclaimed in a low, warning tone.

" And would that be so very terrible ? " Ulrich asked, not without a sharp undertone of mockery at this quickness to take alarm. " However, it wasn't I who went to the lengths of saying so."

Arnheim at once recollected himself and smiled. " One always rejoices to find someone unchanged after one has been away for a long time. It so rarely happens nowadays ! " he said. And indeed, as soon as he felt safe again behind his defensive front of benevolence, he really rejoiced. After all, Ulrich might very well have taken up that offer of a job he had once so rashly made. Arnheim was therefore thankful that Ulrich was so irresponsibly intransigent and scorned all earthly things. " We must have a talk about this some time," he added cordially. " You must explain to me just how you picture this application of our theoretical attitude to practical matters."

Ulrich knew very well that it still needed some explaining. For he did not mean either ' a life of research ' or a life ' by the light of science ' ; what he meant was a ' quest for feeling ' similar to the quest for truth, only with the difference that in this case truth did not matter. He watched Arnheim move in Agathe's direction. Diotima was there too. Tuzzi and Count Leinsdorf kept coming in and going out.

Agathe chatted with everyone, thinking: ' Why does he talk to everyone ? He ought to have gone away with me ! He's devaluing what he said to me ! ' Many of the things she heard him say were after her own heart, but they somehow caused her pain. Everything that Ulrich did had begun to cause her pain again, and once more, within this one day, she suddenly felt she must escape from him. She had no hope that she, one-sided as she was, could ever be all he wanted; and the idea that after a while they would be just like any other two people going home, chatting about the evening's party, was unendurable.

But Ulrich was thinking: ' Arnheim will never understand that.' And he went on:

" The man of science is limited precisely in his feelings. To say nothing of the practical man ! They have to be. It's like having to have a firm foothold if you're to lift something with your arms."

It was the way he usually was himself. The moment he began

thinking about anything, even though it might be the very subject of feeling, he was wary about letting any feeling in. Agathe said this was ' cold '. But he knew: if one wanted to be entirely the other thing, one must begin, as on a life-and-death adventure, by being prepared to lose one's life, for one has no notion where it is going to lead. He felt drawn to this; for the moment he had ceased to be afraid of it.

He was gazing at his sister, watching the lively play of conversational expressions on her face and, below the surface, the real face still untouched. He was on the point of asking her to come home with him now; but before he could move he was rejoined by Stumm, who again had something to say.

The good little General was very fond of Ulrich. He had already forgiven him his flippancies about the report for the War Ministry, and indeed he was rather taken with the expression ' religious war ': there was something festively military about it, like oak leaves on a shako or cheering on the Emperor's birthday. Laying his arm against Ulrich's, he edged him out of earshot of the others.

" You know, I think it's very nice what you say about all events originating in the imagination," he said. " Of course that's more my private than my official attitude to it."

He offered Ulrich a cigarette.

" I must go home," Ulrich said.

" Your sister's having a jolly good time, don't go taking her away now," Stumm said. " Arnheim's laying himself out like anything to make an impression on her. But as I was going to say: nobody really takes any pleasure any more in mankind's great ideas. You ought to put some life into things again. I mean: the time is getting a new spirit, and you're the fellow to take it in hand."

" What makes you think that ? " Ulrich asked mistrustfully.

" It's just how it strikes me." Stumm let it go at that and went on persuasively: " Look, you're for order too, aren't you ? It's obvious from everything you say. So I ask myself: is man more good or does he more need a strong hand ? It's symptomatic of our present-day need for decisiveness. The long and the short of it is what I've told you before, it'd put my mind at rest if you'd really take over leadership of the Campaign again. I mean, with all this talk that goes on there's no knowing what things may come to."

Ulrich laughed. " You know what I'm going to do now ? I'm not coming here any more ! " he answered happily.

" But why ? ! " Stumm exclaimed, appalled. " Everyone'll say the people were quite right who said you were never really the man to get things done."

" If I told people what I really think about things, they'd have all the more reason to say so ! " Ulrich retorted, still laughing. And he disengaged himself from his friend.

Stumm was vexed, but then his natural good humour prevailed, and he said in valediction:

" All these goings-on are so damn complicated. Sometimes I've actually thought to myself the best way out of all insoluble problems would be if some thorough-going booby came along, I mean sort of a Joan of Arc, you know—it's the only thing that might help."

Ulrich's eyes went in search of his sister and did not find her. While he was asking Diotima if she had seen her, Leinsdorf and Tuzzi made another entry from the drawing-room, announcing that the last guests were now leaving.

" I said all along," His Highness remarked cheerfully to the lady of the house, " what those people were saying wasn't their true opinion. And Frau Drangsal has had a really saving inspiration: we ought to continue this evening's gathering another time. But next time Feuermaul, or whatever his name is, is to read some long poem of his, so that'll keep things quieter. I took it upon myself to say, my dear, that I was quite sure you would agree."

Only after this did Ulrich learn that Agathe had suddenly said goodnight and gone without him. She had left a message for him, saying that she did not want her resolve to disturb him.